THE HONOLULU PACT

THE HONOLULU PACT

Michael S. Koyama

LONDON NEW YORK CALCUTTA

Seagull Books, 2013

© Michael S. Koyama / Kozo Yamamura

ISBN 978 0 8574 2 105 0

British Library Cataloguing-in-Publication Data
A catalogue record for this book is available from the British Library

Typeset in Sabon LT Standard and DIN-Bold/Regular by Seagull Books, Calcutta, India
Printed and bound by Maple Press, York, Pennsylvania, USA

To Susan B. Hanley, who co-authored this book as she has the previous two novels, but who has declined my entreaty to be co-author, saying, 'All I have done is what a loyal wife does. That you use "S" as your middle initial to acknowledge my contribution is more than I could ask for.'

CAST OF PRINCIPAL CHARACTERS

FROM HAWAII

Lisa Higashiguchi, *lieutenant in the Honolulu Police Department*
Captain Kalani, *Lisa's superior officer*
Pat Foletta, *HPD sergeant and Lisa's friend*
Steve Sasaki, *Democratic candidate for Congress from Hawaii*
Matthew Chance, *senator from Hawaii, Democratic presidential candidate*

CHARACTERS CONNECTED TO SIMON POWERS, REPUBLICAN SENATOR FROM MASSACHUSETTS

Peri (Experience) Powers, *daughter of Simon Powers*
Anita Faga, *Simon Powers' private secretary*
Lou Parelli, *treasurer of the New American Destiny Forum*
Ginko Parelli, *Lou's wife*
Karen McPherson, professor, *friend of Simon Powers*
Bradley Bond, *governor of Minnesota, Republican presidential candidate*
Evelyn Barrington, *congresswoman from southern California*

CHARACTERS CONNECTED TO PERI POWERS

Alexander Jouvenet (Alex), *Peri's French lover*
Bess Browne, *electronic communications specialist at Rubin Associates*
Nick Koyama, *international finance specialist at Rubin Associates*
Charles DeMello, *private detective*
Claude Martin, *French painter*

FBI PERSONNEL

Sam Ogden, *special agent in the Seattle office*
Dan Bronfenbrenner, *assistant director of the FBI's Criminal Investigation Division*
Eleanor Simmons, *executive assistant to the director of the FBI*
Ben Perez, *senior assistant to the director of the FBI's Cyber Division*
Donna Fletcher, *FBI agent*

FROM JAPAN

Junji (Jun) Taira, *Japanese dietman*
Tomiko (Tomi) Taira, *Jun's wife*
Masaharu Sada, *retired professor of economics, advisor to Taira and his group*

I hope no one dies tonight, Lisa fervently wished as the car rounded the curved drive to an oceanfront mansion. Her sister stopped the car in front of two large Oriental stone dogs guarding the entrance. Lisa thanked her and got out, barely managing not to trip over the long skirt of her borrowed evening gown.

'Lieutenant Higashiguchi! I almost didn't recognize you,' called out one of the two guards in dark civilian suits, who were standing in front of the walled property on Honolulu's famed Kahala Avenue.

Lisa smiled. 'Hi, Bruce, don't let anyone suspicious slip into the party tonight,' she said to the young off-duty colleague from the Honolulu Police Department. As she walked through the gate, she thought, *I almost didn't recognize myself in my sister's black gown, my mother's pearls and a Tahitian gardenia in my hair.*

At the door, an elderly woman, elegant in a cobalt-blue kaftan with gold brocade, warmly greeted Lisa.

'Lieutenant Higashiguchi? Mr Sasaki was right when he said you would be the perfect person to provide security on the inside for tonight's fundraiser for him. After what happened to poor Senator Kwon, less than half a mile from here, I'm really so nervous,' she chattered on. 'And everyone who reads the *Star Advertiser* will know that Senator Chance and the top CEOs in Honolulu will be here tonight to show their support for Steve Sasaki.'

'Please rest assured, Mrs Albinson, that with five members of the Honolulu Police Department here tonight, we should be able to keep any intruders out.' Mrs Albinson didn't need to know Lisa had been called to the scene last week when a deranged man claiming to be a member of the Patriot Party had broken into Senator Kwon's apartment, resulting in the death of both the senator and the intruder.

Selma Albinson, the most generous supporter of the Democratic Party in Honolulu, ushered Lisa into the mansion and said, 'Of course, you know all this. I asked that you come early so you could take a look at our security arrangements and familiarize yourself with the layout of the house and property.'

Lisa entered the huge open living–dining area of a home that had been featured in *Architectural Digest*. She had never thought she would be a dinner guest at one of the multi-million-dollar beachfront mansions that lined Kahala Avenue. She had been in a couple of these houses during her tenure in the HPD, but as an officer investigating break-ins, certainly not as a guest. She wasn't quite a guest tonight, but she was to act like one. She hadn't made the two-thousand-dollar campaign contribution the other guests had ponied up, but she was donating her time as the de facto leader of the security team.

Lisa forced herself to keep her mind on her job—to stop admiring the residence and look at it from the perspective of security. The living area and adjoining terrace had been set up with tables for some fifty diners, a place card at each setting. She walked out onto the terrace decorated with hanging orchids. Beyond lay a lawn, and to its right were a swimming pool and tennis courts. Both were surrounded by a high fence, as was the entire property, but the fence was hidden by abundant bougainvillaea with red, pink and white flowers. At the far end of the property, Lisa could hear the rhythmic waves of the Pacific Ocean. The entire compound was well lit tonight and Lisa was satisfied by the security of the grounds. She chatted briefly with the two off-duty HPD policemen out on the grounds.

Lisa returned to the dining area. She looked for her place card. Hers wasn't a good seat, she decided. She found Mrs Albinson and asked to be re-seated at the side of the dining room from where she could see all of the other tables, the door to the kitchen, the entire living area and, to her left, the grounds. Mrs Albinson readily agreed. While her hostess was dithering about the new seating arrangements, the Sasakis arrived.

Lisa had known the Sasakis for several years now. She had met Steve Sasaki's wife, Sophie, at a yoga class and they had become fast friends. And she had known Steve, a civil rights lawyer, for even longer through his pro bono work for indigent defendants. She had no doubt at all that Sasaki, on whose campaign she had been spending the little free time she had, would make a wonderful congressman.

The next guests to arrive were Senator Matthew Chance and his wife. Lisa was truly in awe of this second-term senator who was now running for President, a long shot but his campaign for 'a just capitalism' to replace 'our jungle capitalism' was catching on. He wanted to rein in the excesses of the current system in which the 'strong' eat the 'weak'. Chance had made an unexpectedly strong showing in several states in the recent Super Tuesday primaries. He was still lagging well behind Senator Rachel Samuelson of California in the total delegate count, but he now had more delegates than did the maverick Oregon senator, Jacob Nelson.

On the heels of the Chances, the CEOs—the makers and shakers of Honolulu—began to pour in, the men in evening dress, and the women in designer gowns with lots of bling. Lisa now fully understood why Mrs Albinson, already so worried because of what had happened to Senator Kwon, was so very security conscious.

Lisa accepted a glass of champagne from a roving waiter, but merely sipped at it. Had she been careless? She hadn't gone into the kitchen and met the caterer and his staff or Mrs Albinson's household help. Now she took pains to check out the appearance of all the servers. She was mollified by the fact that the middle-aged headwaiter seemed very capable and very much in charge.

When dinner was served, Lisa found herself at a table with three prominent businessmen and the wives of two of them. When one of the wives asked what she did, she responded, 'I work for the city.' Hearing this, the others quickly went on to topics of their interest except for the man who came alone, who kept gawking at her lasciviously. As Lisa ate her way through salad, delicately seasoned *opakapaka* and, finally, coconut cake, she was amused by the conversations going on round her.

She didn't correct one of the wives who declared that the intruder to Senator Kwon's apartment had beaten the senator to death. Lisa was surprised at how distorted media accounts were of the horrible incident in which she had been a participant. She had been the stand-by officer on night duty two weeks ago when a homeless man claiming to be a Patriot had broken into Senator Kwon's apartment 'to tell the senator to drop out of the race for his fourth term'. Senator Kwon had managed to call 911 from his mobile phone after locking himself in a bathroom. When she arrived, the man had pointed his gun at her, and a patrolman just behind her had shot the intruder, gravely wounding him. After one of the ambulance teams managed to open the locked bathroom, they found the senator dead in a shower stall. Because of Senator Kwon's age and because he had heart problems, the police doctor, who saw no need for a forensic autopsy, had certified he died of a heart attack caused by shock. The Patriot died of his gunshot wounds a week later and there had been demonstrations by several hundred Patriots against 'police brutality' and 'the HPD, lackey of the rich'.

Lisa also held her tongue when her tablemates sharply criticized the Patriot Party. To her, many of those in the Patriot Party were very different from the Tea Party followers of several years ago. They were far angrier and prone to resort to violence. But she was also aware that a majority of the Patriot Party members were in hopeless situations, with no job, no more unemployment benefits, no health insurance, and a sizeable number among them homeless. She certainly abhorred the violence to which more and more of them seemed to be resorting to during the past year. But she thought these rich Democrats showed a lack of understanding, let alone sympathy for the very serious plight of so many in Honolulu who, she believed, were joining the Patriot Party out of sheer desperation.

So she refrained from joining in the conversation and enjoyed her dinner, all the while discreetly surveying the dining area. In her peripheral vision, her attention was caught by one of the waiters who didn't seem to be as professional as the others. He was somehow clumsy and could collect only half the number of used dishes compared to the others. His left arm seemed stiff, and he favoured it. As he hovered near Steve Sasaki when coffee was being served, the head of the team came over and ordered him to serve at Lisa's table where guests were waiting for coffee. *Was he a fill-in for a regular?*

Lisa continued to observe the waiter unobtrusively as the speechmaking began. He was in his thirties, had dark hair, was of medium build, and, like so many people in Hawaii, it was impossible to tell what his racial mix was. Clearly *hapa* or mixed. The only thing about him that seemed out of the ordinary were his eyes. She couldn't quite put it into words, but the adjectives cold, hard, and even eerie came to her mind. While Senator Chance gave an unqualified endorsement to Steve, and Steve thanked everyone for their generous support, the waiter hovered near the main table. At one point, Lisa caught his eye and saw a cold, calculating glance, in contrast to the relaxed or semi-bored expression on the faces of the other servers who were standing along one side of the room.

At last the speeches were over and people began to push back their chairs and chat. Steve motioned with his cup for a refill of coffee, and instantly the waiter with the creepy eyes was at his side. The waiter rested the cup and saucer on the edge of the table, holding it with his left hand while he refilled it with his right. More drinks were served, then there was more chitchat, and finally the evening was over.

The following morning Lisa leant on her kitchen counter, sipping a cup of instant coffee. She turned on the radio to catch the morning weather and traffic reports. She caught the familiar female voice ending the traffic report with 'The accident on Likelike Highway should be cleared by nine this morning.' There was a brief pause and the same voice said, 'I've just been handed breaking news. Mr Steven Sasaki, a candidate for the House of Representatives, died of an apparent heart attack late last night.'

'No way!!' Lisa cried out, and spilt hot coffee down the front of her clean shirt. She had to hear more. She changed to another news station. A male announcer read the most recent poll result of the Republican primary to be held in Hawaii the next day. Then, he gave the same one-line report of Sasaki's death.

She just couldn't believe Sasaki was dead. And certainly not from a heart attack! She knew that men in their forties could have heart attacks, even men in seemingly good physical condition. But when she had greeted the Sasakis last evening, Steve had said he had swum a mile that morning in the ocean off Waikiki because 'I gotta stay in shape for this campaign.' He couldn't be dead. And *certainly not* from a heart attack!

Lisa poured her coffee into the sink with a trembling hand. She changed her shirt, and drove to work fighting back tears. She stormed into her captain's office and implored she be allowed to investigate *immediately* the circumstances surrounding Sasaki's death.

'Lisa, calm down,' said Captain Kalani. 'The doc said he is sure Sasaki died of a heart attack. Unless the autopsy finds otherwise, it's not a murder case.'

'Captain, something's not right—I just know it! I was at the party and he was perfectly well and in fine form all evening,' insisted Lisa. 'And if we wait for the autopsy report, which could easily take a week or more, any clues we might find today will be gone. Can't I at least spend today looking into what happened?'

Kalani leant back, looked hard at Lisa, and after a long moment said, 'OK, we don't have anything urgent on the docket for you today. Since Sasaki was such a prominent figure, it won't hurt to look into all possibilities, just in case the autopsy comes up with something we can't anticipate. All right, go ahead.'

Lisa checked her emails, cleared her desk and drove to Sasaki's house in Manoa Valley. She would start her investigation with Sophie, her good friend. She knew it would be a painful interview, but she was sure that Sophie would be cooperative to help try to find the *real* cause of her husband's death.

Through tears, Sophie said, 'Steve was perfectly OK all day. He said the swim invigorated him as always, and you could see how energetic and on top of things he was at the party. When we left at about ten, Steve was a bit quiet, but I thought he was just tired after making a speech at the end of a long day. We got home just before ten-thirty and Steve said he would go straight to bed. I paid the babysitter, chatted with her a minute or two and locked up. Then I went to check on our daughter. Marisa was sound asleep so I went straight to our bedroom. I found Steve collapsed on the bed, unconscious. I hadn't been away from him for more than about ten minutes. He was fully dressed, so he must have collapsed immediately after I had left him. I dialled 911 and tried to resuscitate him, but it was useless.' She put her head in her hands and sobbed. 'Whatever will I do without him?' she wailed.

Lisa could think of no way to comfort her. She took Sophie in her arms and let her cry. As Sophie's sobs lessened, Lisa said, 'I really did come to offer my sympathy. But I find it impossible to think that Steve died of a heart attack. So . . . I want to find out all I can to make sure, on the off chance that he didn't. I have been authorized to conduct a preliminary investigation.'

'Nothing will bring him back,' murmured a tearful Sophie, 'but I too find it impossible to believe he died of a heart attack. I would like to know what happened . . . if you find anything.'

After Lisa had shared a cup of tea with Sophie and talked with her about the funeral arrangements, she set out for Mrs Albinson's mansion on Kahala Avenue. She arrived just before noon, and pushed the buzzer on the gate. 'Yes? May I ask who it is?' queried an accented voice through the intercom. Lisa introduced herself and asked if she could talk to Mrs Albinson for a few minutes. The gate swung open and Lisa entered the grounds for the second time in less than twenty-four hours.

Mrs Albinson was surprised by the unannounced visit. As Lisa rightly guessed, she hadn't heard about Sasaki's sudden death.

The old lady was stunned by the news. 'Oh no! He was so full of life last night. Why . . . how did he die? A car accident?'

Lisa explained Sasaki had suddenly died of what was believed to be a heart attack after he arrived home the night before. She added, 'Because Steve Sasaki was a candidate for Congress, we are conducting an investigation.'

Mrs Albinson's expression was a mixture of consternation and confusion, seeing which Lisa decided to ask the question that had first come to her when she heard the news of Sasaki's death and had been bothering her ever since.

'Mrs Albinson, please forgive me for asking, but could you tell me who your caterers were?'

'Island Caterers,' responded the baffled old lady. 'I've used them for my large parties for the past half a dozen years. Their work is excellent.'

To deflect Mrs Albinson from asking 'Why the question?' Lisa praised the dinner, saying it was the best she had eaten in a long while. And then she asked, 'Do you always have the same team of servers?'

'Gary Borges has been the head of the team since I started using this firm, but there's a lot of coming and going in that business, as I'm sure you know. So I recognized some of the waiters and waitresses, but not all.'

Mrs Albinson was now very puzzled by Lisa's questions. But she expanded on her answer as if anticipating Lisa's follow-up questions.

'There was a small Asian woman last night whom I have never seen before, but she was very efficient. And then there was a man with cold eyes I couldn't help noticing—I couldn't tell what race he was. I presumed he was new because he wasn't up to the usual standards of the firm. But I know they often have new people, and there weren't any real problems. So I didn't complain to Gary.'

Lisa knew she had got all she could from Mrs Albinson so she borrowed from her a business card of the catering firm. She was certain that the man who wasn't up to the usual standards, with the cold eyes, was the same man she had observed and wondered about the previous night, though she had to admit she wasn't sure why this waiter preyed on her mind so.

Lisa set off for Island Caterers, located not far from Ala Moana Center, to talk to Gary Borges, but her stomach made her realize that she hadn't had anything but black coffee all day and it was now past one o'clock. She stopped to get a quick sushi lunch, and while eating called and made an appointment with Borges without explaining why.

On being introduced, the caterer gave Lisa a long stare when she said she was from the Criminal Investigation Division of the HPD. 'You sure look different in a ponytail and your work clothes. I had no idea last night that you were a detective,' he said.

He had heard that Sasaki had died, and when Lisa started asking questions, he was immediately on the defensive. 'I heard on TV that Mr Sasaki died of a heart attack. So it absolutely cannot be a case of food poisoning,' he declared.

'Hang on,' Lisa said, 'nobody is saying anything about food poisoning. Besides, as far as I know, food poisoning doesn't usually kill someone so suddenly. The doctor said Sasaki died of a heart attack. There may be an autopsy to determine exactly what he died of, but because he was a candidate for Congress, we do have to look into the circumstances of his sudden death. I just want to ask a few questions for the record. OK?'

'Sorry, Lieutenant. OK, shoot.' Borges became almost deferential.

'Tell me about your team last night. Were they all regulars?'

'Yes, though one woman was a new hire who has only been with us for about two weeks. But she's very good. She was the smallest server, just five feet tall. You may have noticed her.'

'Yes. What about the thinnish man who waited primarily on the head table? I couldn't determine his race. He didn't seem very good at the job. Had trouble clearing tables . . . could only take a few dishes at a time. Was he a regular?'

'Him? He's not on my team. He was a new man Mrs Albinson hired. I had to keep prompting him about what to do. He told me he'd been hired recently as her butler to take charge of small gatherings and she wanted him to see how she expected her parties to be handled. I can't imagine why she hired someone so lacking in experience.'

'Of course, you asked her about him?'

'No, Lieutenant. I didn't. Over the years, I've learned never to question her decisions. Like most rich ladies, she is a woman to be obeyed. I decided if she wanted him for a butler, so be it. She is a very generous tipper and I want to keep her happy.'

'Would you be surprised to hear that Mrs Albinson hadn't hired him, that she thought he was a member of your team?'

'What!?' Borges was clearly astounded. 'So why did he crash the party?'

'That's what I would like to know,' responded Lisa, 'particularly in light of Sasaki's death. Look, tell me everything you can about the man, starting with what he looked like. I want to make sure we are talking about the same person.'

'He wasn't tall, but might have seemed taller than he was because he was so lanky. He was maybe five feet nine. Short, dark hair, but not as short as a crew cut, but so short he didn't have to comb it. I couldn't tell what his racial mix was. Certainly he had both Caucasian and Asian blood. He said his name was Tanabe, Barry Tanabe, so I assumed he was part Japanese.'

Listening to Borges, Lisa felt two conflicting emotions: satisfaction that he was confirming her suspicions that the man with the hard, creepy eyes could somehow be involved in Sasaki's death along with regret for not having done something the night before when she was first suspicious about the man's actions.

Controlling her emotions, Lisa asked, 'What kind of accent did he have?'

'Oh, clearly local. Probably that's why we didn't find him suspicious. You can't fake the local accent for long. He's definitely from the Islands.'

'You talked to him—was he friendly?'

'No, not what you would call friendly. He would ask questions about the work and respond when we talked to him. But he didn't chat while setting up like the rest of us do. I thought it was because he was new and unsure of himself. He didn't seem the talkative type either. Anyway, he was an odd fish. Looking at him, I had the distinct feeling he was anxious about something.'

Borges thought for a moment and then added, 'Possibly because I now know he didn't belong at Mrs Albinson's. But I didn't take to the guy. He had a very, creepy cold look in his eyes even when saying something perfectly ordinary. Did you ever see the Hitchcock movie *Psycho*? The original one with Tony Perkins? I saw it on late-night TV a few weeks ago.'

'I only saw the remake in the late nineties. What about it?'

'Well, this guy, though he was dark and part Asian, he somehow reminded me of the psychotic killer. Tony Perkins didn't have the eerie eyes Barry Tanabe did, but . . . you know what I'm trying to say?'

'Yes, I think I know what you mean. How do you think he got into the house, if he wasn't part of your team?'

'I know how he got in. Brandon, my second in command, let him in. I stayed behind to pick up the cakes from our baker. When I got to the house, I asked Brandon who the guy was, and Brandon said that he had walked up to the service entrance just as our van arrived. He said he had come to help with the party, and he was dressed as a waiter, so when the gate was opened to let the van in, he walked through. I can't fault Brandon for assuming the guy had been hired by Mrs Albinson.'

By now Borges was looking slightly abashed as he seemed to realize that, knowing how security conscious Mrs Albinson was at the party, he should have checked with security or the maid, if not with Mrs Albinson, as to who the man was.

As if to defend himself, Borges said, 'You know, he was really very good . . . slick . . . so none of us thought he could be an interloper. He had a lot of nerve . . . a really cool customer!'

'Why do you think he did what he did? I mean . . . crashing the party and waiting on a table. He wasn't a thief—nothing was stolen as far as I know.'

Before Borges could answer, Lisa decided to re-state the question and ask him directly what was on her mind.

'Is there any way he could have slipped something into what Steve Sasaki ate or drank?'

Borges, surprised, eyes popping, looked at Lisa, and responded deliberately.

'I don't see how he could have. All of the food was served plated from the kitchen and randomly set in front of the guests. I can't imagine how he could have put anything onto Mr Sasaki's plate.'

'What about the drinks?'

'Well . . . as you know, we didn't serve cocktails, just champagne before dinner and wine with each course, and water and coffee, of course. Some wanted tea, but if I remember correctly, everyone at the head table had either coffee or nothing with dessert. And the coffee was poured from carafes. No, I really can't think of how anything could have been doctored. I will admit that the guy did his best to serve the head table. I had to keep instructing him to look after guests at other tables as well. He was sort of a nuisance. But . . . to have put something into a drink . . . I doubt he or anyone else could've done that when serving, with so many people around.'

'Can you think of anything else at all? Anything unusual about the evening? Even something only a little different, perhaps?'

Borges bit his lips together and looked at a wall calendar featuring a naked woman with a lei strategically draped over her body. After a long minute he shook his head and said reflectively, 'Nothing at the moment. Lieutenant. But

I was really running my feet off between the kitchen and the dining area. This was a really important event for us and we hoped some of the guests might hire us in the future if we excelled.'

After thanking Borges for his time, Lisa drove back to headquarters on South Beretania. She was no further in knowing the cause of Sasaki's sudden death. But should the autopsy be performed and show he died by anything but natural causes, she would certainly find out all she could about the interloper at Mrs Albinson's. She had been taken aback when Borges said the man reminded him of a murderer in a Hitchcock film. Now recalling what Borges said, she saw in her mind's eye the interloper's creepy look. As she drove up Ward Avenue back towards headquarters, she muttered, 'I'm not going to let the murderer of a wonderful man go unpunished. I do not want to live in a society where assassins can kill politicians or candidates for office.'

In the Boston suburb of Chestnut Hill, preparations were underway for the birthday dinner of Senator Simon Powers, Republican of Massachusetts. His daughter Peri had returned from Paris three days ago to join in the celebration of her father's sixty-fifth birthday. This afternoon she had picked up from Logan Airport her French lover, Alexandre Jouvenet, whom she had invited to attend with the intention of introducing him to her family. But things were not going according to plan.

Peri had seen almost nothing of her father since her return. When she arrived, she had been surprised to find that he was unexpectedly in New York. She had had a hurried conversation with him at breakfast this morning and only learnt then who had been invited to the birthday dinner.

As she sat in her home's sun porch waiting for Alex to join her, she pondered the strange guest list for her father's party. Alex walked in a little later, plopped down in a wicker chair and gratefully accepted a cup of tea and some cookies. Then he took a long look at Peri's face and said, 'You look *tracassé* . . . preoccupied. Is something worrying you?'

'The guest list for my father's birthday dinner,' Peri answered, doing her best to smile but not quite succeeding.

'You don't like someone on the list?'

'It's not that. What's disconcerting is that while some very strange people have been invited, none of his family—my grandmother and cousins—and none of our family friends or close friends of my father is coming. I had suggested you combine your research trip to Columbia University with a visit here so that I could introduce you to my family and friends, but none of them have been invited!'

'So, who *is* coming?'

'This morning Dad told me there will be only nine of us. Besides my father, you and me, there's someone called Lou Parelli, a former banker who's now the treasurer of the New American Destiny Forum my father created—it's an organization for public education, whatever that is. Parelli's coming with his wife. Then there's a professor of political science, a widow named Karen McPherson, whom I've heard about. If I remember correctly, she's very conservative and very wealthy. And a Japanese dietman—I think he is equivalent to our congressman—who's also coming with his wife. Dad told me the

Japanese politician's name but I can't remember it. Oh, and Dad's private secretary. I don't understand why the treasurer, Professor McPherson and the Japanese dietman have been invited for a very private birthday party. Can you imagine the son not inviting his own mother who lives nearby?'

'*Très drôle*! And you've never met any of them?'

'I know Anita Faga, my father's secretary, who has been with him for almost four years now. I've met her a couple of times on my visits home.'

Looking puzzled, Alex asked, 'Peri, do you think there could be some purpose for this gathering besides celebrating your father's birthday, such as the US elections or something? You've told me your father is very actively supporting a presidential candidate.'

'Yes, he's backing Governor Bond. That could explain why Parelli and Professor McPherson are invited. Parelli works for the NAD Forum, which I think is helping Governor Bond and other Republican candidates, and I gather Professor McPherson is active in the forum. But it doesn't explain why a Japanese politician and his wife have been invited.'

'Curious indeed.' Alex put down his teacup, leant back and looked round. 'Peri, this is a wonderful old house your father has. It has a real sense of space, of quiet, of history. Even after seeing you in your very bourgeois apartment in Paris, I had no idea you lived in such a *grande maison* in the US.'

'Actually it's not my father's house,' Peri said in a small voice. 'It was my mother's and she left it to me. It's not old by European standards. My great-grandfather built it just before the Second World War. He established the insurance company that my grandfather—my mother's father—made into one of the biggest insurance companies in America.'

'Well, you're very lucky,' Alex said and then yawned.

'Oh Alex, poor you, you're still jet-lagged. Why don't you go take a nap for a couple of hours? I'd love to join you,' Peri said with a grin, 'but I should go help Maria with the party preparations.'

After sending Alex upstairs to the guest suite, Peri put the finishing touches to the dinner table and went to the kitchen to chat with Maria, who had been the housekeeper for the family since Peri was a child. When the butler-couple who were to help Maria serve at the party arrived, Peri went up to her room to change for the evening. As she slid a black cocktail dress over her head, she heard a car pass by the side of the house. She peeped out a window that faced the rear yard and garage and saw a small Volkswagen go round the back of the house and park in the turnaround. Anita Faga got out. Swishing her long dark curls and wearing a beige evening coat, she strode up to the rear entrance in dressy sandals with two-inch heels. She went into the house so quickly that

Peri realized her father's secretary had a key. Peri finished dressing and went down the rear stairs to the kitchen in time to hear Anita giving orders to Maria in a peremptory tone that she herself would never have used in speaking to their long-time family retainer.

Before Peri could enter the kitchen, she heard the doorbell ring and so turned left to the front hall where she let in a distinguished-looking Japanese man and his wife, both fashionably dressed reflecting impeccable taste. They introduced themselves as Junji and Tomiko Taira. 'But please call us Jun and Tomi, the American way,' Jun said in excellent English with only a trace of an accent.

Almost as soon as the Tairas' taxi drove off, Senator Simon Powers arrived in a limousine with Karen McPherson, immediately after which the Parellis drove up in a shiny new Lexus.

It was all rather a crush in the hall with Anita and Peri trying to take guests' coats and Powers greeting each guest in turn. As the senator ushered everyone into the living room, Mrs Parelli, who turned out to be Japanese, whispered to Peri that she would like to use the powder room to freshen up. Peri directed her to the first door on the right, just beyond the stairs.

In the chaos of drinks being served while introductions were made, Peri realized that Alex was missing. She decided she had better wake him to give him time to get ready before dinner was announced. She hurried up the stairs and saw Mrs Parelli quietly coming out of her bedroom, closing the door behind her without realizing Peri was watching. Peri was confounded and couldn't help wondering what the woman was doing in her bedroom.

Startled to see Peri as she turned round, Mrs Parelli gave a little laugh and said, 'I didn't quite get your directions right. I thought you said it was just up the stairs.'

Peri was seething, but politely told the woman to go back down the stairs and through the first door on the right. Troubled by Mrs Parelli's snooping, Peri climbed up to the guest suite on the third floor to find Alex putting on his tie. 'Sorry, the alarm on my mobile didn't go off,' he apologized.

The couple made their way downstairs and Peri introduced Alex to the guests. Powers seemed a bit annoyed when his daughter introduced Alex to him, though she had informed him she was inviting her friend to the party. He was frostily cordial, making it obvious that he wasn't terribly happy to have Alex join the party.

But tonight the senator was more concerned with his guests than with his daughter and her young man. It quickly became evident to Peri that Karen McPherson was the guest of honour. Powers sat next to her on the sofa. A tall, angular woman in her forties, she wore her mousy brown hair in an outmoded style, pulled back from her face with combs and bundled into a chignon at her neck. Dressed in an obviously expensive purple silk dress, she looked like a woman from a 1940s movie, Peri thought.

Karen McPherson was introduced to the group as a professor of political science at a prestigious women's college in northern New York and the president of the Kendrick Foundation, which provided grants to students in journalism. Peri recalled more of what she had read about McPherson in some magazine article. The woman was the widow of Evan McPherson, a billionaire banker who had died three years ago in a bewildering plane accident. His small Gulfstream had crashed into a river. The media had made much about his widow who had not only inherited her husband's wealth but was also the sole heiress of her father, Wendell Kendrick, the founder of Kendrick Corporation, a media conglomerate that controlled numerous TV and radio stations and a score of newspapers.

Peri realized that Professor McPherson was triply valuable to her father with her similar political views, her billions in wealth and her influence over a media conglomerate. She was now almost certain that the odd guest list had been drawn up because her father wanted to use his birthday for fundraising.

But Peri was still puzzled about why the Tairas had been invited. A Japanese congressman would be of little help in the US elections and, even if he was very rich, she was sure it was illegal for foreigners to contribute to American political campaigns. But she thought the Tairas an extremely attractive couple, both slim, well dressed and quite at ease with Americans.

As drinks were handed round, Peri and Alex found themselves with the Tairas, and Peri was determined to find out what she could about them.

'How did your paths cross with my father's?' Peri asked, instead of what she really wanted to ask—*Why do you think my father invited you tonight?*

The Japanese congressman answered with ease.

'We met because I sought him out. I read his book, *The New American Destiny*, and realized his ideas were very close to those of my party in Japan. When I was at State Department meetings in Washington, I called your father's office and he generously invited me to dinner with him. We discussed at length the issues facing our countries. Your father is a very well-informed cosmopolitan senator. It wouldn't surprise me in the least if Governor Bond, when he gets the nomination, picks him to be his secretary of state.'

Peri thought Jun Taira's reply was a very polite answer by a savvy politician. She found Taira and his wife intelligent, articulate and with no overt social pretensions. So different from the Parellis, whom she had taken an immediate dislike to. Lou Parelli was an unattractive man—short, paunchy, and with strands of hair combed over his bald pate. He had spoken to Peri unctuously when they had been introduced. His wife, Ginko, was loud in dress and voice, and a snoop!

When the butlers hired for the party announced dinner, the senator moved the group into the dining room, impressive with its large antique furniture, the table adorned with heavy silver candlesticks and other silverware as old as the house. Looking down on the scene were the oil portraits of the senator's dead wife's parents and grandparents. Powers, like the two-star general he had been, told everyone where to sit round the large table. Karen was seated in the guest of honour's place to the senator's right, Jun Taira was put next to Ginko, and Peri ended up next to Lou Parelli; Tomi Taira sat between Alex and Anita on the other side of the table. She couldn't think of a worse seating arrangement, but then, given the odd assortment of people assembled for the party, how else would they have been seated?

While the butlers were serving a white wine to go with the shrimp and avocado appetizer, Jun leant round Ginko and asked Peri, 'Why are you called Perry? I thought it was a last name. Are you related to Commodore Perry who came to Japan in 1853 to open the country to foreigners?'

Peri smiled as she replied, 'Peri is actually a nickname for Experience. It's spelt P–E–R–I, not P–E–R–R–Y, though both are pronounced the same.'

Tomi Taira had heard Peri's answer from across the table and asked tentatively, 'Your name is Experience? What an unusual name!'

'Yes, isn't it? I've had to explain it all of my life. Experience was my great-grandmother's name. It dates from a time when girls in New England were given names like Thankful, Faithful and Patience.'

Parelli's wife suddenly spoke up.

'My name is unusual too. *Gin* means silver and *ko* means child in Japanese. So my name means silver child. But many Japanese think my name is funny because Ginko with a long "O" means bank. In any case, I think my name means I must be destined to be rich,' she added with a hollow little laugh.

No one said anything for a long moment after Ginko's inane remarks. Powers broke the silence. 'All of you maybe interested in what Karen and I were discussing earlier,' he said, relating the gist of a lecture a professor had given recently on the American fiscal crisis at an NAD Forum public lecture in Boston funded by Karen's foundation.

Alex was puzzled. 'Senator, what else does this NAD Forum do?'

Before the senator could reply, Karen McPherson gave a cogent and, Peri thought well-practised, explanation.

'The NAD Forum is the New American Destiny Forum. It's a multipurpose organization—we organize conferences and seminars, publish books and get articles into major newspapers. We also have a website that we keep up to date, plus of course Twitter, Facebook and more. We have a young man who makes sure we have an active presence on the web. Many of our members go on talk shows too.'

Powers interjected, 'We're not a large group, but we think we can be an influential one. We have nearly two hundred leaders from business, the media and universities who contribute money and time to help us. And just in the last month, we have added twelve more members.' He looked over at Parelli and added, 'Lou here is our treasurer. I don't know what we'd do without him!'

Parelli smirked and gave a little bow in the direction of Powers.

Peri spoke up. 'Dad, I'm not familiar with political organizations, so I'm wondering why you established the NAD Forum as an independent organization. Why can't the Republican National Committee, with its huge set-up, do everything Professor McPherson just told us the forum does?'

McPherson replied in a tone that Peri thought almost condescending.

'Peri, the RNC is a large, diverse group with multiple points of views, and various factions back different candidates. The NAD Forum wants to make the public aware of the ideals of the true conservatives, so the forum makes a special effort to support Governor Bond who we believe is the best candidate to lead our country into a better future.'

Alex, hoping his ideological hostility didn't show, asked in an interested but bland tone, 'So I understand your group is very conservative. We've been reading about the Patriot Party in the French press. Is your forum connected with that group in any way?'

Before McPherson could reply, Peri blurted out, 'Before I left Paris, the *International Herald Tribune* carried an article about a man claiming to represent the Patriots who got into a senator's apartment in Honolulu and literally scared him to death before being eventually shot by a police officer. The article said the Patriots claim to represent the true conservatives. How is your group different?'

The room went silent. Even before Peri had finished, she knew her blunt question was inappropriate at this party and that her remark would rile her father. But she was so annoyed by McPherson's sanctimonious response to the question about the forum and her father's uncharacteristic kowtowing to the professor all evening she simply didn't care.

Powers gave Peri a look she knew well—his lips compressed, his eyes an expression of anger and exasperation. Raising his hand to stop McPherson from responding to Peri, he quietly said, 'Peri, the NAD Forum is definitely *not* connected to, nor does it support, the Patriot Party in any way. We created the forum because we needed an organization with focus, a smaller organization than the RNC. During my lifetime, I've seen the US, the unquestioned superpower in the post-war years, gradually become a debt-ridden country without the economic wherewithal or the military capability to effectively lead the world. We've had misguided, left-leaning governments that have stifled the entrepreneurial energy of our business sector through high taxes and too many regulations. I founded the forum to reverse this trend and make America great again, make it an unchallenged superpower. When I was a general . . .'

He stopped mid-sentence, suddenly realizing everyone in the room was no longer eating or chatting, just staring at him.

McPherson, with satisfaction and amusement in her voice, said, 'Simon, I'm glad you're saying so clearly that we've nothing to do with the Patriots. But no speeches tonight . . . we are here to celebrate your birthday!'

Still looking exasperated, Powers said to his daughter, 'Peri, we'll talk about this tomorrow. As Karen has reminded me, tonight is an occasion to celebrate. So let's relax and enjoy the evening.'

At Powers' behest, everyone began to talk as if trying to make the evening a sudden success. Conversations ranged over disparate topics. Lou Parelli talked about how sophisticated the ways to wire money round the world had become; Ginko kept bringing up what the rich and the famous were buying; and Peri's father, Karen and Jun Taira discussed the unsustainable, very large, national debts of the rich countries.

Peri found herself fascinated trying to figure out the various relationships among the celebrants. She was especially intrigued by Anita, who gave Karen odd, jaundiced glances from time to time, making Peri feel that Anita considered the older woman her rival for the senator's attention. It was funny to think that Anita might be jealous of the professor because Peri just couldn't imagine her father finding Karen sexually appealing. But she quickly dismissed the thought because Anita—stunningly beautiful, with her dark eyes, jet black hair framing her face and a slim, curvy figure—couldn't possibly have any amorous feelings towards her father who was at least three decades older than she was.

As the group chatted through the various courses, Peri felt she had to hand it to her father for holding together a group of people poles apart from each other, and amicably too. Maybe, she thought, she might have underestimated him. After all, he had not only become a major general but had also won a Republican senate seat twice in a usually Democratic state.

Conversation was abruptly interrupted when the lights suddenly dimmed as the butler carried in a huge birthday cake topped with lit candles. The party grew very merry as everyone toasted the senator with champagne.

After dinner, the group moved to the living room for liqueurs, and Powers turned the conversation to art. Peri was not sure if her father was doing this because he thought art would be an uncontroversial topic everyone at the party could discuss or because he wanted to draw out Alex, who he had been told was a professor of art history.

On hearing that both Alex and Peri were specialists of the French Impressionists, the dinner guests started to discuss their favourite artists of the genre. Ginko claimed hers was Monet. 'I wish we were rich enough to own a real painting by Monet. His paintings are so wonderful!' she wistfully exclaimed.

Peri felt like saying *Monet's name popped into your head because you sneaked into my room and saw my Monet reproductions, didn't you?*, but instead she agreed with Ginko, complimenting her on her taste. The butler came to refill the drinks, and as often the case at the end of a party, that broke it up.

The Tairas, the Parellis and McPherson bid farewell and Powers went into his office with Anita, saying they had some business to discuss. Peri and Alex climbed upstairs to turn in. Alex was so weary that he barely kissed Peri good-night before going on up to his guest suite.

As soon as she was in her room, Peri quickly got ready for bed. But she found she was not at all sleepy despite her lingering jet lag. Her mind was at full tilt as she recalled all the incidents of her long day. She soon realized what was really keeping her awake was that several things today seemed so strange, especially after being away for nearly a year.

Why was this sleazy Parelli, with his snoopy wife, such a close associate of her father? Why was a Japanese politician invited to this very small gathering? Surely not just because he admired her father's book or liked his ideas. Why did her father and Karen McPherson sound so adamant when they said the NAD Forum was *not* connected in any way to the Patriot Party? And why was her father so very attentive to Karen McPherson, to the point of making Anita seem upset?

The questions went round and round in her head, and, at last, with no answers, she began to feel drowsy and fell into a troubled sleep.

The following morning, Peri took Alex to meet her grandmother at her modest apartment in Watertown, only a short drive from Chestnut Hill. As soon as she had introduced him to Sandra Powers, she pounced on her grandmother with the question: 'Gran, why weren't you at Dad's birthday party last night? You're his mother, for heaven's sake!'

'Honey, your father talked to me about it and we agreed it would be better if I didn't attend. You know I don't mix well with Simon's political friends. And a long, late dinner is not for someone in their late eighties.'

'It was such an unusual affair. I came back to the US and invited Alex to join me because I was sure we'd be celebrating the birthday with you and our relatives and friends. Instead there were only nine of us, and it was a very odd collection of people. We even had a Japanese congressman and his wife. Gran, with me off in Paris, I'm worried that you're terribly neglected.'

'Peri, it's an election year and I've been reading how busy Simon is with helping Governor Bond win the Republican nomination. You're a dear to worry about me, but you can be assured that I am well taken care of. A woman comes in five days a week to clean, run errands for me, take me to the doctor, anything I need. And I'm a rich old lady compared to the years after your grandfather died and while Simon was still in school. The income from a trust fund Simon made for me enables me to live very comfortably now.'

Peri pressed her lips together and forbore to mention that it was not her son who had set up the trust fund that provided the annuity to make certain Grandma Powers would never be in financial need. It had been his wife, Peri's mother. Her grandmother smiled at Peri as she said, 'You take after your mother, don't you, always thinking of others.'

Unspoken was the idea that her father did not always. It stung a little, as she respected her father for what he had made of himself from humble origins and loved him despite his political views, which she found ultra-conservative, if not reactionary. Thinking of her father, Peri asked, 'Was Dad always so driven, I mean even as a boy? To become a general, he had to be ambitious, but what made him that way? My mother said she was swept off her feet by the tall, military attaché she met at a party in Paris. He always knew just what to do, she said.'

'Your parents met in Paris?' Alex was very surprised.

'Yes. My mother was crazy about everything French. She spent her junior year and two more after graduation in Paris. She was invited to an embassy party where she met this handsome man in uniform with an air of authority. He was ten years older than her, and I guess at first she just liked having someone who seemed to know everything, but I know that she eventually found him overbearing. Was he always like that, Gran?'

'Why are you suddenly asking me all these questions?' Grandma Powers said, clearly trying to stall.

'Well, after seeing virtually nothing of him for the past few years, I realized last night that I don't think I really know him. He's never talked about his childhood, and I have never lived with him after the age of ten.'

Then Peri turned to explain to Alex. 'After Mom was diagnosed with MS—multiple sclerosis I mean—she returned to Boston to get therapy. She moved into her parents' house in Chestnut Hill and brought me with her. So after that I saw Dad only on some of my vacations and not much at all after I went away to college and then grad school.'

Peri's grandmother looked at her thoughtfully, glanced at Alex, and then said ruefully, 'Life wasn't easy for Simon when he was young. In one way, he was too much like his father for the two of them to get along easily. They were both headstrong, absolutely sure they were right, and so they were in constant battle. And then your grandfather had so many problems at work—he always seemed to be on the wrong side of any altercation with his superiors. If he had worked for a private company instead of the post office, I'm sure he would've been fired.'

Sandra Powers paused as if reluctant to say more, but she looked down at her hands and finally said, 'Our life at home became very difficult. Your grandfather was so frustrated after being passed over for promotion time and again that he began to drink rather too much. And he quarrelled more and more with your father. I hate to say this, but your grandfather dying in the one-car accident was . . .'

Peri, seeing her grandmother's eyes moisten, didn't let her finish the sentence.

'So you think my father becoming a conservative was the outcome of his rebelling against Grandpa? I know from all the books in your house that Grandpa was a liberal, even a socialist. You have well-read copies of George Bernard Shaw and Beatrice and Sydney Webb—you lent them to me so I have seen Grandpa's notes in the margins.'

'I think Simon was determined to be a success in life and so he set out to be the opposite of his father. He got top grades in school, never openly rebelled against authority, and was such a model student that his principal recommended him to Senator Tobin as a candidate for West Point. He graduated near the top of his class and went on to have a flawless military career, rather quickly becoming a two-star general.'

'Yes, I know the rest,' Peri said impassively. 'Flawless until he made the mistake of criticizing President Bush for recklessly increasing our national debt. He was talking with several close friends, but what he said leaked and reached the president's ears. He had to resign, of course. But not bad, to go from a major general to a senator!'

Peri's grandmother clearly didn't like the exclamatory remark, which she must have thought a bit too sarcastic. Changing the subject, she asked, 'Alex, how did you meet my granddaughter?'

The Frenchman laughed and said, 'Though we were both living in the same Fifth Arrondissement . . . I mean the same part of Paris . . . and were in the same art-history world, we actually met in Aix-en-Provence, down in the south of France. Peri was working on her doctoral dissertation and went to Aix to consult my friend Claude Martin, who is the curator of a small museum there.'

Peri added to what Alex said, explaining that Claude had been a forger who went straight and was now making a meagre living as a curator. Finally, Alex nudged Peri and said they really ought to be going if they didn't want to be late for lunch at the Hutchinsons', Alex's old friends in Newton.

As the couple walked out to the car, Alex stopped and slapped his forehead. '*Mon Dieu*! I forgot to get a good bottle of wine for the Hutchinson's. His wife learnt to cook well when they lived in Paris and she puts out a superb French meal whenever she has guests.'

'No problem, Alex,' said Peri. 'My father has quite a wine cellar. Chestnut Hill is almost on the way to Newton and we'll stop at my house and grab a bottle.'

As the couple drove up to the Powers' house, Peri noticed her father's car parked in the turnaround. She went through the back door and padded down the carpeted hall to say hello to her father and tell him she had dropped home unexpectedly and hoped he wouldn't mind if she took a bottle of wine for the couple who had invited Alex and her to lunch.

As she neared her father's study, she could hear him talking in his usual loud voice, today rather strident. She couldn't hear what he was saying even though the door was ajar. She thought he must be on the phone. Approaching the door, thinking, *well, at least I can wave at him to let him know I'm back*, she heard a second voice, which she instantly recognized as Lou Parelli's.

Deciding there was no way she was going to enter her father's study while the two were having what sounded like a rather unfriendly conversation, Peri turned to leave. As she was about to back down the hall, their voices grew louder and she stopped in her tracks and caught the tail end of something her father said, '. . . problems? That's just what we don't need now. What's Barrington been doing?'

Peri couldn't quite catch Parelli's reply and without a thought took two steps closer to the door to hear better.

'Barrington is asking us to send more than ten thou at a time, Senator. FinCEN is going to catch on sooner or later. And I've got too many Swift codes. I'm not sure if I should phase out some of those in Zug and George Town.'

'As I've told you repeatedly, you can't get me involved in this at all . . . it's your neck,' her father replied.

'But Senator, that's what I'm trying to do . . . keep you out of it. I want you to stay above it all. But can we at least replace Barrington with someone else and phase out some Swift codes? I'm a little overwhelmed by the number of accounts in foreign banks and by the amount of money coming in and going out.'

'Just keep me out of it. I told you when I hired you . . . you can never get me mixed up in what you're doing. Never! In my position, I can't afford to be connected to anything shady or illegal. I have to stay above reproach! Don't make me repeat this. Dealing with Barrington is your job. Barrington is the best pipeline we've got. And you knew from the beginning you'd be dealing with a significant amount of money. Don't try to drag me into this. You handle it.'

Peri could hear a chair being scraped back and decided she'd better beat a retreat. She hastened down the hall and went through the swinging door to the service area. She grabbed a bottle of wine from the top rack in the pantry where she knew her father kept his best red wines. Then she quietly let herself out the back door.

As she got into the car, she handed the bottle to Alex. 'I just grabbed one. I hope this is good enough for the Hutchinsons.'

Alex, reading the label of the bottle, exclaimed, '*Mon Dieu*, Peri, this is Chateau Puy-Blanquet, St Emilion, 2007. This is more than good enough. It's one of the top Bordeaux wines . . . and 2007 was a very good year.'

Alex realized Peri wasn't reacting, took a good look at her and asked, 'Peri, is something the matter?'

'Umm, no. But why don't you drive.'

As the couple set out to Newton, Peri was quiet, disturbing questions running through her mind. What was her father arguing about with the sleazy banker he'd made the treasurer of his new organization? And it had sounded as if this former banker was involved in something unethical, if not illegal, and he was trying to involve her father in whatever it was he was up to. Her father seemed worried that he would be blamed for what Parelli was doing. What was FinCEN? Who was this Barrington? What was the important pipeline? And where were Zug and Georgetown? Surely, the latter was in Washington DC. What was a Swift code? Some code that made something go fast?

The more she thought about what she had just heard the more it sounded like Parelli was trying to drag her father into something illegal despite saying he wanted her father to stay above it all. Peri was unable to conceive of her father, a former upstanding general turned principled senator, doing anything unethical, let alone illegal. To prove she was correct, she decided she had to understand these mysterious financial terms and decipher what the conversation was really about. If there was anything at all she could do to prevent her father being dragged into Parelli's mess, she had to do it.

Peri was aware that Alex was casting anxious glances at her, but she didn't want to tell him anything yet. What she regretted above all else at the moment was having gone home to fetch the wine and having unwittingly eavesdropped on the conversation between her father and Parelli.

'Zender. Now that's an unusual name, isn't it?' chatted the genial hotel clerk as she looked at the registration form on the counter in front of her. She glanced up at the man checking in and saw the piercing look in his eyes. She immediately clammed up, accepted the guest's Visa card and finished registering him. Then she handed over the key to the room he had requested at the back of the hotel, near the entrance to the car park.

As he walked to his room, he wondered if he had better start asking for IDs and credit cards with more common names, even if they were nothing like his real one. After all, he selected these chain hotels near airports to try to remain inconspicuous. That was why he had chosen the Holiday Inn near the Buffalo Niagara International Airport for this assignment.

Once in his room, he plunked down his carry-on and started the checks that had become routine since he started these assignments. First he checked the window and the door locks. Then he went out to the corridor and made a thorough study of the hotel, from the inside and the outside. Assured that he now knew how to swiftly get in and out of the hotel, he returned to his room and made himself a brew using the electric water heater and a packet of instant coffee the hotel had supplied. He sipped it, set the cup down on the bedside table, and plopped on the bed. From his jacket pocket he took out a folded piece of paper with the information for his assignment. He had received it three days ago via email and had printed it out. His target was a Democratic candidate for Congress, Anthony d'Abruzzio. He had already read the sheet of paper three or four times, and had also looked up d'Abruzzio on YouTube. His target was a tough-looking burly man of fifty-six.

Tony d'Abruzzio had been a truck driver with a high school education. He had clawed his way up to become a union leader in the Buffalo area. For the past twelve years he had served as a state representative, and was now running for a seat in the House of Representatives. Tony had been investigated a few times, but never prosecuted, on suspicion of embezzlement of union funds and extortion of several businessmen.

His stomach reminded him that it was past lunchtime. He took his clothes out of his carry-on and put them away, put his smaller shoulder bag into the suitcase, locked it and set it in the back of the closet. Then he was out the door to the car park and on his way to West Seneca—d'Abruzzio's campaign headquarters. He easily found it on Union Road, and not far from it a small Mexican restaurant. He ordered tacos and a Coke and sat down at a table near the counter. The lunch crowd was leaving, so when a middle-aged man, who looked like he might be the owner, came round to clear tables, he asked, 'I see Tony d'Abruzzio's headquarters are just up the street. Do you get much business from them?'

'Naw, there's only a couple of people on his staff. They come in occasionally, but I guess Tony doesn't like Mexican food.'

'What are his chances of winning in November?'

The restaurant owner stopped wiping tables and faced his customer. 'Pretty good, I'd say. People have wanted him in Congress for years but he refused to run until this year when old Jim Cogan went too far and got censured by the House Ethics Committee for misusing government funds. If a Democrat could win the primary, he'd be a shoo-in in November.'

'You mean things have changed?'

'Yeah, well, the so-called Patriot Party has a lot of support here right now. The popular host of a local radio talk show has been making speeches. The usual Patriot stuff about doing more for the unemployed, eliminating a lot of regulations, lowering the national debt . . . that sort of thing. This talk show guy used to be very popular with the Tea Party and now has a big following among the Patriots. He's been trying to sway the Democrats away from Tony to the Republican candidate, but Tony is so popular I think he'll win. Say, can I get you anything else?'

'Black coffee, please,' he replied to keep the conversation going. The owner went behind the counter and poured out a cup of coffee from a thermos and brought it round.

'You're not from these parts, I take it,' the man said as he put the coffee down on the table and pushed the sugar holder over to his customer.

'No, I work out of New York, but I like to know a bit about the areas I come to.' He didn't want to talk about himself, so he asked another question.

'Well, if Tony doesn't eat here, where does he go?'

'He likes Italian food as we'd expect of a good Italian American. He and his good-looking young wife are regulars at Alonzo's over on Center Road. A posh Italian place with white tablecloths. So what business are you in that brings you all the way to West Seneca?'

It was definitely time to leave.

'Insurance.' He pointedly looked at his watch. 'I've got to run.'

He handed the owner twenty dollars and told him to keep the change. Then he was out the door.

Odd man that, thought the owner. *If he wasn't going to drink the coffee, why did he order it?*

Once outside, the man who was in such a hurry to leave the restaurant put on sunglasses and slowly strolled down the street past d'Abruzzio's campaign headquarters. He stopped to read a poster and looked inside. Not a soul was in sight. He returned to his rented car, got in and pulled out his mobile phone. He called Alonzo's and made a reservation for that evening for six-thirty. Then he drove round West Seneca to get a feel of the town and found it to be a singularly uninteresting though pleasant bedroom town. So he headed back to his hotel where he worked out in his room and then carefully checked all the things he always carried on his assignments. At six, he was back on the road again, this time heading for Alonzo's. He parked a short distance away and sauntered into the restaurant. He arrived to find only three tables occupied— two older couples and a family of four. He ordered a glass of the house red. When it came, he stopped the waiter and asked questions about the menu, though he had already decided he would order steak.

'I was told this is Mr d'Abruzzio's favourite restaurant. How often does he come here?' the man asked idly.

'At least a few times every week. But if you're hoping to see him today, he never comes in on Wednesdays—has some kind of union meeting in Buffalo. Most often, he's here with his wife on Fridays.'

So the man's assignment remained incomplete tonight, but he had a very good chance of finishing it on Friday, in just two days. He polished off his meal, complimented the waiter and the manager for the excellent food and service, and reserved a table for Friday.

But this meant he had time to kill, a whole forty-eight hours before he got a chance to finish his assignment. It really wasn't worth going back to New York for a day. In the end he decided to visit Niagara Falls the next day. To his surprise, the day went very quickly because he chatted up two young Japanese women, one of who looked very much like Kim, his girlfriend from years ago. The women were surprised he spoke passable Japanese and accepted his invitation for lunch.

Friday evening the man returned to Alonzo's at half past six. The restaurant was much busier and he was told it was a good thing he had made a reservation.

He sat down and ordered a glass of red wine again. He looked round the restaurant but there was no sign of d'Abruzzio. He kept his eyes on the door, wondering if it would be another wasted evening. And then a burly man with a mane of grey hair appeared from the men's room and headed for what was clearly the best table in the room. *D'Abruzzio*!

As Tony sat down, just two tables away from the man, a waiter hastened over and said, 'Your wife called. Said she'd be a bit delayed. Can I get you your usual Chianti Classico?'

'Thanks, Mario. And I'll wait to order until my wife shows up.'

The man breathed in deeply and waited until d'Abruzzio was alone and settled. Then he walked slowly up to his table with a new briefcase in his hand.

'Mr d'Abruzzio, may I speak to you for a couple of minutes? This won't take long. I tried to catch you at your headquarters but it was closed when I stopped by. Sorry, my name is Chad Lopez and I represent a group of gentlemen who wish to make sure the Democratic candidates do well in November.'

D'Abruzzio, more than a little surprised, looked at the man for a long moment and said, 'What is this? Who did you say you work for?'

'Some very rich gentlemen who must remain anonymous but who want to make a sizeable contribution to your campaign. They want as many Democrats as possible to win in November.'

After a pause even longer than the last, d'Abruzzio said tauntingly, 'Well, well. That's very interesting. The Democrats always win in this district. I know my Republican opponent thinks he can beat me with the help of these nutty Patriots. But they don't have a prayer. So . . . do your gentlemen know something I don't? For all I know, you could be wearing a wire for the Feds. Scram.'

He stayed where he was and waited.

D'Abruzzio stared at him. 'Whatever you said your name is, your eyes remind me of a crooked truck driver in New Jersey I used to know and I don't believe in fucking fairy tales.'

The man took a step closer to the table and spoke rapidly into d'Abruzzio's left ear as he opened his briefcase and put it onto d'Abruzzio's lap.

D'Abruzzio was startled by this move. He looked into a case filled with bundles of one-hundred-dollar bills. His mouth gaped open.

Before d'Abruzzio said anything, the man started the spiel he had carefully prepared. In a low voice, he said they could go to the men's room where he could be frisked for any wires or microphones. Or they could meet tomorrow at d'Abruzzio's headquarters or at his home after dinner or anytime tomorrow. He knew what he was offering might sound dubious, but the rich gentlemen were retired senators and very rich businessmen, all staunch Democrats who wanted to do everything they could to prevent the Republicans from taking over Congress. Then he added, 'Sir, these gentlemen know your Republican opponent isn't likely to win even with the support of the crazy Patriot Party, but they want to be doubly sure you get elected.'

The man continued to deliver his prepared speech: 'Sir, if you want, these gentlemen can provide a foolproof document attesting that the money came from nearly a hundred donors, each giving less than the legally permitted campaign contribution. The money in the briefcase is five hundred, mostly used, one-hundred-dollar bills. All are unmarked, chemically or otherwise. Most are old and none have consecutive serial numbers. I assure you that the donors ask for absolutely nothing in return for the money. Sir, this isn't a fairy tale. The money you see is real. All fifty grand!'

As the man talked on, he could see d'Abruzzio's expression change from his initial anger to bewilderment and then, as he fingered the bundles of bills, to an impish and knowing grin. The man knew he had the Congressional candidate hooked.

D'Abruzzio saw the waiter approach with the wine before the man did, and hurriedly closed the flap of the briefcase and put it on the floor between his leg and the leg of the table. When the waiter showed him the bottle, he said coolly, 'Thanks, Mario. Just open it.'

The donor of the briefcase, more than a little impressed by the imperturbability of the candidate, said, 'Thank you, Mr D'Abruzzio, for your time. I apologize for intruding on your evening.'

As Mario opened the bottle of wine, the man straightened up as if preparing to leave. He could hardly breathe, knowing his chances of being asked to have dinner or at least a drink with d'Abruzzio were riding on the latter behaving normally.

'Wait, don't go. Do sit down and have a drink with me. Mario, please pour two glasses of wine.'

The man took a deep breath and sat down. 'Thank you, sir.'

As the waiter poured the wine, d'Abruzzio asked, 'What did you say your name was?'

'Chad Lopez, sir.'

'Well, Chad, let's toast the Democratic Party and all of its benefactors!' So saying d'Abruzzio raised his glass of wine, Chad quickly picked up his, and they clinked glasses. They had barely sipped their wine when another waiter came to the table with a platter of Calamari Fritti compliments of Alonzo.

'Dig in, Chad. This is the best calamari west of Italy.'

D'Abruzzio was clearly in ebullient spirits and Chad egged him on, asking questions about where the d'Abruzzios would live while in Washington and how many terms he envisioned serving in Congress.

Soon d'Abruzzio's glass of wine needed to be topped, and, before Mario could return to fill it, Chad grabbed his opportunity. He picked up the bottle of wine, stood up and went round the table to refill his host's glass. Ignoring d'Abruzzio, who was rather surprised by this, he held onto the glass with his left hand, pouring wine with his right. At least that's what d'Abruzzio saw, completely missing Chad's magician-like quick release of a stream of pale gold liquid into the wine. He returned to his place and poured wine into his own glass too.

Just as d'Abruzzio picked up his glass, a very attractive young woman waltzed up to the table. She kissed d'Abruzzio, said 'Jeez, what a day. Sorry I'm late,' snatched the glass from his hand and gulped half of it, all without taking a breath. 'Boy, did I need that! *Molto delizioso*!' she exclaimed and sat down. D'Abruzzio did the introductions: 'Chad, this is my wife, Amanda. Amanda, meet Chad. A good friend.'

With the half-full glass of wine still in her hand, she smiled at Chad and said hello. Her husband picked up the bottle, grabbed a glass from the next table and poured wine for himself. He began to sip it, and turned to his new friend: 'You must stay for dinner. I insist. The Piccata Milanese is their signature dish.'

Chad's head was spinning, and he managed a shaky 'Thank you'. All he could think of was *Christ, the young wife*, not *the target, is going to die*!

Mario returned to the table. Tony d'Abruzzio ordered for all three of them and asked for a second bottle of wine. The rest of the meal was a blur for Chad but he didn't think his hosts noticed. He wasn't listening to Amanda's chatter and he barely registered what her husband said, talking so excitedly because of the contents of the briefcase at his feet.

While pretending to listen to the couple, Chad tried to calculate how long it would take Amanda to die. She was probably half the weight of her husband, and the amount of golden liquid he had squeezed into the wine glass by the unnoticed bend of his left arm was calculated for a man of well over two hundred pounds. How long would it be before Amanda began to show the effects of what she had consumed? Perhaps two hours before she experienced chest pains? And now how was he going to get his actual target? Even if he managed to get at his wine glass, if both husband and wife died from heart attacks the same evening, all hell would break loose and it would make all future assignments difficult, if not impossible, to carry out. Chad couldn't think of what he should do.

During dinner, d'Abruzzio drained his glass three times. Chad debated what he should do, but Mario kept his valued customer's glass full. So Chad nibbled at the veal, merely sipped the wine and gave monosyllabic answers when either the husband or the wife spoke to him. He was now resigned to a botched assignment.

Before after-dinner coffee arrived, Chad looked at his watch and excused himself, saying he had to get back to New York. Amanda suggested he spend the night in their guest room, but he firmly declined the unexpected offer. As he stood up to leave, d'Abruzzio too got up, albeit a bit shakily. He shook hands and said, 'Nice getting to know you, Chad. If you come to DC after January, do look me up. And thank your friends for me for the campaign contribution.'

From the restaurant, Chad strode the three blocks to his rented Nissan. He was shivering in the wind blowing in from Lake Erie and despondent because he knew he had failed. In a couple of hours his target, the overweight Congressional candidate, would still be alive, but his young wife would be dead.

But as he started his car, he knew he would be long gone by the time she died and when the police decided to look for him after talking to her husband and possibly the waiter. Then, as usual, he put the thought of what he had done out of his mind and concentrated on what he had to do next. Despite what he had said to d'Abruzzio, he had no intention of going to the airport. There were no flights to New York after nine. He would stick to his original plan: spend the night at the Holiday Inn and fly out tomorrow morning. Too obvious if he checked out now, and there wasn't the remotest possibility of either d'Abruzzio or the police immediately connecting Greg Zender to Amanda's sudden death. He was very confident that the chance of anyone, even the FBI, finding him was a big fat zero. And if they did start looking for the man at the d'Abruzzio's table, it would be for a man named Chad Lopez.

Twenty minutes later he was back in the car park behind the hotel. He went to the front desk and asked to settle his bill tonight because he would be leaving early in the morning. Then he went back to his room. He quickly undressed down to his underwear and carefully lifted two long, thin slips of adhesive tape from his left wrist and the inside of his left arm to remove a long thin rubber tube and a thumb-sized rubber ball attached to the end of the tube. These he put in a small case in his carry-on.

The next morning Greg Zender returned his rented Nissan to the airport rental agency, paid the extra charges with a Visa card and took the agency's shuttle to the terminal building. That was the last anyone would ever be able to trace of a man named Greg Zender.

Simon Powers once again glanced at his watch. It was now twelve past nine. Where was Governor Bond? The meeting of the Eagle Society had been set to start at nine sharp. What could possibly be holding him up on a Sunday morning? Some urgent state business or something pressing related to his presidential campaign? Powers had to keep himself from drumming his fingers on the dinner table, a nervous habit.

The other members of the Eagle Society had already arrived and were waiting in Bond's dining room. Professor Karen McPherson was chatting quietly with Senator Tom Jameson from Texas, a former professor. Congresswoman Evelyn Barrington from Southern California was texting on her iPhone. Gordon J. Brewster, now board chairman of the Brewster Corporation, was talking on his mobile, while Senator Christian Herrmann from Wyoming sipped coffee.

Powers turned a page of the *St. Paul Pioneer Press*, but he wasn't reading the paper. As he impatiently waited for Bond, he thought back to when he had created the Eagle Society, the very reason he was sitting this morning in the large dining room of the governor's official residence in St Paul.

In early spring of last year, the polls had shown that Powers' possible run for the Republican nomination was doomed to fail. In virtually all the polls, he had come either last or next to last among the seven likely candidates. Realizing that this meant he had no chance of leading a real conservative revolution, the likes of which the US had never before seen, he had pursued a carefully planned strategy to become the vice president, the man only a heartbeat away from the presidency.

In July, he had published, with the able assistance of Anita Faga, *The New American Destiny*, which spelt out his vision of the new America, which would be 'debt-free, have far lower taxes and fewer regulations, and possess military power that would make the US the unquestioned hegemonic power in the world'. Then, in September, he had created The New American Destiny Forum, a tax-exempt educational organization with two goals. One goal was to hold forums, publish books and pamphlets, contribute op-ed articles to national and local papers and send its members—truly conservative academics and other opinion leaders—to appear on talk shows, give speeches at colleges and the like. The second, and far more important, was to have the forum act as a covert conduit for funnelling money to the presidential candidate who would agree to pick him for his running mate. In addition, the forum would provide covert financial support to Republican Congressional candidates in tight races and also to the Patriots in order to sway them to vote for Republican candidates. Sending money to the Patriots had to be done as surreptitiously as possible. Should anyone, especially the Independents who would decide the outcome of the election, find out the forum was funding the Patriots, the conservative Republican candidates, Bond included, would be severely punished come November.

Powers thought his idea of creating the forum to send money covertly to the Republican candidates was a stroke of genius. The Super PACs, the political action committees, were allowed to raise unlimited amounts of money but they were prohibited from providing money to candidates and were much more rigorously audited than Powers' educational forum would be.

Powers then had to undertake two more tasks. One was to select an ideologically like-minded presidential candidate who had a good chance of winning the Republican nomination and who would agree to pick him as his running mate, in return for receiving campaign funding via the NAD Forum. The other was to create a small clandestine group who shared his political ideology and who would help him raise and distribute huge amounts of money to various candidates and to the Patriot Party.

The first of the two tasks turned out to be rather delicate but not too difficult. Since Powers knew Bradley Bond was the only candidate for the Republican nomination who was his ideological kin and had a good chance of winning, he had approached him. The two had not been acquainted, so it took four lengthy meetings during October for Bond to finally agree to use the NAD Forum in the way Powers had planned and to join Powers' group for raising money. At the fourth meeting, Bond agreed to pick Powers for vice president provided it remained absolutely secret until he won the nomination. It had been Bond who proposed the group be named the 'Eagle Society'. He had said, 'It sounds very patriotic and very American.'

Forming the Eagle Society proved not difficult at all. It happened almost naturally. Earlier, in August, Powers had contacted Karen McPherson, whose political views he knew well because her publications had been indispensable in writing his book. He wanted her in the group both because of her influence as a professor and pundit and because she was a multibillionaire. She was the sole heiress of her husband, a billionaire banker. And she had inherited at least four billion dollars from her father Wendell Kendrick. Like her husband and her father, Karen was well known as a generous contributor to the Republican

Party, especially to candidates who really believed in the 'true free enterprise system'. One evening, last September, she promised Powers ten million dollars, to be wired as soon as he gave her the account information, saying, 'I hope this is enough for you to put the New American Destiny Forum into the wider public view. We really need to get the right people into office. If you need more, we can discuss it.' She had readily agreed to be a member of his secret society for fundraising.

At Karen's suggestion, Powers contacted Gordon Brewster, founder of Brewster Corporation, the world's third largest maker of machinery of all types, from small precision machines used in surgeries to huge machines used in building dams and skyscrapers. Powers had no idea exactly how rich the crusty and well-read old man was, but he knew Brewster had assets of at least two billion dollars. When Powers had approached him saying, 'Karen McPherson suggested I tell you what a few friends and I are doing' and explained the forum and the Eagle Society, Brewster had immediately agreed to join the group. He had matched Karen's contribution of ten million dollars to 'an enterprise our country really needs'.

Powers looked up from his newspaper and glanced at Brewster. He was sure that he could get a lot more from him if he hinted that such support would surely bring him the ambassadorship to the Court of St James when Bond became president.

With Bond and the two major contributors on board, getting the final three members of the Eagle Society was quite easy. Powers had approached Senator Tom Jameson, who was known for his political acumen and muscle, and had got an unqualified and enthusiastic 'Yes, of course, Simon.' Powers genuinely liked Jameson, who was a close colleague in the Senate and nearly always voted as Powers did. He valued Jameson's counsel on almost all issues. Jameson also agreed to serve as the vice chair of the executive committee of the NAD Forum. He had worked tirelessly to recruit members for the forum, from CEOs of large firms to leaders in many fields including academia.

The last two members of the Eagle Society were unanimously agreed on by Powers, Bond and Jameson.

One was Christian Herrmann, the sixty-eight-year-old senior senator from Wyoming who had served as Secretary of Commerce in a past Republican administration. Powers found him a little too earthy but valued his strong convictions in the vision they shared. Herrmann was the strongest supporter of the NRA in the Senate and he had a nose for money—he was an unabashed fundraiser who knew how to get round all the legal restrictions on raising and dispensing funds. Since he was not up for re-election this year, he had already raised and found safe ways to channel almost fifteen million dollars to the coffers of the NAD Forum. Powers had no doubt that he could come up with a lot more cash.

The last member recruited was Evelyn Barrington. She was an indefatigable, veteran congresswoman from San Diego who could work as liaison with the Patriot Party because of her strong right-wing views and her personality. She would be an indispensable pipeline to the Patriot Party. Barrington was the only person in the Eagle Society towards whom Powers felt a visceral dislike, for a reason he couldn't quite pin down, but he knew they needed a pipeline to the Patriots. The NAD Forum was already funnelling money through her— to pay for rent and wages—to several candidates and local groups, and she had proven to be good at fundraising from small donors, particularly in the Western states. Despite his dislike of the brash, homely woman, Powers had come to appreciate her ability to act as the behind-the-scenes puppeteer of many, if not most, of the leaders of the Patriot Party, adroitly providing guidance to them with regard to their activities.

The seven had held their first meeting in Honolulu just after Christmas. The members had all arranged to spend the holidays in the Hawaiian Islands, so no one but they knew of the real purpose of their visit to Honolulu. On the day of the meeting, they each made their way to the three-bedroom luxury condo Powers had purchased near Diamond Head with a magnificent view of the Pacific Ocean. Not all of the seven had met before, though they all knew about each other. After an amiable hour of cocktails, viewing the sunset over the Pacific, they got down to business that lasted through the dinner that followed and most of the next day.

By the end of the Honolulu meeting they had agreed to raise at least two hundred million dollars before August to assure Bond's winning the nomination and to provide funds to Republican candidates and the Patriot Party. They had also had extended discussions on who would be the most likely donors, what the members of the Eagle Society could promise to donors in return for their money, how the forum was to be used and numerous other details. All the members accepted Powers' suggestion to call the list of issues they had agreed upon the Honolulu Pact.

The Eagle Society had its second meeting in early February at Powers' mansion in Chestnut Hill to provide updates on their fundraising efforts and strategize on how the money being raised was going to be distributed. They also discussed what the forum could do to best aid Bond and other candidates.

Today was the third such meeting of all the members. None of the group members wanted to leak out that they were secretly meeting in St Paul. So each pretended to be in the twin cities of Minneapolis–St Paul on a different pretext.

Powers couldn't be happier and prouder of what he had accomplished. He was singularly confident that the ability of the members to raise large sums of money furtively and the talents of the treasurer of the forum to hide all traces of these assets from the authorities would enable the forum to collect and disperse its wealth as Powers wished, and so achieve his own goal of becoming vice president.

Powers looked at his watch again. The gratification the memory gave him was quickly turning into annoyance. His displeasure in waiting for Bond increased as he thought how much he disliked St Paul. He found its downtown a forlorn collection of utilitarian buildings hemmed in by freeways with nothing green in sight. And here he was on a Sunday morning in the governor's mansion just sitting round waiting for Governor Bond to show up. They had important business to discuss and he knew most of the group had planes to catch in the afternoon. This certainly wasn't the way things were run when he was in the army, he thought.

As he began to drum his fingers on the table, Mrs Bond came in with a fresh carafe of coffee—the staff had the day off, allowing the secret Sunday morning meeting—and apologies from her husband. The governor's wife explained that her husband had had a breakfast meeting with key legislators and he would be with them shortly.

Even before Mrs Bond had finished replenishing their cups, Bond breezed in with more apologies and individual greetings for each member. Whenever Powers saw Bradley Bond, he had to try hard not to be envious of him. The Minnesota governor was a tall and handsome man at fifty-two, thirteen years younger than Powers. He had easily won his last two elections, was extremely articulate and, since the Super Tuesday primaries earlier in the month, was now running neck and neck with Governor Higgins, the moderate mainstream candidate from Missouri, in the nomination race for the Republican Party.

Powers made coughing sounds and suggested they begin since they had so much to discuss.

Bond took the chair's seat at the head of the table, but it was Powers who ran the meeting. At six-feet two and weighing two hundred and forty pounds, with a shock of grey hair, Powers radiated the same authority and confidence he had when a major general. Even seated, he looked imposing to the other six people round the table.

Powers wasted no time in coming to the main reason for the meeting: fundraising.

'We need to step up our fundraising because so many of the Congressional races look very close. Our candidates need to be able to buy more TV spots. We need to give more incentives to local TV stations to invite our candidates for interviews by promising to buy more of their airtime. And our candidates can use a lot more money for various campaign expenses. I don't need to go on. I can tell you that they all really appreciate the money they get from us which they don't have to report to the election commission.'

Heads nodded in agreement, and Powers enumerated his second concern.

'In addition to funnelling money to our struggling candidates, we need to send a lot more money to drum up the support of the Patriots. I know they are a black hole, but we must send them more than Evelyn has been able to until now.'

'Simon is absolutely correct,' said Evelyn Barrington, launching into a veritable tirade.

'Looking at the districts in the states where there were Super Tuesday primaries, it's very obvious we need to get more votes from the Patriots. After so many terms in Congress, I've learned to read the mood of these people who constitute about two-thirds of my district. I know . . . I feel . . . how angry, confused and scared they are. Either they've lost jobs, or they have relatives and friends who are looking for work and can't make ends meet. Do you know that the average number of people per household in my district has risen significantly because of multiple families pooling their resources and living together? They need a target to vent their anger . . . and their target is the politician. The only politicians they don't hate are those who are as critical as they are of most of the Democrats and what the media call mainstream Republicans. The trick we have to pull off is to convince these people that Brad is a real conservative like them . . . a man with a new vision who can set the mainstream Republicans straight. They may be a little prone to violence, unlike the Tea Party people, but we can't win the election without them!'

Powers nodded in agreement and said, 'Evelyn is right.'

Before he could say more, Barrington added with vehemence: 'Have you seen the successes they've had? I often send a dozen Patriots to some of the campaign speeches to whip up excitement for our candidates or to shout out some questions or broadsides at the candidates we need to defeat. And you might have seen on TV news that some of my people have totally disrupted several recent campaign speeches by Democratic candidates.'

Professor McPherson spoke up: 'The Patriots certainly aren't very rational in their outlook. I applaud their demand for smaller government and huge budget cuts. But how can they demand at the same time increased spending for Medicare and Medicaid, Social Security, school lunches, unemployment benefits and more. Most of them are a bunch of nuts and dolts.'

Hearing the words 'nuts and dolts,' Evelyn Barrington's nostrils flared.

'Karen, if you talk to them, you'll find them quite well informed. Many of them are well educated . . . some of them are accountants, teachers and nurses. I admit their views can be nutty at times but I wouldn't call them dolts. That's insulting to those whose votes we need.'

'Well, I shouldn't have called them dolts. Evelyn, I apologize if I offended you.'

Ever the diplomat, Bond said, 'Well, ladies, the bottom line is we need them no matter what you call them. We can't have them swaying the outcome of the remaining primaries away from me . . . to Congressman Fulton, our Libertarian friend who is again trying to win our party's nomination. So, we have to walk a tightrope. We can't lean too far to the right, as the Patriots want us to do, lest we lose the moderates in the primaries and the Independents in November. But we have to lean as far in their direction as we can. And that means, as Simon and Evelyn have said, sending them more money.'

Powers smiled for the first time since the meeting had begun. 'So let's get back to the main issue,' he said. 'We've done well so far. To date we've raised more than two hundred million dollars, thanks in no small part to very generous gifts from Karen and Gordon. But I'd feel a lot better if we could raise at least another two hundred million to make sure Brad gets nominated in August and then elected in November.'

Powers kept mum about the forty million dollars Brad and he had raised from the CEOs of thirty-two of the largest financial institutions and companies in the country. Because these donations were strictly illegal, the money had been raised with extreme caution. Donors had been met at out-of-the-way places in total secrecy, and, most important, the emissaries of the CEOs and Parelli, the crafty treasurer, had worked out myriad complicated arrangements that often made use of offshore banks. In virtually every case, Bond and Powers had promised the CEO that they would do their utmost to amend or even gut several laws the donors disliked and enact ones they wanted.

'We get the message, Simon,' Senator Jameson said. 'Each of us has been at this game for a long time so we know how to wrestle up donations. It may not be easy, but we can do it.'

Herrmann agreed. 'Tom is right. We've already tapped our usual donors. But if we make the right promises, thirty million is not an unrealistic target for each of us. We can get new donors if we promise something they want from the Bond administration.'

'Promise anything . . . within reason,' instructed Powers. 'I'm sure what our donors want is what we want too.'

Barrington said she didn't think she could raise that sum. Brewster and Herrmann promised to help her achieve her quota. The discussion turned to details.

An hour later, many were getting restive. Tom Jameson looked at his watch, jumped up and declared that he really had to get to the airport to catch his flight back to DC. 'Sorry to break up the meeting,' he said, but Powers could see that the white-haired man was tired.

The governor invited the rest of the group to stay on. 'Join me for a drink and a light meal. My wife has gone to pick up the best Thai food in St Paul.'

But one by one the others apologized and excused themselves.

'Well, Simon, that leaves just the two of us,' Bond said jovially.

Powers and Bond had planned an afternoon *tête-à-tête*. Powers was willing to suffer a few more hours with the Governor of Minnesota for whom he had no special fondness but who was indispensable to his shot at the vice presidency. But he hadn't anticipated having to suffer Thai food as well—his least favourite ethnic cuisine. But longing for that second-highest office he replied, 'Thanks, Brad. That's very kind of you and your wife.'

'Lisa, it's official . . . Sasaki died of a heart attack.' Captain Kalani tapped a document on the top of his desk. 'The initial autopsy report just came in this morning.'

'Did the forensic pathologist test for any foreign substances . . . poisons or anything?'

'Yes. The report says she found only a small amount of alcohol in his system, but no drugs for which she tested. The doctor who signed the death certificate and the pathologist said all signs point to a heart attack. Lots of seemingly healthy men in their forties die suddenly. So you can stop obsessing about a man who shouldn't have been at the party. He could've been just another bored local guy acting on a dare or a bet, or perhaps he wanted to see what a party at a mansion in Kahala was like. Who knows?'

Disheartened, Lisa went back to her desk, leant on it with her elbows and put her head in her hands. She just knew something was wrong. Steve had bragged about having swum a kilometre on the morning of the fundraising party and he had been running the Honolulu Marathon for the past several years. He had been the picture of health! She had no idea how the man with the creepy eyes could have done it, but her gut told her that he had done something, somehow to cause the heart attack.

Her pal Sergeant Pat Foletta found her slouched over her desk some minutes later and invited her out to lunch to cheer her up. But Lisa declined, went down to the snack shop, bought a sandwich and coffee and brought them back to her desk. And as she sipped her coffee, an image came unbidden to her mind. It was of that waiter refilling Steve's cup, clumsily pouring coffee with his right hand while his left hand held the cup, which he had set on the edge of the table. Had he looked clumsy because he was putting something into the coffee? But how could he have put something into the coffee in full view of so many people? What about some unusual substance the pathologist hadn't tested for or for which she didn't yet have the results? Was there sophisticated enough equipment in Hawaii to do an advanced test to find the residue of some unusual poison? She knew she didn't know enough about these things and her imagination could be running amok.

She finished eating and turned on her computer to browse through the news as she often did at midday. Most of the headlines were the same old stuff, but then an item on CNN caught her eye: the wife of a candidate for Congress had suddenly died in some place called West Seneca near Buffalo, New York. Why would this make national news? She read on further and found the reason: the police were looking for a man 'most likely in his thirties', who had had dinner with the couple a few hours before her death. Though the certifying doctor had said her death was due to a heart attack, 'the police wanted to cover all bases' the report said.

Well, Captain Kalani was wrong. Lisa couldn't get rid of her obsession just yet. The woman who died in New York State was only thirty-seven, even younger than Steve. But it was her husband who was running for Congress. Could something have gone wrong? The question made Lisa realize that in the back of her mind she was formulating a hypothesis: the man with the eerie eyes was killing political candidates by somehow causing a heart attack. But since the candidate hadn't died in West Seneca, she wondered if his wife had been murdered by mistake.

Lisa sat up straight. Despite what her captain said, she wasn't going to forget about this case. She would investigate it on her own time and on her own dime. She looked at her watch. It was almost six on the East Coast. Someone in the West Seneca Police Department might be still at work and could answer her questions. She looked up the number for them and placed a call on her mobile.

'Honolulu Police Department? You're calling from Hawaii?' was the surprised question of the man to whom Lisa's call had been directed. 'What can I do for you? I'm Detective Geoff Cohen, by the way.'

Lisa introduced herself and explained that she was calling because of the similarities in the death of Stephan Sasaki and Amanda d'Abruzzio. 'I know they were both certified as having died from a heart attack, but there seems to be a mysterious man involved in both cases and I'm calling to get a good description of the man who had dinner with the d'Abruzzios. I'm also wondering if you can tell me more than was in the news item I read online.'

Detective Cohen sounded taken aback, but he gave her the description she wanted: 'D'Abruzzio said the guy was in his thirties, five–eight, maybe a bit taller, on the lanky side, black hair, spoke American English, definitely not with an East Coast accent—couldn't tell from where. He was rather ordinary except for two things. First, neither Tony d'Abruzzio nor the waiter could tell what race the guy was. One thought he was part Asian, the other possibly Mexican—he gave his name as Chad Lopez. But both agreed that, 'he had piercing dark eyes, rather scary when you looked directly at him.'

Lisa thanked the detective, excitement in her voice. Reacting to Lisa's tone, the West Seneca detective said, 'You think these deaths are connected? The one in Honolulu and the one here? How could the guy have caused a heart attack? The physician who signed Amanda d'Abruzzio's death certificate was certain it was her heart. And it was the wife who died, not the candidate.'

'So why are you seeking the man who had dinner with them?' enquired Lisa.

'It's really just to clear things up. When Mrs d'Abruzzio suddenly collapsed late in the evening, her husband called 911 to get an ambulance. She had already passed away by the time it got there, so the police were called in. It seemed to everyone to be from natural causes—an aneurysm, heart attack, something like that. So the physician who was called in certified the death and there was no autopsy. But Tony D, as he's affectionately known here, is a local bigwig, and so I was asked to follow up the next morning. I went through the events of the day with him and that's when I learnt about the man who had dinner with the couple, a guy they'd never met before. I thought this rather odd, so I went to the restaurant and interviewed the staff.'

'And so you couldn't just drop it?' asked Lisa.

'You got it. We're a small, local police force, but once someone sets the ball rolling—this time, inadvertently me—we have to follow up. But we sure never expected to get a call from out in the Pacific Ocean regarding a death here in West Seneca! So,' he said thoughtfully, 'you think someone is trying to take down Democratic candidates for Congress? People who are sure to win? Then why Mrs D, and not Tony?'

'Well, if this mysterious guy administered some kind of slow-acting poison and managed to get it into something the victim ate or drank, isn't it possible that the wrong person somehow took the poison? That it was Tony d'Abruzzio who was the intended victim?'

'Wow! That's quite a thought! What could the killer be using that would get past doctors and pathologists? Was your candidate—Sasaki, was it?— autopsied?'

Lisa filled him in on the initial results, but said she didn't know what tests the pathologist had conducted.

'I'll check and see if we can still perform one on Mrs D.'

'Thank you,' said Lisa, very grateful that this detective in West Seneca didn't think she was some crazy obsessive nut from a tropical island. So far he was taking her theory far more seriously than her captain. With promises on both sides to keep in touch, Lisa ended the call. She checked her watch: time to get going on investigating the series of jewellery-store robberies in Waikiki and Ala Moana Center that had put one of the managers into the Intensive Care Unit at Queen's.

★

Lisa didn't get home until nearly eight. She took the Chinese chicken salad she'd picked up at the Diamond Head Market out to her lanai. As she sipped a glass of Pinot Grigio, she tried to unwind from a tiring and unproductive afternoon. Soon her thoughts went back to Steve Sasaki's death. She pushed aside her salad and got out her mobile phone. She wasn't sure if she should do it, but she called Senator Matthew Chance's home.

Mrs Chance answered the phone. When she heard it was an officer from the HPD calling, she got her husband on the line immediately.

'Senator Chance, I'm Lieutenant Lisa Higashiguchi from the HPD. I'm a friend of the Sasakis and it was Steve who suggested I be asked to Mrs Albinson's party when she wanted to beef up security. We were introduced briefly, but I'm not sure if you remember me . . .'

'Lieutenant, I know who you are; Steve talked about you. What can I do for you?'

'Well, thank you, Senator,' Lisa said. 'I apologize for disturbing you at home. But from what I have been able to establish, a mysterious man at Mrs Albinson's and the man who had dinner with a woman who died a few days ago in New York—the wife of a man running for Congress—could possibly be the same man. The candidate in New York is a Democrat, like Steve. I'm trying to follow up on it, but it's not yet official. Do you think you could make some time to talk to me for maybe fifteen minutes or so?'

'Steve was a good friend and would have made a wonderful member of the House. If there is any way I can help you, I will. Could you possibly come over tonight? I'm scheduled to return to Washington tomorrow.'

Surprised, Lisa looked at her watch and said, 'I can be at your home by nine, if that's not too late for you.'

'No, not at all. This must be important or you wouldn't be calling me now. I live in Makiki Heights . . . do you need directions?'

Lisa was amused. 'Sir, the Honolulu police know where our senators live. I should be there in half an hour.'

So Senator Chance is also concerned about getting to the bottom of Steve Sasaki's death, she thought, as she set out for Makiki in her little Toyota.

The senator met Lisa at the door when she arrived and led her into his home office off the front hall. He asked her if she wanted anything to drink, and when she refused politely, he plunged right in.

'What makes you think there was something suspicious about Steve's death? I was told by Sophie that the autopsy report confirmed he died of a heart attack. You mentioned a mysterious man—you aren't thinking of the klutzy waiter with the penetrating eyes, are you?

'So you noticed him too!' Lisa cried out so excitedly that the senator was surprised and amused at the same time. Seeing his reaction, Lisa said in a quieter voice, 'Yes, that's the person. I learnt that he told the caterer he had been hired by Mrs Albinson, but Mrs Albinson told me that she was under the impression he was part of the catering team. No one knows who he was. Our initial investigation terminated when the autopsy report came out. But today I learnt that the wife of a Democratic Congressional candidate in West Seneca died under similar circumstances. She and her husband had dinner with an unknown man who approached them in a restaurant. Then Mrs d'Abruzzio died of a supposed heart attack later that same evening.'

The senator, listening raptly, nodded. Lisa continued.

'Senator, what really got me was what the detective in West Seneca I spoke with earlier today told me. When he quizzed the man who had served the d'Abruzzios, the waiter described the guest nearly the same as you did to me—in his mid-thirties, about five–eight, with sinister-looking eyes.'

The senator bolted upright.

'Now I see why you say the same man could be involved. I thought he had penetrating eyes, but one could say they were sinister. I'm sure you have an idea why this man was involved in both deaths.'

'Yes, Senator. I know this may sound far-fetched, but my theory is that the candidate in West Seneca, a Democratic candidate like Steve, was the target, but somehow the poison or drug was administered to his wife by mistake. So the wife ended up dying. But I don't know what the substance was that killed the two or how it was administered. I do suspect that the perpetrator put it into Steve Sasaki's coffee, but it's only a suspicion based on my seeing him clumsily refill Sasaki's coffee and finding out later that he was an interloper.'

'Hmm . . . It's not a bad working hypothesis. But I think you need some serious evidence. I'm wondering . . . is there a poison that is difficult to detect by standard forensic tests, one that is slow-acting and only kills a person a few hours after it's been ingested?'

'If my theory is correct, there ought to be. But, Senator, I admit I've never heard of such a poison.'

'And are the two men really the same guy? I know from court cases I was involved in before I got into politics that physical similarities are notoriously unreliable. Isn't it more reasonable to conjecture that the two deaths an ocean and a continent apart were totally unrelated . . . so we don't have to make the assumption that the target of the murder in West Seneca was the candidate and not his wife?'

'Yes, I know, Senator, that's why I admit my theory . . . hypothesis has a long way to go. But while we are talking about hypotheses, let me bring up the possibility that this guy could be a Patriot, like the intruder who scared Senator Kwon to death two weeks ago. Though this guy is a very different sort from the intruder, I'm wondering if the Patriot Party could be behind these deaths.'

'Hmm . . . The people in the Patriot Party are certainly very different from those in the Tea Party. They are demanding even more irrational policies than the Tea Party people. They are a lot angrier, more desperate, and we know they are having many, often serious, scuffles with the police in many cities, and more and more of them are getting arrested. This sort of thing never happened with the Tea Party. But isn't it pretty unlikely to think that one of them would be devious enough to infiltrate a fundraising party and then go cross country and crash a dinner at a restaurant to administer a poison that an autopsy can't find? This isn't the way the Patriots usually operate. And there would need to be funding and knowledge of esoteric poisons. I don't know. I'll have to think about it.'

'Senator, what I'm most concerned about is whether you have had any threats from the Patriot Party. They haven't made you feel threatened in any way, have they?'

'No, nothing personal. Nothing that scared me so far. And the Patriots are equally vitriolic about the Republicans.'

The senator then looked hard at Lisa and added, 'But you know, you're right. What you have told me has convinced me that it's important to get to the bottom of what's going on. A Democrat and a wife of a Democrat have died under arguably very suspicious circumstances. That means I too must be vigilant . . . stay alert, but I'm not sure what I should look out for except for a guy with creepy eyes. I can assure you if any small piece of information, or even a rumour, comes my way that could help in your effort to get to the bottom of this, I will contact you. Give me your phone number and email address.'

Lisa knew the meeting was over. She hadn't learnt anything useful in helping to strengthen her hypothesis, which was still in need of a lot more supporting evidence. She thanked Senator Chance for giving her his time so late in the evening and said goodbye to the man she very much hoped would be the next president. She couldn't miss the senator's troubled expression on his face as he ushered her out of his house. The main outcome of this meeting seemed to be that she had suitably scared the only senator from Hawaii still alive.

Lisa spent a restless night. Steve Sasaki's death and the attack on Senator Kwon kept infiltrating her dreams. By morning she had come to a decision. She would not keep her hypothesis to herself, especially now that Senator Chance seemed to support it. If someone was trying to kill political candidates, it should be brought to the attention of the FBI. But how? As a lieutenant in a police department that had closed the case on Sasaki's death, she could scarcely call Washington. Captain Kalani would have a fit when he found out, and find out he would.

No, she would have to inform the FBI in a roundabout manner. She quickly realized she actually knew someone she could call. Three years ago she had gone through a course at the FBI's Advanced Forensic Research and Training Center in Quantico, Virginia. There she had met David Porter, a handsome, young FBI agent from Chicago with whom she had gone on a few dates while they were in Quantico. She had been attracted to him, but nothing had come of it, and she hadn't heard from him since. He was probably married by now. But still, she felt she could call him and ask his advice. If he had been transferred and was no longer in Chicago, someone could tell her how to reach him.

In the morning, before she left for work, Lisa called the FBI office in Chicago. *It should be just after lunch there.* A young woman answered on the second ring.

'The FBI. How may I help you?'

'I'm Lieutenant Higashiguchi of the Honolulu Police Department. I'd like to speak to Agent David Porter if he's available.'

'Hold on a second, Lieutenant. I'm pretty sure he's here.'

Porter's resonant voice came on the line immediately.

'When Barb told me a police lieutenant called Higa-Gucci was calling, I knew instantly who it was. How are things in Paradise? Have you got hitched since I last talked to you?'

'I'm fine. But no husband yet.'

'Yeah, I'm not married either. No woman wants a husband who keeps my hours! So what can the FBI do for the Honolulu Police Department?'

'Actually I'm calling on my own about something that's been bugging me and something I think the FBI should know about.' She paused.

'Go on. I'm listening.'

Lisa spelt out what was on her mind about the possible politically motivated serial killer. She admitted that the HPD had closed the case on Sasaki when the autopsy report came in—it was called a preliminary report but she knew it would be the final one—so she was calling as a citizen. She was prepared to hear some probing and pointed questions challenging her hypothesis from the young FBI agent who she remembered as being very intelligent.

But Porter surprised her. He launched into a long disquisition that amounted to support for her hypothesis. He described what the FBI was already doing and also what he intended to do.

'You may not be aware of it, but statistically there have been far too many deaths among candidates this election year. Not just heart attacks, which may or may not be from natural causes, but also suspicious car accidents and the like. Each one seems explainable in itself, but the numbers are too high. So I can assure you that we are keeping an eye out. I'll make certain that Washington is aware of this mysterious man. Probably Washington will want more information. I'll alert them not to mention your call to me. But I will tell them how to contact you if they need to. Will that work? I'll make sure you don't get into trouble. And Lisa,' Porter added, 'I know from a friend at Headquarters that they are worried and have been talking about informally warning candidates for Congress to be extra careful this year. Your report about the same unidentified man possibly having been seen with the two victims hours before their deaths might just tip the FBI to put out these warnings. Don't think your call has been for nought.'

Lisa was overwhelmed, not just that Porter had taken her hypothesis seriously, but that there seemed to have been other suspicious deaths of candidates she was unaware of. What was happening in America?

Instead of being told that her fears were for nought, or that this was the first the FBI had heard about the deaths of candidates, she was being told that something very ominous might be occurring in the country that liked to think it was the most democratic in the world, deciding who governed by the ballot box not by assassination. She had frightened Senator Chance, and now Porter had scared her. She knew that from now on she would wake up with trepidation every morning, and even before she had coffee, she would check the news to see if there had been further deaths among would-be senators and congressmen.

Special Agent Sam Ogden knew the smell. It was the same odour he had smelt a dozen times in Kosovo back in 1999. That was when he was serving in the army in the NATO intervention to protect the Albanians who were being subjected to brutal ethnic cleansing by the Serbs. The Serbs had often used Czech-made C-4 *plastique* to blow up cars driven by Albanians. Ogden had been a young lieutenant in a military police company that was frequently dispatched to these bombings. He had never forgotten the faintly cloying, sweet scent every time he came across a charred vehicle that more often than not held a charred body or two.

It was past midnight before Ogden arrived at Felts Field outside Spokane, the scene of the bomb site he had been sent to investigate. Tonight it wasn't an automobile that had been bombed. Instead, it was a Cessna Mustang whose passengers had been Kathryn Myers, the Republican candidate in the race for the Senatorial seat in the State of Washington, her campaign manager and her secretary. All three, along with the pilot, had perished when the plane went up in flames just five hours ago.

Ogden was helping the twins with their homework when he got the call. The caller ID on his phone told him the relaxed evening with his wife and sons was over. Even though he was the SAC—special agent in-charge—of the FBI's Seattle field office, he had decided because of his experience to go to the bomb site himself instead of sending a younger agent.

He was flown from Seattle's Boeing Field to Spokane International Airport on a small jet—a standby arrangement the FBI had for such instances. At Spokane International, he was met by two detectives from the Spokane police department and driven to Felts Field, the original airport for the city of Spokane, now used chiefly by charter and private planes.

The airstrip was lit up by a strong beam of light from a fire engine, revealing the charred remains of the plane surrounded by the foam that had finally put out the flames. The bodies had already been pulled out from the plane, so the site was no longer intact. Two policemen were guarding the site and warding off a few persistent ghoulish onlookers, who had arrived after hearing the explosion and seeing the smoke rising from the bombed Cessna. Ogden was told that the flames had been visible four miles away in the city.

Ogden stood on the field and scanned the horrific scene. He rubbed his hand over the stubble on his chin and bit his upper lip. He knew that the experts would examine the plane and eventually report what he already knew: the plane had been bombed with *plastique*. His job was to find out everything he could about who had been responsible for this heinous act. He knew it was a daunting task but he was going to give it his best try.

'OK,' he said to the two detectives, 'let's go see the eyewitnesses and the staff present at the time—anyone you haven't sent home.'

The older of the two detectives answered. 'We have their names and where each of them were at the time. But we asked the two people who we think saw the perpetrator to stay. They're waiting in that building to our left,' he said, pointing to a desolate-looking building nearby.

The detectives walked Ogden over to a rather bleak office in the desolate building. Ogden took one look at the young man slumped in a chair, almost comatose with shock and fatigue, and asked for coffee for all of them. Then he pulled up a chair and sat down next to the airport worker, who was still in his work coveralls.

'Hello. I'm Sam Ogden from the FBI. I'm so sorry you have been kept waiting until I could come in from Seattle. We want to talk to you while the incident is still fresh in your mind.'

'How can I ever forget what I saw? I don't think it was my fault. I did everything by the book. I remember securing the cap of the fuel tank and checking everything else I'm supposed to. I've been doing this for two years and I can't afford to lose my job,' the dejected young man almost wailed.

'From the brief the Spokane detectives gave me on the way in, and from what I can tell of the remains, I'm certain the plane was bombed—someone put a bomb on the plane. It couldn't have been your fault at all. What's your name?'

'Fred. Fred Minton,' answered the airport worker, his face brightening as he straightened up in his chair.

'Fred. Now let me ask you a few questions. OK?'

'Yes, sir,' Fred, noticeably calmer, responded.

'OK, Fred, you were the last person to work on the plane. Did you see anyone near the plane besides the pilot and the three passengers?'

'Not while I was working on it. But, yeah, at the last moment a woman delivered a box. It was just before the plane started to taxi out to the runway.'

Ogden was startled. 'A woman? Can you describe her?'

'Well, I was some distance off as I had taken the hoses away. It was getting late and the sky was overcast. Lemme think . . . she was tallish, with a lot of curly black hair. She wore a black raincoat, black pants and . . . and high heels. She ran over to the plane after the pilot had just closed the door and waved madly at the plane. After a minute, the door of the plane opened, and the woman said something. She handed the box she was carrying to the man who opened the door. Then she ran back to the building and I didn't see her again. The pilot started up the plane and taxied to the runway. The plane was just picking up speed, and then it slowed down as if it was aborting take-off. And BOOM!! The plane just exploded. It just went up in flames and into a million pieces. No one had a chance.'

As Fred spoke he became so agitated that Ogden had to calm him down by offering him the coffee that had now arrived. The FBI agent spent another ten minutes asking more questions. When he had finished, he told Fred that his guess was that the plane had tried to abort take-off, either because they had found the box contained a bomb or because they were afraid it might.

Ogden thanked Fred and bade the exhausted man goodnight.

'Did anyone else see that woman?' Ogden asked Craig Fuentes, the younger detective.

'Yes, sir, and he's waiting in his office here to see you. He was in charge of the airfield when the explosion occurred. Shall I bring him in?'

'No I'll go see him.' Ogden gulped down the rest of his coffee and followed Craig into the operations office where he was introduced to Ted Gilson, a red-haired, slightly overweight man in his mid-thirties. He looked very composed, but the mountain of cigarettes in his tin ashtray said something else. Ogden asked him the same questions he asked Fred Minton and got a different picture.

'I didn't see the explosion but I did see the woman. I was outside when she ran up about fifteen feet from me and breathlessly asked if Mrs Myers' plane was still on the ground. She had a sort of gravelly Lauren Bacall voice— you know, the woman who starred with Humphrey Bogart in the old movies.'

'Did she say anything else?'

'She held up a small box, but from the way she was holding it, it seemed sort of heavy. She said she had something important for Mrs Myers. Really important. I pointed to the plane preparing to take-off, and without saying another word she ran towards it. The door was opened and her box was accepted by someone in the plane.'

'What did she do after that?' asked Ogden.

'She ran out of the airfield. I noticed she ran awfully fast even in the heels she was wearing.'

'Can you describe her for us?'

'She was wearing a black trench coat, belted but rather loose. She had on black pants and shoes with medium heels. She had a big mop of black hair that seemed all over the place. And she was wearing those big designer dark glasses so I can't describe her face.'

'You are very observant, Ted. Did you notice anything else about her? Anything at all that comes to mind?'

'Well, she was tall and not fat. At least from what I could see of her. What was odd, I thought, was the way she ran. She ran really fast, but I got the distinct impression she wasn't used to wearing heels. I almost thought she looked like a man in drag. So I kept staring at her instead of coming back into my office right away.'

'At what point did you come into the building again?'

'When the woman disappeared from sight. I had only just got back inside and sat down when the explosion occurred. It made helluva noise, rattled the windows and lit the place up like midday. I knew it was the plane. So I dialled 911 before I went back outside. Two men were already hauling fire extinguishers towards the plane, but the fire was so intense with all that fuel burning that they couldn't do anything to put it out. Everyone on the plane must've died before they even knew what had happened. What a tragedy!'

By now it was well after two in the morning, and even all the coffee he had drunk couldn't keep Ogden fully alert. But his mind was sharp enough to conjecture that the woman Fred and Ted had seen had to be a man—'a man in drag' as Ted had put it. Someone who knew how to make a bomb and explode it by remote control or by a rigged timing device. But was the bomb meant for the senator?

Special Agent Sam Ogden couldn't do more tonight. He had to get a few hours sleep, before he could return to the daunting task of finding out who had committed the carefully premeditated, heinous crime of murdering four innocent people.

'Hey, nice digs! This is a great pad you have,' exclaimed Tomohide Ikeda in English, as Junji Taira let his fellow dietman into his new apartment.

'Is that the way you talked at Wharton? Pretty old-fashioned slang, isn't it?' Taira asked, laughing. Then switching to Japanese, he said, 'Come on in and see the rest of it, Tom. Sada Sensei is already here.'

The banter revealed how close these two dietmen were, though Ikeda had graduated from the University of Tokyo a decade later than Taira. The university was where the now retired Masaharu Sada had been a professor—*sensei*—to both. Ikeda had acquired the nickname Tom while studying for his MBA at Wharton, the University of Pennsylvania's business school. Now a second-term dietman from Osaka, he had joined the small group who were working to form a new party.

Ikeda took off his shoes, put on the slippers set out for him at the entrance (as customary in Japanese homes), and went into the living room with Taira and then out onto the penthouse patio where Sada Sensei was leaning on the railing, looking out over the city. Tom greeted his former professor and said, 'Quite a view it is!'

Sada turned to Taira and replied nostalgically, with sadness in his voice, 'Aah, but I do miss the old family home with its Japanese garden and koi pond. I could forget I was in the middle of Tokyo when I visited you there.'

Taira agreed. 'Sensei, I know how you feel,' and added ruefully, 'but it just isn't possible to keep up a large private estate in the centre of the city these days. We managed the upkeep of the old house while my father was still alive, but my brother and I had to sell the property after his death. You know what the inheritance tax is like in our country.'

Ikeda chimed in, sounding astonished, 'Even though your brother is head of one of the largest banks in Japan?' Ikeda was from a long line of saké wholesalers in Osaka and, though his family was well off by all standards, he had been surprised by the wealth of the Taira family when he had first visited Taira's old home.

Taira looked at Tom, laughed and said, 'You've been reading too much about what CEOs in the US are paid. You should know that, in Japan, even a bank president doesn't make anywhere near what an American CEO does. Come, let's go inside. I'm sure my wife has lunch ready.'

'Isn't Hori joining us today?' asked Sada. Shinji Hori was the third member of the group leading the formation of the new party and also a student of Sada Sensei.

'He called about an hour ago,' Taira answered. 'He had a breakfast meeting with his constituents today and missed the train he had planned on taking. He should be here soon, but the sushi has arrived, so let's start. Hori can join us when he comes.'

This was the first meeting the four had set up to formally discuss their new party. The three dietmen—Taira from Tokyo, Hori from Niigata in northern Japan and Ikeda from Osaka—were the leaders of the forty-odd dietmen in the Reform Conservative Party now in power who had decided to bolt from their party and launch a new party in January of the coming year. They had been holding meetings for a year now, and a few months earlier they had asked Sada Sensei, also a close friend of the Taira family, to join them.

Sada was a widely respected author of many books and had served as the president of the Japanese Association of Economists. The three dietmen thought him the best person to advise them on developing a platform for their new party that would be solidly conservative but not mired in the old, corrupt politics that kowtowed to traditional interest groups, something they had come to believe the elders in their party were doing. They wanted to help the economy grow again and inject a fresh air of optimism into a society now ridden with gloom and anxiety.

The trio sat down in the Taira dining room. A large, square lacquer box lay on each place mat. Tomiko Taira poured tea for all of them and disappeared. As the men lifted the covers from their lunch boxes and began to eat, Tom said to Taira, 'You sent me a few cryptic emails saying you had met with Senator Powers when you were in the US. Is he really going to be useful in getting our new party started? Tell us more.'

'I met the senator for the first time when I sought him out after the Washington meetings I attended at the State Department. I had read his book and liked his ideas very much, but I had some questions. When I asked if I could have a short meeting with him, he invited me to dinner and we ended up talking for nearly two hours. Then, a few days after I returned to Japan, I got an invitation from him for my wife and me to attend his birthday party at his home in a Boston suburb.'

'Why would an American senator want to spend so much time with a Japanese politician whom he has barely met? What's in it for him?' Tom asked, quizzically.

Taira laughed. 'At first, I thought it was his ego, that he was pleased a Japanese dietman had liked his book enough to seek him out to discuss his ideas.

But when we met at the Hay-Adams for our first dinner together, he grilled me about my background. From the questions he asked, I got the distinct feeling he had had someone check up on me before inviting me to dinner. He already knew a lot about the Taira Bank and other things I had never mentioned.'

'So then, it wasn't his ego after all. He just smelt money like all good politicians! But as a foreigner, you can't contribute to his campaign, can you?'

'You're right, Tom. I can't contribute money directly to him. But Powers has formed an organization called the New American Destiny Forum, which claims to be for educational purposes. Under American law, he can solicit funds from anywhere for this kind of non-profit organization. And, as you said, he did smell money . . . enough to invite me to his birthday party.'

'Did he ask you to make a donation to his forum?'

'You know how these things go. He didn't explicitly ask me to donate, but he did take me aside at his party and told me that people who support his forum are donating millions of dollars. He even spelt out that those as well off as me were giving five million dollars.'

'Five million dollars!?' Tom gasped. 'I'd say he was pretty explicit. What did you tell him?'

'Well, I said if I *were* to make a donation of that size, I would have to think about it. He understood. At the end of the evening, he asked me to consider doing so in the fall when his organization will need the money to get really actively involved in political education to get a true conservative like Governor Bond elected president.'

Sada, who had been quietly eating sushi, now spoke up. 'Five million dollars is a lot of money to invest in an American political campaign. How would your new party get its money's worth? Wouldn't it be better to spend the money here in Japan?'

'Sensei, I think a large donation would give our new party a direct pipeline to the new US administration if Bond were to win—I've read that he stands a good chance. I wouldn't have to make the donation until I see what the polls say months from now. Our new party could use our close relationship with the US in various ways, and it'll even impress our media and might do wonders in getting our candidates voted into office in the forthcoming election in July next year.'

'I can see why I was a professor and not a politician,' Sada said with a smile.

'Well, I may be cynical, but whatever the media and we say about America, it is true that all new prime ministers in Japan visit Washington as soon as a new government is formed. So having an in with the American administration would go a long way to help our new party.'

The conversation turned to a discussion of the proposed five per cent hike in the consumption tax when Taira's wife ushered in Shinji Hori, who apologized for being late. Tomiko poured tea for everyone and again left the men to talk business.

As Hori ate his way through his box of sushi, he listened hard to catch up on what he had missed. He was as curious about the Taira–Powers meeting as Ikeda had been. 'Why did you want to meet him?' he asked through a mouthful of sushi.

'I read his book and had questions about it.'

Sada said, 'I've read it too. *The New American Destiny*—a powerful book and very well written.'

'I haven't read it yet,' said Hori, sounding almost ashamed. 'Reading English takes too much time and I've been too busy. Sensei, if you could quickly give me the gist of the book, I'd be most grateful.'

Taira nodded, agreeing to the request. 'Yes, please do. I'm also interested in what you thought of the book.'

Sada put down his chopsticks and started speaking in his lecture voice: 'Put simply, I was impressed by the senator's book. It spells out what it means to be a real conservative and how to reinvigorate the American economy and society. He wants to stop America from sliding into socialism while piling up more and more national debt. He thinks it's time to stop mollycoddling people when they ought to be standing on their own two feet, to build a strong America without depending on the purchase by foreigners of increasing amounts of Treasury bonds.

'What specifically does Powers recommend?' asked Hori.

'He strongly believes in a free economy in which the profit incentive is almost sacrosanct. He considers it the sole engine to ensure prosperity and enrich the lives of all citizens. The economy prospers by becoming more efficient in production and services, and this efficiency is maximized when investors reap the highest returns from their investments in free and least-regulated markets. So government intrusion into how people spend their income and wealth—in other words, taxation—must be kept at a minimum and regulations of all kinds must be limited. Powers argues forcefully that all misguided, left-leaning administrations have stifled the entrepreneurial energy of American businesses by overtaxing and over-regulating. Only a really free market system can make a country prosper and become militarily strong.'

Sada took a sip of tea and continued: 'The book is an excellent one, but I think he goes too far. What I mean is that, even though I'm a life-long conservative, I have a serious problem with the seemingly ultra-conservative tone of some of his views, those of a rigid ideologue. He believes in the total, unconditional supremacy of the market and the desirability of having the smallest possible government. But what concerned me most is what we can read between the lines. To me, it is unmistakable that he thinks ordinary people are likely to have difficulty in understanding how the world really works. He claims people need a leader who can explain things to them and show them the way. And it is rather obvious that he thinks he is that leader. I'm a conservative but I also believe in democracy.'

Taira nodded in understanding and said, 'Sensei, you have hit upon the point that troubled me at the birthday party: despite being among friends and being able to speak his mind much more freely than in public, Powers behaved more like a general in charge of an army than like a senator in a democracy.'

Sada exhaled loudly in a sigh. 'One way to put it is that he is the product of the *zeitgeist*—a reflection of the crisis of capitalism . . . and also of democracy . . . faced by all of the advanced, democratic, capitalist economies,' said Sada thoughtfully.

Professor Sada, sounding more and more like he was running a seminar with his graduate students, carried on about how all the rich economies are growing so slowly and suffering from high unemployment, fiscal deficits and other social ills, including the increasing inequality of income and wealth. This has made these economies the natural incubators of demagogues, who like Powers are convinced their solutions to the slow economic growth are the only right ones. Such solutions, according to Sada, included lower corporate and income taxes, even for the richest, in order to increase the supply of capital needed to invest, and thus create more jobs. 'Even for me, a confirmed conservative,' he said, 'such so-called solutions are wrongheaded because what is needed is not more capital but more demand. And demand can be created both by adopting policies to make income distribution more equal and by enacting demand-stimulating programmes of the government.'

Taira was surprised to hear Sada sound like Senator Chance, the most liberal among the presidential candidates in the Democratic Party. But he held his tongue. He was sure both Hori and Tom were equally surprised.

Finally, Taira spoke up: 'Sensei, I'm surprised to hear you talk of increasing taxes and of having the government do more . . . and being so concerned with income distribution.'

Sada wasn't displeased as Taira had feared he might be. Instead, he said with a smile, 'A good conservative is someone who knows how to keep the essential institutions of capitalism—markets, private property, risk taking and the innovative spirit—even if some institutions and practices have to be modified for the sake of the long-term survival of the system. We did that in the late nineteenth and early twentieth centuries by accepting the income tax and anti-trust laws and by allowing more union activities, for instance. And we made a slew of changes during the Great Depression in the 1930s. I'm still a traditionalist but I am aware that we are again at a crossroad and we have to make some serious changes for capitalism to survive in the future. I hope all of you will keep in mind what I'm saying as you inaugurate your new party next year.'

There was pin-drop silence in the room. Hori stopped eating. Tom raised his hand, just as he had always done in Sada's class, and asked, 'Sensei, you said earlier that we are now facing a crisis of democracy as well as of capitalism. Do you mean the crisis of capitalism is endangering democracy?'

'In a way, yes. The demagogues today are very effective in swaying people's minds and votes. Since the demagogues are the products of the crisis of capitalism, one can come to that conclusion. I am not saying that we are in the crisis Germany was after World War I, but nevertheless something has to change. And not just in the economy but in education too.'

'I don't quite follow you, Sensei,' said Hori. 'I know there have long been problems with the Japanese education system, but are you talking about a broader problem?'

'Yes. In all the advanced rich economies of the world, more and more young people are studying only what will get them jobs, such as economics, business, computer science, engineering and so on. Subjects such as philosophy, history, literature and political science are seen as useless. What with young people spending so much time on the Internet and playing online games, they are reading fewer books that make them think about the meaning of life, about humanity and social well-being. And even when they study economics, they take courses in, say, econometrics and learn how to make money from derivatives rather than read Adam Smith, Joseph Schumpeter or Karl Marx.'

Taira nodded. 'So you are directly linking slow growth in the economy—resulting in high unemployment of the young—to changes in education, which makes demagoguery more effective?'

'Yes, and technology isn't helping in the way it could. While the Internet has broadened political participation, it doesn't lead to a thoughtful exchange of ideas. I feel all we are getting are one-sided shallow arguments—sound bites perhaps—on Twitter and on blogs. So, today we have more and more voters who are susceptible to such sound bites from politicians too.'

Ikeda spoke up, 'Sada Sensei is correct. I was talking to a group of young executives from my constituency in Osaka. They are dead set against raising the consumption tax again. All the arguments they gave me were nothing but selfish. I tried to tell them why Japan can't go on piling up more national debt but they won't listen. Their rationale is that if the consumption tax goes up, their businesses will suffer. So, I wonder, do I vote for the tax and lose the next election or do I vote against it to keep my seat in the Diet?'

'The questions you are asking are "do I want to keep my seat respecting the voters' wishes—that is, being democratic, even though you know it'll bankrupt the economy sooner than we think—or do I vote against the voters' wishes for the good of the country and lose my seat?"' Sada responded quietly.

'Precisely!' said Ikeda. 'And if I don't follow the wishes of voters, who don't realize what the economy—and the country—needs, then I can lose the election and open the door to the demagogues on the right or on the left. And then what, Sensei?'

'I could give you a long discourse about what thinkers such as John Stuart Mill and David Hume and Edmund Burke have said on the questions you've raised. But I don't have an answer for you,' replied the professor despondently.

'This is a depressing conversation,' said Taira, 'but it will now make us think about what our new party will have to offer in the way of solutions and how it must market our ideas to appeal to voters. Quite a job we have ahead of us!'

The four fell silent again, furiously thoughtful. Taira's mind was spinning. He felt Sada Sensei had changed ideologically from being the professor who gave passionate lectures extolling the work of Ludwig von Mises, the Austrian economist who had written a bible for free markets and freedom, to a man who was taking a stand against the very virtues of an unconditionally free market. He found Sada's observations of Powers a bit too harsh. Ikeda, who had barely won the last election, couldn't stop worrying about how he would vote on the consumption tax. Hori wondered why the professor had lost his former intellectual zest and hadn't made any concrete suggestions as to what should or could be done. And Sada too was aware that he might have gone too far in saying he had no answer to Ikeda's questions, but he had been feeling quite pessimistic about the situation.

The silence was broken by Tomiko coming into the room with coffee, a platter of tropical fruit and the professor's favourite Baumkuchen, which she had obtained from a famous German bakery.

After everyone had been served dessert, Taira began the conversation, bringing up the subject of Powers again: 'Senator Powers has invited me to participate in a forum in Washington in early May to discuss the future of American diplomacy in Asia. I've pretty much decided to accept the invitation. The topic is "Whither American Diplomacy in Asia". I'd like to talk about how Asia, especially China, has changed and how it will—and should—affect American policy towards Asia.'

'And what will you say about China?' asked Ikeda. 'I recently heard a talk by Professor Goto from Kyoto University who suggested the possibility of a Chinese Spring similar to the Arab Spring that began in late 2010. He argued China could have another Taiping Rebellion like that of the 1850s—years marked by horrendous corruption, income disparity, and a bloody ethnic feud over land rights between the better-off Cantonese speakers and the poor Hakkas who spoke only Hakka. The rebellion started in the southern part of China but gained momentum very quickly in the northern part of the country. In the end, it claimed twenty million lives. It took eleven years to quell the rebellion, exposing how weak, corrupt and impotent the Qing Dynasty was, though it didn't collapse until 1912. Professor Goto was very persuasive in suggesting that something very similar could happen in China today because of government corruption, the huge income disparity and demands by the people for more freedom.'

Hori shot back, 'I know Goto's right-wing line which he constantly spouts on TV. But it's just wishful thinking. He would love to see the political system of China implode. But you can't compare China in the nineteenth century to the China of today. The Communist party in China has done a miraculous job since the 1980s of increasing the standard of living; people are enjoying more and more freedom and the government is no longer as corrupt as it once was, especially after 2012 when they began to weed out the corrupt officials. Goto aggravates me no end because he uses what little history of China he knows to concoct a wild, self-serving speculation about the country's future. Like many older Japanese, he just can't accept that the Chinese economy is doing so much better than our own.'

Taira, who was listening to the exchange with a smile, commented, 'Tom, I agree with Hori. Goto never talks about all the changes that have been taking place in China: the creation of stronger labour unions, more advanced new technologies that are being patented, more aggressive efforts being made to clean up the environment, to name only a few. And don't forget that the financial markets of all the rich economies will face a major crisis if Professor Goto is proved right. Should China implode politically, there will be economic chaos. China will likely have to sell almost three trillion dollars of US Treasury bonds it now holds, which in turn will cause the bond price to plummet. This will not only make the interest rate the US has to pay to finance its profligate ways skyrocket, but will also cause financial chaos globally.'

'Sada Sensei is right. Both capitalism and democracy in the advanced economies are now in a critical transitional phase. This means we must really think through the kind of new party we want to create. Conservative for sure, but humane, far-sighted and aware of the political and economic changes taking place all round the world, aware of the changing *zeitgeist*,' remarked Hori. Their discussion finally ended with Hori's observation. The three guests made their way out, thanking the Tairas for having them over and promising to keep in touch and meet again for further discussions.

After the guests had left, Tomiko asked her husband, 'Are you really thinking of giving five million to Senator Powers? Wouldn't it mean borrowing money from your brother?'

'What? How do you know about that? I haven't discussed it with you?'

Taira's wife laughed. 'Haven't you noticed the service window in the wall between the dining room and the kitchen? I always keep the window open a crack so I can tell when to bring in dessert. I could monitor diners in the old house through the paper sliding doors, but here the service window does the trick!'

Taira chuckled. 'My eavesdropping wife! I'm sorry to have worried you. I hadn't mentioned the request Powers made because I think it won't come to anything. I do want to have an in with the candidate likely to win the Republican nomination and possibly the presidency, but I'm sure I can do it for less money than that. And I won't donate anything until I know how the wind is blowing.'

'So is that why you're planning on giving a presentation at the Washington meeting?'

'Yes. You have to be in America to find out what's really going on in politics. And I'm sure I will meet Powers at the conference in May. I need to know more about Powers to find out whether he is, as Sada Sensei thinks, a rigid, anti-democratic, reactionary ideologue and demagogue or whether he is a sincere conservative politician who is forcefully advancing his views. If Bond, supported by Powers, does become the president, my new party will benefit immensely by having a close tie with him and his administration. I can give Powers only a million or two, but I have to get something in return.'

'My husband is making a cold-hearted political calculation that has nothing to do with principles and morality?' Tomiko exclaimed, sounding a little surprised.

Taira responded, clearly pained, 'I'm doing this for our new party, which I believe can do an immense amount of good for Japan. The two conservative parties we have now are constantly squabbling for acquiring or retaining power. Meanwhile we are piling up national debt, holding back economic growth, and creating all sorts of problems which are making our people lose hope. I am making what you call a political calculation for the sake of my country.'

'Good grief! Look at all the people,' Peri whispered to Alex as she turned round from her seat in the front row to survey the lecture hall at the Metropolitan Museum of Art. Alex could tell Peri was nervous.

'I've never given a talk to such a big crowd. I'm sure there are at least a dozen art history professors and art critics among these people. They must know more about the Impressionists than I do. And I recognize a couple of art historians from Princeton and Columbia too!'

'Calm down,' Alex said reassuringly. 'You've been researching your topic for years, and the two weeks you've just spent drafting your talk means you must be well prepared. Just focus on a couple of friendly faces, talk to them, and you'll do fine.'

Before Peri could do more than squeeze his hand in appreciation of his support, the moderator, a scholarly looking, middle-aged curator of the museum, came up to the podium and opened the session. He gave Peri a wonderful introduction.

'Our speaker today is Dr Experience Powers who holds a doctorate in the History of Art from Yale University. She now lives in Paris where she gives lectures and continues her research on the nineteenth-century Impressionists. She has also just completed a book, forthcoming from Yale University Press—quite an accomplishment because we all know the press has the best list of books on art history in the country. Dr Powers will talk to us today about how circumstances in the lives of some of the best-known Impressionist painters might have influenced their work.'

During a polite round of applause, Peri went up to the podium, adjusted the mike, took a deep breath and began. Within minutes of having begun to speak on her subject, she was no longer nervous. For the next hour, she expounded on how their birthplaces and the places to which they had travelled influenced the works of Monet, Renoir, Cezanne and Degas. She showed wonderful photos of Normandy, Limoges, Aix-en-Provence, Paris and numerous other locations to illustrate the beauty of the places reflected in their works. She spoke so knowledgeably and with such emotion that the audience listened, rapt. When she finished, the applause was long and enthusiastic.

The moderator opened the Q&A session, asking people who had questions or comments to introduce themselves first. Several professors and art history students asked intelligent questions that Peri answered with aplomb. Then an attractive woman in her late twenties stood up and introduced herself.

'Bess Browne. I work for Rubin Associates, an international financial consulting firm. Dr Powers, I agree with you that place affects what and how artists paint. But you might also consider that the Impressionists lived at a time when artists were exposed to an explosion of new information about the world through many new newspapers and magazines and through world exhibitions. Paris held four or five international expositions in the second half of the nineteenth century. So artists not only travelled but also lived in a new age when all kinds of visual, scientific, socioeconomic and other kinds of information became available because of the Industrial Revolution. How did these developments affect what and how artists painted? My apologies for framing such a long question.'

Peri took a good look at the woman in the fourth row, next to a man of similar age who might or might not be Asian—it was hard to tell. Then she replied, 'Ms Browne, your question is a very good one. Yes, these developments you mentioned did affect what they painted. This is another much longer topic of discussion, so I didn't get into it deliberately. But to answer your question: I can give you two examples now, both painted by Monet in 1877. The first, called 'Flowered Riverbank in Argenteuil', is a painting of a riverbank with a lot of beautiful flowers, but across the river is a huge factory spewing smoke. A second example is Monet's 'Train Tracks at the St Lazare Station', which is a scene of a train with a huge plume of steam. These subjects are more gritty, not what we usually associate with Monet. I could give you many more examples. And, of course, there is the important influence of Asia, particularly Japan, which I can't go into here. This is a very brief answer, I'm afraid, but you've raised a very important point.'

Peri smiled and continued: 'You said you work for a firm that does financial consulting. So is painting your avocation?'

'No, Dr Powers. I'm actually a specialist in electronic communications security. But a lover of art—I did a minor in it in college. Thank you for a wonderful lecture.'

Peri fielded four last questions about the Impressionists and the session was brought to a close. The hall was packed and so movement towards the door was slow. Just before Bess Browne and her companion reached it, Alex pushed his way through the crowd and addressed Bess in what she thought was good English but with an unmistakeable French accent.

'Ms Browne? Peri . . . Dr Powers would like to invite you and your companion to have dinner with us. Are you free?'

Bess was surprised by the unexpected invitation, but was delighted to have the chance to talk more with the impressive and charming Dr Powers. She looked at her companion who nodded and said, 'With pleasure.' Alex asked them to wait for a few minutes while Peri packed her things and bade farewell to the organizers.

Ten minutes later, Peri joined them and introductions were made. Peri learnt that the man Bess was with was her colleague, an economist who worked at the same firm. Bess introduced him as Nick Koyama, the associate director at Rubin Associates.

Alex had made reservations for four at Lumière, a small French restaurant a few blocks from Central Park. They chatted about Peri's lecture as they walked to the restaurant a short distance away. Once seated, their orders taken and wine served, Peri slowly broached the reason for the invitation.

'Forgive me for springing this meeting on you. I shouldn't be bothering you in the first place, but I have a few questions that have been troubling me a great deal for the past few weeks. I'm going back to Paris in a few days and I'm not sure if I can find someone among my friends, here or in Paris, who can answer my questions. I would really appreciate it if you could help in any way. I apologize for imposing on you, but I believe you will be able to answer my queries because of your work.'

'What would you like to know?' Bess asked, quite puzzled.

'I don't mean to be rude, but you must promise not to ask why I am raising these questions.'

Bess and Nick looked at each other. Bess said, 'Sure. Go ahead. We're used to this kind of request. Discretion is our trademark at Rubin Associates.'

'Thank you. I'd like you to explain some things about finance that I don't quite understand. Let me start with the first: what are Swift codes?'

'That's easy,' replied Bess. 'Swift codes are one of the three international codes that help identify banks. Swift stands for the Society for Worldwide Interbank Financial Telecommunication, an organization based in Belgium that facilitates wiring money round the world. A Swift code consists of eight to eleven characters that identify the bank, its location and the branch. If you want to send money internationally from one bank to another, you need to have the Swift code of the bank you are wiring the money to. Does that make sense?'

'So then each bank has a different code. Is that right? If you have lots of Swift codes, it means you are dealing with lots of different banks abroad, correct?'

'Right,' replied Bess and asked, 'what's the next question?'

'What's FinCEN?'

'FinCEN . . . hmm . . . that's the Financial Crimes Enforcement Network of the Treasury Department. They do a lot of things to combat financial crimes. One of the most important steps they have taken is to require all banks to notify the Treasury when they wire more than 10,000 dollars at a time, to ensure the money being sent is for legitimate purposes. For example, that it isn't large sums of drug money being laundered or sent to terrorist groups.'

Bess could tell from the expression on Peri's face that she was already struggling to keep up with the information. But Peri plowed on.

'Forgive me for all these questions, but where is Tsoog? I know it's a place because I heard it mentioned along with Georgetown.'

Bess looked perplexed, but Nick figured out immediately what Peri was referring to. He said, 'If you're talking finances, and especially the wiring of money internationally, then what you've pronounced as Tsoog, I'm sure it's Zug in Switzerland. It's spelt Z-U-G, but in German "zee" is pronounced "ts". And I bet George Town refers to another financial centre . . . the largest city in the Cayman Islands, located in the northeast of the Caribbean. Both cities are known for being overfriendly to people who need lax bank regulations.'

'I see,' said Peri, raising her eyebrows. 'OK, a final question. Does the Barrington pipeline mean anything to you? Does the name perhaps mean something in the financial world?'

Nick and Bess looked at each other and shook their heads. Alex, looking uncomfortable, said, '*Alors*, I don't understand what's going on. Peri . . . ?'

The waiter came with their salads. Peri whispered something to Alex who was sitting next to her. Bess figured she was telling Alex that she'd explain things later. As everyone began to eat, Peri asked, 'You know who my father is, right?'

'Yes,' Bess responded. 'He's often in the news these days.'

Peri looked at Bess and Nick and said, 'I'd like to tell you why I've been asking these questions and I hope you can help me understand what's going on. I know you agreed you'd keep things confidential, but I really have to rely on your discretion. If you don't want to hear more, tell me and I won't go on.'

Bess, now overwhelmed by curiosity, said, 'Go on, tell us. You can count on our discretion. We hope we can help you.'

Peri looked at her lover and said, 'You too, Alex. You won't tell anyone either, will you?'

'I haven't a clue what's going on, but I would never break your confidence. You know that, Peri,' assured Alex.

Peri related the conversation she had heard accidentally between her father and Parelli. She explained who Lou Parelli was and what she thought the

NAD Forum did. While Bess and Nick listened fascinated, Alex was agape, bewildered by the facts.

Peri continued, 'Now, can you tell me what the Barrington pipeline is?'

Nick responded in a quiet voice, 'The name Barrington . . . and the Barrington pipeline . . . these don't mean anything in the financial world. But the name is familiar and I wonder if it could refer to Evelyn Barrington, a long-time Republican congresswoman from the San Diego area. I've recently seen her on TV, and she surprised me because she sounded like the leaders of the Patriot Party who have such preposterous ideas and who are getting a lot of media coverage these days. At the moment, the only explanation that makes sense to me is that Parelli—or the forum, if you like—has been sending money to the Patriot Party using her as the conduit, the pipeline. Of course, this is just a guess and I could be totally wrong. I'm sorry, Peri, but given what you heard, I suspect your father might be involved in some way in sending money to the Patriot Party.'

Peri had stopped pretending to eat her coq au vin and bit her upper lip. Neither Bess nor Nick could read her reaction to what Nick had just said. Bess decided to say what was on her mind instead.

'Peri, from what you've told us it seems as though Parelli is dealing with far more money than he had expected to when he became treasurer of the forum your father created. I think the forum is using offshore banks to send, and possibly receive, money. Since FinCEN came up in the conversation, Parelli must know that at least some of the money is illegal, probably skirting campaign laws on finance. He is not sure he can keep this up without getting into some serious legal trouble and sooner or later having to involve your father.'

Peri shook her head and said very determinedly, 'Bess, if Parelli gets into legal trouble, what's crucial is that he doesn't involve my father. My father's career depends on it. And he's always been totally straight, very law-abiding. I was severely punished for telling the smallest of lies when I was a child. And you didn't hear the conversation . . . how angry and agitated he was . . . I'm certain he was trying to make sure he won't get dragged into what Parelli's been doing.'

Peri paused, and her shoulders sagged. She let out a long sigh and added, 'Well, at least that's what I want to believe. I've played the conversation I overheard so many times in my head that I don't know what to think of it any more. I really want to find out what exactly Parelli is up to. And whether or not it's legal. I think . . . I hope . . . if I can find out what Parelli is doing, if I can confirm that he is the lawbreaker and not my father, and that my father is being asked to help get him out of the mess he has created . . . then . . .'

As Peri's voice trailed off, Alex started to say, 'Peri . . .' but stopped on seeing her intertwine her fingers and squeeze them tightly. He knew this was what she did when she was trying to make an important decision.

Finally, Peri slowly said, 'OK. I've made up my mind. Would it be possible to . . . I don't know the right word . . . to um . . . *retain* both of you? I mean, I'd like to pay you to find out all you can about Parelli and what he is up to, because if he is doing something illegal—which I'm sure he is—the forum will be in trouble. And that means my dad's name will be sullied. I want to help him . . . before it's too late.'

Bess answered, equally slowly, 'Peri, I'm not sure what Nick or I can do. This really isn't the kind of consulting our firm does. I don't think Rubin Associates would approve of us taking on something freelance and snooping about Parelli and his schemes . . .'

Nick jumped in. 'But when we have to do background checks on people—potential recruits by our clients or an employee of a client suspected of doing something illegal—we often hire a guy named Charles DeMello, a former FBI agent, to investigate for us. He doesn't come cheap, but he could make the right enquiries about Parelli. Of course, Bess and I can make some discreet enquiries too. But to find out things like to whom and how much money Parelli wires, we'd have to hack into his computer. Bess can do that but it's illegal.'

Before Peri could reply to Nick, Alex piped in, 'Peri, I know you're worried about how all this could embarrass your father. I suggest you talk to your father directly about everything you overheard before Nick and Bess hire this DeMello fellow. I just can't imagine your father doing anything fraudulent.'

Peri shot back, 'I *know* Dad wouldn't do anything unscrupulous, let alone commit financial crimes, Alex. But I just can't go up to him and question him outright on a conversation I wasn't even supposed to have heard. I just can't do that.' Alex remained silent.

Peri sat with her fork in her hand, thinking. She couldn't disclose to the others her instinctive dislike for Parelli right from the first time she saw him on her father's birthday. He seemed so irritatingly deferential to everyone at the party, especially to her father, except when the two were arguing. And catching Ginko Parelli surreptitiously walking out of her room didn't help how Peri felt about Lou Parelli.

Peri gave up trying to eat and put down her fork. 'I've made up my mind,' she announced. 'Please get in touch with DeMello and ask him to find out what he can. I would be most grateful if the two of you would ask round too and find out whatever you can about Parelli—of course, without doing anything you or your firm consider unethical.'

Bess smiled and said, 'Peri, I think hiring Charlie is the way to go. He'll find out something useful for sure. I doubt he can learn everything you want to know, but he is very resourceful.'

Nick added, 'I agree, Charlie is your best bet. Give me your phone number and email address and I'll have Charlie get in touch with you.' Nick looked at Bess for agreement, saw her smiling to herself, and knew Bess was thinking *I too can hack into Parelli's computer and I wouldn't charge as much as Charlie is going to*!

Having made her decision, Peri relaxed and finally began to eat. For the rest of the meal, they talked about other things. Both Nick and Bess surprised Peri and Alex with their knowledge of the French Impressionists. After a pleasant conversation and two bottles of wine, Alex asked what had been on Peri's mind since she had first looked at Bess and Nick in the audience: 'Isn't Koyama a Japanese name? You seem to speak good English without an accent, and you don't look Japanese at all. I realize this isn't a politically correct question . . . but . . .'

Nick looked amused and broke in to forestall Alex feeling further embarrassed. 'You're right, Alex, Koyama is a Japanese name. My father is half-Japanese, half-Thai. My mother is originally from Minnesota. I'm half-Asian, half-Caucasian, and I speak English without an accent because I'm American.'

The group enjoyed each other's company through dessert, coffee and after-dinner drinks. The two couples finally parted ways with Bess promising to email DeMello's response to Peri's request as soon as she heard from him.

When Nick was alone with Bess, he asked, 'Are you thinking what I'm thinking?'

'You mean that Peri really suspects her father is involved in what Parelli is doing and she's afraid he will be implicated? Well, she will definitely need some evidence to clear him. Personally, I don't think Parelli would have said what he did to Powers unless he was working closely with Powers . . . possibly even under his direction.'

'We're on the same page, Bess. If what we think is accurate, Powers is sending money to Patriot Party groups round the country through Barrington. We know she's one of the leaders in the Republican Party who is very close to that loopy offshoot. Powers recently endorsed Bond for the Republican nomination, but Bond needs to keep his distance from the Patriot Party to get the votes of mainstream Republicans and Independents in the November election. I'd be willing to bet that the NAD Forum is a front to buy Patriot Party members who have the political muscle to pressure right-wing Republicans to get Bond nominated.'

'Well, let's see what Charlie finds if he agrees to take on this case,' said Bess. 'I wouldn't mind looking into Parelli's computer myself and see what I find.'

'I knew that's what you were thinking when I said Charlie was our best bet. Don't even think about it!'

'Just kidding! But it'd be delicious if I found something that would seriously embarrass the sanctimonious, reactionary Senator Powers . . . even if he is the father of such a wonderful daughter. Poor Peri.'

'Poor Peri is right. I'm sure Charlie will find out what the treasurer of the NAD Forum has been doing. The NAD Forum sounds like the Nut Forum, doesn't it?'

Bess laughed but quickly became serious.

'I wouldn't have dreamt that asking a question about how the age of new information in society affected the Impressionists would lead to our getting involved in an investigation of probable money laundering and the violation of campaign laws on finance. And more so because it's very likely being masterminded by a self-righteous senator from Massachusetts. What a world we live in!'

What a sexy man! thought Evelyn Barrington for the *n*th time as she looked at Jose Reyes across the table. If he wasn't ten years younger than she was, if she wasn't married to a physician with whom she'd had three children, if he wasn't married to the stunningly beautiful Mariella, if-if-if . . . But Jose had stopped talking and looked at her as if awaiting an answer. Evelyn brought her mind back to the argument the two had been having for months.

Evelyn took a messy bite out of her taco and looked at Jose. 'Come again?' she said.

'You haven't been listening,' he accused her. 'And those tacos aren't really Mexican food. Or Spanish. They're very American. You should see what Mariella can cook up!'

Jose patted his flat stomach. He was stocky, of only medium height, but he didn't have an ounce of fat on him. And that dark black hair that kept falling onto his irresistible dark eyes . . . And Evelyn was off again. But she could guess what he had been saying, and she had begun to think he was now continuing the argument just to tease her. Yet she could never be certain whether he was serious.

She had met Jose at one of the rallies the Patriot Party had held at Balboa Park in San Diego. Jose, the owner of a small trucking company and the leader of the Patriot Party in the San Diego area, had impressed her with his ability to whip up support for Republican candidates whom the Eagle Society wanted elected for the House and the Senate. She was amazed at how eloquent a second-generation Mexican American who hadn't gone to college could be.

On that cool autumn day, Jose had approached her.

'Congresswoman Barrington, what we are trying to do is to have a real revolution in American politics. Throw out all the bums in Congress who are trampling on our Constitution and making the USA into a USSA—the United Socialist States of America!'

He had gone on at length about what he wanted to do to oppose the Democrats, whom he called 'those socialist bastards'. He had also said, 'As solid conservative revolutionaries, we shouldn't worry about running afoul of a few laws.'

Evelyn had agreed with him, but not entirely. 'Don't quote me, but skirting a few laws doesn't bother me too much. We have to get as many of the Patriot votes in November as possible. But we have to make sure we don't go too far.'

'I get your point. The question is how far is too far. Assuming we can be sure of not getting caught, would it be going too far if we were to cause a few accidents that might result in a few of the socialist candidates dropping out of the race for Congress?'

'Cause accidents? You mean physical harm? Jose! You *know* that's going too far. Breaking into campaign headquarters and finding some dirt we can use against the Democrats and the so-called moderate Republicans is one thing—I don't worry too much about flouting silly laws on campaign funding. But . . .'

'But being unable to prevent the death of a candidate is something you don't approve of?'

'Unable to prevent a death? Jose, really! There is no such thing as causing the perfect accident. Or the perfect murder. In any case, chances are the police will find the culprits. And they will work extra hard to do so if the victim were running for high office.'

'I wouldn't bet on the ability of the cops to catch the guys who cause the accidents. In my business, we know all too well how mishaps can occur. I've got a lot of friends in the San Diego Police Department and they are no geniuses, nor are they especially hardworking. So chances are pretty good the police will never find out who caused what. From the days when I did the long hauls myself, I made friends all over the country and many of them are in the Patriot Party. I'd be very surprised if most of them wouldn't help us get those bastards out of Congress. But nobody's got any money these days. And that's a real problem. So I can help you stir up the opposition . . . do something more to make sure fewer socialist candidates get elected . . . if I can get some big-time financial help.'

Evelyn still remembered how she had responded, feeling like she was crossing the Rubicon.

'Don't worry about money, Jose. There are always enough rich conservative revolutionaries who'll be happy to finance smart and dedicated revolutionaries willing to take risks for the cause. Mind you, I'm not saying I approve of anything violent. All I'm saying is money isn't a problem.'

With a wide grin, Jose had said, 'You just tell me what you want done—which of the Democrat candidates are likely to take a House seat away from the kind of Republican candidates we want in Congress. I'll have them taken care of. I can arrange for the disruption of rallies, TV debates that favour us, digging up dirt, true or false, on candidates—anything you like. I'll take care of the local cops too. And other things you don't need to know. None of my friends will end up in jail for anything. You just tell me who to focus on and I'll figure out the details. You can count on me and my buddies.'

Evelyn forced herself back to the present. Jose stopped grinning and continued in a serious, almost self-pitying tone: 'We really have to do something to change this . . . system—you fill in the adjectives. We have to make absolutely certain that guys like Chance in Hawaii and Nelson in Oregon don't get elected, no matter what!'

Evelyn was not fazed by Jose's vehemence. He and many of his friends had really experienced the worst the American system could mete out. And with his intelligence and his network, she knew she needed him. She just wouldn't ask too many questions. A veteran congresswoman knew better.

The only thing that worried her now was how many of Jose's old friends to whom he was going to send the money she would give him were genuine Patriots, genuine enough to do anything to defend the Constitution. Or were they merely telling Jose things he wanted to hear and pocketing the money.

She was very disturbed by recent accidents—the fatal car crash in Maine, the small plane that blew up in Spokane, and other such incidents that had taken the lives of both Democrat and Republican candidates. When she had looked into the case of the bombed plane, she found the Republican candidate who was killed was a moderate—the kind Jose and the Patriots despised even more than the Democrats. But she had never discussed the case with Jose. She knew, even if she asked, Jose wouldn't tell her anything. He would protect her. Despite his brash outward demeanour, he was an intelligent man who knew how the game needed to be played.

'So what?' she thought. Not only had she violated campaign funding laws and played felonious dirty tricks for the past thirty years, she was now the pipeline to transmit thirty to fifty thousand dollars a week to the leaders of over thirty regional Patriot groups. She was also helping Parelli of the NAD Forum send tens of millions of dollars to Republican candidates in tight races. So there wasn't very much wrong in her financially helping Jose, she argued to herself. *Hell*, she thought, *the Eagle Society can raise tens of millions every month*.

She was snapped out of it as she suddenly heard Jose change his tone.

'So how much can you give me during the next couple of months? I've got more buddies out of work all over the country and they will do almost anything I tell them to. Of course, I have to let them skim off a bit of what I send them so they can buy groceries and gas.'

Evelyn pulled out a list from her capacious handbag and started to concentrate. Jose pushed aside his empty plate and pulled up his chair next to hers. He mentioned a score of new names of his revolutionary buddies round the country to be added to her list of those already receiving the money she had been giving him. He promised the new buddies would do everything the old buddies had been doing. And he suggested they get paid the same. Evelyn agreed in all cases but one, explaining that the guy was already a local Patriot leader who was receiving thirty thousand dollars a month directly from her for his activities and to pay his associates. Jose laughed, saying, 'Excellent! This proves that our ideas of who is a good revolutionary are the same.'

When they had finished, Jose said, 'Just keep the dough coming my way. I give you my solemn promise all the money will be used for the revolution we want in the US . . . the kind Senator Powers has written about in his book . . . and not a penny will end up in my pocket, I promise!'

Evelyn's instinct as a multi-term congresswoman who had chaired several sub-committees over the years still told her she needed to ask Jose about the things his buddies were doing. But she was smart enough to know the only way not to be told things she would be better off not knowing was not to ask.

'So who do you think will win the election for Congress in this district?' a hotel guest idly asked the bartender in the lobby lounge of the Ritz Carlton in Clayton, Missouri.

The rather overweight, middle-aged bartender handed the man a glass of beer and took a closer look at him. His customer was in his mid-thirties, tallish, dark hair cut short, and of mixed blood—the bartender couldn't tell his racial origin. But he spoke English fluently with a hint of a regional accent. West Coast perhaps. The bar was nearly empty before the businessmen at the hotel descended upon it after work hours, so the slightly bored bartender took his time to answer the man.

'Oh, the incumbent Arnold Roper, I suppose. He's been in Congress now for a couple of decades. A Republican. He's been our congressman as long as I can remember, but he's over seventy now and the Patriot Party wants to get rid of him. I guess a lot of other folk would like some new blood as well, but the party can't tell Roper not to run.'

'So you mean his Democratic opponent has a chance of winning?'

'Yeah, if the people on the right don't come out and vote for Roper as they've been doing for years. He's managed to stay in office by straddling the fence and bringing home the pork, but he's become less effective. He's not in good health either, and the former attorney general, Gwen Sanders—who's the Democrat candidate—is really popular. So she could beat Roper this time. This state is neither blue nor red, so it's unusual for a guy to stay in office for so long. I've heard a lot of people say that young Ron Weller has a better chance— he barely lost to Roper in the primary. Hey, you in politics or something?'

'No, nothing like that. Sales. But I like to find out about the places my company sends me to.'

The man suddenly seemed to be in a hurry. He downed the last of his drink and asked for the tab. He signed it, leaving a generous tip, and walked out quickly.

Twenty-two hours later, the same man, today dressed in an inexpensive dark blue suit and innocuous necktie and carrying an attaché case, walked out the front door of the Ritz Carlton, refused the offer of a taxi, and walked over to Hanley Road where he turned right and went north towards Westmoreland Avenue, the heart of old Clayton. In fifteen minutes of leaving the hotel, the man arrived at the home of Arnold Roper.

The man liked what he saw. The yard was full of leafy trees and bushes. Overgrown shrubbery hid the windows on the ground floor. The wooden fence along the street was almost as tall as he was. No one was in sight in the early afternoon of this weekday and there were no signs of life in the house. But the man knew the congressman was there.

He had got the information—always reliable—by email. But it was a little unusual because it included information he didn't usually get in the emails for his assignments. The message had read:

Arnold Roper will be either at his office in downtown Clayton or at home between 13 and 17 April because no key votes will be taken then and neither of his committees will be meeting. He is always back in Clayton whenever possible because of his health problems. He lives with his unmarried forty-three-year-old daughter who works for the city of Clayton. There is no full-time staff in his home.

Before he left the hotel, he had called Roper's office. The woman who answered the phone said the congressman was not in but refused to say where he could be reached. She suggested making an appointment, but the man declined and hung up. Then he called the congressman's house and when a gruff voice answered the phone, he said 'Wrong number. Sorry.' He knew the voice was Roper's because he had watched YouTube videos of the congressman's speeches so he would be able to recognize his voice and his face when required.

The man entered the congressman's yard, halted behind a stand of trees and removed a long, flat cardboard package from the attaché case he was carrying. From this he took out a long knife in a leather sleeve and inserted it carefully at the left side of his waist between his belt and shirt and then pulled his jacket over it. He knew the non-metallic knife did the job as well as a steel one. It cost well under a hundred dollars, it was legal to purchase one in most states, and it was also available online. Best of all, though it was illegal to carry one on board a plane, the Transportation Security Administration still hadn't found a way to detect the presence of non-metallic knives in luggage.

He stepped out from behind the trees and approached the front door. He pushed a bell above a small brass plate on which 'Roper' was etched in black letters.

Nothing happened. The man was patient. After almost a minute, a tired voice crackled through the intercom: 'Yes?'

'My name is Adam Zeller. I work for a group of gentlemen who are eager to help . . . uh . . . provide campaign money to Republican candidates. I wish to speak with you, Congressman, I need only about ten minutes of your time.'

The voice said, 'If it's only about a campaign donation, you are most welcome to see me in my downtown office tomorrow. I will be there from two to six in the afternoon.'

'Congressman, I came to your home because our conversation has to be absolutely private. Our group is not a Super PAC . . . it's not a known political action committee in that sense . . . it's totally private. We make donations directly to candidates, which Super PACs can't do. We make contributions of up to three million dollars to conservative politicians who need help getting elected. Of course, the money doesn't get reported to anyone, and we ask nothing in return.'

The congressman asked, 'Three million, did you say?' and after a long pause asked again, 'And did you say your group is not a Super PAC and the money isn't reported to anyone?'

'Yes, sir. And we ask for nothing in return. I need only ten minutes, sir. Just long enough to tell you where and how you can get the money. We very much want to make sure you beat Ms Sanders in November.'

There was another long pause. This one even longer than the first.

'All right. I'll give you ten minutes.'

Then there was the sound of a chain being released and a deadbolt lock turned. The oak front door opened.

An old, white-haired, haggard-looking man stood in the doorway. The younger man was surprised because the congressman seemed to have aged a decade since the video clips he had viewed, which were taken not long ago. But Roper almost flinched at the sight of this young man because of his piercing cold eyes.

'Well, come in. Follow me to my study.' The congressman haltingly led the way to a room to the left of the large front hall. He went round his desk and sat down, pointing to a chair facing the desk and said, 'Please sit down.' The man nodded and did as he was told. He sat quietly, waiting to see what the congressman would say next. He was also straining his ears to pick up the slightest noise that might indicate they were not alone. He wanted no surprises.

Roper hadn't been able to raise even half the campaign funds he needed and decided he had better give a warm welcome to this young man. 'I'm sorry I can't offer you a cup of coffee or something, my maid's left for the day,' he said. 'So about your group . . . could you explain in more detail who you represent? We have to be very careful about our fundraising, as I'm sure you're aware.'

The visitor opened his attaché case and pulled out a thick manila folder.

'Sir,' he said, pointing to the sofa behind a large coffee table along one side of the room, 'perhaps we could move over to the sofa so I can spread out the paperwork to show you; it'll tell you who I represent and how careful we are.'

The congressman seemed to relax slightly at the sight of a sheaf of papers. It was good if something was in print. He got up, came round his desk to the sofa and sat down, unaware that the visitor had made certain he sat to the right of Roper.

Roper sank back into the soft cushions, while his visitor, perched on its edge, opened the folder and pulled out at least a dozen pages of typescript. The topmost sheet looked like a contract, but just as the curious congressman leant forward to grasp the papers, the young visitor deftly pulled out his knife and thrust its point at Roper.

The old man, frightened out of his wits, emitted a guttural shout, pushed his hands against the sofa's edge for support, stood up and backed away, just out of reach of the young man. Although taken by surprise by the unexpected strength and agility of the old man, the young man reacted instantly. He stood up, raising his knife, and glared at the old man. The old man tried to jump away again but momentarily lost balance and fell back onto his desk, the back of his right hand hitting hard against the edge of the wooden desk. He shrieked in pain and stole a quick glance at his raised right hand. Crimson streams flowed down his arm. The young man was momentarily frozen.

But he was swift. He jumped round the coffee table with the knife still pointed at Roper. The old man tried to get away and lost his balance yet again, falling hard, this time hitting his head—a distinct crack was heard—on the edge of the coffee table. The young man lowered the knife and stood staring as the old man slid onto the floor, his head almost bathed in a pool of blood. The old man lay still.

The young man with the cold eyes was puzzled by the unusually large amount of blood that continued to ooze from the old man's injuries. Why was there so much blood? He had, after all, just knocked his hand against the desk and bumped his head a little hard perhaps.

Then he suddenly remembered something his great-uncle had once told him: 'You can kill someone by giving the person an overdose of anticoagulants.' He no longer remembered the names of the medicines but he vaguely recalled they were often prescribed to patients to prevent strokes by thinning the blood and impeding blockages. He was certain the congressman must be on this medication.

He muttered a curse, went over to Roper and knelt down to check on his condition. Roper was unconscious and still haemorrhaging steadily. The young man looked at his watch. It was before three. The daughter shouldn't arrive home for another two hours or so. At the rate the old man was bleeding, there was no way he would survive the head injury. And if he did, the young man was reasonably confident he wouldn't be able to say who his visitor was.

He stood up and stared down at the old man. Yes, he would take the chance. If he left now, the death would be put down to natural causes. It would save work for the police. The young man was pleased with himself: he had carried out the assignment in Clayton without causing a suspicious death.

He began to methodically erase any sign of his presence. With his handkerchief he wiped his fingerprints from all the surfaces he'd touched and plumped up the sofa cushions to make it look like no one had sat on the sofa since the cleaner had come in last. Then he packed the papers into his attaché case.

He looked round a last time and, using his handkerchief, shut the door to the study behind him, then opened and closed the front door, ensuring the latch was on so the door would get locked shut. Stuffing his handkerchief in his trouser pocket, he walked calmly down the front path and out onto the sidewalk. Then he picked up his pace and briskly made his way back to the Ritz Carlton the same way he had come.

Once back in his room, the man phoned the front desk and arranged to check out. He readily agreed to pay for the extra half day as it was past checkout time. He tossed his few clothes and shaving kit into his suitcase, scanned the room for other belongings, took his luggage down to the lobby, checked out and took a taxi to the St Louis airport.

At Lambert International, the man booked a round-trip flight to Denver on United Airlines using a California driving licence as ID and a Bank of America Visa card. Then he went to the men's room where, on his way out, he ditched a narrow, flat cardboard box in the trash, burying it beneath a lot of used paper towels.

He had two hours until his flight, so he bought a newspaper, got a cup of coffee and a sandwich and sat down in a corner, making himself as inconspicuous as possible. Online he booked a room at the Holiday Inn near the Denver Airport.

He didn't arrive at his hotel until late evening. He checked in using a different credit card and ID. When he reached his room, he ordered a pizza from room service. He turned on the TV, looking for news, but found no mention of a congressman's death. He went onto the Internet and cancelled his return flight to St Louis, booking instead a flight to San Francisco for the following day on Frontier Airlines, using yet another credit card and a different driving licence with another name. Unfortunately, he couldn't get a flight until half past ten in the morning. He was exhausted and fell fast asleep as soon as his head hit the pillow.

At a few minutes before ten, the man sat in the lounge at the gate in Denver Airport waiting to board. He glanced at the TV monitor overhead, which was blaring out something about high unemployment rates in the country. He paid little attention. When a young woman at the Frontier desk announced that boarding was starting, he joined the line of passengers waiting to board. It was then that he heard a man announce breaking news.

'Congressman Roper of the Second Congressional District in Missouri died at his home in Clayton yesterday afternoon. The details are still sketchy, but the cause of death is believed to be the result of a fall. The police are certain no foul play was involved.'

The young man suppressed a smile and followed the passenger in front of him to the boarding gate.

Lisa had taken three steps away from her desk when her phone rang. She looked at it, debating whether to answer the call. She was already late for her lunch date with Pat, but curiosity got the better of her and she answered the call. When she heard the caller identify himself as Sam Ogden, special agent in charge of the FBI's Seattle office, her heart began to race. She was sure he was calling her because David Porter, the FBI agent in Chicago she had talked to over a month ago, had carried out his promise and spoken to someone in the head office about her concerns over the deaths of the Congressional candidates. *But why an agent in Seattle and not in Washington?* she wondered.

Ogden immediately answered her unspoken question. David Porter in Chicago had called the FBI headquarters in DC to relay her concerns. Headquarters was already in the process of creating a special task force to investigate the unusual number of deaths of candidates before the media began to speculate about the serial murders of candidates. They had alerted candidates informally to be extra cautious about their security. Ogden, who was already involved in the investigation of the Cessna bombing in Spokane, had been asked to lead a preliminary investigation into these deaths.

When Lisa began to wonder where this was going, Ogden asked, 'Have you heard about the highly decorated Iraq war veteran, Paul Robinson, who was running for Congress in Ohio? The day before yesterday, a truck rammed into his car and he was killed—just like that, a hit and run.'

'Yes, this morning's *Star Advertiser* here had a short article on his death and I read a longer one online. I understand he was a former sergeant who had received two purple hearts and had won a highly contested Republican primary against a candidate who was strongly supported by the local Patriots.'

'Right,' said Ogden. 'The truck was found yesterday near Lancaster, a small town near Columbus. It was a rental, and the guy who rented it did so late at night paying cash and using a fake driver's license. The only thing the woman who processed the rental agreement remembers is that the guy wore a pair of very thick glasses and spoke little. As you might expect from this, the places the driver would have touched were wiped free of fingerprints.'

Before Lisa could react, he went on.

'Nate Kimpel, special agent in charge of the Columbus office, called me this morning because he knows I'm leading the preliminary investigation team.

He suspects this case may not be an ordinary hit and run. He interviewed Robinson's wife and she said she'd seen a dark-haired young man wearing sunglasses lurking in front of their house a couple of days before her husband was killed. Their twelve-year-old daughter too had seen a man with the same description sitting on a bench at a bus stop two blocks from their house. She thought it was odd because it was a cloudy day.'

'Hmm . . . Sam, I can guess why you called me. You think he sounds like the same guy I told David about . . . the guy I saw at the party just before Steve Sasaki died of a supposed heart attack.'

'Right, Lisa. So . . . here is my request. Could you fly to Seattle as soon as possible? Tonight if you can. We really have to try to prevent more deaths and we need to get some kind of picture of this guy which we can circulate.'

'What? Tonight?' Lisa was surprised but managed to agree: 'Yes, I guess so. But what can I do in Seattle that I can't do here?'

'We have the newest FBI computer program that does wonders in coming up with a surprisingly good likeness of a face on limited information. Much better than the Identi-Kit everyone's been using. We call it the "generative algorithmic program". Don't ask me how it works. All I know is that you work with an artist and the program does the rest, using what they call an evolutionary approach: you get an equation, you put in what a person remembers about a face into the equation, then the equation tells you how to modify the face. It works brilliantly . . . almost spooky.'

'You want me to tell your artist what I remember about the guy I saw at the party the night Steve Sasaki died?'

'Yes. I think it's worth a try. I'm not yet sold on the idea you told Porter about, that only one guy might be doing all these killings. But so far the only descriptions we have are the same as yours. And you've been trained as an observer. I also want to have a thorough discussion with you on the information we've gathered so far on all the deaths of Congressional candidates this year. I have a small budget but I'll cover your airfare and the cost of a hotel.'

'OK, I'll try to book a flight for tonight. There's no reason I can't take sick leave if I have to. I'll call you back as soon as I can, certainly within an hour. But can I ask you a question?'

'Of course. Shoot.'

'You said the FBI is informally alerting the candidates to be careful. What does that mean exactly?'

'Oh! Well, our agents in various field offices are unofficially telling candidates or their campaign managers to use more caution than usual. We don't want to send out a written warning because these things invariably end up in the hands of the media and we don't want that, do we?'

'No, certainly not. As I said, I'll call you in an hour.'

A very excited Lisa worked quickly. Captain Kalani approved her request to go to Seattle for two days. Hawaiian Air had a seat for her. Lisa called Ogden to confirm. He sounded very pleased. After lunch, Lisa cleared her desk, went home to pack and was at the gate long before her plane boarded. Thanks to an empty seat next to hers, she managed to sleep for almost three hours.

Lisa shivered when she left the Seattle–Tacoma terminal. At half past six in the morning the air was much colder than it ever got in Honolulu. A cab took her to a small downtown hotel only a couple of blocks from the Third Avenue field office of the FBI. Knowing how tight budgets were everywhere, Lisa was unfazed by the shabby-looking hotel. In a small third-floor room, she showered quickly, dressed in what she called her mainland winter clothes— wool slacks and a light cashmere sweater—and went down to the ground floor for breakfast.

Walking briskly, she barely made her nine o'clock appointment with Ogden. As she had judged from his voice, Ogden was in his mid-forties. He was tall, almost six-feet two, and handsome, if she ignored his visibly receding reddish hair.

Ogden took her to a little office on the second floor and introduced her to an attractive, plump, young woman called Anne, a portrait painter and also a genius computer-aided-design specialist from the *Seattle Times* who helped the FBI from time to time. Lisa and Anne worked together for nearly an hour. As Anne listened to Lisa, she drew a rough sketch on the screen using a pen-like gadget. Then, following Lisa's suggestions, Anne touched up the sketch with the help of the new computer program. By the end of the hour, Anne had succeeded in coming up with the face that Lisa believed resembled that of the young man with the chilling eyes whom she had seen at Mrs Albinson's fundraiser.

Ogden, who came to fetch Lisa, took one look at the face on the screen and said, 'Christ, he looks both handsome and creepy at the same time! We'll send the picture to the field offices who have witnesses of someone suspicious and see if we get a match.'

Ogden led Lisa to his office, telling his secretary not to disturb them. As soon as Lisa was seated, he put in front of her a list of thirteen names, each followed by a condensed description of how Congressional candidates running for seats in the coming election had died. Ogden said, 'It starts from January of this year. We can start earlier . . . sometime last year . . . if we decide we should. One of them is not the name of a candidate but his dead wife. I'm going to get us some coffee and then we'll discuss this.'

Lisa asked for a latte and then got to work. The bulleted list contained the date of death, name and age of the deceased, place of death, party affiliation and whether they were running for the House or the Senate, presumed cause of death and additional remarks. Lisa began to read each entry carefully.

- January 14, Kendrick Mitchell, 62, Tucson, Arizona, Democrat, House, heart attack. Suffered a mild heart attack four years prior to his death. Tucson field office established that a stranger—a young man of uncertain ethnicity, about 5´8˝—was seen near Mitchell's campaign office. Had no opponent for the Democratic primary election.

- January 20, Arlene Schmidt, 58, Scottsdale, Arizona, Republican, House, car accident. Car careered into a valley. Known to have been a good, cautious driver. No rain in area during the week prior to the accident. No reliable report of any stranger being seen near Schmidt's house or campaign office during days preceding accident. A moderate with a strong challenger in the Republican primary in February.

- January 21, Silas Fuller, 81, Providence, Rhode Island, Republican, Senate, heart attack. Hospitalized with pneumonia last October. Had two serious challengers, one male and one female, in the Republican primary. No reports of possible foul play.

- February 10, Kent Harrison, 48, Bangor, Maine, Democrat, House, car accident. State police concluded the accident most likely occurred when Harrison tried to avoid a car coming at him, driving in the same lane in the wrong direction. Fog reported on morning of accident. Unfamiliar driver or with impaired vision probably crossed centre lane inadvertently. Had no challenger in the February primary.

- February 19, Vera Nelson-Berg, 52, Hartford, Vermont, Democrat, House, freak accident. Fell down icy steps of campaign manager's building late at night. Female aide, who left building a short time before incident, reported seeing man about 5´7˝ moving away in the dark from the bottom of the steps as she left.

- March 1, Samuel Krueger, 64, Yuba City, California, Democrat, House, cerebral aneurysm. Had physical check-up two weeks before death. In robust health. Wife convinced that 'a young right-wing nut', who Krueger had complained was pestering him—how she didn't know—had a hand in husband's death. No autopsy performed. Police convinced no foul play involved. Krueger was unopposed in the primary election.

Lisa glanced at the content of the next entry. She had been right to arrive at Mrs Albinson's fundraiser hoping no one would die that night. Going by this list it was evident Congress had already lost far too many candidates since the year began.

- March 8, Stephen Sasaki, 43, Honolulu, Hawaii, Democrat, House, heart attack. . . .

She knew the rest of the details of the Sasaki death—there wasn't very much else to add—and moved on to the next entry.

- March 18, Amanda d'Abruzzio, 38, wife of Anthony d'Abruzzio, West Seneca, New York, 62, Democrat, House, heart attack. (NB: Only case of death of a non-candidate, but in this list for obvious reasons.) Totally unexpected heart attack after having dinner at a restaurant with her husband and a man her husband described as 'a stranger who came up to say he was going to make a campaign contribution'. Anthony and a waiter described stranger as 'about 35, 135–140 lbs, 5′8″, perhaps an inch or two more'. Most notable feature was piercing hard eyes. Gave name as Chad Lopez. Police failed to locate anyone by that name. Amanda's doctor confirmed a sudden heart attack. Anthony running for seat in district that hasn't elected a Republican since 1982.

- April 5, Kathryn Myers, 54, Spokane, Washington, Republican, Senate, plane accident. Died with three others when her plane was bombed just before take-off at Felts Field. Complete file, CI-187, is available in Seattle field office.

- April 14, Arnold Roper, 72, Clayton, Missouri, Republican, House. Bled to death at home after hitting his head accidentally. Police in Clayton and St Louis did thorough joint investigation of death because of recent rash of deaths of Congressional candidates. Roper had history of serious health problems: was taking Coumadin, a blood thinner, to prevent a stroke. Died alone, indoors, house locked. No autopsy conducted. Doctor who signed death certificate declared death due to natural causes. Full report is available in the St. Louis office.

- April 18, Sandra Montoya, 42, Daytona Beach, Florida, Republican, House, hypoglycaemia. Police concluded the obese candidate with diabetes must have been careless about maintaining glucose levels because of her hectic campaign schedule. Nothing to indicate possible foul play. At time of death, Montoya was polling 8 points above her Democratic opponent.

- April 20, Wayne Gustafson, 63, Madison Wisconsin, Democrat, House, heart attack. 'Totally unexpected' is how his wife described it. Said her husband, who had taught at University of Wisconsin, 'went to dinner with a former student who wanted to make a sizeable campaign contribution. Two hours after he came home he complained of chest pains and died.' Wife has no idea who former student was. Gustafson was expected to win the election easily for the second time beating same Republican opponent.

- 25 April, Paul Robinson, Ohio, Republican . . .

Lisa's reading was interrupted by a light knock on the door. Ogden walked in, carefully balancing two cups. He handed one to Lisa and asked, 'Well, what do you think? Anything strike you?'

'If my theory is right, Agent Ogden . . .'

'Sam, please,' Ogden interrupted.

Lisa smiled and continued: 'I was saying, Sam, if my theory is right and one guy is behind all these killings, we can throw out three cases right off the bat.' Lisa looked down at the list. 'First the death of Fuller on 21 January. I don't know the time of Schmidt's car accident in Arizona, but it would seem virtually impossible for a killer to cause her accident, fly across the country to Rhode Island, and somehow murder the elderly senator the following day. And I think the car accident is more suspicious than the death of a man in his eighties and in delicate health. What do you say?'

'I'm with you on that one. I checked the time of the deaths. Couldn't be done. The second case . . . ?' Sam prompted.

'The one on 14 April, Roper, the congressman from Clayton. He was old and was taking Coumadin. Sounds more like the case of an old man on strong blood thinners accidentally hitting his head and bleeding to death. And we have to remember he reportedly died alone and in a locked house. Our suspect couldn't have had anything to do with it.'

'I agree. And the last case . . . ?'

'The last one is the death of the Republican candidate in Florida, Sandra Montoya, who died of hypoglycaemia on April 18. Again, the timing between this and the next death makes it difficult, if not impossible, to pin both deaths on one man. It's far more likely that Gustafson was a murder victim. He died two hours after having a meal with someone no one really knew.'

'How about Krueger in California who died of a cerebral aneurysm on March 1?'

'Hmm . . . your list says he wasn't autopsied, and his wife said he was being pestered by a young right-wing nut. I think we should keep it on the list of suspicious deaths.'

'I'll go along with you on that. So what do you think the motive could be?'

'That's what's stumps me,' Lisa admitted. 'Up till now, I've been thinking of a Patriot, like the guy who tried to dissuade Senator Kwon from staying in the race for re-election. Of course, the assassin must be much smarter than the guy who broke into Senator Kwon's apartment. And he either has to be rich himself or more likely has a rich sponsor, someone who hates all Republican and Democratic politicians.'

'Lisa, your theory has gaping holes in it. If he hates the politicians of both parties, why kill these candidates and not others in office at present?'

'Maybe his rich sponsor tells him whom to go after. I know the motivation is definitely political . . . but I've no idea why the specific targets were chosen. But since everyone who died was a candidate, the motivation is clearly the coming election. And, Sam, you sound like you're not convinced one guy could be doing this.'

'I'm not saying you're wrong. But I need stronger evidence before I can be convinced. More than one guy of similar physique could very well be going to different parts of the country to kill. To be honest, I'm having a hard time believing one guy is killing all these people and using so many different methods. A serial killer—if your theory is correct—usually follows a single trademark style. What we can be certain of is that we have one or more murderers out there. After all, it's unusual to have more than one candidate die during an election year, and here we have thirteen since the beginning of the year!'

'Sam, if you're right, it might explain why the modus operandi is different in each case. Perhaps there's one guy who's using some kind of impossible-to-detect poison that metabolizes quickly, causing a heart attack soon after it's administered, explaining what happened to Sasaki, and another guy who's staging accidents, bombings and so on.'

'Hmm . . . from the methods of killing, I actually think there could well be a number of guys involved . . . you know, Lisa, there are many who fit the description we have and who are just plain psychos.'

'But, Sam, something still doesn't make sense. It seems unlikely that the mastermind behind these killings would be able to go out and find several men of roughly the same age and appearance willing to be paid killers. I'd still put my bet on one very resourceful, clever—cunning, I mean—man committing all these murders, changing modus operandi to make the deaths seem less suspicious.'

Sam nodded. 'You do have a point there. And, yes, there could be simple explanations for the change of technique. He might have been forced to orchestrate an accident instead of using poison as the latter would've meant getting near the target, and we've warned them to be extra cautious about security. The problem is that we need more evidence. I'll send our field offices the face Anne and you came up with; let's hope we hear something important we don't know yet. I'm going to get a couple of my staff to do more on-site checking while our field agents continue to dig on. You keep this list and mull over it. Let's try and figure out the motive; that should help us determine the next likely target, and perhaps get closer to catching the culprit.'

Sam looked at his watch. 'Come on, Lisa. I'll treat you to a decent lunch. That's the least I can do,' he said with a smile.

After a satisfying meal at Wild Ginger, a trendy Asian restaurant, Lisa leant back, teacup in hand. Relaxed, she failed to stifle a huge yawn.

Sam laughed and suggested she go crash in her hotel room. 'You can stay there until check-out tomorrow,' he said.

Lisa looked at her watch and thought a minute. 'If you're through with me, I think I'd rather go back and crash in my own bed. Let me see if I can get a seat on the five forty-five flight to Honolulu,' she said.

'You really are a fiend for punishment,' Sam observed. 'But if that's what you want, I'll drive you to Sea-Tac.'

O

Lisa boarded her plane, made herself comfortable in the window seat and was about to doze off when a middle-aged woman plonked down in the middle seat and began talking:

'You're a good-looking girl. What do you do?'

'I work for the city . . . the city of Honolulu.' Lisa wasn't really up to idle chatter.

'Lucky you.'

'Why? My pay isn't great and my hours . . . you wouldn't believe.'

'Honey, the most important thing is that you've got a job . . . unlike most of my family. We've got lousy jobs, if any at all, in hotels and restaurants that ain't doin' too good in this damn recession. We're all hard up, so everyone chipped in to send me here for our uncle's funeral yesterday in Tacoma.'

Lisa couldn't think of an appropriate response, but the woman carried on.

'It's not our fault, you know. And housing is so expensive in Honolulu. Fourteen of us live in a three-bedroom house that's a firetrap. It's the government I tell you! The Republicans, the Democrats, they're all the same.'

Lisa, now intrigued, was about to ask why, but the woman didn't stop.

'The politicians . . . they're all in cahoots with the big banks and corporations. They rig the system so we stay poor. They tax us but don't do *anything* for us. But things never change, they just get worse.'

'We can make it change. Have you listened to Senator Chance? He wants to change the jungle capitalism we have now into just capitalism . . . so . . . if you vote for him, we can change America, we can unrig the system,' Lisa responded.

'No way, honey!' the woman exclaimed. 'My friends tell me he's a socialist who wants to make another Russia here. All the Democrats and Republicans say nice things when they run for office. But I've been around long enough not to believe what they promise. No matter what they say they'll change, when they get into office they just run things the same old way. The rich get richer while we live on food stamps and food banks and minimum wages. We need better everything . . . houses, health care and jobs. And fewer taxes. Taxes only make the rich richer and the politicians more corrupt. So we've got to raise hell! We'll get change only by a revolution . . . a Patriot revolution! We sure ain't like those tame Tea Party folks. We will rise in revolution!'

As the woman ranted on in an agitated and increasingly loud voice, Lisa could feel the disapproval of fellow passengers. After a night with only a few hours' nap on a plane and an intense morning at the FBI, she couldn't cope with all this blathering. She pulled out her Bose headphones and said, 'I didn't sleep last night and I'm exhausted. Forgive me, but I *have* to take a nap.'

'You'll be sorry if you forget you're one of us,' the woman said petulantly and looked away. Lisa leant back and closed her eyes, so exhausted she hadn't even noticed take-off. She dozed off wondering, *Could we be looking for a Patriot murderer?*

Peri sat in her room on the second floor of her Chestnut Hill home and looked down on the spacious lawn at the far end of which stood a dozen mature trees her grandfather had planted. In the twilight, the garden was quiet and peaceful. What a contrast this was to the view from her flat in Paris—a busy street and a tiny park in front of the tall, ivy-covered wall of a university building. It was as if she entered a different world whenever she returned to her family home.

She was alone until Alex drove down from giving a presentation at a college in Waterville, Maine. Maria, the family's housekeeper, was off for the weekend. And her father was in New York.

As she thought of Alex, she grew aware of how their relationship had become increasingly serious over the past few months. Despite busy schedules, they had been doing their best to spend as much time together as they could. When Peri had to be in the US, Alex had made arrangements to give talks and hold seminars in the New England area. She knew his standing in the art history world made it easy for his friends to arrange presentations, but she was very happy that Alex had taken so much trouble to be with her.

This afternoon Peri had returned home after giving a job talk—the presentation of a paper by all prospective candidates to get a professorial appointment—at a liberal arts college in upstate New York. She had debated coming all the way back to the US just for one interview, but she had decided she wanted a position as soon as possible to establish herself in her profession. For the same reason, she had also accepted an invitation by the University of Lyon to give another job talk in the coming week.

However, she faced a quandary, one not uncommon to young academics, especially women: if the position she got was in the US, it would mean she would be an ocean away from Alex; if she got a job in Lyon, it would still mean they'd be hundreds of miles apart. As a very rich heiress, she had the luxury of not having to worry about money, but location was certainly an issue. It had already become clear to her that her chance of finding a job where she could be near Alex was remote. Peri did realize that Alex hadn't been very vocal about his feelings for her nor had he broached marriage yet, and perhaps fretting about where a job would take her and her future with Alex wasn't of much use. Yet, she found herself thinking about this frequently.

It was growing dark and Peri was beginning to feel hungry, so she went downstairs, got herself an apple and turned on the TV while she waited for Alex. As she flipped channels, she suddenly heard the name of Senator Powers. She went back a channel and discovered that CSPAN was holding a debate among the contenders for the Democratic nomination. She quickly understood why her father's name had come up: the moderator was asking the contenders to comment on the bill to abolish all inheritance taxes, introduced by Senators Jameson and Powers of the Republican Party. 'This bill was introduced in the last session of Congress and defeated. But the senators plan to reintroduce it in the next session after the election,' the moderator said.

This was the first that Peri had heard of the bill. *I really am spending too much time outside the US!* What was her father trying to do? She sat back on the sofa to listen, her apple forgotten in her hand.

Senator Rachel Samuelson of California was asked for her view on the bill. She spoke vehemently. 'This is an old canard these reactionary Republican senators trot out every session. To argue that there should be no inheritance tax at all because the money in an estate has already been taxed when it was earned is ridiculous. Why should the heirs of the richest Americans pay no inheritance tax? They did absolutely nothing to earn that money. Jameson and Powers argue that the rich should keep their money to invest and create jobs, but it's already been shown that this doesn't work. What they cold-heartedly ignore is the fact that in our country the rich are getting richer every year while the poor and the middle class continue to struggle. All this tells me is that we Democrats must ensure we get a majority in both Houses of Congress in November!'

Despite being an heiress, Peri couldn't agree more with Senator Samuelson. During the past few years, every time she came back to the US, she found an increasing number of beggars in Boston and New York, and she read how hard the lives of the middle class Americans had become. She was well aware the rich were indulging in luxuries she too thought excessive, and that the increased disparity in income was steadily swelling the ranks of the Patriot Party.

While she was thinking she ought to question her father on how he could justify co-sponsoring such a bill, scholarly-looking Senator Nelson from Oregon was given the mike. He essentially echoed what Senator Samuelson had said, using words such as 'plutocracy' and 'impecunious'.

Senator Maxwell Chance from Hawaii was asked for his view next. From the minute he began to speak, Peri realized that he had given this very denunciation countless times before, but she had to admit he was a charismatic speaker.

'What the Jameson–Powers bill intends to do is to safeguard the jungle capitalism of the United States, an economic system rigged to preserve the current pattern of income and wealth distribution, which is the most unequal in the industrialized world. Jungle capitalism sacrifices the welfare of more than three-quarters of our citizens for the sake of higher corporate profits and the obscene salaries and bonuses CEOs and bankers receive. This brand of capitalism operates on the self-serving and totally fallacious premise that when the rich become richer, their gains will eventually trickle down to the poorest.' Senator Chance had hit his stride, and went on.

'Senators Jameson and Powers have their logic backwards! What we need is to increase demand, which will make manufacturers increase the supply of goods to meet the rising demand. The rich ought to understand that when demand increases, so does supply, causing the economy to grow and everyone to gain. Unemployment rates drop and wages rise. The rich profit too, for as corporate profits increase with increasing sales, the price of stocks rises and dividends go up. But no one, no matter how rich, is going to hire more workers and increase the supply of goods and services if there is no demand for them. In jungle capitalism everyone loses. But in the just capitalist system I'm fighting for, everyone gains!'

There was a roar of approval for Senator Chance, and Peri watched the cameras pan to a crowd of young people standing at the back of a large auditorium, clapping and yelling. Someone yelled, 'Chance for President! Chance for President!' and the crowd took it up.

Through the noise from the TV, Peri was suddenly aware of the ringing doorbell. She hurriedly switched off the TV and went to open the door. It was Alex. The lovers greeted each other as if they hadn't met for months, though it had been a mere three days. When they finally broke apart, Alex announced, '*J'ai une faim de loup*—I could eat a wolf!' Peri laughed and said, 'You mean a horse,' and sent him to wash up.

When Alex joined Peri in the kitchen, she was laying out on the table a cold meal of roast deli chicken, a hearty salad she had made earlier and a large baguette. She added a lightly chilled bottle of Pouilly-Fuissé from her father's cellar.

'I didn't know what time you'd come back, so it's only a cold meal,' Peri said apologetically. 'No complaints,' said Alex as he sat down.

'So how did your talk go?' Peri asked.

'*Ça va*. Fine. But judging from the questions I got after my presentation, I gather that I made the best impression—no pun intended!—when I talked about Cezanne's *The Card Players* being purchased in 2011 by the royal family of Qatar. It sold for over two hundred and fifty million dollars, the highest price ever paid for a painting. From the reaction of some in the audience, I must have sounded more like a socialist outraged by the extraordinary price than like an art historian discussing a Cézanne painting.'

'Why? What did you say?'

'Well, as you know, Cézanne's paintings didn't bring him immense wealth in his lifetime—I'd consider him poor by that yardstick; he even died in a rented house. But *The Card Players* sold for what it did because Qatar is obscenely rich. It has oil you know. You don't need to be a socialist to see how ironic this is.'

'I don't get it, Alex. That Qatar has oil is an accident of geography. Paul Cézanne died in Aix-en-Provence, a poor man—if you say so—over a hundred years ago. What's ironic about that?'

'What I'm trying to say is that the sale of this painting at such a high price epitomizes the fact that the price of art is determined not by its intrinsic worth but by who can outbid other buyers. And how much a person or a country is willing to pay to outbid others is determined by how big a disparity in income or wealth exists in an economy and how capitalistic or despotic an economy is. Qatar is despotic. If it were a social democratic country like France where income is more equally distributed, no one would be able to bid that much because no one is rich enough.'

'And you're unhappy because in France—and other large parts of Europe—income is more equally distributed than in Qatar or even the US? And since many rich Arabs and Americans can outbid French buyers in most auctions your art heritage is leaving the country?'

'OK! I admit it, that too,' said Alex a little sheepishly. 'But it can apply to any country. My theory about the price of art is that the amount of the highest bid is inversely correlated with the degree of equality of income distribution. Not the first time I've said this. But most of the questions I got were on why the painting fetched over two hundred and fifty million dollars, and whether this meant that it was intrinsically better than those that didn't fetch such a high price.'

'You know,' said Peri, 'it's interesting you bring this up. When you arrived I was watching a debate among Democratic candidates for the presidency. I didn't see much of it, but I did hear what they had to say about a law the Republicans want to enact to completely abolish the inheritance tax. I didn't take economics in college, but what Senator Chance said made so much sense. He called our current system "jungle capitalism", and said that letting the rich get richer isn't good for the country and won't encourage economic growth because everyone else will be too poor to buy anything.'

'That's an argument we hear in France at every election. Our right-wing politicians always argue like the Republicans here, that unregulated capitalism is the most efficient and productive system because there's nothing like profit incentive—greed, if you like—to unleash the entrepreneurial spirit to create new products and new ways of making everything more efficiently. But, of course, eventually, the entrepreneurs will have to find new markets because the rest of us won't be able to buy their products on our low wages—or no wages—as more and more goods are produced offshore. However, money speaks far louder in America than it does in Europe in terms of shaping national policies.'

'What really disturbed me about the programme was that the candidates were discussing a bill that my father has co-sponsored in the Senate, not once but a few times already,' Peri said, sounding abashed.

'What? You mean your father has sponsored a bill to abolish all inheritance taxes? I'm a cynical socialist, so I guess I shouldn't be surprised. He must be trying to pay for the campaign money he raises by passing laws the donors want. I have to say that political candidates in the US seem willing to do almost anything these days to get elected!'

'That's why Senator Chance from Hawaii made so much sense. He wants to fundamentally reform our capitalist structure to prevent the kind of economic debacle we had in 2008 and to eliminate the terrible income disparities we have now. He claims this will benefit everyone, even capitalists whose profits will go up when demand rises.'

Alex said quietly, 'I think your Senator Chance is too optimistic about the ability of any one politician to transform American capitalism.'

'But why, Alex? . . .' Peri began in protest.

'Should Chance get elected in November, he's sure to run up against a huge brick wall—a wall of the devout admirers of the current system, such as big business and banks. They'll do all they can to prevent Chance from getting his way. Money talks far louder and in more insidious ways here than in France. Even some Democratic members of Congress, who're very conservative by European standards, will block many things Chance wants to do. Millions of people who vote for Chance, hoping their life will improve overnight if he is elected, will find their life doesn't change much. So they'll get mad and kick the Democrats out of the House at the next election in two years, just as happened in 2010 when voters derailed many of Obama's policies—similar in many ways to Chance's—by voting in a Republican majority in the House. And . . .'

Alex stopped as he realized Peri was beginning to look depressed with the bleak picture. He picked up her wine glass and said, 'Here, have another glass of wine and tell me how your job talk went.'

Peri gave a little laugh and replied, 'Very well actually. The individual interviews were the problem.'

'Let me guess. They asked things like "Why do you want to leave Paris and come to a small rural college town?" Or, "When your book from Yale comes out, won't you want to leave for a position at a large research university?" I learned in Waterville that a large percentage of the faculty live in Portland, especially the younger, unmarried lot. They can't cope with a life without the bright city lights,' Alex said with a big smile.

'You're right. And my hesitation must've shown. The chair of one of the smaller art programmes was almost unfriendly over dinner last night. I thought he felt rather threatened by my degree and my forthcoming book from Yale.'

'Peri, you seem so set on getting a regular academic position, no matter where in the world it takes you. Why do you want to leave Paris? And me? I'm spending so much time drumming up lectures and presentations so that I can be near you. I do want you to become an academic success, but will taking up a teaching job with long hours in the classroom, lots of duties and little free time make your name in the art history world?'

Peri was astounded. This was the first time Alex had been so blunt about wanting to be near her.

'It's what I've always been told someone with a PhD in art history should do. I love my life in Paris. And I don't know what's going on in my own country any more. I do love my father but I loathe the Senator Powers who wants to introduce the Jameson–Powers bill.' Her face clouded with conflicting emotions.

'Peri, I love you. *Je t'aime vraiment.* Come back to Paris with me and stay there. But for now, let's go to bed.'

Peri couldn't ask for more at the moment. Alex hadn't mentioned marriage but he had expressed his feelings for her.

While Peri and Alex were getting ready for bed in Chestnut Hill, her father was getting out of a king-sized bed in an ornately decorated bedroom of a luxury flat in upper Manhattan.

'Where are you going?' Karen McPherson asked in a sleepy voice.

'To get a glass of water. Would you like one?'

'Yes, thanks, Simon,' and she rolled over and pulled up the sheet.

Powers slipped on a robe and padded barefoot down the long hall to the kitchen where he slowly took two glasses from a cupboard and filled them with ice and filtered water. He sat down on a stool facing a long counter, picked up one of the glasses and took three small sips.

He was peculiarly depressed, unusual for him. What was he getting into? He needed ten million dollars from McPherson as soon as possible to assure that Bond would pick him as his running mate. If he became vice president, he might have a chance of creating the America he had outlined in his book. But what was he doing feigning romantic interest in Karen? The word marriage hadn't yet come into their conversation, but he was sure it was in the air.

Yet, all the while he made love to her—if that was the right phrase—he kept thinking of the much younger Anita, whom he didn't have to worry about marrying. He had had numerous affairs and a number of mistresses during his lifetime, but this was the first time he had an ulterior motive. But was there a reason to feel ashamed? Wasn't this just a different version of what he had been doing for the past year—raising money by promising legal changes he doubted would ever be passed and leaning on people who owed him for past favours?

Maybe he was just feeling low because of his humiliating experience yesterday. He slumped down on the stool as he thought: *I should have seen it coming when Ernst Wessel agreed to meet me only after three calls, and then at the Harvard Club where Ernst Wessel, Jr is a member. I wasn't even offered lunch. But who would've thought the billionaire grain trader would turn down my proposal to amend the Commodity Futures Trading Act to save his corporation tens of millions of dollars each year?*

Wessel Jr had come with his father and dominated the conversation, but Wessel Sr had echoed his son a number of times. Powers thought over their conversation for the *n*th time. *Maybe I did go too far in declaring that Chance is a socialist, but I didn't expect the head of a major corporation to go all righteous and claim he wouldn't channel money to Bond through the forum. His operations must be involved in all kinds of tax shenanigans, so why did he turn me down on a mere technicality? Clearly, that was just a pretext. I know Wessel is a diehard Republican, so why doesn't he want to support Bond? He spoke like he's been brainwashed by his son who graduated from that rabidly left-wing university in Cambridge.*

This wasn't the first time Powers had been turned down. But he was concerned that a staunch Republican wouldn't support his ideas or Bond, and he had counted on Wessel's money. Now, it was essential that he get a big donation from Karen. He was certain that others in the Eagle Society were using the same tactics, and all for the good of the country. But maybe they hadn't been reduced to using sex. Was that why he felt so grubby now?

Powers drained his glass and put it down on the counter. He wished he could just leave the flat now. But he knew he couldn't. Parelli was coming to see the two of them early the next morning to figure out how Karen could donate ten million dollars to the NAD Forum while burying all footprints of the money by using offshore banks so that no one at Treasury ever got wise. Besides, he couldn't ask Karen to go to Parelli's office in Boston and her flat was as secure as could be from any prying eyes.

He knew he ought to return to the bedroom. But fear suddenly gripped him, rooting him to the spot. What kind of a human being was he? A man who couldn't wait for his very sick wife to die, the very wife who left him a fortune to do as he pleased. An apparently moral man who had half a dozen mistresses while he was in the army, and continued to have them as a politician. An upright, law-abiding citizen who had engaged in devious and illegal practices to win his Senatorial elections and was now routinely lying to donors and violating campaign finance and other laws. And here he was in Karen's flat acting like an old gigolo.

He slid off the stool to stop his thoughts, and went slowly back to the bedroom carrying a glass of ice water. His robe, damp with sweat, was cold and unpleasant. As he walked down the long hall, the ice cubes in the glass made clinking noises, loud in the hushed multi-million-dollar flat.

He couldn't believe it was his fourth day in West Covina. What a dump! And he was no nearer to finishing the assignment than on his first day. He had thought it would be so easy. His target, Congressman Gregory Pang, who was running for the fourth term, was a third-generation Chinese American. He lived twenty miles from downtown Los Angeles in what was essentially a lower-middle-class suburb. With the population nearly two-thirds Latino and Asian, he had the comfort of being inconspicuous. But he had no wish to stay in this dreary place any longer than absolutely necessary.

He had flown into Los Angeles International Airport, picked up a black Nissan and driven to West Covina where he checked into the Best Western, which was located right next to the San Bernardino Freeway. It didn't even have a restaurant. He'd gone out for a meal and discovered that the nearby restaurants were all inexpensive chains, with a lot of Mexican joints. He had settled on a burger, and then as dusk fell, he had set out to locate both Pang's office and his home.

He had had no trouble finding either. The office was in a two-storey building downtown that reminded him of Hilo on the Big Island, which he had once visited. Pang had a staff of at least three people who worked long hours. The candidate never seemed to be there alone.

Next, he had driven out to the congressman's home. He had seen online that Pang lived in a new housing development. So far there seemed to be no landscaping in the area; everywhere there was bare dirt. But what surprised him was finding that the houses on either side of Pang's were still unfinished and remained unoccupied. He could see the lights on both in the front and on one side of the Pang home. He had been informed that Pang lived here with his elderly mother and an older sister who was wheelchair-bound due to a stroke, and that both rarely left the house.

Having no occupants in the neighbouring houses was a piece of luck, but the lack of cover was not good. He would have to take cover in one of the partially built houses after the workmen had left if he was to do the job here. His best bet was to get Pang alone.

The following morning he had called the congressman's office and asked for a private appointment. The young woman who answered the phone asked him to hold while she got Pang's personal assistant on the line. After the assistant asked him a few questions, he was finally put through to the congressman. He told the congressman that he had just come to the area because he had got a job and was a lifelong and ardent supporter of the Democratic Party.

'I hear you have stiff competition this year because of the Patriot Party's strong support for your Republican opponent. I want to help you out if I can. I have some ideas for fundraising and would like to share them.'

'That would be terrific,' responded Pang, sounding truly grateful. 'I can make an appointment to see you almost any time. Can you find my office?'

'Yes, but I'd like to see you privately.'

'Oh, don't worry. I have a large private office and I can easily arrange it so no one disturbs us.'

'Well,' the ardent supporter said hesitantly, 'my problem is that my new boss is a dyed-in-the-wool conservative, and I really can't let anyone from my office see me anywhere near your office. Could you come to my hotel room instead? I haven't been able to rent a place yet.'

'Yes, I could manage that, but I ought to tell you that I will have to bring my aide with me. He's the bodyguard I hired after my campaign manager . . . you see I have received several threatening calls from the Patriots. Knowing how batty they are, I can't take chances, and the local police don't want me going anywhere alone.'

'Okay. Excuse me, I have a call coming in. I'll get back to you on a time and date,' said the man, hurriedly ending the call. He was irritated by this new hitch in his plan. *Why does he have a bodyguard?* But an assignment was an assignment, and he had to do his best to carry it out using his initiative.

For the next three days he had tailed the congressman, but the man never seemed to go anywhere without a very fit, young Hispanic-looking man at his side. Pang himself was under forty and looked very trim. He had to be caught alone.

Trying to keep track of the congressman's whereabouts was really more than a job for one man. To try to remain undetected, he had turned in the Nissan and had rented a white Honda from a different agency. But parking was at a premium opposite Pang's office and the only places to get food near the office were a couple of fast food shops. When he had tried to stake out Pang's house, he was able to park unobtrusively down the street along with the cars of the construction workers. But by late afternoon these were gone, and a woman in one of the houses kept peering out of her window as he sat in his car. On the third day, he rented a black Ford just in case the woman or someone else had become suspicious and reported seeing the Honda to the police. One never knew what people might do in such a place where he was sure there were many break-ins.

And then the weather turned against him. When he arrived on Sunday, strong winds had been blowing the dirt round in swirls on the bare ground at the housing development. By the end of his second day, torrential downpours had made driving difficult and the heavy rain had caused flooding and erosion on the hillsides of the development.

So he finally decided that he would have to resort to the very risky plan of carrying out his assignment in the minutes between when the bodyguard dropped off Pang at home at night and before he entered the front door. It was a pity he wasn't a sharpshooter.

So tonight, his fourth in this godforsaken town, he drove his black rental car to the street on which Pang lived, and parked three houses down from the congressman's house. He walked to the unfinished house to the right of Pang's. It was nearly complete and had a carport on one side with a partial wall at the inner end where he could stay out of sight.

He had arrived just before six and stood with his back against the corner of the carport and wall. Intermittent rain saw to it that there was no place to sit or rest. After an hour he was cold and damp, but he stood motionless in his dark clothing.

It seemed to get darker by the minute and it rained steadily now. His feet hurt and he was growing stiff. Suddenly a car came round the bend, slowed and stopped in front of Pang's house.

There were two men in the front seat. *So far so good*, he thought. The bodyguard had driven Pang home, as he had done the evening before. The man in the passenger seat got out, pulling an anorak over his head. As he slammed the car door shut, the rain suddenly began to come down in sheets. Though he could barely see, the man in hiding sprang out of the carport, knife in hand, and ran to Pang's yard. He nearly slipped in the mud about five feet from Pang, but managed to maintain his footing and rushed towards his target, the knife aimed at the heart of the silhouette he could just make out in the downpour.

But before he could plunge the knife in, the silhouette jumped to the left and behind of him, grabbed the right hand holding the knife and twisted it in one quick fluid motion. Continuing to twist his right arm, a loud voice yelled, 'Greg, I got a guy . . . someone trying to kill you!' The voice wasn't Pang's. An excruciating pain ran through the assailant's right arm almost making him drop the knife. At the same time, he heard someone run up the path, calling, 'Jack, are you OK?'

How careless of him to have assumed Pang's bodyguard had dropped him off and driven away and that the man who got out of the car was Pang. He had tried to kill the bodyguard! He now had to free his arm and get away. He grunted, twisted his body in a deft move and kicked the bodyguard hard in the groin. Tears ran down his cheeks because of the wracking pain in his right arm. The bodyguard staggered, yelping in pain. Pang was just a few feet away when he heard the siren of a police car.

The assailant turned and sprinted back in the direction from which he had come. He ran slipping and sliding across the muddy front yards of three or four houses, his shoes squelching as he tried to run. He could hear voices yelling behind him and the police siren closing in and he knew he didn't have time to reach his car and make a getaway. At the last house on the street, he veered to the left and down a gentle slope, and suddenly found himself sliding down into a ditch.

What had been an empty ditch a few days ago was now filled with more than two feet of water and mud. With all the building debris also in the ditch, he had to struggle to keep his head above water. Just as he managed to stand in the cold water, he heard the sound of several feet running on the muddy ground, getting closer every second. And then, despite the heavy rain, he saw a powerful torch searching the area.

He did the only thing he could: he took a deep breath and plunged his head into the cold, mucky water. When he couldn't hold his breath any longer, he emerged from the water and gulped in a lungful of air. He wiped and shielded his eyes using his hands. The light from the torch had moved further down the incline.

The man slowly dragged himself to the side of the ditch, and laboriously climbed its side, slipping and sliding even though it was no more than four feet to the top. Though the men searching were now nowhere near, he knew they would have to come back sooner or later. He made for the rear of the nearest house and hid behind a pile of lumber. Standing in the heavy rain, he did his best to clean the muck off his head and face.

He sat there for a long time, shivering in his drenched, smelly clothes. He had no idea how long he had been there, but he finally heard voices dispersing and engines starting up from the direction of Pang's house. He decided it was probably safe to leave.

Slowly, he got up and made his way down the street to his car, making ugly squishy sounds with each step. Both the patrol car and the car that had brought Pang home were gone. He climbed into the driver's seat and slowly drove back to the Best Western. But he couldn't go into the hotel looking the mess he did. What was he to do?

He parked at the very end of the deserted parking strip. He walked to the front entrance, stood to one side and peered into the lobby. He could see no one except for a single man at the reception. He waited. After a few minutes, the receptionist turned and went into the back, out of sight. Taking this opportunity the man dashed into the lobby and headed for the elevators.

In his room he hurriedly showered, put on clean clothes and packed his small suitcase. On his way out, he dumped his filthy, wet clothes in a bin in the service area and went to the reception. By now it was after ten, but the bored clerk at the reception didn't seem surprised that he wanted to check out, and merely told him that he would have to pay for the night even though he wasn't going to sleep there. The man readily agreed, paid, handed over the keys and walked out. Leaving the black Ford in the car park, he stowed his suitcase in the white Honda and drove off towards the city.

He did a lot of thinking as he drove. Something had gone terribly wrong. Why had the bodyguard pretended to be Pang returning home? What had warned them to make such a switch? Could the bodyguard have seen him keeping watch on Pang? And how had the police managed to arrive so quickly? Too soon for Pang or the guard or anyone in the house to have called them. Perhaps the man with the dog had seen him lurking in the carport and called the police.

He couldn't take the chance of the police tracing the number plate of the car he was in now since he'd had to register the cars with the hotel in order to park. He wouldn't return the car at the airport. Nor could he risk flying out. Where should he spend the night? What would be the best way to get back to San Francisco undetected? If he couldn't risk flying or driving, he had to take either the train or the bus. He pulled out his iPhone and checked the timetable for Amtrak. He found that at this time of night, he would have to take a combination of buses and trains to get to San Francisco. There was a Greyhound bus departing at a quarter past one in the morning, which would arrive in San Francisco just before noon the next day.

Now he had to figure out how to dump the Honda so the police wouldn't be able to guess how, or if at all, he had left the city. If he left the car near the bus terminal, it would be a dead giveaway. He ended up parking a few blocks from the downtown Marriott, where he picked up a taxi to take him to the Greyhound terminal. The Marriott wasn't near either the Amtrak station or the Greyhound terminal, and he could easily have taken a taxi from the Marriott to the airport. He was quite sure that by the time the car was found, the police would be sufficiently flummoxed. He should be able to reach San Francisco before anyone could track him down.

All the while he couldn't stop wondering why and how things had gone so wrong. Was someone getting wise to what he was doing or was his luck running out? He didn't like bungling an assignment, so knowing he hadn't killed at all, let alone kill the wrong person, didn't console him, but instead left him angry.

In the cab on his way to the Woodrow Wilson Center, Dietman Jun Taira was already regretting that he had agreed to give a speech at a conference sponsored by the NAD Forum. In mid-March, he had accepted the invitation from Senator Powers to be a participant at the conference on 'Whither American diplomacy in Asia?' He thought it politic to find out more about the forum and also keep abreast of developments to see whether he really wanted to commit to funding it. So he had agreed to make the presentation, but he hadn't seen the detailed programme until he arrived in Washington. The order of events gave him the distinct impression that the conference was all eyewash and the event was more of a fundraiser, but it was too late to back out. Besides, he had another reason to be in Washington.

Two weeks after he had accepted Powers' invitation, his elder brother, Sei'ichi, now running the Taira Bank, had called.

'Jun, Mike Carvin, my friend for over two decades, is an ardent supporter of Paul Higgins, the Republican governor of Missouri, who as you know is running for the presidency. Governor Higgins, I am told, intends to announce the removal of all American bases in Japan, should he win the nomination. His reasons are fiscal retrenchment and the expansion of American bases in Guam and Hawaii to increase American employment. Apparently, Higgins asked Dr Lee Morimoto in Washington to write an in-depth study of all political and economic effects of the removal of American bases from the US and Japan, especially Okinawa. But Dr Morimoto can't do this without Japanese help. Mike asked me to recommend someone in Japan who knows about the issues relating to these bases—someone with the connections to get government information is essential. I thought you'd be interested in this project.'

His brother was right. The remaining American bases in Japan were one of Jun's major interests, an issue he meant to use in starting the new party he planned to inaugurate in January. If he could come up with a strong argument with Dr Morimoto's help for the removal of the US bases, instead of the vacillating policy of the current government, he was sure it would go a long way in gathering supporters for his new party. This meant he had to meet Dr Morimoto in Washington. But with this thought came the feeling that this would be a betrayal of Powers, who was supporting Governor Bond, the main political rival of Governor Higgins.

However, his brother was persuasive and had got him an appointment with Dr Morimoto for the day after the conference. But first he had to get through his presentation.

When Taira reached the conference venue, he was escorted up to a room on the second floor where the other speakers had gathered. He spotted Karen McPherson, whom he had met at Powers' birthday party, and they began to chat. A stout young man with sandy hair and freckles bustled into the room, looked round and made a beeline for Taira. He introduced himself as a staff member of the NAD forum and said he had a message for Mr Taira from Senator Powers. 'The senator has said he will meet you at the end of the session and has arranged to take you for a private lunch with Governor Bond,' the young man said, making a statement, not seeking consent. Taira said he would be pleased to join the senator. Then the young man turned round and announced to the group that everyone should move to the auditorium so the session could begin.

The conference was opened by Senator Jameson, the vice chair of the forum's board and a former professor. Everything he said was suited more to a political rally than to an academic conference. For the next hour, Taira listened to two speakers tout thinly disguised America-centric views bordering on a strange mix of anti-Chinese propaganda and American triumphalism.

A middle-aged man from a right-wing think tank argued stridently: 'The US must at all costs maintain its military might in the Pacific to ensure the enduring stability and prosperity of Asia, which is being threatened by China.' His view was blatantly anti-Chinese, but the audience seemed to love it. The second speaker, a short, plump professor who wore a bowtie that seemed to choke him, was insistent that 'America must lead the Asian nations because their traditions and history continue to shackle them, preventing the emergence of truly free market economies in the region.' Taira was offended and wondered how the professor could spout such nonsense when most Asian economies were steadily growing while the American economy continued to stagnate. Besides, American politics remained mired in persistent gridlock, as its two parties seemed to be more interested in ideological confrontations than in solving the many critical issues the country had been facing during the past two decades.

Then it was Taira's turn to speak. He was tempted to discard his prepared text and rebut some of the central points made by the first two speakers, but he resisted from giving in to the thought. He summarized his long-held view that all governments, American as well as Asian, must do more to reduce trade barriers. 'Only free markets can sustain the prosperity of all of us,' he said in conclusion. It did not surprise him that the audience's response to his speech was noticeably restrained. In sharp contrast to the other speakers, he was given only brief applause.

The final speaker was Karen McPherson. Given her stature as a professor, McPherson's talk astounded Taira. She didn't give a reasoned or well-researched academic lecture on the different conservative and liberal positions. Instead, she argued for a nationalistic and self-serving position favoured by the extreme right-wing groups. The audience loved her.

Having listened to all the speakers, Taira was left puzzled by the principal thrust of the presentations: that the American way was the only way and the US was the geopolitically ordained suzerain of the Asian nations. The only possible explanation, he thought, was that the NAD forum had carefully selected speakers whose views matched those of its board members and that most of the audience shared the same views. The purpose of the so-called conference was not to educate people on the issues, but to stir up the audience to build up a political base for Governor Bond's campaign. Taira was sorely unhappy to have been involved in this event.

As soon as the presentations were over, Taira found Senator Powers at his side. The senator apologized for not having heard Taira's presentation, but thanked him for joining Bond and him for lunch. They took a taxi to the Hay Adams, where Bond was staying.

They entered Bond's suite just as a waiter was finishing laying out a cold lunch at a table set for three. Powers introduced Taira to Bond, who said he was delighted to have the opportunity to meet such a distinguished—and con-servative—Japanese dietman. Bond was cordial. But Taira couldn't help notice the governor was making only a skin-deep effort to be polite. The three men sat down to eat and the talk immediately turned to politics.

Taira knew Bond's chance of getting the nomination was still uncertain. In the most recent primaries in five eastern states, including New York and Pennsylvania, Bond had got fewer delegates than Higgins, the two-term gov-ernor of Missouri who was supported by the moderate wing of the Republican Party. But Higgins' margin was narrow enough for Bond to win, despite the increasing media and expert criticism of Bond's political stance being 'too close to the Patriots' views'.

'Well, we could've done better,' the governor responded jovially to Taira's comment on how well Bond had come out of the most recent primaries. 'But thanks to Simon and a lot of other people, we are doing well. We've sent out a feeler to Ed Fulton, the party's Libertarian candidate, asking what he wants in exchange for dropping out of the race in the interests of the conservative wing of our party. He hasn't responded yet, but by the latest count, I think we have only forty, possibly forty-five fewer delegate votes than Higgins, a number we think we can more than make up when the super-delegates—the congressmen, the senators and others who are not legally bound to any specific candidates—vote for us at the convention as they have promised.'

'So, you are very optimistic about winning the nomination,' Taira said to Bond with a smile.

It was Powers who responded: 'That's right. We are. Brad definitely has the nomination in hand. Our worry is not what happens at the convention, but whether we'll have enough ammunition to get through the campaign against the Democratic contender—most likely Senator Samuelson of California, though the Democrats could surprise us by picking Senator Chance from Hawaii.'

'Simon means Senator Samuelson has raised more money than Senator Chance has to date, though he's using the Internet for fund-raising so effectively. But Senator Samuelson also has the support of all the labour unions and the misguided Hollywood millionaires. So to beat her in November, our campaign needs at least another two to three hundred million dollars.'

Powers didn't mince words, making clear why he'd arranged for Taira to be at this meeting. 'Jun, we are hoping you can consider doubling to ten million the donation we discussed in spring. We can arrange for you to send the money to an offshore account so it won't be traced. We know the Taira Bank is the fourth largest in Japan. We know about the magnificent new house your brother has just built. I know you need money to start your new party too, but . . . how about it? If you can do this for us, President Bond will do anything you ask of him.'

Although he had anticipated this, Taira was disconcerted. He wondered how Powers had had the nerve to check his wealth and to ask him to cough up so much to an American political campaign. He didn't know how to respond politely so he said nothing.

Bond broke the uneasy silence, not in the least embarrassed.

'Simon is right. If I get elected, I'll do all I can—for you and your new party—if you just tell me what you want. We will be on a first name basis, you know, and at the launch of your party you can announce our commitment to resolving old bilateral issues of importance to you.'

Finally, Taira had to say something. He said very slowly, 'I think ten million will be very difficult. . .'

'But do think about it,' pressed Powers. 'Jun, it's extremely important. We are working day and night to raise as much money as we can. We really could do with some help.' Powers sounded uncharacteristically deferential.

Taira decided to make a tactical retreat. There was no point in getting badgered or making them plead more than they already had.

'I'll seriously consider it.' He knew the Americans would take his statement at face value, unlike the Japanese who would know right away he was politely turning them down.

Bond, smiling broadly, said 'Excellent! Let us know when you've decided . . . soon I hope. We'll be most grateful and my administration will do whatever you ask.'

After a few awkward minutes, Taira left the suite. He was angry. The more he thought about the lunch meeting, the more annoyed he grew. *How could a pair of their stature be so brazen about illegal funding? And so demanding!* He wondered why he had become involved with Powers in the first place.

The following morning Taira took another short cab ride, this time to a nondescript four-story brick building on Massachusetts Avenue. The building looked decades old on the outside, but the minute he stepped into the lobby, he knew he was on high-tech premises with high security. The guard at the door checked to see if he was on the list of visitors for the day, asked for his photo ID and had him sign in before escorting him to the lift.

He followed the guard's directions to Dr Morimoto's office—the first door on the left as he came out of the lift—which he found open. Three people were in the room carrying on what sounded like a very intense conversation. A casually dressed young Asian man seemed very upset. Taira wondered if he should interrupt—he didn't want to eavesdrop.

As he put his hand up to knock on the open door, a short, middle-aged woman saw him and asked, 'Mr Taira?'

'Yes, I've come to see Dr Lee Morimoto.'

'That's me,' she said with a smile. She came forward with her hand outstretched to greet him. She had seen the brief look of surprise on her visitor's face and, continuing to smile, added, 'Yes, most people don't realize Lee can be a woman too. Welcome! Do come in. We're just finishing up here.'

She turned to a tall, rather grizzled man and said, 'Giles, I think that's all we can tell you for now. Please ask your staff to be extra vigilant about whom they sign into the building.'

Giles nodded and left. Dr Morimoto turned to Taira and said, 'This is Peter Huang, my research assistant. He's a graduate student in political science at Georgetown and he's a great help as he's fluent in Chinese. Peter, Mr Taira is a member of the Diet in Japan, the equivalent of our House of Representatives.'

The two men briefly acknowledged the introduction, and Dr Morimoto continued: 'Peter, thank you very much for coming in this morning. Before you leave for the day, do bring me a description of the man as soon as you've typed it out—don't worry about interrupting us. Oh, and remember you can move into the vacant apartment at your convenience. Just let me know.'

When Peter left, Dr Morimoto took a deep breath and said, 'If you don't mind, I'd like a cup of coffee before we start. It's been quite a morning. What about you?'

'Thanks. Black please,' Taira said. And then as she turned to the coffee machine on a side table, he asked, 'Dr Morimoto, do I gather you've had a security problem?' Normally he wouldn't have asked such a question, but what he had been asked to do with Dr Morimoto had to be kept completely confidential.

Morimoto handed him a cup of coffee and said, 'Lee, please.'

Taira said, 'And I'm Jun in the United States.'

She sat down opposite him, took a sip of her coffee and sighed. 'Yes, we could have had a serious problem, but Peter is very loyal. He came in this morning just to tell me about an incident yesterday evening. As he was return-ing home from the library, he was approached by a man who introduced him-self as James Cox. The man revealed he knew all about Peter's dire financial situation as a student, and gave him a proposition: if Peter gave him useful information on what my office is doing for Governor Higgins, he would be paid ten thousand dollars in cash. Peter asked who was paying that kind of money and was told a rich supporter of the next president. Peter said he hoped it was a Republican and was told it was a *real* Republican, a true conservative. The man asked Peter to meet him on Friday at a cafe at Dupont Circle. To get rid of him, Peter agreed.'

'Do you think Peter ever intended to give some information for the money?'

'No. Peter's been terribly agitated. That's why he came in though it's his day off. He told me he hadn't slept at all. What really bothered him was how this man had got so much personal information about him. He thinks one of his housemates must have given out the information, and he regrets having talked to them about his job, particularly as he doesn't know them too well. The least I can do to help is give him a rent-free place for a few months—I have a place over my garage I use for visitors. Now shall we turn to Governor Higgins' project? I'm sorry to have involved you in our security issue.'

Taira was still concerned. 'I have one more question. Which candidate do you think this James Cox is working for?'

'We're guessing Bond, because his campaign already has the reputation of being involved in sleazy acts. But it could even be a Democrat. Cox might have said he was working for a Republican because he knows Peter is working for Governor Higgins.'

Just as they started to discuss the information Governor Higgins needed on the US bases in Japan, there was a light tap on the door.

'Yes, come in,' responded Lee.

Peter poked his head round the door. 'Sorry to interrupt, but here's the description of the guy who approached me. I made some copies too.' He came in and handed a few sheets of paper to Lee.

'Thanks again, Peter,' Lee said, as the young man slipped back out the door.

'Here, do you want to see this?' asked Lee, beginning to read over one copy and handing another sheet to Taira.

Taira took the sheet and read through. James Cox was in his early thirties, somewhat overweight—'slightly rotund' was Peter's expression. He had medium-length sandy hair, parted on one side, and light skin with freckles that matched his hair. He had been dressed in chinos, a dark blue jacket and a red and blue striped tie.

Taira was stunned for a moment.

'I think I've met this man,' he said.

'What? Where?' Lee was astonished.

'Yesterday I gave a talk at a conference of the NAD Forum which turned out to be a fundraiser for Governor Bond—I didn't know what I was getting into, until it was too late to back out. A man of this description was working as staff at yesterday's conference. The sandy hair and freckles are a definite match, even the necktie is the same. So I think your guess is correct. I'm sorry, but I never caught his name.'

Taira and Morimoto managed to tear themselves away from discussing the freckled man and spent over an hour discussing how best to prepare a report for Governor Higgins. Taira agreed to do a considerable amount of homework to get the necessary data and to send her a memo putting down his own views on various issues she had raised during their discussion.

After the meeting they went to an early lunch at Lee's favourite restaurant, Le Petit Bistro, a few blocks from her building. At the end of lunch, Lee made a surprising suggestion.

'You said you're leaving tomorrow, right? How about if I call the chief of staff for Governor Higgins? Would you like to meet the governor? As far as I know, he's in town to meet with some senators from the western states. Why don't I ask if he can see you? He may be able to spare only fifteen minutes or so, but I'm sure you'll enjoy meeting him and you can have a brief word about the things we've talked about. I'll call to let you know if the governor can see you.'

Pleased with the possibility of meeting Higgins, Taira readily agreed. He went back to his hotel, packed to leave the next day and constantly checked his messages for one from Lee. He had just begun to think about where to have dinner when his phone rang. It was Lee.

'Jun, I've arranged for you to have dinner with Governor Higgins!' she said excitedly.

And so, unexpectedly, Taira had dinner with Governor Higgins at the Willard Hotel, not far from the White House. Taira was impressed by the governor. Unlike Bond, he came across as an unpretentious, genuine person. Taira liked Higgins' earnest expressions of concern about 'making the economy grow in a way that will really benefit everyone'. By the end of the meal, Taira was convinced that Higgins' desire to remove all the US bases from Japan was sincere and based on the well-reasoned logic of economic necessity and 'the need to get out of the rut the US defence policy has fallen into'. He was the sort of politician Taira most admired, not an ideologue like Powers. And he certainly hadn't tried to get money out of Taira.

The two shook hands and parted warmly, Governor Higgins saying, 'Congressman, please do all you can to help Dr Morimoto, so I can carry out my plan to remove all our bases in Japan at the earliest.'

Taira didn't need to think it over any longer. He had seen the real face of the Bond campaign with its multiple illegal operations, and Powers was clearly using him for his money. He had mulled over making a token donation to the NAD Forum, but what with first-hand knowledge of the sham conferences and the outright demand for ten million dollars, he had already had second thoughts. And the Bond camp henchman propositioning Peter with a bribe put the nail in the coffin, as his English tutor would have said.

A day after he returned to Tokyo, Jun Taira sent a check of ten thousand dollars to Dr Lee Morimoto, asking her to give it to Peter and tell him it was an anonymous gift from someone who admired his honesty and integrity.

'So now we are going to read proof of Parelli the Criminal!' exclaimed Bess as she sat in the living room of Nick's apartment. Nick, holding the report that Peri had commissioned from Charlie DeMello, chuckled as he read a note attached to it.

Bess asked, 'What's so funny?'

'Charlie says he is sending this report by private courier instead of via email because there are too many people like Bess Browne who can hack into computers!'

Bess laughed and together they started reading the report, Nick handing her each page as he finished. 'Peri really got her money's worth,' remarked Nick. 'When she agreed to pay Charlie twenty-five thousand dollars to look into the doings of Lou Parelli, I thought she might be wasting her money.'

Peri had been so pleased to have Charlie take on the job that she hadn't negotiated his fee. Charlie had delivered what he promised. In just three weeks, he had produced a succinctly written twenty-four-page report that included eleven pages of records of international and domestic wired money transfers, something only a former FBI agent could come up with in such a short time.

'You're right, Nick. This really is an exhaustive report,' said Bess. 'He's definitely had someone hack into Parelli's computer or done it himself. He's also managed to interview many of Parelli's former superiors and colleagues at the banks in New York and Kansas and even Parelli's neighbours. And it's also obvious that he's read a lot of public records, including those of the Senate hearings, not easy to access electronically.'

'We now know Parelli grew up in Pittsburgh and graduated from the University of Pittsburgh with a degree in finance and computer science. He was the head of the International Division of the Federal Bank of New York when he was grilled at the Senate hearing,' said Nick.

'And Parelli was the key witness at that hearing on money laundering and tax evasion and he sang freely after getting immunity from prosecution. He had worked for the bank for over twenty years until the Senate hearing, but after the hearing he ended up at a small bank in Topeka, Kansas. After that setback, who would've expected him to be offered the treasurer's job at the NAD Forum? Oh and I love this description of Ginko here,' Bess said, pointing at a section on the sheet in her hand.

Seven years after the subject was hired by the FBNY, he was sent to the Tokyo branch for four years to help upgrade its electronic communication capabilities and security. While in Tokyo, the subject married Ginko Iwamoto, a college grad who was working in the branch (unable to establish her exact position). An employee of FBNY recalls Ginko as 'a smart, pushy woman from a well-to-do family in Ishigakijima Island in Okinawa Prefecture.

As soon as he finished skimming the paragraph, Nick said, 'Why should we care about the island the wife came from?'

'No idea. Just to make a thorough report I guess. Listen to this . . . Charlie doesn't miss a thing!' Another of Parelli's former colleagues recalls Parelli as "a good tennis player but a poor dancer and swimmer" and his wife as "an aspiring nouveau riche".'

Nick laughed. 'An interesting way of saying she wants to be rich or is plain greedy.'

Bess nodded and said, 'They live in the posh Boston suburb of Newton in a pseudo-Tudor house that Parelli paid a whopping one and a half million dollars for. Multiple sources confirm the couple lives well. They have both a Mercedes and a brand new Lexus.'

'Look, here Charlie's report begins to explain what he learnt by scrutinizing the files in the "subject's" computer,' said Nick, handing a sheet to Bess.

Several files confirm Parelli's main job as the treasurer of the NAD Forum is to do two things: one to receive millions of dollars (Calculations show the forum received a little over 200 million dollars since last October, mostly in units of a few to 5,000 dollars. Exceptions were the 27 receipts that ranged from 2.5 million dollars to as much as 10 million dollars.); the other is to disburse money (all via wire transfers) in units usually less than 10,000 dollars (some exceptions of over 10,000 dollars noted, where disbursements ranged from 20,000 to 30,000 dollars) to an increasing number of accounts in domestic and foreign banks (in Switzerland, Singapore, Jersey and the Cayman Islands). The total disbursement since last October is a little over 200 million dollars. The NAD Forum's main function does not seem to be educational but to be a clandestine and efficient conduit for huge amounts of money.

'You know what this means, don't you, Bess?'

'Yes, I do. Since the NAD is supposed to be a tax-exempt educational organization, they're clearly violating all kinds of laws, especially campaign laws on finance,' she said.

'Exactly. And I wouldn't be surprised if a good chunk of the money has gone to the Patriots. Remember the reference to the Barrington pipeline? What intrigues me is how it was possible for the forum to have raised over two hundred million dollars in a little over six months. I've read that CEOs and others donate to the forum, but in amounts of five thousand dollars or less, according to Charlie. I wonder who the big donors are, the ones donating in millions. They're obviously not the ones who're supporting the forum just for its educational activities,' remarked Nick.

'I agree,' said Bess in response. 'If we find out who these donors are, we can find out who's buying the elections, trampling on democracy using the forum as a front.'

'Right, Bess. It's a sham organization. To find out who these donors are, we need Parelli's secret list. But from what the report says, this could be an uphill task.' Nick pointed at a paragraph.

The senders and recipients of money are identified only by account numbers and SWIFT codes and/or BIC codes, when foreign and/or domestic banks are involved, respectively. Unable to trace file containing a list identifying the name of a person or an organization to which the account numbers belong. Without this list, it is impossible to identify either the senders or the recipients of the money. A few banks in the US might be coaxed into disclosing the names of the account holders, but no foreign bank, especially in the places Parelli has accounts, is likely to do so. My educated guess is that the subject does not keep such a list in his computer. What Parelli runs is an operation that necessitates keeping the names of the account holders absolutely secret.

Bess reread the page and said with a sigh, 'Charlie's done a good job, but I don't think his findings are going to help Peri. She needs names. Where do you suppose she can get them? Where do you think Parelli might keep such a list?'

'If I were Parelli, I'd have the names on paper and keep it in a home safe or in a safe deposit box—someplace only I had access to.'

'Do you think anyone might have a duplicate? Perhaps Powers, since he's so involved?'

'Parelli might keep a duplicate himself. I don't think Powers or anyone else would have one. Remember Peri said she'd heard Powers telling Parelli he didn't want to be involved in his activities. I'm sure he meant the nitty-gritty of day-to-day operations. Besides, the list can't be static—there would be changes each time the money comes in and goes out. I'd actually bet my money on the only list being in Parelli's possession.'

Bess sighed again. 'So, it's impossible for Peri to get it. Well, Peri ought to stop worrying about her father being embarrassed or getting into legal troubles. If one hires a shady person for his shady talents, you can't expect him to become an upright citizen, can you?'

'We shouldn't lose sleep over this either. Peri must have gone through the report too by now. Let's see what she thinks. And for all you know, she might agree with us and drop this whole thing.'

While Nick and Bess had decided nothing further could be done, Peri had come to a decision that was to surprise them.

Peri had found Charlie DeMello's report fascinating. She was now certain she had to get the missing list of names at any cost. If she proved Parelli was doing something illegal her father didn't know about, she was sure her father would fire him, and he wouldn't be able to drag her father into any mess. It bothered her that such large sums might be flowing through the NAD Forum.

Peri read the report a second time. As she finished, the kernel of an idea emerged. She mulled over her plan to get the list of names for a long time. It was risky and would mean spending a lot more money, but she wasn't concerned about that as she could easily afford a larger sum than she had already given DeMello. The next thing to do was to call Bess, but a glance at her clock told her it was too late to call anyone now. She set her alarm for seven and went to bed.

The first thing the next morning, Peri phoned Bess and came right to the point: 'You've read the report, right? I think I've come up with a plan to get the list of names from . . .'

Bess cut her off mid-sentence. 'Wait, Peri. Let's not talk now. You're calling from home, right?'

'Yes, from my cellphone.'

'I know I'm being overly cautious because of the kind of work I do, but I'd like to discuss this when you're away from home and from any phones you normally use. A public telephone, if you can find one any more, would be good. Could you call me at my office between eleven and twelve? I've got meetings earlier, but that will give you time to find a phone.'

Peri was surprised at Bess' request but readily agreed. She dressed, and had breakfast with Maria because her father was away in Washington. At a quarter to ten, she drove off to the Chestnut Hill Shopping Center and purchased a prepaid phone. She thought it pointless to try to find a public phone for a long conversation. Then she drove to Cutler Park in Needham, parked and got out with her new phone. In hundreds of acres of parkland, there couldn't be danger of anyone overhearing her conversation or bugging her new phone, if that was what concerned Bess.

At a few minutes past eleven, Peri called Bess. Several minutes into the conversation, it became clear to Bess that Peri was determined to get the list of names and that she could not be dissuaded. As Bess listened, she too became convinced Peri's idea was feasible despite the risks and costs involved. She made a few suggestions to refine Peri's plan and promised to consult Nick.

The conversation ended with Peri saying, 'OK, Bess, I'll ring up Alex right away and ask him to contact his friend in Aix-en-Provence to see if he'll agree to our plan. I'm keeping my fingers crossed he will. When I hear from Alex, I'll fly down to New York to work out the details with you and Nick. We'll be in touch. *Au revoir.*'

Peri sat next to the open window of her flat in the Fifth Arrondissement and looked down on the tiny park nestled between the busy street and the tall, ivy-covered wall of the Science Politechnique, one of a very small number of Les Grandes Écoles, France's most prestigious universities. A little blond boy was playing with a stick, watched over by a young woman wearing a white scarf. The soft spring sun on this mid-May morning made the boy's hair gleam. The scene reminded Peri of Gauguin's 1886 painting, *Pont Aven Woman and Child*.

Peri had flown into Paris from the US the previous night so as to travel down to Aix-en-Provence today to put into action the plan she had finalized with Bess. Alex was to come to her flat in half an hour. After lunch at her favourite cafe on nearby Boulevard St Germain, they were to take the TGV to Aix, where they had arranged to meet Claude Martin, the curator of a small museum in that city. Years ago, Martin had served time in prison for art forgery. Although he had long since gone straight, Peri wanted to persuade him to copy an Impressionist masterpiece to carry out her scheme.

Waiting for Alex, she was too nervous to settle to anything. She had packed and was ready to leave, so she stared out of the window, her eyes on the blond boy at play but her mind on the scheme. She really needed it to work. Peri had been pleased with Alex's support when she called him from Boston. He had listened to her plan and agreed to go with her to Aix, provided she went over a weekend. He knew Claude and believed he would take this on for a good cause. 'Your plan should work, Peri. Tell me more in detail when we meet,' he had said.

Peri thought of how lucky she was to have met Alex, just over a year ago now. And it had been Claude Martin who introduced them. A long article on Claude's talent and imprisonment, in the art section of *Le Figaro*, had made her look him up. Claude had been very forthcoming in answering her questions about the brush strokes and colour compositions of Monet, Corot, Sisley and other Impressionist painters whose works he had once forged. He was a superb source of information she couldn't get easily from scholarly texts. She was at Claude's one afternoon when Alex had walked into the museum and into her life.

As she looked out of the window, she saw the No. 6 bus pull up. Among several university students who got out she caught a glimpse of Alex carrying a small suitcase. He crossed the street and came towards her building. Without waiting for him to ring the bell, she ran down the stairs in the hall to let him in. They greeted each other with a tight embrace, but eventually pulled apart. They had a train to catch, and lunch before that.

After a quick meal, they hailed a taxi to the station. Their taxi got caught in the Friday afternoon traffic, and so Peri and Alex ended up making a mad dash for their high-speed train to Aix. It was only once they'd found their seats and sat down that they caught their breath. As the train left the Gare de Lyon and Paris, and began to speed through the French countryside, their conversation turned to what dominated Peri's thoughts.

'Alex, you became friends with Claude after meeting him in an art gallery in Montmartre before he was sent to the Santé Prison. So you must know a lot more than what was in the article I read in *Le Figaro*. How did he come to be called "as good a forger as Han van Meegeren", the world-famous Dutch forger of Vermeers?'

'Don't let his straggly appearance and nonchalant manner fool you. He's a very clever and methodical man. He studied in great detail how to produce authentic old masters. He went to a great deal of trouble to use paints that didn't contain anachronistic pigments. He searched for canvases from the correct period and then very carefully scraped off the original painting so an X-ray wouldn't reveal anything underneath.'

'It must have taken him an incredible amount of time and effort. Do you know how he reproduced the *craquelures* you see on centuries-old paintings?'

'He told me he used to dab the surface of the painting with a mixture of formaldehyde and something else—I forget what it was—something one could easily buy at a pharmacy. Then he dried the painting in an oven . . . not on high heat or for too long. *Voila!*, he succeeded in producing very authentic-looking fractures in the paint in his forgeries.'

'Where did he get a large enough oven? He must have been living in a small apartment.'

'A crooked art-dealer had one—the guy who was making good money by helping Claude peddle his forgeries.'

'It seems ironic to me that despite all the advanced tests and checks we now have, selling forgeries is not all that difficult.'

'*Oui*. I had many discussions with Claude and other friends about how easy it is to sell forgeries and how large the market is for them. Despite all the time and trouble it takes to make a forgery that can pass as the real thing, painters make far more money selling forgeries than their own paintings. Claude is an excellent painter in his own right and he's sold his paintings too, but never in large numbers or at prices to make ends meet. And there are always many well-heeled buyers—individuals and museums—for imitations.'

Peri sighed. 'I guess Machiavelli was right when he said "men are so simple and yield so readily to the desires of the moment that he who will trick will always find another who will suffer to be tricked." I've read that at least twenty, maybe even forty per cent, of the paintings in art galleries and museums round the world are forgeries. Even the Rijksmuseum in Amsterdam and the Metropolitan Museum of Art in New York for years showed numerous paintings that turned out to be forgeries, including the van Meegeren ones. So you can bet that in small museums a lot of the paintings admired by millions of people are actually modern copies.'

'*Oui*, and neither the watchful eyes of art critics nor the demand by buyers for a painting's certificate of authentication seems to have reduced the number of fakes in the market.'

'Well, provenances can be faked, you know. And what do you do about the painting that suddenly appears, say from someone's attic?'

Alex laughed. 'That's one reason Claude's forgeries sold so well. His crooked art dealer was very good at cooking up likely stories of why provenances had been lost or never existed.'

'And art critics depend on their intuition and hubris in making the final decision on a painting, and they often disagree. This reminds me of the film about the supposed Jackson Pollock painting. A woman bought a painting for five dollars, which later someone said must be by Jackson Pollock. She had it examined, and despite positive forensic evidence some very famous art experts said it just didn't seem like a Pollock. Yet, these same experts authenticate paintings that later turn out to be forgeries.'

'You know, Peri, the reason Claude was caught wasn't because his paintings were judged to be forgeries. He's really good!'

'So then how did he wind up in prison?'

'His dealer sold too many forgeries, and Claude was caught in the same net. He had a really hard time in prison, which is why he decided to go straight, even if it meant living in penury. I gather that these days he just manages to scrape by.'

'Alex, then the question is not whether Claude is a good enough painter to copy an Impressionist master but whether he will be willing to do it?'

'That's why I agreed to come with you. I'm not sure you could persuade him on your own. But you do have a good reason for wanting a forgery, and you're not trying to make money from it or pass it off to a museum.'

'I'm willing to make it worth his while.'

'I think the money will help convince him. The fine he had to pay cleaned him out and the museum is paying him only a pittance. It can't afford to pay more . . . it doesn't attract a lot of visitors. The only painting the museum has that's included in the reliable *catalogues raisonné* is Monet's *Le Coucher du Soleil en Provence*, done in the mid-1880s.'

'Then that's the painting I should ask Claude to copy. *Sunset in Provence*. I'll bet Ginko Parelli would do almost anything to get that painting for herself! Not because she understands or likes the painting especially, but because of how much she thinks she can get for it when she sells it!'

When the train pulled into the Aix TGV Station in the middle of nowhere, they found Claude, still looking unkempt, waiting for them. They had almost an hour's ride to the city, which Peri found quite uncomfortable in the back seat of Claude's very old Peugeot. Claude was very pleased to see his old friend Alex and remembered Peri as 'the beautiful and smart Mademoiselle who asked sharp questions'.

Claude took them for dinner at a small Italian restaurant in one of the winding lanes in the heart of the charming old city. They indulged in general convivial conversation over an excellent dinner and parted ways for the night, promising to meet the next day to discuss work.

The next morning, Peri and Alex met Claude at his museum. It was as Peri remembered: an unimpressive two-storey building on the narrow rue Cardinale, three blocks south of Cours Mirabeau. The three met in Claude's messy and cramped office.

Peri got straight to the point and explained what she wanted and why. Claude listened attentively without interrupting her. But when she said she was prepared to pay twenty thousand dollars for two copies of *Le Coucher du Soleil en Provence*, Claude's jaw dropped.

'Two copies? For ten thousand dollars each? *Les bras m'en tombent . . .* I don't know what to say, Mademoiselle! I don't fully understand . . . Mademoiselle's scheme sounds very complicated but it could work. Two copies . . . they would naturally take time, but yes, I can do them easily. *Pourqui pas*, it is for a good cause after all. And since the museum will be showing one of my copies while the real Monet is on loan to Mademoiselle, I can guarantee no one will suspect they are seeing a copy.'

Claude went on talking, almost as if to himself. 'Hmm . . . the only problem might be finding two canvases of the right age quickly. I'll have to go to Paris for them and they'll be expensive.'

Peri said quickly, 'Claude, just bill me for all the costs—the canvases, the travel and stay, the special paints you need, everything.'

Alex looked astonished by Peri's generous offer but didn't say anything. Peri added, 'The most important question I have is when can I expect the two copies?'

Claude thought a minute and said, 'I need at least a month . . . could be a little longer. I may have to spend some time in Paris. And I can't rush the job. Both copies have to be not just like genuine Monets but identical too. So, I can't rush.'

'I understand. *Marché conclu*! It's a deal, Claude. I'd like to have them sooner, but I know you're right, you can't hurry when copying Monet.'

Peri made arrangements with Claude to pay him cash in instalments, and handed him a cheque for five thousand dollars to start with. Despite his initial feeble protests, he gratefully accepted the cheque.

'Do you know how this small museum got this magnificent Monet piece?' Alex asked Claude.

'Aix is where Paul Cézanne was born and did a lot of work, so all the museums here hold one or more of his works. Monsieur Dillard who funded— I mean owns—this small museum bought a Monet to make his museum stand out.'

'Do you know how much he paid for the painting and from whom he bought it?' Peri asked.

'He told me he paid *beaucoup* French francs more than twenty years ago. I don't know the actual price. He said he bought it from a woman somewhere in Normandy who got it from her grandmother who may have been Monet's mistress when he lived there for several years.'

'I wonder how much the painting wourld be worth today,' said Alex, looking at Peri.

'Well, Monsieur Dillard said that in 1988 he got two bids within a couple of weeks. A Japanese art gallery in Tokyo offered him almost two-and-a-half million dollars and a large Japanese bank, close to three million. It was the time when the Japanese economy was booming and a lot of Japan's rich people and companies were buying French Impressionists.'

'Three million dollars?!' Peri exclaimed, 'but obviously he didn't sell. Why?'

'He said before he confirmed with the bank he'd sell the painting, he heard a Japanese insurance company had just paid forty-two million dollars for van Gogh's *Sunflower*, so he decided to wait and see if someone else in Japan would offer a lot more. But the boom in the Japanese economy suddenly collapsed in

1990. The highest offer he's had since then is only two million dollars. So he told me he'll keep the painting until somebody else comes along offering more.'

'Well, it's nice to know this. I can tell Parelli a doctored version of what you've just told me. As prices of art have been rising recently despite the recession, we should be able to convince him the painting is worth at least five million on the market.'

Later, as the couple enjoyed chilled champagne at Le Pigonnet, Peri remarked, 'You seemed surprised when I offered to pay for all of Claude's costs as well as the paintings.'

'I was surprised because the twenty grand you offered was more than enough. He once told me he often was paid as little as five hundred euros for a forgery—just enough to pay his rent in Montmartre in Paris. He said he got a few thousand euros several times, but his agents took close to half in commission. In France we say *Le crime ne paie pas* for good reason!'

'We have that in English as well—crime doesn't pay. But this time he's not committing a crime. He's helping me nail someone I'm sure is committing crimes and has the nerve to try and involve my father. Claude deserves the pay.'

'It's an amazing plan you and Bess worked out. No one else would have thought of using two forgeries to trap this man.'

'I'm just crossing my fingers the scheme works,' said Peri, as the waiter arrived with their appetizers. And for the time being her worries were forgotten.

Rodney Watson was an angry man. Ever since he had resigned his commission and been forced to work at low-paying jobs, the former captain had raged against what he called 'rigged American capitalism'. He was furious at his gutless superior, Colonel Elbert Frank, who had threatened to give him a performance grade low enough to ensure he would never become a major unless he went easy on the murderous Afghan civilians in Kandahar who he knew were hiding terrorists. Watson was called Ramrod Rodney by his fellow officers and even behind his back by the enlisted men because he was so gung-ho and did everything by the book. He was never going to compromise, and as the pressures became increasingly difficult he quit the army and returned to Montgomery, his hometown.

However, his life had been nothing but a series of disasters since his return. His father-in-law had found him a job as a production manager of a poultry company just before he left the army, but the job had disappeared in the recession by the time he came home. The only work he was able to find was in what he called 'demeaning sales jobs'. He began by selling shoes, then electronic products—what he thought of as a 'marginally better job'—with a promise of pay raises. The promised raises, of course, didn't materialize. After his daughter was born eight years ago while he was overseas, his wife had worked on and off as a cashier in a department store. But for months now the family had relied on his meagre wages. He could no longer afford the mortgage on his house and its market value was under water.

In early February, Watson had attended a meeting of people worried about losing their homes by foreclosure. After the meeting, he chatted with a number of men in the same circumstances and was invited to join a group of local Patriots. He initially hesitated because he had always voted for the Democrats and he knew that a number of the local Patriots were racists and hothead Republicans.

A few weeks later, his bank sent him a foreclosure notice as he had failed to pay his mortgage for six months. He had medical bills for his daughter's tonsillectomy which was complicated by a staph infection. With inadequate medical insurance, he owed tens of thousands of dollars for his daughter's surgery and her week-long hospital stay. His bank refused to renegotiate the mortgage and the hospital had begun to hound him for payment. At the end of February, Ramrod Rodney was on the verge of tears.

By March, he was desperate and hopping mad at the bank, the hospital and the whole system, including the US Army. And then there were the politicians who promised everything and delivered so little while, he was sure, they lined their own pockets. He believed even the courts were in the pockets of the banks. So when Art Redder, his high school teacher and the leader of the local Patriot group, dropped in one day, Watson listened to him for nearly two hours as he tried to convince Watson to run for Congress as a Patriot.

Finances were Watson's biggest concern in running against a seemingly well-funded Republican congressman, rather than any ideological differences. He knew it would cost a small fortune to run for Congress, and he was not only broke but also nearly homeless.

'Rodney, the Patriots will do everything to get you on the ballot and then get you elected. We need a lot of signatures, but we also have a lot of volunteers. And George Simpson of Simpson Development and Real Estate has promised to fund your campaign, secretly of course. Mr Simpson will keep his word. He is worth about three hundred and fifty million dollars and he thinks even the Republicans supporting Governor Bond for the presidency have lost their way. Folks here like and respect you, especially your high school buddies who remember you as the best quarterback they ever had! You have a darn good shot at becoming a congressman,' assured Redder.

'Why don't you run yourself? You're much better known than I am,' retorted Watson.

'I'm sixty-seven. We need a young man, full of vim and vigour. It's a good job . . . being a congressman. Pays over a hundred grand and comes with a lot of perks. And when the bank finds out you're running for Congress, I bet my pension they will negotiate with you and let you keep your house.'

Redder was persuasive. Watson agreed to run. His teacher had convinced him he could beat the sixth-term Republican congressman whose popularity among the electorate was waning. As Redder promised, his Patriot group, the ranks of which had grown steadily during the ongoing recession, did all the work needed to get Ramrod Rodney on the ballot. At Redder's suggestion, Watson would run for what was to be named the Justice Party, instead of for the Patriot Party, so as to garner as many votes as possible from the Democrats who were in favour of Senator Chance of Hawaii because of his ideas of just capitalism.

In mid-April, Redder gave Watson a hundred and seventy-five thousand dollars, saying, 'This is from Simpson. You don't need to report it to anyone. He'll give you more as required.' The former captain used this to print and distribute campaign posters, flyers and yard signs. Almost everyday he met one group or another and made speeches. He didn't find talking in front of people difficult. After all, as an officer he was used to addressing groups; besides, all he had to say at any meeting or rally was how mad he was at 'the whole damn system'. Everything seemed to be going so well that his wife began to worry about how they would find a place to live in Washington.

But on the morning of 21 May, Ramrod Rodney had good reason not just for being surprised but for becoming more hopping mad than usual.

He walked over to his eight-year-old Ford in the driveway to go to a meeting with his supporters at the Embassy Suites Hotel in Montgomery. He was late and in a foul mood after an argument with his daughter. As he opened the car door, he was hit by a strong stench. There on the driver's seat, perched on what looked like a small cardboard box, was a dead black cat smeared with dried blood.

'Damn! When I find out who did this, I'll wring his neck,' yelled Rodney. He made a grab for the cardboard box to remove it from the car, and even as he did so a memory flashed before him, of Afghan terrorists putting a dead dog on an improvised explosive device as bait for the curious, animal-loving GIs. It was nanoseconds too late.

The dead cat slid out onto the driveway at the same time the box blew up with a thunderous noise. Rodney Watson, candidate for Congress, was blown backwards nearly five feet as his old Ford burst into flames. His shocked wife ran out of the house to find half his face blown away. Her hysterical screams could be heard a block away.

Five days later, in Jackson, Mississippi, only two hundred and fifty miles west of Montgomery, Megan Abbott was feeling giddy and guilty at the same time.

What was on her mind were her newfound riches of two hundred dollars in her wallet—two fifty-dollar bills and five twenties. Since her family lived from hand to mouth as far back as she could remember, and these days she had to give all but forty dollars of her meagre weekly earnings to her mother, she couldn't recall having had so much cash at any time in her life. Thinking about so much money made her feel dizzy.

But her Cheshire cat smile didn't last long as she started thinking about how she had come by the money.

Two days ago, while on duty at the New West Hotel, Megan had to take up dinner for Congresswoman Iris Hudson, who was staying in a suite on the sixth floor. Megan knew the Democratic congresswoman because she often stayed at the hotel when in Jackson. She had heard that Hudson was running for office for the fourth time and everyone expected her to win again, even though it could be close as her Republican opponent was picking up support from the Patriots. Megan didn't know exactly who the Patriots were; she wasn't interested in politics.

Megan had come out of the service lift pushing a cart carrying the congresswoman's dinner. She had been walking down the corridor when a waiter of about thirty-five suddenly appeared in front of her.

'Hi, my name is James. I just started work today. I know you're taking dinner to Congresswoman Hudson. I've never met the congresswoman and everyone is talking about her. Could I take the cart and serve her dinner today?'

'Dunno. This is my job. How come you weren't introduced to us when we came on duty today?'

'I was filling out forms and got late. Hey, I really want to meet the congresswoman and her dinner is going to get cold if we keep talking! To show you how eager I am to see her, how about letting me serve her dinner for twenty dollars?'

'Dunno. I'd consider it if you gave me two hundred! Or no deal. I could get into big trouble.'

'Done. I think I have two hundred.'

'What?! Are you serious? No one would pay that kind of money just to take in her dinner. If you attend one of her rallies, she'll talk to you.'

'Yes, but I want to have a nice little chat with her.'

Megan remembered looking at the young man with strange deep-set eyes as he pulled out his wallet and counted out the bills. She sighed as she thought again about the article in the *Clarion-Ledger* her mother had brought to her attention early this morning.

'Megan, there was a death in the hotel yesterday. Congresswoman Iris Hudson was found dead in her suite yesterday morning. Did you see her when you were on duty two nights ago?'

Megan rarely read the paper, but she had grabbed it from her mother and skimmed the article that reported the apparent cause of death to have been 'a sudden heart attack'. It said there would be an investigation.

She had been scared all day. She'd had the day before off, and when she went to work this morning, she hadn't seen any sign of the man and was afraid to ask anyone about him lest she was asked why she wanted to know. She didn't even want to think about the possibility that he had something to do with the congresswoman's death. She dismissed the idea quickly as she had never heard of anyone being able to cause a healthy person to have a heart attack.

By the time she finished her shift, Megan had resolved not to say a word to anyone about the odd man. She was terrified she would end up being asked a lot of questions, more so of the police getting involved. And she knew her chances of being able to keep the much-needed money would take a nosedive. She had never had so much cash in her wallet and she was determined not to lose it. She didn't want to think about the strange man and her newfound wealth but it seemed as if she couldn't get him out of her mind.

Lisa was doing her best to look calm and collected. She was in the third-floor conference room of the FBI headquarters in Washington DC, waiting for the meeting of the task force to begin. She couldn't believe that the FBI was seeking her help on a case that was increasingly appearing to be serial murders with major consequences on national politics. After all, she was only a city police detective from Honolulu.

On Friday, Captain Kalani had told her that the FBI wanted her in Washington on Tuesday to help with the investigation. 'I don't know how they know you're obsessed about these killings or why they want you. But the chief says it's good for the HPD to have someone asked by the FBI to help them. So you should go, Lisa. It's all expenses paid too.'

A dozen people were at the meeting. Lisa found it impossible to remember all their names and titles when she was introduced to them before the meeting started and while everyone was milling round drinking coffee, nibbling on doughnuts and chatting. The only person she had met before was Sam Ogden from the Seattle office, now assigned to the task force for the duration of the investigation. But Lisa did manage to figure out who the key people were.

Dan Bronfenbrenner, the assistant director of the Criminal Investigation Division, was leading the task force. He looked about forty and was extremely handsome. While Sam had a well-settled middle-aged look and a receding hairline, Dan had the physique of someone a decade younger and a full head of wavy brown hair. The only giveaways to his age were the lines round his eyes and mouth, which Lisa thought only added to his attractiveness. Lisa liked Dan almost instantly because he had made her feel at ease as soon as they met, saying, 'I'm going to call you Lisa, and you can call me Dan. We can take off fifteen minutes from our meeting time if we don't use our long last names.'

It was Dan who introduced Lisa to Dr Eleanor Simmons, the executive assistant to the director of the FBI. She appeared an intelligent woman in her late forties, professionally dressed and rather stern in demeanour. Lisa had felt intimidated by her, but found Dr Simmons to be friendly. At first, Lisa couldn't figure out who held a higher rank, but as the meeting progressed, she figured Dan and Eleanor were about equal. It was clear, though, that Dan was in charge of both the task force and the meeting.

The youngest person at the meeting, as far as Lisa could determine, was Ben Perez, an FBI officer from the elite Cyber Division. Ben seemed not more than about thirty, had bronzed skin and bedroom hair that must have taken him a long time to arrange.

The meeting started with Eleanor Simmons explaining what everyone at the table already knew: why the task force had been created and that the last two deaths in Alabama and Mississippi had finally made the director decide the investigation was to be conducted on top priority. Using PowerPoint, she went on to summarize all the deaths since January. She added to the list the death of a candidate's wife and the attack on a candidate's bodyguard. The group round the table looked a bit bored because everyone had the following handout with everything Dr Simmons was talking about.

Suspected Victims of Politically Motivated Homicides and Attacks					
Name	Age	Affiliation	Apparent Cause of Death	Location	Date
Kendrick Mitchell	62	Democrat (House)	Heart attack	Tucson, Arizona	14 January
Arlene Schmidt	58	Republican (House)	One-car accident	Scottsdale, Arizona	20 January
Silas Fuller	81	Republican (Senate)	Heart attack	Providence, Rhode Island	21 January
Kent Harrison	48	Democrat (House)	One-car accident	Bangor, Maine	10 February
Vera Nelson-Berg	52	Democrat (House)	Fall, down icy steps	Hartford, Vermont	19 February
Samuel Krueger	64	Democrat (House)	Cerebral aneurysm	Yuba City, California	1 March
Stephen Sasaki	43	Democrat (House)	Heart attack	Honolulu, Hawaii	8 March
Amanda d'Abruzzio (Tony's wife)	38	Democrat (House)	Heart attack	West Seneca, New York	18 March
Kathryn Myers (three others died with her)	54	Republican (Senate)	Plane bombing	Spokane, Washington	5 April
Arnold Roper	72	Republican (House)	Bled to death from fall	Clayton, Missouri	14 April
Sandra Montoya	42	Republican (House)	Hypo-glycaemia (was diabetic)	Daytona Beach, Florida	18 April

Wayne Gustafson	63	Democrat (House)	Heart attack	Madison, Wisconsin	20 April
Paul Robinson	42	Republican (House)	Car rammed by truck	Ohio	25 April
Jack Diaz (Gregory Pang's bodyguard)	37	Democrat (House)	Knifed with intent to kill	West Covina, California	4 May
Rodney Watson	38	Justice Party (really Patriot; House)	Car bomb	Montgomery, Alabama	21 May
Iris Hudson	57	Democrat (House)	Heart attack	Jackson, Mississippi	25 May

Finally, Dr Simmons turned to Dan: 'Do you have any new information on Hudson's death? Was an autopsy performed?'

Dan looked at Ogden: 'Sam?'

'Unfortunately, Iris Hudson's body was immediately released to her family after the doctor signed the death certificate and the remains were cremated before our request for an autopsy reached the Jackson Police Department,' replied Sam. 'I did manage to get our field office in Jackson to investigate the circumstances of Hudson's death, though. Senior Agent Martha Fisher reported that the congresswoman had given an important speech on the afternoon of her death and then checked into the hotel, retired to her room and ordered dinner from room service. She seemed in good health when she checked in. A waitress took dinner to the room. The next morning, Hudson was found dead. The Alabama police are satisfied with the findings of a doctor who was called by the hotel—that she died of a heart attack.'

'Did the police check the wine glass . . . the coffee cup . . . the dishes she ate off?' Lisa blurted out, and then wondered if she should have.

Sam responded right away. 'No. Agent Fisher told me the dinner cart was left outside the room sometime during the evening, and it was taken down to the kitchen late at night. Everything on the cart was washed by the night staff. The next morning, when several phone calls to Congresswoman Hudson went unanswered, the manager went up to her room with a master key and found her dead in bed. The room had been locked but not bolted, and there were no signs of anything being out of place.'

'Did anyone in the hotel see someone or something suspicious the day Hudson came to stay at the hotel?' asked Lisa.

Sam laughed, but replied seriously. 'No. Agent Fisher asked round. She interviewed the waitress who took dinner to Hudson. The young woman swore she saw no one she didn't know in or round the hotel that day or the day before the death.'

Dan took over the meeting. 'Let's leave the Hudson case for now. Thank you, Eleanor and Sam. The first thing on our agenda is to try to determine which of these deaths are definitely homicides, which are almost certainly due to natural causes and which can be considered suspicious. Agreed?'

Everyone nodded, and Dan continued: 'Certainly the two deaths by bombing in Spokane and Montgomery were murders. And the knife attack on Congressman Pang's bodyguard was attempted murder. That's three of the sixteen cases before us. Let's look at the remaining ones and figure out which, if any, can be attributed to natural causes. Anyone?'

A man whose name Lisa didn't remember spoke up. 'I'd classify Arnold Roper's death as due to natural causes. He was old, in ill health, and we know he hit his head and bled to death because of the blood thinner he was taking to prevent a stroke.'

'Everyone agrees?' Everyone nodded. 'Any others?' Dan asked.

A female agent, several seats away from Lisa, spoke up. 'I would put Sandra Montoya's death too in that category, without knowing more than we already do about the circumstances of her death. Again, her health was poor.'

Almost everyone in the room said yes or just nodded.

Sam looked up from the notes in front of him, and said, 'You know, of the thirteen people we're talking about, three died from car accidents and one from a fall, all while alone. None of these people were elderly. I would put these deaths in the suspicious category. That leaves ten to account for. Of these, six have been certified as having died from a heart attack, one from a stroke, one from a cerebral aneurysm and one from hypoglycaemia . . .'

Before Sam could say more, Ben broke in. 'We checked and this pattern of deaths is way outside statistical probability. Particularly since only two of the deaths were of people over seventy. This is not normal.'

Sam was a bit annoyed at the interruption. 'That's my point, Ben. Since few autopsies have been performed and none have used advanced techniques to detect obscure poisons and the likes, I think it's possible that any of the deaths attributed to natural causes could've been due to some kind of poison.'

Lisa felt pleased that Sam was beginning to see her point of view, even if it had taken a month and a half.

A man across the table from Lisa objected to Sam's statement. 'There is no way all the deaths could be murders. Look at the dates. Schmidt died in

Arizona on 20 January and Fuller died a day later in Rhode Island, way across the country. Montoya died in Florida on 18 April and Gustafson died two days later in Wisconsin. The killer not only would have had to travel but also would have to get in touch with his victim and commit the crime.'

'What if there's more than one killer?' asked Sam. 'Look at the different methods. At least three different MOs are evident: heart attacks, perhaps due to poisoning; car accidents, a fall and a knife attack, which could have all been deliberate; and the bombings. The first and last MOs would require specialized knowledge. Oddly enough, we haven't seen the use of a gun. Perhaps, because it wouldn't be classified as a natural death or an accident.'

'Sam,' Dan said calmly, 'we can't determine the number of killers at this stage. Shawn here just pointed out that at least two sets of deaths occurred on days in close succession. But we have to remember that both Montoya and Fuller were in poor health, so their deaths could well have been natural.'

'But maybe not, if there is more than one killer,' Sam said.

'Why do you think there is only one killer, Lisa?' Dan asked, turning towards her.

'In every case in which someone suspicious was spotted, the description is the same: a man in his mid-thirties of medium height and build, with dark hair and penetrating, strange eyes, and of undeterminable, possibly mixed, race. I saw a man of this description pour out a cup of coffee for Steve Sasaki hours before Sasaki died. The description also matches that of the man who had dinner with Amanda d'Abruzzio just hours before she died and of the man who was hanging round near Robinson's place before his truck was rammed. It could well be the description of the man seen in the dark by Nelson-Berg's assistant and perhaps in disguise as the woman with the wig and dark glasses who bombed Myers' plane in Spokane. Different MOs, same descriptions.'

Lisa paused briefly and looked round. Everyone was listening attentively. 'And I would like to know the description of the man who had dinner with Gustafson before he died and the nut who was bothering Krueger before his death. I think we have three MOs but the same description in every case.'

'You're very persuasive, Lisa,' said Bronfenbrenner. 'But there are a couple of problems. There are innumerable men in their thirties, of medium build, with dark hair. And saying he looks to be of mixed race or has penetrating, odd eyes is subjective.'

'Then, what about Occam's razor?' asked Lisa.

'What's that?' asked Shawn.

'It's the scientific and philosophical rule stating that the hypothesis that makes the fewest assumptions and therefore offers the simplest explanation of unknown phenomena is likely to be the most plausible and so ought to be sought first.'

'So, you mean it's more likely there's only one killer rather than two or more?' Shawn asked, insistent on getting it straight.

'Right. But it doesn't make any difference whether we are looking for one or more killers. We should try to stop candidates from being murdered,' said Lisa, looking a little flustered.

'If we are looking for motives and trying to find out who is behind the killings,' said Dr Simmons, 'it's important to determine whether it is one man or whether we're dealing with a larger, perhaps powerful, group that can pay several persons to commit these murders. Let's look at motive. If people in Congress or candidates for Congress are being killed, what could be the motive?'

Someone Lisa couldn't see from her seat spoke up. 'The deaths seem random. Of the sixteen dead candidates, nine belong to the Democratic Party, but the rest are from the right—ranging from moderate Republicans to the extreme right-wing Patriots. So, isn't it possible that someone who hates all politicians is committing these murders? Anyone running for Congress is an easy target. And it wouldn't surprise me if there were more than one such person.'

'It certainly looks like that on the surface,' said Lisa. 'But if you examine what kind of a Republican the candidate was, how well he or she was doing in the polls and who might move ahead by that candidate's death, I think the motive is to put right-wing Republicans, but not Patriots, into Congress. That would be an obvious motive for getting rid of a Democrat, but it could also mean getting in a Republican who would have a stronger chance of getting elected or one with the right ideological leaning. Besides . . .'

Before Lisa could finish her sentence, Dr Simmons, distinctly annoyed, interrupted her. 'Precisely. I think this is the key to finding out who the killer is and who's funding them. After I was asked to be on this task force two weeks ago, I started looking into the political leanings and the electoral situation in the districts of the deceased candidates, with the help of Ben here. And here's what I've found . . .'

She glanced down at her laptop and continued.

'The candidates who were killed or died under suspicious circumstances were a Democrat or a moderate Republican or someone getting support from the Patriots and likely to jeopardize the chances of a conservative Republican. So if a candidate dies, either a moderate or a very conservative Republican candidate will likely win in the general election. Even the case of Watson in Alabama who was running for Congress as a candidate of the Justice Party fits this pattern. He was running against a right-wing Republican congressman who is supporting Governor Bond. Watson would probably have split the Republican votes and a Democrat would get elected. So Watson had to go.'

'So, you're suggesting super-rich reactionaries may be funding these homicides to ensure as many right-wing Republicans as possible get elected both in the House and in the Senate, right? It makes sense actually . . . a group of rich nuts . . . maybe, a rogue, reactionary Super PAC ordering all these killings,' a woman of about thirty said quietly.

Eleanor nodded. 'One way to catch the murderers is for us to *chercher l'argent*. We have been keeping tabs on the flow of money into and out of the Super PACs, but they are spending their money on TV ads and research. I thought we'd look into how the well-known leaders of the Patriot Party in the three large cities of Seattle, Buffalo and Los Angeles plus Montgomery—where we are sure someone killed a candidate—were getting their hands on money to pay for office space, staff, rallies and so on. But so far we've come up with nothing. We can't trace any of their funds—sources or destinations,' she added, sounding rather frustrated.

There were murmurs as she finished. Someone got up and brought a thermos pot of coffee over to the table. Dan looked at his watch and took charge of the meeting again.

'Okay, so tracing funding sources for these murders is one way of going about finding out who the killers are, but so far it hasn't led to much. Eleanor, I'm hoping you will work with Tabitha and Shawn to pursue this line of investigation. Now, let's turn to where we should go from here. I'm sure you've all noticed that the methods are getting more violent and less subtle over time because the candidates are becoming wary. Who knows what will be next. I've been reliably informed that some major newspapers, including the *Los Angeles Times* and the *New York Times*, and even a reporter from the CNN, are seriously probing these deaths. The director is going to come down hard on me—on us—especially if the damn journalists find out something we don't know, unless we get cracking on this and nail the guy or guys as soon as we can.'

Dan looked down at his notes and continued. 'For starters, I want to re-investigate the circumstances of all the deaths certified as being from natural causes, and I want to investigate more thoroughly all the ones that have already had some kind of local enquiries made. From what we've concluded, the only deaths we will exclude are Roper's in Missouri and, for the time being, Montoya and Fuller's.'

Dan looked at Lisa and carried on. 'One of the reasons I brought Officer Lisa Higashiguchi all of the way from Hawaii is because she is the only law enforcement officer who has seen the possible culprit without any sort of mask, dark glasses, wig or some such disguise. You've all been given the sketch Lisa helped us draw up in Seattle. I'd like her to add anything she wants to and answer any questions you have. We are going to circulate her sketch and use it when talking to witnesses. Lisa?'

For the next half an hour Lisa described Suspect X and answered a variety of questions. When there were no more questions, Dan asked for suggestions as to how the FBI might better protect candidates given the impossibility of knowing what method the killer or killers might use, the large number of candidates at risk and the scarcity of FBI resources. Several people made some suggestions, and then Lisa spoke up again: 'This may be a very wild idea, but expanding a bit on what Dr Simmons was saying earlier about determining the kinds of candidates getting killed, I think we might be able to make a reasonably good guess as to which candidates would likely be the next targets. So, besides all the thorough investigations, we could also try and plan to trap the assassin and protect the candidates at the same time.'

Dr Simmons cut in. 'You really are sharp. I'm in the preliminary stage of trying to identify the next potential targets. I'm using a computer program some political scientists have developed to analyse who will likely win the election in each district by feeding in several variables such as the ideological leaning of the candidate, the current poll results, the past results of elections and the demographic composition of each district. I'm going with the assumption that whoever is behind these homicides is doing what amounts to the same thing based on educated guesses and even hunches.'

Lisa spoke up. 'I've been using the Internet to try to come up with a guess as to which candidate is most at risk. I didn't consider candidates for the House because there are too many of them. But there are only thirty-four candidates for the Senate. So, I looked for a Democrat or a moderate Republican who would most likely be the next target.'

Everyone looked at her intently.

'And you've come up with a candidate?' a surprised Dan asked. 'Who is it?'

'Senator Thomas Greenfield from Idaho. He's a moderate Republican. He was ahead by a few points in the last poll taken two weeks ago. And he's been in office for years. Should he die, there is a far stauncher right-wing candidate whom the senator barely beat in the primary.'

'Right. I've read the Patriot Party is very unhappy with Senator Greenfield and some in the party leadership would definitely like to replace him,' commented Dr Simmons.

'While we wait for Eleanor and the Cyber Division to come up with names for possible targets, we should offer protection to Senator Greenfield immediately' said Dan. 'We shouldn't take any chances. We'll do it on the QT and hope the press won't get wind of it. We'll just have to pick our agents very carefully because we don't know what the next MO will be.'

A little hesitant, Lisa continued when she found Dan looking at her encouragingly. 'Dan, I realize I said I couldn't deal with candidates for the House as there are too many, but I wonder whether you could provide some protection for Congresswoman Harriet Hanson, a Democrat in Portland who is running for a second term. My colleague, Sergeant Pat Foletta, has a sister living in Portland who said she is very worried about Congresswoman Hanson. This year Hanson is in a very tight race against a Republican candidate who is being backed by the Patriots, several of whom have made threatening calls to the congresswoman, telling her to drop out of the race.'

A little surprised, Dan answered immediately. 'Sure, Lisa. I'll see that she gets protection. Eleanor and I will discuss everything we've talked about today with the director this afternoon. I'm sure he'll give us the go-ahead on protection for both Senator Greenfield and Congresswoman Hanson.'

Turning to the group Dan addressed everyone. 'I'll be meeting with all of you individually or in the teams to which you've been assigned. It's past noon, so this meeting is adjourned.'

Chairs scraped loudly as people stood up, and the room filled with the buzz of conversation. Lisa stood looking round, unsure of what to do. Just then Dan came up to her and invited her to join a few of them for lunch. Lisa was delighted and accepted immediately.

Sam and Ben joined Dan and Lisa at a table in the cafeteria. While Sam and Ben quickly became involved in a heated argument over the probable number of assassins, Dan engaged Lisa in conversation, asking if she would brief the FBI agents in Honolulu on Sasaki's death. She was very pleased when he said he wished she were on his task force, and said she would be happy to cooperate with the FBI on her own time.

When lunch was over, they shook hands and Dan offered to take Lisa down to the entrance and get her a cab.

As they approached the front entrance, Dan said, 'Lisa, since you're leaving tomorrow morning, I'd like to invite you to dinner at my favourite French restaurant.' Then he hesitated. 'Of course, that's providing you don't have other plans . . .'

Lisa beamed at him. 'I'd love to have dinner together. No other plans—I don't know anyone in DC. Thank you for the invitation.'

She agreed to be picked up at seven from her hotel and said she would be waiting in the lobby. They smiled warmly at each other as they parted, their eyes meeting for a second too long perhaps.

Lisa went shopping that afternoon and ended up with an outrageously expensive black silk dress to wear to dinner. Then she went back to the hotel and took a long bath, dreaming about Dan, all the while reminding herself he'd only asked her to dinner and that she'd go back to Honolulu and probably never see him again. *But I intend to enjoy this evening*, she said to herself with a smile.

He sank back into the pillows on his bed, arms behind his head. Usually, he appreciated a good hotel and a pleasant city when on assignment, and the River Place Hotel certainly was a good place. But tonight he only glanced out the large window, staring at the Willamette River reflecting the moonlight. He was too tired and too frustrated to appreciate Portland's beauty or the hotel's comfort.

Three days ago, late at night, he had flown in from Boise, where he had been unable to carry out an assignment. However desperately he tried, he was unable to find a way to get anywhere near his target in solitude. A ferret-faced giant of a man in his early forties, who didn't try to hide his revolver's bulge under his jacket, was never more than a few steps away from Republican Senator Thomas Greenfield. He even went to the toilet with the senator and stayed at the senator's house at night. And every one of the senator's campaign staff seemed to be constantly on alert, as if they had been warned of possible danger.

So he had been forced to abandon that assignment and come to Portland on another. But he faced the same problem here. This time Democratic Congresswoman Harriet Hanson had a six-feet tall female guard in her thirties constantly by her side. Although he didn't think she carried a gun, he could tell from the way her eyes never stopped moving and her restrained movements that she was a trained policewoman or government agent whose job was to protect VIPs. Besides, the congresswoman left her campaign headquarters and her house only four times during the two days he watched her.

In Boise, he thought the senator might simply be an overly cautious man or even slightly paranoid, but he was now convinced they had both been warned about a possible threat to life and been asked to remain extra vigilant.

He sighed and reached for his phone on the bedside table. The email he sent was short and succinct:

NEITHER PACKAGE CAN BE OPENED.
BOTH ARE PROFESSIONALLY SEALED. 15-DAY R&R
REQUESTED. KEKOA

When he checked his email before going down to breakfast the next morning, he had a five-word response.

MESSAGE UNDERSTOOD. REQUEST GRANTED. KEKOA

Over a breakfast of bacon and eggs in the hotel's restaurant, he decided to take the train back to his hideout in Sausalito instead of flying. He was tired of all the cramped planes, airport security and bad airline food he had endured over months of assignments. So while munching toast, he browsed on his phone and found an Amtrak train—the Coast Starlight—that travelled from Portland to the Bay area overnight. He booked a first-class sleeper compartment on the train leaving that afternoon, paying extra to have the compartment to himself.

Then, on his way back to his room, he wheeled a cardboard carton from the pretty receptionist in the lobby and set about packing his clothes, wigs, knife, a long rubber tube attached to a small rubber ball and other such tools of his trade. He would take the box to UPS to have mailed to his apartment in Sausalito. Amtrak didn't carry out the rigorous security checks that airlines did, but one couldn't know for sure when and where there would be one. The four very small plastic containers of pale, gold liquid he carefully packed and put into his carry-on. Next, he put in a large box of Godiva chocolates, at the bottom of which was hidden a pound and a half of *plastique* wrapped in aluminium foil.

By early afternoon he was on his way to California. He relaxed in his compartment and took out a copy of the *Oregonian*. He found nothing in the newspaper to indicate any warnings given to political candidates. The front-page news was of Senator Chance holding a big rally in Eugene. The rest was a lot of boring local stuff. Now that he was on R&R, he began to realize just how exhausted the past several months of tense work had made him. He spent the rest of the afternoon just staring out at the changing scenery.

At six, he made his way to the dining car reserved for first-class passengers. As he entered the car, he did a double take. *No! It can't be Dr Ito*, he thought. The resemblance was uncanny—the same round face, the same narrow slits for eyes and the full head of white hair. The old man looked up and nodded and then went back to his book. The book was in Chinese. As he glanced over the old man into the book, he noticed that the pages were in Chinese characters, without any Japanese *katakana* or *hiragana* syllabaries. So it couldn't be his great-uncle. Had the book been in Japanese, he knew he would have spoken to the old man.

The sight of the old man left him feeling disconcerted throughout dinner and later he couldn't recall what he had eaten. He returned to his compartment to find the porter had made the bed. Feeling exhausted, he lay down.

Soon, the rhythmic sway of the train lulled him into drowsiness, a twilight state in the haze of which a two-storey Japanese house, set in a large garden, drifted into mind.

When he had been discharged from the army, he had spent a month travelling in Japan. His mother had said he must visit her uncle, and so, for the first time, he had travelled north to Sendai. She said her uncle had retired early because he had lost his medical licence and then his wife died, but he had written that he was managing all right. 'He should be able to put you up for a few days at least,' his mother had said.

'Surely that's unusual—to lose one's licence to practice? Why?'

'Cousin Teruko in Kobe told me Uncle Ito had been under suspicion because he was paid a lot of insurance money when his great-aunt and, soon after, two of his patients all died from heart attacks. It was rumoured he had somehow caused these heart attacks.'

'Didn't the police and the insurance company investigate?'

'Yes. Teruko said they did. But nobody could pin anything on him. And in Japan the dead are cremated very soon after death so there were no remains to autopsy. In the end the government took away his licence under the pretext that he was an alcoholic. But lots of people die of heart attacks and some do leave money to their doctors,' explained his mother.

'So how does Uncle Ito make his living these days?'

'He says he is doing a lot of research and advising pharmaceutical companies. I've no idea what that means. I doubt he is making much. But Teruko said he has a woman who keeps house for him. She suspects the woman does more than just cook for him because she is much younger and pretty too.'

He still remembered very vividly the day he had first visited his mother's uncle. When he rang the buzzer on the gate, an attractive woman of about forty came out and greeted him.

'We've been waiting for you. I'm Misako.'

She showed him to a large study with floor to ceiling bookcases overloaded with books and documents. An old man in his late seventies, with narrow eyes and a mop of white hair stood up and welcomed him warmly, saying in Japanese, 'So, you are my niece's boy from Hawaii. Welcome.'

The three days he was Dr Ito's house guest were full of surprises. He tried calling Dr Ito 'uncle' but Misako said he was to call the old man 'Dr Ito'. He couldn't figure out how Dr Ito made his money—he did live in a sprawling house that was in rather good condition and obviously maintained. Perhaps, the insurance stories were true.

After dinner on his first evening, he was surprised when Dr Ito spoke to him in good English instead of the simple Japanese they had been using. He complimented the doctor's English and asked where he had learnt it.

'In London, where I studied cardiology,' the doctor tersely replied, adding that he had many friends who spoke and read English well, but didn't say whether these friends were in London or in Japan.

On his second day came yet another surprise.

Just after breakfast, Dr Ito asked out of the blue, 'Do you know the Japanese phrase *menkyo kaiden?*'

When he shook his head, Dr Ito said, 'It means a teacher or master of a technique or some specific knowledge has taught everything he knows to a student, and this gives permission to the student to pass on this knowledge to others.'

Dr Ito ignored the perplexed expression on his face.

'You know, I've been waiting for you ever since your mother wrote to me about how smart you are and how you were a medic in the army. I've long waited for someone like you, someone who can help me preserve and use the fruits of my research.'

'Use the fruits of your research? Me?'

'Yes, you. My favourite niece's only son. I want to give you the *menkyo kaiden* on the many years of research I've done on *torikabuto.*'

For the rest of that day and through most of the next, except when he took a long nap in the afternoon, Dr Ito talked to him about *torikabuto*. As Dr Ito lectured on, he began to wonder whether the doctor was sound in the head. What he was learning fascinated him, but many things were plain outlandish and left him very puzzled.

'I got interested in *torikabuto* more than fifteen years ago when a patient of mine ate it thinking it was mugwort—*yomogi*—even though it tasted bitter. It made him vomit, his heart palpitated very fast and it became very difficult for him to breathe. He thought he was having a heart attack. But he hadn't eaten much. So when I cleaned out his stomach, his heart rate slowed down and he got better,' Dr Ito said, with an almost childish grin.

'You must be wondering what *torikabuto* is. A perennial weed that grows in mountain forests, it has a helmet-shaped, small purple-blue flower—very beautiful. *Tori* means bird and *kabuto* helmet. We call them bird's helmet as the flower is shaped like the hat worn in traditional *bugaku* performances. The plant grows almost anywhere in Japan, although you see more of it in northern Japan, such as here in Sendai.'

'I grew interested in this weed and read up on it. It has a long and fascinating history. The ancient Greeks knew about it, naming it *Aconitum*, and used it in their practice of early medicine. The sorceress Medea is said to have tried to kill her lover with it, but she failed because her lover didn't eat enough of it.

In the mediaeval period, the English called this plant wolfsbane or monkshood; in recent times, in most parts of England, it is commonly known as the helmet flower. I think the English also used the weed for its poison, but I haven't read anything that said so explicitly.'

'In Japan, too, this plant and its poisonous properties were known in ancient times. Some sources say Yamato Takeru-no-mikoto, the legendary prince who pacified eastern Japan, was poisoned to death by this plant. And in mediaeval times, the plant's poison was used effectively on the tips of arrows.'

Seeing how engrossed his pupil was, Dr Ito rattled on. Not all of what he said was comprehensible, but the doctor repeated himself so often that finally the gist of the matter became clear.

'The poison of this weed is the highly poisonous alkaloid "aconitine", often called the "queen of poisons" in contrast to arsenic, the "king of poisons". Its chemical formula is $C_{34}H_{47}NO_{11}$ and it's more soluble in alcohol than in water.'

'I experimented with birds, cats, and dogs and established that three milligrams per kilogram of weight is all that's needed to kill any living being. So three hundred milligrams—a mere point three grams—will kill a person weighing a hundred kilograms. More importantly, I found that if you boil the dried root of the plant in water and then distil the poison, the telltale sign of its bitterness goes away and you can get far more poison than you get from squeezing the same amount from fresh weeds.'

'By diluting the poison with water in the right proportion and administering carefully measured quantities of the mixture, you can kill a person very quickly or you can delay death for about two to four hours. It is almost impossible to detect that the person didn't die from a natural heart attack unless you are looking specifically for the minutest amount of aconitine residue in the kidneys and liver. Aconitine is a marvellous poison—virtually all of it metabolizes within six hours!' exclaimed Dr Ito.

Dr Ito went on endlessly about the most advanced scientific tests necessary to detect the faintest signs of aconitine and how few forensic laboratories in the world could undertake such tests. He talked in detail about several tests, such as gas–liquid chromatography, that help find residues in the body. All of this was too complicated for the man to understand. Finally, he ended by explaining how, after four years of round-the-clock study, he had successfully determined which variety of *torikabuto* contained the most poisonous aconitine that metabolized the most quickly.

The man was shocked with all the details, yet fascinated with his newly acquired knowledge. He couldn't stop listening or say anything through all of this. He now knew what had killed the people who had made his great-uncle the beneficiary of their life insurance policies.

At dinner the second day, Dr Ito had a lot to drink. His English became garbled and he increasingly used Japanese as he rambled on about his views on who deserved to die and on various other deadly poisons.

'There are a few other ways of getting rid of people besides using the *Ito torikabuto* poison. Many people don't deserve to live . . . people who've got too old . . . they contribute nothing and cost too much money and time to society. A lot of crooks . . . criminals . . . and most politicians and bankers . . . we need to get rid of them. By other ways even . . .'

A refill of saké and several swigs later, Dr Ito continued: 'Remember, insulin . . . intravenously . . . a lot . . .—I mean inject it—will cause hypogly-caemia. Deficiency of glucose . . . think sugar . . . in the bloodstream. The brain runs out of glucose first . . . the person gets disoriented . . . tremors . . . becomes dizzy . . . and death is not too long if not treated soon enough. Difficult . . . for even a forensic doctor . . . to find a tiny needle mark . . . will lead one to con-clude . . . massive amounts of insulin. If diabetic, no one will ever think the death wasn't accidental.'

Dr Ito was already speaking in half sentences and phrases. Several more swigs of saké later the doctor talked about injecting potassium chloride or KCl—the stuff that's used in some American states to execute prisoners with—and using anticoagulants or blood thinners, which, in his opinion, worked wonderfully to achieve the same results.

'Used medically . . . quite often to deal with thrombosis . . . clotting of blood in the veins, you know? Sold under the names of Coumadin, Heparin and Plavix . . . I think . . . and they're very easy to get. Give drugs slowly. Any of them will cause massive haemorrhage . . . sooner or later . . . kill person. Little chance . . . anyone finding overdose . . . anticoagulants,' slurred Dr Ito.

Suddenly Dr Ito stopped, looked straight at him and, for the first time, asked his pupil what he thought about his work.

The man was too embarrassed to tell his great-uncle that he was rather horrified by his revelations, especially since it was now obvious that the doctor had murdered relatives and patients for money. He just said that the *Ito torik-abuto* sounded like the safest method to get rid of someone without getting caught.

The doctor was delighted by his response. 'You can write to me any time to get dried roots of the *Ito torikabuto* It will be sent as a Chinese-style medic-inal weed. But never forget that you have to be very, very careful about the dosage.'

The next morning, Dr Ito took his pupil to the laboratory and taught him how to distil the poison from the plant, showing him the chart of dosages by weight of target and the desired time between the administration of the poison and death.

By that afternoon, the man had had enough of his great-uncle who, he was convinced, was unhinged. So, while Dr Ito napped, he went on an excursion into Sendai, as he had the day before, but today he bought a train ticket back to Tokyo. He had to get away from his madcap great-uncle.

After dinner on the third evening, when Dr Ito had fallen asleep from too much saké, the man went back to his room and packed. At breakfast the following morning, he announced he had to go back to Tokyo. The doctor looked crestfallen. He thanked his great-uncle for all he had taught him, and, to cheer up the old man, promised to stay in touch and visit again. Dr Ito insisted he take the formulas for the dosages he had perfected, and thrust a small notebook into his hands before they parted.

The man hadn't realized then how valuable this gift would be. At his mother's insistence he had written to Dr Ito, thanking him for making his visit to Sendai so interesting and memorable. He had meant to stay in touch with Dr Ito, but hadn't, and then his mother died a few years later.

Last December, when he had called Dr Ito, to his delight his great-uncle remembered him well. From their conversation, he wasn't sure if the old man would send him what he had asked for. But a week later, he received an air-mailed packet marked 'Chinese-style medicine—dried weed roots'. The packet contained four pounds of the bird-helmet weed roots. He carefully followed the instructions in the little notebook and boiled the roots, producing the pale gold crystals. Then, using the formulas, he had diluted these in water to obtain a pale gold liquid. He tried it on a neighbour's cat and learnt he never again had to listen to its noisy caterwauling at night.

Nick parked the Ford in front of the Parellis' ersatz Tudor house in Newton. Bess got out and waited while Nick opened the door to the backseat and pulled out a large oblong object wrapped in brown paper. He looked at Bess who was frowning; both of them were very tense.

'OK, take a deep breath and relax,' he said. 'We need to play this cool.'

Bess managed to smile and Nick flashed a grin back at her as they walked up the flagstone approach to the house.

Bess rang the bell. The door was opened immediately by a short balding man. From Peri's description, they knew the man was Parelli.

'Come in. You people are right on time. So, you're Susan McKnight? I spoke with you two days ago, right?'

'Yes, Mr Parelli. And this is Mr Nick Tabata. I told you he would come with me.'

'Yes, of course. Come into the living room so you can tell me what this something very important is all about. You said I'd regret it if I didn't meet you. Sounded like a threat, so this must be crucial!'

'I apologize. I didn't mean to sound threatening. But, yes, you will regret it if you don't grab the opportunity we're going to offer you,' said Bess.

In the living room, Bess immediately noticed two very good reproductions of Monet's *Champs de Tulipes en Hollande* showing a windmill in a field of red flowers and *Régate à Argenteuil* showing boats in a lake. She thought this a good omen.

Parelli motioned to the pair to seat themselves on a sofa. He stared at the bulky packet that Nick had in front of him.

'What's that?' he bluntly asked.

Before Nick could respond, Bess said, 'We'll soon explain. Let me first tell you why we're here.'

She paused and then said, 'Actually . . . the simplest way to proceed is to say we came here to do a trade.'

'Trade? Like stocks and bonds . . . currencies?'

'No, Mr Parelli. We are here to trade a genuine Monet painting for a list of names.'

As Bess expected, Parelli looked confused. After a long moment he said, 'What? I don't follow you. We already have Monet paintings, as you can see. And I've no idea what you mean by a list of names.'

Bess said in a quiet voice. 'Yes, but the paintings on your wall are reproductions. Mr Tabata is holding an original Monet worth more than five million dollars. And the list I refer to is the one with all the names of people holding accounts in both domestic and offshore banks and their corresponding account and Swift numbers.'

'What the . . . ,' Parelli started.

Looking at his shocked expression, Bess continued calmly.

'Please listen. I'll try and explain better. The NAD Forum, of which we know you're the treasurer, has a lot of money coming in. Well over two hundred million dollars in donations since last October, some as large as ten million dollars. But we found that the forum reported to the Treasury only a small percentage of the actual amount it received since it obtained its tax-exempt status last fall.'

His eyes bulging, Parelli almost shrieked, 'How did you . . .?'

Bess held her hand up to stop him in mid-sentence and continued.

'We know you wire money to banks in the Cayman Islands, Singapore, Jersey, even Zug in Switzerland—all hotbeds of tax evaders and money launderers. And we know you've wired a lot of money to banks in the US in batches of just under ten thousand dollars so that the banks don't need to report these to the Treasury. I hardly think you can call any of this legitimate.'

Parelli was agog. His face reddened and he clasped his hands together to try to stop them from shaking. After several seconds of awkward silence, Parelli sputtered, 'You bastards! You hacked into my computer! I'm just the treasurer of a legitimate educational organization doing my job. Who are you?!'

Bess spoke firmly. 'Who we are isn't important, Mr Parelli. All that matters is that you accept our offer. You give us what we want and we'll give you an original Monet worth at least five and a half million in today's market.'

Parelli stared at her, his lips pressed together. She braced for what he would say next.

He was belligerent, as she had expected. 'I don't understand what you want. Even if I had such a list, no one would give away a painting worth so much in exchange for it. You're wasting your time and mine. Get out! This conversation is over.'

Before Bess could respond, the French doors leading to another room opened and a middle-aged Asian woman, wearing a tightly fitted pink dress, rushed in and addressed Parelli in a hysterical voice: 'Lou! I'm sure a real

Monet is worth more than five and a half million dollars. At least look at the painting. Do you have the list of names they want? It's stupid not to make the trade they're proposing. No list you have can be worth so much . . . and they're only asking for a list of names and account numbers. Just think, Lou, how well we could live with five million dollars!'

'You don't know what you're talking about,' Parelli snapped at his wife. 'As treasurer, I have numerous confidential files and documents. If I traded any of them for money or an expensive painting, Powers would come down on me like a ton of bricks. He is not a man to make angry. Besides *these* two hacked into *my* computer . . . the painting's got to be fake.'

'Mr Parelli, you haven't said you can't do the trade because you don't have the list we want. That's progress. Before we go any further, I suggest you take a look at the painting we have here.' As Nick spoke, he untied the string round the painting and, with Bess' help, carefully pulled off the paper wrapping and the white cloth covering the oil painting. When he turned the painting round to face the Parellis, Ginko caught her breath.

'Lou, this is a real Monet! Oh, my! I've seen this in a book on French Impressionist paintings.'

Watching Ginko approach and lift the painting close to her face to admire it, Bess was thankful Ginko, like herself, was unable to distinguish Claude's copied Monet from a real one.

'It's a forgery . . . a good forgery. Don't you know lots of excellent forgeries exist even in the top museums?' growled her husband.

'It has to be authentic, Lou. Just look at it. Oh Lou, we must have it! We can sell it for five million . . . maybe more. We can invest some and spend some. With that kind of money, you won't need to work any more. We can move to a beautiful island for the rest of our lives! Why can't you give them what they want? We'll disappear . . . be long gone before Senator Powers finds out.' Ginko was giddy with the very thought of this new wealth.

'Mr Parelli,' Nick said, 'of course, we don't expect you to agree to this deal without having the painting authenticated. And by an expert of your choice, not ours, if you so wish.'

Parelli stared at Nick, his mind clearly buzzing at top speed.

Nick continued: 'Mr Parelli, we also have suggestions on how you can avoid Senator Powers' wrath. You accept our offer, and disappear like your wife just said—go somewhere where Senator Powers can't find you. You can leave in a week . . . ten days . . . as soon as you'd like really . . . just as soon as you have the painting authenticated by someone and find a real-estate agent who will sell your house and wire the money to one of your many offshore bank accounts.'

'And if I don't take you up on your so-called offer?' asked Parelli.

'The information we have is in the hands of others now, and it could well end up with the FBI or FinCEN or the Federal Election Commission,' Nick said casually.

Bess could see Parelli was thinking hard. She knew he was weighing the very serious consequences of handing over critical information to two strangers and its effect on Powers and the forum against the life he could have with five million dollars. Parelli's wife was now shaking her husband's right arm fretfully.

Parelli moved away from his wife wordlessly. Then he turned to Bess and asked, 'You said the painting is worth over five million. What makes you think so? There is a recession, you know.'

Bess had her answer ready. 'As Mr Tabata has said, you can have the painting authenticated by an expert you choose. Any expert will tell you that, despite the economy, prices of paintings by the best-known French Impressionists have been going up, not down, during recent years.'

She acknowledged Ginko's presence and continued: 'Mrs Parelli, I'm sure, knows that Van Gogh's *Still Life: Vase with Fifteen Sunflowers* was sold to Japanese magnate Yasuo Goto for close to forty million dollars in the 1980s—the Japanese love good Western paintings! A Japanese art gallery and an insurance company also wanted to buy this Monet for five million dollars about a decade ago. And prices have certainly gone up since then. So I'm quite sure you'll have no trouble in selling this painting for closer to six million, possibly more. So, as you said, it will be more than enough money for both of you to live comfortably for the rest of your lives. I suggest you try selling the painting in Japan where you'll definitely find a buyer and are sure to get the best price for an authenticated Monet.'

'Something else for you to think about, Mr Parelli,' said Nick. 'I think it is safe to assume that the NAD Forum will be disbanded right after the election in November, if not sooner. That means you'll be out of a job. Then your little fortune will come in mighty handy.'

Mrs Parelli sidled up to her husband and whispered into his ear. When she leant away, Parelli said to Bess and Nick, 'Give us a few minutes. We want to talk privately.'

'Of course, take your time. We'll wait,' said Bess and Nick, almost in unison.

Within five minutes, the Parellis were back. Lou Parelli looked oddly agitated and excited.

'OK, give us a week to have the painting authenticated. If it is genuine, you'll get the list you want. We have just one question: Where does the painting come from? We can't sell it if it's stolen,' Lou said, sounding rather concerned.

Nick smiled to himself and said, '*Le Coucher du Soleil en Provence* was painted in 1886. The granddaughter of a woman in Aix-en-Provence who received the painting from Monet sold it to a small museum in Aix sometime ago. The museum in turn agreed to let a very rich American keep it for up to a month with the understanding that he would buy it for five and a half million dollars as soon as it was authenticated; the man deposited five hundred thousand dollars in the Aix branch of BNP Paribas, France's largest bank, as a security deposit for borrowing the painting for a month. The museum was satisfied with the arrangement because the man was a well-known multi-billionaire.' Nick had given their well-prepared answer, carefully crafted the night before with the help of Peri, in anticipation of this very question.

'Why did the museum willingly do this?' asked Parelli, obviously hooked.

'A fair market price was offered and the museum was in dire straits and needed the money. So a few weeks ago, it quietly let the rich American purchase the painting. If you look up a catalogue you will find this Monet painting still listed as being in possession of the museum in Aix. Obviously, the buyer had it authenticated before he shelled out millions,' answered Bess.

'Who is the rich American? Why is he giving this several-million-dollar painting to you so you can trade it with me?'

'All I can tell you is that he is a fanatic right-wing Republican who wants to see Libertarian-Republican Congressman Fulton of Arkansas win the Republican nomination. Five and a half million is pocket change for him. He wants to discredit . . . er . . . let's say, destroy . . . the NAD Forum and Senator Powers, who is supporting Governor Bond. He thinks Bond isn't a real conservative. He wants the list so he can turn it over to the authorities,' explained Nick.

'What's his name? We may have heard of him.' Ginko asked.

'I'm sorry, Mrs Parelli. We are not authorized to disclose his name. He is a very private man,' Bess responded quickly.

Parelli nodded slowly 'I see. It's all politics, isn't it?' he said ponderously, as if he was trying to convince himself. 'The forum goes kaput and won't be able to help Bond. That would boost the likelihood of Fulton getting nominated and elected president.'

'You got it, Mr Parelli. So, you see, five and a half million dollars is a very good investment for this billionaire,' said Nick.

Parelli, looking canny and puzzled at the same time, had a thought. 'Wait. Why all this rigmarole involving a rich guy and the painting? Why don't you two just go to the authorities with what you've already got from my computer? And tell them about the money coming in to the NAD Forum and the places

I'm wiring it to? That would get them asking questions that neither Senator Powers nor I could answer easily.'

'You're a very astute man, Mr Parelli,' said Bess. 'What we already have will certainly start the authorities asking some tough questions. It's clear that the NAD Forum has been carrying on illegal financial transactions. But since it will be a very politically sensitive investigation, Justice or Treasury or whoever else is involved will have to be very careful. To make a stronger case, they will want the names of the people giving and receiving the money. Fulton's supporter wants to get all this into the open as quickly as possible with the maximum media coverage to swing as many voters as possible. He wants names. But since the information we already have is damaging to you as the treasurer of the NAD Forum, the end result will be the same for you whether or not you hand over the information—a long prison sentence! So, why don't we make this easy: you accept our proposal, we do the deal and you disappear with the precious painting. What do you say?'

Breaking a prolonged silence, Ginko said, 'The most important thing for us is to find out whether this painting is real. We have to find someone to . . . what do you call it . . . ?'

'Authenticate,' Bess filled in.

'Yes, authenticate this painting. So can you leave the painting with us for about three days?'

'I'm sorry we can't do that, Mrs Parelli,' Nick answered immediately. 'We will put the painting back in safekeeping at a bank. When you have found someone to authenticate it, please email Bess, and we will meet you and the expert with the painting. After the painting has been authenticated, we will examine the list and if all is in order, we will complete the exchange. Do you want us to help you find an expert?'

Parelli, who was listening carefully, smiled at Nick's last words. 'No. We'll find someone ourselves,' he said and added, 'The arrangement is fine with me.'

Bess gave Parelli the new email address she had created specially for this assignment. The pair left the Parelli house with Claude's Monet, which they carefully stowed in the car. As soon as they were a few blocks away, Bess pulled out her mobile and called Peri. She was feeling exhausted from the strain of their visit to the Parellis, but as soon as she heard Peri's voice, she was exhilarated: 'Peri, they bit! And you know what, they had the nerve to ask us to leave the painting with them!'

Peri, sounding very pleased, responded, 'That doesn't surprise me at all. Well done, guys. But the hardest part is Act II. I hope everything goes according to script as it did in Act I.'

The thin, dark-haired man pulling a black carry-on looked round as he entered the baggage area of Frankfurt Airport. He was sombrely dressed in black pants and an open-collared white shirt, and carried a dark jacket slung over his shoulder. To those round him, he looked unruffled, a seasoned traveller, yet one who had never been to this airport.

This impression was correct because, though he flew frequently, this was his first visit to Europe. An observant man who caught on quickly, he saw the sign for 'Nothing to Declare' and was soon on his way to his destination: the Villa Kennedy, one of Frankfurt's five-star hotels. In less than two hours after his plane from San Francisco had landed, he had signed in as Aaron Zobel and was taken to a room on the second floor. His windows overlooked the huge courtyard surrounded by the four connected buildings comprising the hotel.

It was now lunchtime in Germany. First, he followed his standard practice when checking into a new hotel: he went out of the hotel and walked round it, making careful note of his surroundings. Then, he went back to the courtyard where a dozen people were eating lunch. He liked the look of a sandwich a young couple at the next table were eating—with fresh tomatoes and oozing melted cheese—and asked a waiter for the same sandwich and a beer. As he waited for his meal, he thought about his first assignment abroad.

After his two weeks of R&R, he had been told to go to Germany, much to his surprise. He instantly recognized the name of his target. It was the subject of his failed mission a couple of weeks ago when the man had been so closely guarded that he hadn't had any room for manoeuvre.

The email with details of his target had been unusual: the information had clearly been garnered from private, not public, sources.

Senator Thomas Greenfield of Idaho is making private two-day trip to meet board chairman of Seidelmann A.G., one of world's largest pharmaceutical firms. Making trip suddenly on behalf of the president of Greenfield & Klein, third largest pharmaceutical company in US. Senator will be travelling incognito, unaccompanied by full-time security guard he's had for past several weeks.

Two days later, a FedEx parcel was delivered to him. It contained a US passport with his photo on it, in the name of Aaron Zobel, a name for which he already had a credit card; a round-trip business class ticket on Lufthansa from San Francisco to Frankfurt, arriving in Frankfurt on 2 July; and a slip of paper with 'Villa Kennedy' scribbled on it. He booked himself a room there.

He relished both the sandwich and the German beer but didn't linger over his meal. It was time to get busy. He went to the reception to ask if Mr Greenfield had checked in yet. A blond, young man informed him in stilted English that no person with that name had checked in or was expected. 'I must've got the hotel wrong,' he said. Realizing the senator must be using an alias, he went to his room, waited fifteen minutes and then called the reception from his mobile, disguising his voice. This time he asked whether the board chairman of Seidelmann A.G. had arrived, in response to which he was told Herr Seidelmann was expected the following morning.

He spent the rest of the afternoon familiarizing himself with the hotel. He scouted round the stairs, lifts, service areas, the restaurant and bar, the lobby, spa and exits. He located the public toilets and found a very small room on each floor that housed cleaning equipment. By five in the evening, he was so hungry and sleepy he called for room service, devoured his meal quickly and turned in.

After ten hours of sound sleep, he got up early and took a brisk walk round the neighbourhood and went as far as the Main River, almost a mile away. He returned to the hotel for breakfast and then reconnoitred the hotel again. Then he took up a post in one of the many sitting areas lining the route to the lifts, and pretended to read the *International Herald Tribune*. Before leaving the US he had googled Herr Seidelmann. He hadn't found a photograph of the German but did learn that he was eighty-two and the former CEO of his firm. He was familiar with the senator's appearance having shadowed him in Boise.

As he waited, he ruled out the possibility of using his favourite gold liquid in this assignment. He still hadn't figured out how to get close enough to the senator. There was no reason to think Greenfield would be any less cautious in Frankfurt than he was in Boise. If the senator took a swim in the pool, he could drown him. But the chance of no one else being at the pool was nil. He was sorry he had had to ditch his plastic knife in the amnesty bin at San Francisco International. He had no choice because, for some reason, the TSA agents were going through every carry-on by hand. The X-ray machines wouldn't find his knife but a hand search could. The more he thought about it, the more certain he was that the only way to carry out his assignment was to go to the senator's room at night when he would presumably be alone.

Two hours went by and neither Greenfield nor Seidelmann passed down the corridor. He gave up waiting when the bellmen began to look at him suspiciously for having sat there for so long. On the way back to his room, he thought of asking one of the bellmen about both men, but decided against it because they might be warned about someone making enquiries about them.

Back in his room, he sat down at the window and surveyed the courtyard. By noon, the tables in the courtyard were beginning to fill up. And then he saw a waiter set up a table for two in a quiet corner away from the other tables. He kept watching, and at half past twelve he saw a tall male attendant push in a wheelchair with a very old man and seat him at this table.

No sooner had the attendant left than a middle-aged, slightly overweight man strode up to the table. He recognized Senator Greenfield immediately. The old man and the senator shook hands and the senator sat down. He watched for a while as their food was served. Every time the waiter left, the two men would lean towards each other in earnest discussion.

He thought of going down to the courtyard, but decided it would be pointless as there were no seats that would enable him to eavesdrop. And it was likely the two men were conversing in German. So, he took a bag of peanuts and a bottle of beer from the mini-bar in his room and made a meal of it, while patiently watching his target.

At last, the old man pulled out his mobile and said something very briefly. In less than a minute, the attendant arrived and wheeled him away, while Senator Greenfield signalled for the bill. He signed it and walked out of the courtyard heading towards the lifts.

The man in the room suddenly had an idea. He quickly ran down the stairs to the courtyard and sought out the waiter who had served the two men.

'Excuse me . . . I'm the assistant of the American who just had lunch with Herr Seidelmann. My boss says he thinks he forgot to leave a tip when he signed. May I see the cheque to make sure he did?'

'Oh these Americans! They always worry about how much to tip. Here, take a look,' the waiter said as he handed over the bill.

It was signed illegibly, but below the signature the name Adam Field was written in block letters along with room number 404. The senator had added a generous tip. He thanked the waiter and left with a smile on his face.

He killed the afternoon swimming in the pool and watching the English news on TV. Unable to give up on the idea of using his prized gold liquid, at dinnertime, he put the liquid in a tiny rubber ball and taped to his left arm a long, thin rubber tube attached to it. Then, he put on a coat and tie and went down to the restaurant. He hoped the two men would come down for dinner and not go out. At forty past seven when he was beginning to lose hope, the senator was shown to a table and, a few minutes later, Seidelmann's wheelchair was pushed into the restaurant by the same tall, young attendant.

He dawdled through his meal, biding time in the restaurant, but realized he wasn't going to have the slightest window of opportunity to administer the liquid. It was also clear from their expressions and body language that the discussion between the two men was not as amicable as it had been at lunch.

Declining coffee, he left the restaurant and returned to his room. There was now only one way to accomplish the assignment. He would also have to leave the hotel as soon as he was done. He checked flights back to the US and booked a seat on one leaving just after eight in the morning. To take the first flight out, he would have to fly economy to Chicago. There was no way he was going to use the business class ticket he had as it meant having to hang round in Frankfurt to take the afternoon flight. He packed his carry-on and was ready to do the job. He was still unable to forego the possibility of using the pale gold liquid, so he took out a small plastic container from his suitcase and put it in his pocket.

Just after midnight he made his way to the senator's room in the East wing. He inhaled deeply and rang the doorbell. He could hear it from outside in the hall but there was no response. So he rang it twice again. *Is the senator not in his room?* he wondered.

He looked down the corridor and saw no one. He tried one more time.

Finally, he heard a voice approach the door mumbling, 'For Christ's sake. Who is it?' Then the door opened a few inches and the senator said, 'What is it? I was dead asleep.'

'Sir, we have an emergency message for you from your Washington office. We were asked to give it to you as soon as we could.'

'How on earth do they know I'm here? Christ! Let me have it.' The senator opened the door a bit further and extended his hand.

His visitor shoved the door with his right shoulder as hard as he could with all his might. The door flung open, causing the senator to tumble onto the floor. He kicked the door shut behind him, flung his coat over the senator's head as the senator struggled to get up. He hit the senator's face and chest as hard as he could, causing him to fall back on the ground. The senator whimpered as he collapsed on the floor, and then was quiet.

The man uncovered the senator's head and stared at his glazed eyes.

He dragged the body to the bed and managed to lift him onto it, no mean feat as the senator must have weighed well over two hundred pounds. He changed his mind about asphyxiating the senator with a pillow. Instead, he took out the small plastic container from his pocket and leant over the inert man.

To his extreme surprise, the senator suddenly opened his eyes and looked at the face peering down at him. The senator surprised him again by letting out a protracted scream of terror, piercing the quiet of the night. He shifted the plastic container to his left hand and hit the senator's head with his right hand as hard as he could. The senator's head slumped back onto the bed. He quickly unscrewed the top of the container and poured all the liquid into the senator's mouth. The senator gagged, but all the liquid went down. One plastic container of the liquid would kill the senator in less than two hours.

He put the empty container in his pocket and moved quickly back to the door. With his left hand, he pushed the door open a little and surveyed the corridor. Seeing no one, he came out of the room and pulled the door behind him. As the lock clicked shut, a middle-aged woman emerged from the adjacent room, a hotel robe over her nightgown.

Taken aback, he stood frozen. The woman approached him, looked up and when their eyes met, she stifled a gasp. Then she said in a torrent, '*Ich hörte einen gellenden Schrei. Es war eine Männerstimme, sehr laut, von Raum nebenen. Was passiert?*'

Seeing the man's blank expression, the woman said in English, 'I heard a loud scream. A man's voice . . . very loud . . . so close. What happened?'

As soon as she finished speaking, she caught her breath audibly as he saw fear wash over her face. He was aware she knew he was the cause of the scream. She gathered the collar of her robe with trembling hands and turned to go back to her room, her hand already on the doorknob.

Almost involuntarily he yanked the woman's arm, spun her body round, and clamped his hand down over her mouth, simultaneously twisting her neck hard and pushing it down to her shoulder. She had no time to cry out. The only sound he heard was a distinct crack that came from breaking bones. He held her for several seconds. Her body quivered and then went limp. He caught her from falling and then wondered what to do. When he had pulled her away from the door, it had shut so he couldn't put her body back into her room. Thankfully no one else had come into the corridor. He thought a moment, and then, holding the lifeless body from behind with his arms under hers, he lugged her down the hall to a closet he had seen earlier. He moved the vacuum cleaner aside and shoved the woman's body behind the housekeeper's cart.

He closed the door of the closet, took the stairs and got back to his room without being seen. Shutting the door behind him, he leant against it, breathing rapidly. It took him a few minutes to calm himself down, quickly change into his travel clothes and leave with his suitcase. At the reception desk, he woke up a sleepy clerk. He rapidly explained he had just got a phone call telling him his mother had had a heart attack and he had to leave immediately. The clerk was most sympathetic, quickly settled the bill and called a taxi for Herr Zobel. He didn't ask how Herr Zobel planned to travel at two in the morning.

'I still can't believe we got away with it!' Bess said ecstatically as soon as she greeted Peri, who had just entered the suite Bess and Nick were staying in at the Four Seasons Boston.

Peri plopped down in an easy chair, sat back against the cushions and demanded, 'Now, tell me *everything*! I've been on pins and needles all day.'

Bess responded, 'OK, you know we had an appointment this morning at nine-thirty with Dr Mary Furness—a professor at Boston College.'

'Yes. By the way, the Parellis made an excellent choice,' Peri said with a laugh. 'I used Professor Furness' marvellous book on the early Impressionists as a reference while writing my dissertation. So, how did it go?'

'Well, we took the genuine Monet with us and found the Parellis waiting with Professor Furness when we arrived at her office. She spent over an hour going over every inch of the painting with a magnifying glass, tilting the painting in every angle, referring to a few books and even feeling various parts of the painting with her fingers. All the while we sat on hard chairs and waited. Parelli was expressionless, but his wife kept jumping up and asking silly questions, but most of the time she got only monosyllabic answers. I was ready to bite off all my nails. Finally, Professor Furness looked up at us and pronounced the painting genuine as far as she could tell without having done any scientific tests. She said she had seen the painting in the museum in Aix and she was almost a hundred per cent sure this was the same one,' said Bess with a gleam in her eyes.

Nick continued: 'While Parelli paid Dr Furness and his wife danced round the office, Bess and I carefully packed up the painting exactly as you'd done last week—with all the protective cardboard, bubble wrap and paper. Then we left with the Parellis. We refused to let them take the painting right away, saying we had to examine the list first. We followed them home in Charlie's Toyota, with the painting on the floor of the trunk. Parelli wanted to take the painting into their house on arrival, but I refused again. I went in with them, leaving Bess and the painting in the Toyota. And finally I got to see the list.'

Peri gave a slight gasp. 'Go on,' she said.

Bess spoke up excitedly: 'It seemed like an eternity before Nick came to the front door and signalled me to bring in the painting. I opened the trunk and pulled out Claude's painting in identical packing from under the false bottom of the trunk, which Charlie and his assistant Bruno had rigged up for us. And believe me, that needed some practise! It was tricky pulling out Claude's Monet from the false bottom, without anyone noticing, especially with Parelli and his wife likely to keep a close watch. Bruno helped me master it in one smooth motion. I have to admit I did panic at the thought of Parelli coming out of the house to watch me get the painting. So when Nick signalled to me, I jumped into action instantly.'

'When I got the painting into the house, Ginko hurriedly unwrapped it and propped it up on the sofa. Parelli had been peering out the window intently as if he knew I was going to switch the painting and wanted to catch me red-handed. When he looked at the painting Ginko had propped up on the sofa, he seemed very nervous. Guess someone who scams others is suspicious of everyone. Ginko ignored him. She leant over and examined the soft wooden frame on the painting, then screamed ecstatically.'

'I can almost hear it. But why did she check the wooden frame?' asked Peri, looking puzzled.

'She'd apparently found proof of authenticity! Last week she'd marked a tiny cross with her fingernail on one side of the frame. "See, it's still there! *Banzai*! At last, this Monet is ours!" she yelled.'

Hearing Bess do her brilliant imitation of Ginko's exuberant voice and Japanese accent, Peri chuckled and said, 'I've heard of many ways to authenticate a painting, but this one takes the cake!'

'While Ginko was jubilant, I could see Parelli wasn't. I don't think he regretted the exchange, but we hightailed it back here before he changed his mind. We even took a roundabout route just in case the devious man had made arrangements to have us followed,' Nick said.

'I'm truly grateful to you two for making this possible, giving up your weekend, putting yourselves in possible danger, and even refusing to be paid for all you've done,' said Peri, appreciatively.

'We did have back-up security in case something went wrong, you know. Bruno was watching out for us the whole time. And Peri, we're only too glad to help,' Nick said. 'It's generous of you to put us up at the Four Seasons, and a suite no less. And don't forget you'll get Charlie's bill!'

'I'm sure Mr DeMello's bill will be reasonable for what he and his assistant have done. As for the suite here, you deserve it. Besides, we needed somewhere we could talk in absolute privacy. I'm sorry I couldn't have you stay with me in Chestnut Hill, but I never know when Anita is going to drop by my father's office. We can't have anyone connecting the two of you with me.' Peri sat up and asked, 'So, where's the original now?'

'It's hidden in the hall closet behind our suitcases,' Bess replied.

'Oh good! That must've been a nerve-wracking morning for you two. Well, you did a great job. Thank you very much! By the way, I met Bruno last night. He told me about the Parellis' telephone conversations he's been tapping. They've been very busy. Their house is up for sale—it'll be advertised this coming week—and they've booked flights to Tokyo. They've made calls to close friends and neighbours saying they're going to Japan because Ginko's mother is dying. And Parelli has continued to work for the NAD Forum. As far as Bruno and DeMello can tell, he hasn't hinted to my father about his plans to leave the country.' Peri bit her lips and added, 'It's amazing what you can find out if you aren't concerned with privacy laws. I admit to feeling a little guilty.'

'I think I should prepare you for something, Peri,' Nick said, looking grim.

'And I think I know what's coming,' she replied, looking equally sombre. 'It's the list, isn't it?'

'I'm afraid so,' said Nick with regret. 'I haven't had time to go through it thoroughly, but certain names jump out. Mitchell Benson—Governor Bond's campaign manager—is one and Congresswoman Evelyn Barrington—the pipeline to the Patriot Party—is another. Some people may have served as conduits for the money. Everything will have to be investigated. It's evident that the NAD Forum as an educational organization is just a front for funding candidates and the Patriot party with illegal large-scale contributions. I agree with Charlie that these amount to almost two hundred million dollars since the forum was created.'

'I can no longer ignore my father's deep involvement in Parelli's shenanigans. Besides Parelli's probably just a puppet. I hate to admit my father may be the puppeteer,' Peri said, glumly, and continuing distraught. 'This past week I've had all the time in the world to mull this over. Dad claims he's trying to educate people about our nation, its politics and culture, and what the country needs. But, in fact, he's undermining the very foundation of our democracy. I've no idea why he thought he could get away with this, and, more importantly, why he's doing it, against all the principles he's preached all his life. So hypocritical, so unlike the father I've known!'

Peri sighed aloud and added, 'My mother was right when she said my father may have been a good general but would be a bad senator because he's authoritarian, dogmatic and self-righteous. She said she felt responsible because when he first ran for the Senate, it was her money and her father's influence that got him elected, rather than the dreadful rumour that his Democratic opponent was a pervert.'

Bess and Nick listened in silence.

'If I have to be unfilial, so be it!' Peri exclaimed, with some force. But I'm not going to be a dishonourable American. I don't want to live in the kind of society my father is trying to create. I've been outside the US for so long that I really don't know whom I want elected president, but I do know that I don't want someone who gets into office by illegal means. I'm going to the FBI!'

'Wait a minute,' said a very surprised Nick. 'I understand your desire to be truthful and I admire your patriotism. But let's think this through. If you go to the FBI and hand over what you have, what do you think will happen? The Republican convention starts in six weeks. From what I've read, Governor Bond still is a viable candidate for the nomination and there have been persistent rumours that your father may be picked for the VP spot if Bond gets the nomination.'

'So isn't it even more important for the FBI to get everything we have on the forum as soon as possible? Why do you seem to be so surprised, Nick?' asked Peri, sounding surprised herself.

'If you send the FBI all the evidence we have, they may turn it over to Treasury or Justice, or they may do the investigation on their own. The problem is that the evidence is tainted . . . and the government will have a difficult time using it. I'm not a lawyer, but I seriously doubt they'd even try to use it.'

'Tainted?' Peri asked, alarmed.

'What Nick means is that Charlie got the most crucial information in his report by hacking into Parelli's computer and that's not likely to be evidence admissible in court. And the list is just a list of names and bank account numbers. A team of good defence lawyers can easily dance round it. You'll also have to explain how you got the list, and we wouldn't be able to hide for long our duping Parelli with a forged Monet. If they're concerned about the legality of acting on the evidence, Bond could be nominated before any decision is taken, and if the FBI decided to act later . . .'

Peri cut off Bess mid-sentence.

'I know, Bess. It'll be nearly as bad as Watergate! I hadn't thought it through. Any suggestions?'

'We've given it some thought,' Nick said hesitantly. 'We think you should send parts of what DeMello got from Parelli's computer along with the list of names and accounts, details of wire transfers and a cover letter to FBI headquarters, all anonymously. Bess and I have no doubt that when the FBI examines what you send them, they will open an investigation. Since they won't know how the information was obtained, they won't worry about whether it was legal or not. They might be very careful and act slowly because of what's involved, but they might want to do all they can very quickly as the Republican convention is coming up and they wouldn't want a political mess later.'

Peri's eyes narrowed briefly as she thought over Nick's proposal. Then, without hesitation, she said, 'OK, let's do it. Nick, can you please draft the cover letter? The FBI will get their packet tomorrow. Then I have to get myself back to Paris and the Monet back to Claude.'

At two on Sunday afternoon, a young woman wearing huge designer dark glasses and an oversized sunhat took a thick envelope to the UPS Store on Mass Ave in Cambridge and had its contents—all twenty-two pages—faxed to the FBI headquarters. She paid for this in cash. Five days later, when the clerk at the UPS Store was questioned about the sender of the fax, all he could say was: 'A young lady wearing expensive clothes and dark glasses. I could tell she was very good-looking, but I've never seen her before.'

The packet landed as a bombshell on Dan Bronfenbrenner's desk at exactly seventeen past eleven. He knew the exact minute because he had just looked at his watch to see if he had time to grab coffee before his eleven-thirty meeting.

'What's this?' he asked Sandy, his assistant.

'I don't know. The Office of Public Affairs just sent it over and I thought you might like to see it immediately, in case it's important.'

Dan looked at his watch again and decided he'd skip coffee to look at the contents of the packet. He pulled out a sheaf of papers, glanced at the cover letter and decided he'd skip the administrative meeting as well.

He read through the contents twice, the second time meticulously. He only got some lunch because Sandy brought him a sandwich and a cup of coffee on her way back from her own lunch break. He thanked her and then asked her to call a meeting with Sam Ogden, Eleanor Simmons and Ben Perez as soon as all of them were free to meet, and to make three copies of the material just received from the OPA.

He was annoyed that it had taken four days for the OPA to send over the packet. Although the Fourth of July had been a holiday, that couldn't excuse the delay. A note from the OPA said the twenty-two pages had been faxed from a UPS store in Cambridge, Massachusetts, and 'because the sender is anonymous, this could be a politically motivated bogus tip-off'. Despite their reservations, the OPA had sent him the fax because that office was acting on standing orders from the director to allow the CID to glance over anything that might possibly have a connection with the investigation of the deaths of Congressional candidates.

The small group couldn't get together until four that afternoon because Simmons had a series of meetings. Dan had sent a copy of the material to all of them, giving them enough time to read through it.

'As you can see, the letter clearly states that the sender believes the FBI ought to take the information in the attached pages very seriously. I believe this information, if verified, constitutes sufficient evidence that the NAD Forum is a front organization serving as a conduit of illegal campaign donations,' began Dan.

He continued excitedly: 'What got my attention was the money wired to and from offshore banks. Dozens of these wire transfers in million dollar units are to companies that most likely change their names soon after getting the money. But most of these transfers were to accounts of individuals, in units of 9,000 and 9,500 dollars—just under the 10,000-dollar mark that needs to be notified to Treasury. These individuals include Bond's campaign manager, Congresswoman Barrington, and several candidates. But a lot of transfers are to people whose names I've never heard of and couldn't find on online searches. There are regular transfers to an A. Favia in Zug since March and to an X. Zeiss in San Francisco since January. And a large number of transfers are to a variety of banks in Switzerland, Hong Kong and the Jersey Islands. If this were all, I'd have told the OPA to send the stuff to Treasury and the Federal Election Commission, but in going over this information I thought of something that made me decide I should call this meeting.'

Eleanor stopped thumbing through her photocopy. Sam and Ben looked at Dan intently as he continued.

'It may be tenuous, but I think we may have a link to the political homicides here. Remember, about a month ago, we said we have to follow the money? Well, if you do, you'll see that one of the primary recipients is Evelyn Barrington, who has a strong link with Patriot groups. And then there are the regular payments—weekly transfers of 9,000 dollars—to X. Zeiss, who's also been getting additional transfers of tens of thousands of dollars. These additional payments began in January. I found a sketchy correlation between the dates of the deaths and the dates when these additional sums were transferred. Usually one of these payments was made a week or ten days after the death, almost like a payment to cover expenses and a commission for committing the murder. It's not a definite correlation, but because it recurs several times, it can't be just coincidental either. I'm saying we ought to take what the OPA sent us very seriously because this could be our first big lead in the investigation of these homicides. And . . .'

Eleanor interrupted Dan.

'Dan, of course, you could be right. Though I only had time to skim through the copy you sent me, I strongly believe the information consists of very carefully concocted disinformation by some leftist group or by a Republican presidential candidate in order to discredit and possibly finish off Governor Bond's chance of getting the Republican nomination. As we all know, the forum is Powers', and he's one of the biggest supporters of Bond. Anyone who knows a little about *how* interbank transfers are done and who has followed the deaths of the candidates could cook up what's in the packet you received. And, Dan, I can think of any number of reasons why additional transfers could have been made. We can't rule out that your sketchy correlation could well be coincidental, though I will have to check that more closely.'

Dan looked troubled, but Eleanor ploughed on.

'Then, they've put in names such as Mitchell Benson and Evelyn Barrington—names everyone knows. But they've also listed strange names like Edward King and Mary Queen. Give me a break! I can almost see someone giggling as they made these names up! The whole thing is like carefully doctored disinformation put together by some Democratic Super PAC, a shameless left-wing group or a campaign strategist of Congressman Fulton or Governor Higgins.'

Sam shook his head vigorously and said, 'I beg to differ, Eleanor. I believe the information is trustworthy. No Democrat or leftist group or Republican campaign would spend the hours needed to come up with these names, account numbers and corresponding domestic and offshore banks. They've even taken the trouble to list the transfers to each account since last October. Some of the names on the handwritten list are so strange that they have to be real! If someone wanted to get the forum and Senator Powers into trouble and derail the chances of Governor Bond getting nominated, they could've sent just a small part of the printouts and a short list of names we would recognize immediately. Besides, it would've been logical to send the information to Treasury or to the Federal Election Commission, but it was sent to the FBI.'

'What do you think, Ben?' Dan asked, turning towards him.

Ben answered thoughtfully. 'I think either point of view is equally plausible. Like Sam said, they could've sent less information with a score of names like Benson and Barrington. But they sent us much, much more. I wouldn't have if I were concocting phoney evidence. And the offshore banks listed are in places like Switzerland, the Cayman Islands and Singapore—the most popular tax havens for crooks worldwide! A little too obvious, don't you think? And the fake names could've been used to hide the names of real people to whom payments were made in overseas accounts.'

'At this point, we can't decide whether all of this is real information or disinformation. All we can do is investigate. And since we can't use anonymous information to get judicial permission to compel the people named here to tell us what we want to know, we have to discuss our plan of action. Where do we go from here?' Dan said, expectantly.

'Dan, can we find out more about the person who sent this to the FBI? I don't mean the group behind it, but the person who went to the UPS store? Wouldn't this person provide a lead?' blurted out Ben.

'Who do you think this person is, Ben?' Dan asked.

'Assuming this document is for real, my guess is that the person is someone inside the forum, someone who is trusted by its board.'

Ignoring a frosty look from Eleanor, Ben went on.

'Someone in the forum could access relevant files in a computer and print it out. But the handwritten list must be top secret, so definitely not in a computer. To have access to this the person has got to be a trusted insider.'

'Ben, can you be clearer?' Eleanor prompted coolly.

'From the top of my head, it's someone who disapproves of what the forum is doing or someone who has a personal grudge against Powers or one or more of the directors of the forum. Or even against Bond. Hell, I don't know! But the person has to be a respected and reliable insider. An outsider could get access to files by hacking into one of the forum's computers, but couldn't have got the handwritten list of names.'

'OK, that should narrow it down. But it doesn't tell us who the insider is. Do you have someone specific in mind, Ben?' Sam interjected.

'Since the information is critical to wire transfers, I think we should start with the treasurer,' responded Ben.

'But the treasurer is probably someone who has been handling the forum's financial arrangements since it was set up,' Dan objected. 'Why would he suddenly, after all this time, send us this information? And it would implicate him and potentially land him in prison. What about a board member or an assistant who has full access to the office and its computers? In short, it could be anyone among a lot of people. But you've hit on a line of investigation we ought to follow up on.'

'All right.' Dan made a decision and declared: 'Ben, do some snooping on the Internet. Find out who works at the forum and see if you can find out anything useful about each person, including the treasurer. Knowing who sent us the info could be very important so I'm going to send Sam and a couple of good agents from the CID to conduct interviews with key people working for the forum and for Senator Powers.'

'OK, Dan. I'll get on it immediately,' Ben responded, sounding pleased.

Sam, who had been quietly leafing through the papers in front of him, spoke up, carefully choosing his words.

'Dan, I've been thinking about the correlation you pointed out between the dates of transfer and the dates of deaths. I agree with you about the possible link. And I'm just thinking aloud now: this correlation doesn't mean the forum is directly involved in the murders, does it? I'd bet on Barrington sending money to the Patriots to commit the murders, possibly without the knowledge of the forum. So Powers and the other board members may not be complicit in these murders. The point I'm trying to make is that, without finding out a lot more, we have no basis for directly connecting the forum itself with the deaths of any of the candidates.'

'If the forum isn't involved, who in San Francisco is getting money so regularly?' asked Ben. 'The amounts add up. Why is the person getting paid so much?'

'You're all making good points,' Dan acknowledged, 'but we aren't going to get anywhere by just speculating. We'll do the interviews and then figure out exactly how we want to proceed. We have to be very careful because should we find that the forum is either directly or indirectly connected to the homicides, our investigation into the serial murders of the candidates could become an unprecedentedly explosive political atom bomb. So what we . . .'

Dan was interrupted by the ringing of his mobile.

'Donna . . .What?! . . . In Frankfurt? Go on . . . yes . . . yes.' Dan listened for a good five minutes, just nodding. When he rang off, he looked a little pale. 'That was Donna. The Frankfurt police called,' he said, addressing everyone in the room. 'Senator Thomas Greenfield of Idaho died in a hotel in Frankfurt on the night of the third. They say it looks like a heart attack, but circumstances suggest foul play, so an autopsy has been ordered and the police are investigating his death as a potential homicide.'

'Good Lord!' Sam exclaimed. 'Why wasn't he travelling with his bodyguard? Why was he in Frankfurt at all? And why are we being informed only now?'

'Hold your horses, Sam, and I'll explain as much as I've been told,' Dan said. 'Since Donna knew we were in a meeting, she called the senator's office and a staff member told her that the senator went to Frankfurt alone on private business and had informed only his chief of staff and a couple of close Senate colleagues about his trip. He's a widower and didn't tell any family members. He went without our guy from the Boise office—the agent who's been his bodyguard since we decided he was a likely target and needed extra security. He used an alias—Adam Field—and I guess he thought that would protect him. That's one reason it took time for the police to learn who he was.'

'And the other reason?' asked Ben.

'We've been told there were two deaths that same night. The first body found was that of an older woman, an Uwe Katzenstein, the widow of the head of one of Germany's largest chemical firms. She was staying in the room next to the senator. The police are sure she was murdered. Her neck was broken and her body was found in a utility closet. The police don't know yet what the connection between the two might be. No one in the hotel knew that the senator was also dead until almost noon on the fourth when the police started questioning other guests in the hotel and found him dead in bed. They thought he died of natural causes until they noticed the bruises on his face and chest.'

'Wow!' Ben was astounded. 'And was our dark-haired odd-eyed suspect in the hotel?'

'I think so,' said Dan. 'According to hotel records, a slim, dark-haired American named Aaron Zobel suddenly checked out of the hotel at two in the morning on the fourth. The police found out he took a flight to Chicago six or seven hours later. Had he taken the later flight he was originally booked on, they would've apprehended him at the airport. Damn! They were so close! They contacted the police in Chicago, but they could find no trace of him leaving O'Hare.'

'Why did Senator Greenfield go alone? Why did he go at all? Who knew he was going?' Sam was upset and had several questions. It was clear he felt responsible for the safety of the candidates and was distressed that he had failed.

'That we have to find out,' Dan responded calmly, with the gravity befitting his position of leadership within the FBI. 'We could speculate all afternoon but let's get going and find the facts. First, we have to determine who knew Senator Greenfield was going to Frankfurt and under an assumed name. Second, as soon as I get back to the office, I'll get more information from Donna and call Frankfurt to find out more about why foul play is suspected. And third, Sam, as I've already said, I'd like you to question the people connected to the forum and have someone look into the wire transfers.'

He then added firmly, 'We'll really scrutinize the forum and everyone involved with it and its financial transactions. We have to find the killer or killers. Senator Greenfield's death is going to be made public tonight. When his death hits the news, the media are going to play up all the suspicious deaths and murders of the candidates. So far, we've only had a few serious investigative reports by the papers but none of them have really dug into the matter because they haven't connected all the dots. The only exception is CNN, where a sharp, young guy—Zach Cunning—aired a pretty good report on the deaths of the candidates a couple of nights ago. I'm sure he'll be on top of it all as soon as he learns of the senator's death. So, let's get to work. We really have to apprehend those behind this as soon as possible. We can't let another person die.'

Sam Ogden was almost sorry he had to subject the attractive woman sitting in front of him to a 'false flag interview'—an FBI euphemism for grilling a person under false pretexts. But he had to learn what Anita Faga knew about her boss Simon Powers' activities. As he glanced over at her desk, he saw the front page of the *New York Times* staring at him.

Anita, noticing him looking at the paper, said, 'I just found out about Senator Greenfield's death in Frankfurt. Apparently he was travelling under an alias, and the German police say the circumstances of his death are suspicious!' Then realizing Sam obviously knew all about it, she asked, 'But what did you want to see me about?'

'We had a few questions for Senator Powers. But I was told he's in New York for a couple of days and then he's going to west to make campaign speeches for Governor Bond and won't be available for a while. So I wondered if you could help me.'

'I will if I can. But I can't imagine what you want to ask the senator.'

'Well, let's see. You've been Senator Powers' secretary for three years, right?'

'Going on four. I'm his private secretary. The senator, not the government, pays me. I work for him wherever I'm needed—here in DC or when he's at home in Boston, and sometimes even on the road. But on this trip he's gone with his chief of staff.'

'My questions are not about him as a senator but about the NAD Forum he founded. We've heard that a lot of money donated to the forum for educational outreach programmes is being diverted to other causes.'

'What? Diverted? What do you mean? Where did you get this information?'

'Our sources are not important,' Sam said quietly, noting Anita's discomfiture in her raised voice and sharp questions.

'I doubt that's true, but even if it were, wouldn't Treasury be the one asking questions? After all, the forum is tax exempt under section 501c of the IRS code.'

'You're right, of course. If we do get more information showing funds are indeed being diverted, we'll hand over the investigation to Treasury. But the FBI decided to make enquiries because our sources told us some of the forum's funds are being sent to Patriot groups in various parts of the country, and these groups are notorious for breaking up Democratic campaign rallies and even for injuring campaign workers. If the forum is sending money to these groups for legitimate educational activities, and the money is being used elsewhere without the forum's knowledge, we think they should know about it. We've also heard whispers about the money being sent to Republican candidates in violation of federal campaign finance laws. We want to be sure this is true before we inform the Federal Election Commission.'

'Mr Ogden, you're not asking me questions but giving me unsubstantiated facts—rumours really.' Sam found it interesting that Anita was being defensive rather than curious.

'I'm telling you what the FBI has learned in the hope that you can help us either substantiate the rumours or prove them groundless. Since you work so closely with Senator Powers, do you have any knowledge of the forum's money being used for anything other than its intended purpose . . . anything at all? And please don't tell me to ask Mr Parelli. Our Boston office has checked and established that he's no longer in Boston. One of his neighbours told us his mother-in-law is dying so they had to go to Japan.'

Anita looked at him but said nothing, so Sam went on. 'And his house is up for sale. Why would they sell their house if they were just going to visit his wife's dying mother?'

Sam had conducted more false flag interviews than he cared to remember and he was certain that Anita already knew Parelli had disappeared. He was also certain that Anita, who a few Senate staff said could well be more than just a secretary, knew a whole lot more about how the forum's money was used than she was letting on. He could tell from her body language that she wasn't going to admit to anything, but that wasn't the only reason he had come to see her. From the look on her face, Sam knew he had rattled her enough so she would report this interview to Powers. His team wanted to see what Powers would do. He doubted the senator would call the director of the FBI to complain about this interview with his secretary. But Sam was just speculating. He had to try everything he could to find out whether the forum and the killer or killers were somehow linked.

Sam left his card, asking Anita to call him at any time of the day if she remembered or heard anything that would help the FBI. Then he was off to Congresswoman Barrington's office in the Rayburn House Office Building.

He found the long-serving congresswoman in a huge second-floor office in the Rayburn Building, with a nice view of dozens of tall trees and the White House behind them. As he entered it, he reminded himself that he could be much more aggressive in interviewing the veteran congresswoman than he had been with Anita.

A young woman led him to a small conference room where he was left to cool his heels for ten minutes. When Congresswoman Barrington came in full of apologies for having kept him waiting, his first thought was that she was even warmer than he remembered from what he had seen of her on TV.

Then the congresswoman's mood changed. 'My secretary said you had a few questions about Senator Powers' NAD Forum,' she said, addressing Sam rather tersely. 'I doubt I can be of much help because I'm not actively involved in the forum, but I'd like to help the FBI in any way I can. I can give you ten minutes.'

'I really appreciate your seeing me. I'll get straight to it. We've learned that the forum has been sending considerable sums of money to your bank account in San Diego—over thirty times during the past several months. If you aren't involved in the forum's activities, why has it been sending you so much money?'

Evelyn Barrington was clearly startled but made a valiant effort to hide it.

'Agent Ogden, I've no idea where you got such misinformation. It sounds like a politically motivated, malicious tip-off to the FBI. If that's all you want to ask me, excuse me . . .'

'Our sources are reliable, Congresswoman Barrington. If you like, I can give you the date and amount of each transfer. This is not an official enquiry, but lying to an FBI agent has consequences I'm sure you wouldn't like. The total amount you've received since the beginning of this year exceeds four million dollars. Need I say more?'

Barrington bit her lower lip and said nothing for a very long moment. Then she responded, 'Well, if you must know . . . I loaned Simon—Senator Powers—money when he created the forum. He needed money before the donations began to come in. The forum is paying me back as and when they get donations.'

'Four million dollars?'

'My husband is a wealthy man and I borrowed some from my relatives too.'

'We have reason to believe the money you've been getting from the forum might be used to pay for the commission of a string of murders of Congressional candidates. I'm afraid if I don't get straight answers from you now, we'll have to go to court and get permission to look into your bank account to track your transactions.'

'A string of murders?! I've absolutely no idea what you're talking about! I'm just getting paid back what I loaned. If you want to ask anything more, make a request for an official interview and I'll get a lawyer before I answer any more of your ridiculous questions.'

The congresswoman stood up abruptly and stalked out of the room. Sam was very sure she was lying and was blustering out of desperation. He would have an FBI agent in DC and another in San Diego watch her closely to see what kind of damage control she would try to put in place.

As soon as Congresswoman Barrington was certain that Sam had left her suite, she firmly closed the door to her office and called Powers' office in the Dirksen Building. When she was informed that he was away, as she had feared, she asked to speak to Anita. Anita sounded uncharacteristically snappish.

'Anita Faga speaking. What do you want?'

'Anita, I must've called you at a bad time. I was told Simon is in New York. Something very important came up and I have to speak with him. Where is he staying?'

Anita couldn't tell her that the reason she was fuming was because she too had been trying to contact Powers to warn him that the FBI was making enquiries about the forum's money and she had just been told by the concierge of the Pierre that the senator had gone out to lunch with Professor McPherson.

'Sorry, Congresswoman, if I sounded sharp. He is staying at the Pierre as usual. Is there anything I can help you with?'

'I don't think so. Someone came to see me a little earlier and asked some outrageous questions about the forum's funds.'

'The diverting of funds, you mean?'

'What? How do you . . .?'

'Agent Sam Ogden came to see me this morning and told me he had information—he didn't say how he got it—that the forum was illegally sending money to candidates and perhaps even to Patriot groups,' Anita clarified.

'This Ogden . . . did he say anything about the possible link between the forum's money being diverted and the recent series of deaths of Congressional candidates? He seemed to suggest a definite link and I thought he hinted at Simon having something to do with these so-called murders.'

'Murders? Senator Powers? No, Agent Ogden didn't say anything to me about any murders. What did he tell you?'

'I wonder what's up. He asked all kinds of questions and made outrageous insinuations. Can you imagine Simon having anything to do with murder? It's a ridiculous thought! But he ought to know the FBI is asking questions before this agent talks to more people and the media gets a whiff of the rumours. By the way, do you know why Parelli isn't responding to my emails? Is he on vacation or something?'

'Mr Parelli is gone, Ms Barrington.'

'Gone? What do you mean *gone*?'

'He just disappeared. Mr Powers is very unhappy but there is nothing we can do. For now, his chief of staff is dealing with the forum's finances. We have to find a replacement for Mr Parelli as soon as possible.'

'Oh, dear, I hope the forum's work won't be disrupted. Anita, do try to reach Simon as soon as you can and tell him to get in touch with me ASAP. This is really very important.'

'I understand. I'll do my best, Ms Barrington.'

After she ended her conversation with the congresswoman, Anita debated what to do next. She was still irritated with Senator Powers who was spending so much time supposedly fundraising in New York, which she knew meant he was spending more and more time with Karen McPherson.

Anita thought about going to lunch but she didn't think she could eat. Her mind was buzzing. The illegal diverting of the forum's money she knew about. But the idea that Simon might have something to do with the murders of Congressional candidates was something else entirely. *My Simon?* She tried to get rid of the thought, but the more she tried, the more she thought about it, and she just couldn't sit still. But apart from flying to New York to ask him, what could she do?

Then, she had an idea. The staff had left the suite to go to lunch. She went to Powers' office and entered it using her copy of the key. She had decided she was going to learn everything she could before she confronted him. She switched on his computer, and while waiting for the few seconds it took to boot, she hoped she would find nothing. The senator hated computers and used this one only occasionally for email. A few months after she had begun to work for him, he had told her he needed to handle his private emails himself and had her set up an email account. She changed the password to his computer and his email account every six months, so accessing this was easy.

There was no email in the Inbox, but there was one in the Sent mail folder to a TGreenfield. It read:

Tom, I do not intend to hold any subcommittee meetings at the beginning of July. Your Frankfurt trip is on. Simon.

Next, she checked his files and found only two: one named XYZ1 and another XYZ2. Both were empty. Before shutting the computer down, she reread the lone sent message. The domain name was freedom.org—the same name used by many of the conservative congressmen and senators. She stared at the name 'TGreenfield'. *This has to be Senator Thomas Greenfield*, she reasoned. *Senator Greenfield! The one whose death was front-page news today!* This meant Powers knew Greenfield would be away and where he would be.

Just a coincidence, she tried to convince herself. But too many questions flooded her. So, why had Powers deleted all his other email messages? Why not this one? He wasn't computer savvy and may have, in a hurry, just forgotten to delete the very last email. Why does he have two empty files? Why are they there in the first place? Anita handled virtually all of his correspondence, even to his daughter in Paris, so what was this email account for?

There was nothing more Anita could find so she turned the computer off. She sat staring at the dark screen, her mind racing. She began to suspect everything had been deleted because Powers wanted to make sure no one, not even she, could read his messages. She was sure he had no idea deleted items could be retrieved.

She felt her chest tighten. *What was going on?* She didn't know the details but she knew Parelli had been handling the receipt and disbursement of illegal funds for Powers. But what she was hearing today was far more sinister. The article in the *New York Times* said it had taken time to learn who the murdered man in Frankfurt was because he had travelled to Germany without telling anyone and had registered at the hotel using an alias.

But Simon knew Greenfield was going to be in Frankfurt! She had to learn what was in the deleted emails and the two empty files. She had to know whether Powers was involved in Greenfield's death. To do this, she had to get someone to help her retrieve the deleted information. But whom could she ask? If she did find someone to help her, what would she say? Senator Powers asked her to retrieve inadvertently deleted files? It would be difficult to get someone to retrieve the files but not read them. That wouldn't work.

Then, she had a brainwave. She could ask Sam Ogden. He had left her his number to call at any time for any reason. If the FBI read all the deleted messages and learnt that Powers had nothing to do with these murders, then they would get off his back. If what Powers had deleted contained something that tied him to the murders, even if it were a chance in a million, she had to know!

She entered Sam's number in her mobile, feeling almost queasy. He was on the line after one ring.

'This is Anita Faga. I have a request . . .'

'. . . What is it?' he interrupted, excitedly.

She told him about her conversation with Congresswoman Barrington and why she wanted to retrieve the deleted items from Powers' computer. He listened attentively.

'OK, I got it,' responded Sam. 'I'll send over one of my colleagues right away. His name is Ben Perez. He'll know what to do.'

'When the agent gets here, tell him to ask for me and to say he's a computer repairman. OK?' Anita didn't want anyone getting suspicious.

Her mind still in a whirl, Anita rang off. She was terribly afraid of what the FBI would find in the deleted emails and files. Her whole future could be at stake too. She was so upset that she didn't even think about what would happen if the FBI only found evidence of the illegal use of funds.

✪

While Anita sat in front of Senator Powers' computer, a short distance away, Congresswoman Barrington was on the phone talking to Governor Bond. He hadn't been eager to take the call.

'I was told something critical had come up. What is it? Give me the short version. I have a press conference to go to.'

'I'm calling to say that, earlier today, an FBI agent came to see me telling me things that could have serious consequences . . . to affect you negatively.'

'An FBI agent? What's going on?' asked Bond, all ears now.

'It has to do with our friend at whose beautiful island condo we made a very important pact last winter. Don't say anything if you understood who I'm talking about. When I'm talking to a presidential candidate, I don't trust the phones these days.'

'I know who you're talking about. Go on.'

'Good. The agent said the FBI knows the donations to an organization this man created have been illegally diverted. Worse still, the agent said the FBI is looking into the possibility of this man funding and possibly being directly involved in . . .'

Congresswoman Barrington's voice trailed off and she didn't finish the sentence.

'In what? Evelyn?'

'Brad, I don't think I should go on . . . on the phone I mean. Could you find ten minutes to see me sometime this evening?'

'Evelyn, my phone is secure. We sweep for security everyday.'

'But is mine? I'd feel a whole lot better if we met and talked. This evening.'

'All right. At a quarter to seven tonight at the Hay Adams. I'm hosting a dinner there at seven.' He agreed but his tone was not very gracious.

'Brad, when you hear what I have to say, you'll be glad you decided to see me.'

Bond mumbled something and cut the line. Evelyn looked worried as she turned off her iPhone and put it in her handbag.

Donna Fletcher knew why she had been chosen for this assignment at the Pentagon as soon as Dan Bronfenbrenner asked her to investigate Senator Powers' military background. Dan wanted to find out whether the senator had known someone while he was in the army whom he trusted completely and who was so beholden to the general that he would commit murder at Powers' behest. 'This is a long shot, but worth looking into,' Dan had said.

Donna had been with the FBI for only two years after graduating from law school, but this was her second career. She had served in the US Army, rising to the rank of captain, and so Dan thought she would be the best member of his team to follow this end of the investigation.

She received the assignment late in the afternoon on Friday. The only thing she could do at the Pentagon before Monday was to make an appointment to see Major Poole, the officer in charge of inter-governmental affairs. But she didn't want to waste the weekend and so spent hours searching the Internet for anything she could find on Senator Powers, and, more importantly, on General Powers. This led her to search the digital version of *Stars and Stripes*, the newspaper for the military, which gave her access to archived editions. Her search turned up an article titled 'CG Powers of Zama Staying on Two More Years'. The article began: 'The Executive Officer of the Base, Col. W. Wilson announced today that . . .' Donna had found her lead fairly quickly.

However, trying to find William Wilson's current whereabouts online had led to a boring and frustrating weekend. There were nearly 8,000 people in the United States with that name. So after making a dozen phone calls, she gave up.

On Monday morning Donna met Major Poole. When she enquired about how to find the service record of a former major general, he had asked, 'Who's the general? And why does the FBI want to see his service record?'

'General Simon Powers. We have good reasons we can't disclose at this moment. Trust us, sir. It's important.'

'Senator Powers? I remember him. He had to retire suddenly because he said President Bush was incompetent!' Poole laughed. 'I kinda liked him. I'm sure you people at the FBI won't find anything useful in his file, but we can let you get access to his non-restricted personnel file. It has everything except the records of personal evaluations by his superiors from when he was a lieutenant and some other stuff the army has to keep confidential. But to get an NRPF, you need an OK from the general in charge. That would be General Fried, the deputy chief of G-1, head of everything related to personnel here. You're from the FBI, so I'm sure he'll give you what you want.'

'Where do I find him?' Donna asked.

She waited close to an hour before General Fried could see her. When she stated her mission, the general looked at her quizzically.

'What's Simon Powers up to now?'

Donna had prepared her answer. 'This is strictly confidential, sir. The director was asked by someone important to scrutinize Senator Powers' military record so nothing that reflects poorly on him comes to light because . . .'

'. . . because if Bond gets the nomination and he gets picked for vice president, and if Powers has done anything that could be construed as unethical, illegal or stupid while he was in the army, it could embarrass him and the country. And, of course, this someone important doesn't want that. Isn't that it?'

'You could say so, sir. Can we see Senator Powers' NRPF?'

'Of course you can. The FBI can always get an NRPF, but it takes at least a week.'

'Sir, we need the file as soon as possible. Is there any way I can bypass the process and get the NRPF today?'

General Fried looked at Donna and said, 'The Republican convention is still about a month away. That Bond will get the nomination is far from certain, and his picking Simon for vice president is only a rumour. So why the urgency?'

'Sir, I've an order from the director to get the file as soon as I can.'

General Fried gave her a long, hard look. 'I don't know why the urgency, but if it's that important, I'm going to bend a few rules and do the FBI a special favour. Come back in about an hour and I'll have a printout for you.'

An hour later Donna had the forty-five-page-long NRPF on General Simon Powers. She took it to a cafeteria, sat down with a cup of coffee, and began to read. The content of some of the pages was in such heavy army lingo that, even with her background, she could barely comprehend it. She learnt that Powers had graduated eleventh in his class from West Point and had held a series of assignments in the US and overseas, including serving as military attaché in Paris and as commanding general of an army base for four years in Japan. The file included all kinds of information—promotions, changes in pay grade, station transfers, commendations and a lot of other mundane army data.

She began to go through the file carefully, looking for names. Dan had said anyone might be a lead to someone who knew Powers well. Donna finally spotted what she was looking for when she came to the section on Powers' posting in Japan: a short entry dated twelve years ago that read 'Approval of request for extension of duty as CG at Zama Base, Japan, and retention of Col. William G. Wilson, 0345851, as Exec. Officer.' She had found a middle initial!

This time she googled Wilson's name with his middle initial. But this still didn't help. The White Pages on the Internet didn't use middle initials in the preliminary search, and there were still thousands of listings on the web. She thought for a while, and then called Major Poole. She thanked him for helping her obtain the file, and told him that, after going through it, she had a question: Could Major Poole tell her whether a William G. Wilson, who had been a colonel in Japan just over a decade ago, was still in the army?

Poole was curious, and Donna thought he might be bored too, because he said he'd look it up for her and told her to call back in five minutes. When she called back, the major told her Colonel Wilson must have retired because he couldn't find his name among currently serving officers. He couldn't say when he had retired without getting the colonel's NRPF. Then he asked, 'Will I ever know why you're making these investigations?'

'Sir, if anything comes of it, you'll read about it in the newspapers. But let's hope it doesn't come to that,' said Donna, thanking him again for all his help.

She went back to her laptop and gathered her thoughts. She now knew Wilson was a civilian. What would he likely be doing and where would he be? She had to narrow down her search. Would he be making use of his army experience? She tried adding various words after his name, and 'defence' worked. In a few minutes she came across a William G. Wilson who was the vice president of Raymond–Wilson Public Relations (Defence Contracts), located on K Street.

This had to be the right guy. She read the firm's home page but it was uninformative. It touted how the firm, started fourteen years ago by former Congressman Owen Raymond, rendered 'the most strategic and effective service'. Donna called and asked for an appointment with the vice president. When the receptionist was told it was about an FBI investigation, Donna was immediately put on hold. Several minutes later, the receptionist came back on the line and said that Mr Wilson was tied up with meetings all afternoon, but he could see her on Wednesday, or, if the matter was urgent, at half past five that evening. Donna was elated. She accepted the appointment for later that same day.

She decided she ought to check in with her office and was told a meeting of the team was scheduled for four-thirty. She asked to speak to Dan to find out how important it was for her to be there. When Dan found out about her appointment with Mr Wilson, he asked her to keep it and report to him first thing in the morning.

Wilson was surprised to learn why Donna wanted to see him. 'Why would you want to investigate Powers? I've never known a man who's such a stickler for the rules. You'd think he upheld the moral integrity of the US Army all on his own.'

'Sir, you must've known him well. After all, you served two terms under him.'

'Just my bad luck that he found me an efficient administrative officer! He was one of the reasons I decided to get out of the army and be my own boss. So, tell me, why *is* the FBI investigating him? He's been in the Senate quite a few years now.'

'Sir, I'm sorry, but I can't disclose what the investigation is about. We'd like to know if he had an officer or someone who was very close to him, whom he trusted to the point that you would notice.'

'Hmm . . . I'm really not the right person to ask because I was in charge of administration and had little to do with personnel. But I can tell you that Powers wasn't the kind of man people were close to. Most of his subordinates were afraid of him and had very businesslike relationships with him. And I never had a social relationship with him, never went drinking with him after hours or anything.'

'So you didn't hear any rumours even? There wasn't any odd incident that might suggest he could've had a special interest in someone?'

'It's interesting that you've asked this question. Yes, there was one soldier Powers seemed to have had a special interest in, to the point of asking to have him transferred to Fort Shafter in Hawaii where Powers was posted after Zama. The soldier was so puzzled by this that he talked to me about it in the mess one day. The guy had very high Battery A and B scores and so a high IQ. But he had been busted down from tech sergeant to private first class two or three times for fighting . . . once he even sent a sergeant to the hospital. He just couldn't figure out why Powers wanted to take him along to Hawaii.'

'You don't by any chance remember his name, do you?' asked Donna, hesitantly.

Wilson laughed. 'That was years ago. Under normal circumstances I wouldn't, but the soldier had an extremely odd name: Xavier Y. Zagalo. Zagalo with a "Z". Notice the initials XYZ. Such an odd name!'

Donna was ecstatic at this new lead. She even had a full name. She asked Wilson if he could remember any other incidents or people, but he couldn't, so after another ten minutes, she took her leave. She decided she would go to G-1 again the following day to ask for Zagalo's records after reporting in to Bronfenbrenner.

Donna almost bounced with every step as she left Wilson's building. It was still early. Dan would like a report, if he was still in his office. She phoned him.

Dan answered on the second ring, sounding a little tired. But when Donna reported that she had a name, he perked up at once.

'Look, Donna, can you come in and tell me what you've found? I know it's after hours, but I want to know everything about your investigation and I can fill you in on our meeting too.'

Donna had barely walked in through the door of Dan's office when he asked, 'What is the name of the guy you found out about?'

'Xavier Y. Zagalo. Zagalo with a Z.'

'XYZ? XYZ!' Dan almost shouted.

Donna was startled at his reaction.

'That's him! That's our man!' he looked at her and shouted out in excitement. 'The serial killer, Donna! Let me fill you in on the meeting.' Dan calmed down and reported, 'Sam interviewed Anita Faga and Evelyn Barrington, hoping they would do something to provide us some leads. It worked. A few hours after Anita was interviewed, she called Sam in rather a panic, worried that Senator Powers might somehow be involved in Senator Greenfield's murder.'

'What?' Donna was startled again. 'Why did she think that?'

'Apparently, Sam scared her so she snooped into the senator's private computer to see what she could find. It was nearly empty except for an email to TGreenfield saying Powers wasn't holding any meetings on the dates Greenfield wanted to be out of town. And there were two empty files named XYZ1 and XYZ2! So she called Sam who sent Ben over to retrieve the contents of the hard drive. And we now have evidence that Simon Powers is the man behind the serial killing of Congressional candidates.'

'A senator! What kind of evidence did Sam find?'

'In January, Powers started sending two kinds of emails: one contained fairly detailed descriptions of candidates—we think he must've had a staff member gather information about specific candidates; the second kind always contained just six numbers and five letters. The numbers changed with each email, but the letters are always K-E-K-O-A. These emails were first sent on the tenth of January when Powers sent a description of Kendrick Mitchell, a Democratic candidate for the House in Tucson. A second email was sent the next day with the numbers 113115. Mitchell died, supposedly of a heart attack on the fourteenth, so it was no trick figuring out the numbers 13 and 15 refer to the target dates for killing him.'

'What do you think K-E-K-O-A stands for?' asked Donna.

'That's easy. Powers was no cyber geek. If you google the five letters, one of the first things that come up is the Hawaiian word for warrior or soldier. We think this was a code to let the recipient know who the email was from and that it was an order to kill.'

'And according to Wilson, Powers had Zagalo transferred to Hawaii with him,' said Donna.

'Right. It all fits. Even though there were no emails to Zagalo about a few of the suspicious deaths, it doesn't mean Powers didn't order them. He could've contacted Zagalo by phone or face to face. But the emails we have verify with certainty that Powers was behind the killings of most of the people on our list. Even Roper, the candidate in Clayton, Missouri, who bled to death after a fall in a locked house.'

'How could Powers be responsible for that?' wondered Donna.

'Well, the killer could've inveigled his way into Roper's house when he was alone and then grappled with him or shoved him hard, causing Roper to fall. And the police report said the house was locked but there was no mention of dead bolts or chains, so the killer could've turned an ordinary lock that would catch when the door was shut.'

'And there's more,' Dan continued. 'The guys in Cyber Division have been looking into the bank transfers. We've managed, with the help of our field offices, to confirm that the NAD Forum has been sending money to Republican candidates, including Evelyn Barrington. And because the information we got in the document faxed anonymously from Cambridge, proved to be accurate, we've made headway in establishing how much money was wired to whom and when. But we still don't know everything because we think a lot of names, especially of the companies that received money, are phoney, as is expected in such cases. The only one that's been puzzling us is the regular payment made to an X. Zeiss. From what you've just told me, I can bet now that it's Zagalo using an alias.'

'Since the payments were made from the NAD Forum, Parelli, the treasurer, must be implicated, right?'

'We don't know whether Parelli knew about the killings or whether he was just acting on Powers' orders to transfer the funds. But given all the illegal transfers, we have asked for a warrant for his arrest, though right now we think he's left the country.'

'Do you have enough evidence to arrest Powers?'

'Yes, I'm sure we do,' said Dan. 'But we want to make the case watertight before making a move. Most importantly, we don't know the whereabouts of this killer and we can't let him escape. We need to plan what to do next. Let's see, what else did we discuss . . .'

'What about the Patriots? Do you think they're involved in any way?'

'I can't say for certain, but probably not in the killings. The evidence all points to a single killer who was given his orders directly by Powers. But I'm sure the Patriots have been involved in all kinds of activities financed by the forum. We've also been keeping tabs on Barrington to see what she does. She had what can only have been a hastily arranged meeting with Bond in the lobby of the Hay Adams, the evening of the same day that Sam interviewed her. She can clearly be implicated in the illegal use of the forum's funds, but that's a job for the Federal Election Commission or Treasury.'

'After what Wilson told me about how General Powers was a stickler for rules and so particular about upholding morals, I'm really quite astonished he could be behind all these killings. A murderer himself!?'

'He's an arrogant bastard!' Dan said, not mincing words. 'Sam dug into his background and found out that he likely won his first election by planting pornographic material in his Democratic opponent's house. The local papers and TV and radio stations were all tipped off that the Democrat was a pervert. To prove he was innocent, the candidate took several reporters to his home, and to his astonishment, the photos were right where the tip had said they'd be. This went viral in the media just a few days before the election. It all sounds like a plant. The Democratic candidate was an upright and principled citizen, a widower and a grandfather. But his reputation was ruined and he lost the election to Powers.'

Dan yawned. 'OK, let's call it a night. I'm exhausted. You must be too. You did a terrific job today, Donna. I'm glad you're on our team. Now, we all have to put our heads together and figure out how to catch the killer.'

Anita was worried, so worried she couldn't sleep. The sleepless nights had started last Thursday, the day she'd made an impetuous decision to call Agent Sam Ogden to find out what Senator Powers had deleted from his computer. The more she thought about it, the more aware she was that her decision was foolhardy, made under the duress of strong apprehension, fear really, that her Simon could be directly involved in the death of Senator Greenfield. And possibly in the deaths of other candidates as well. But tonight she was worried about herself.

By asking the FBI to retrieve deleted emails and messages from the senator's computer, she had opened the door to an investigation of the NAD Forum, its funds and the people who managed it. No matter what the FBI found in the senator's computer, the forum would without doubt be vigorously investigated now that Parelli had scarpered. And there was all that money that Parelli had transferred for her into a Swiss account. She had a growing feeling that she too ought to disappear.

A year ago she had dreamt about becoming Mrs Powers. The wife of a powerful senator or perhaps even the wife of the vice president! Heady stuff for a girl who had worked her way through the University of New Hampshire. She had delighted in her dream, though now she thought she had little chance of competing with Karen McPherson. However, she was certain the professor wouldn't have anything more to do with Powers the minute his reputation was sullied by NAD Forum scandal, which was sure to break sooner or later.

Anita had spent sleepless hours on Thursday night, dithering over what to do next. By Friday morning, she had decided it was time to make herself scarce. Powers was out of town, so she had gone to his Senate office and had cleared out all the private papers from her desk, leaving behind the personal items on top—her coffee mug, paperweight and photos, so it would look as if she planned to return. She left the office early to go to her bank where she withdrew five thousand dollars.

By Friday night she had worked herself into a frenzy. She knew all about Powers' illegal monetary dealings, but she couldn't quite see him as a murderer. She spent the weekend in nervous activity, cleaning out her apartment, donating large quantities of clothes and household goods to charity and packing up all her books. She told friends she was coming down with something and cancelled plans to meet them. On Monday morning, she called the assistant to Powers' chief-of-staff and told her she was taking some personal leave while the senator was out of town. Then, she mailed six boxes of books and papers to her mother in New Hampshire, and arranged for her post to be forwarded there as well. By eleven in the morning, she had cleared her furnished apartment of all of her personal belongings and was on her way to Boston. She spent Monday night at the pied-à-terre in Cambridge that Powers had rented for her to use. Yesterday, Tuesday, she had packed up the few personal items she kept there and closed her local bank account.

All along, she wondered when she would hear from the FBI. Finally yesterday, at midday, she had received the promised call from Agent Ogden, who clearly thought she was still in DC, but he hadn't told her anything of significance. She was sure he had been prevaricating.

'Perez managed to retrieve the deleted data from the files, but much of it is in code and we haven't managed to make much sense of it yet,' he had said. 'When we figure out what's going on, I'll tell you more. At this stage, I can't say more than thank you. I hope you understand. We really do appreciate your contacting us.'

She spent a second night in the apartment in Cambridge. Though she had gone to bed early, she couldn't fall asleep. Suddenly her mobile rang. Her bedside clock said two. Who could be calling her in the wee hours? She saw Simon's name flash on the screen. Powers spoke to her rapidly in a groggy voice she hadn't heard before. She wondered whether he was drunk.

'Anita, the bastard dumped me after all the money the forum gave his campaign. I'm going to hibernate in my Honolulu condo for a while. No nosey press, no idiotic interviews. Get me a plane ticket to Honolulu, tell the condominium manager to get the damn place ready for me, and have someone pick me up at the airport. Got it?' he said almost in one breath.

'Simon, what do you mean the bastard dumped you?' Anita wanted to corroborate her hunch. She guessed Bond had told Powers he wouldn't be his running mate even if Bond got the nomination, but she had to make certain.

'Bond the bastard! Who else could it be?' yelled Powers, slurring his words. 'He called me three hours ago to inform me he can no longer consider me for vice president. He said the FBI knows the forum's been sending millions of dollars to candidates in violation of a bunch of laws and he can't afford to have me anywhere near him any more, let alone put me on the ticket. An absolute coward! He couldn't tell me to my face even though we are staying at the same hotel. He had to do it over the phone! I've got to clear my head. You got everything I told you to do? Call me back when you've made the arrangements.'

Before she could utter a word, the line went dead. She sat up in bed. So the unravelling had begun. It was just like him to call in the dead of night and take her for granted.

Now she was wide awake. So many emotions played in her head that she couldn't think clearly. She knew how badly Powers wanted to be a heartbeat away from the presidency and how hard he had been working to raise money. She even felt sorry for him. At the same time, she knew she had to face reality. Her decision was irrevocable: she wasn't going to stick around, even if Powers still wanted her. In any case, he could well wind up in prison. And so could she! She shivered at the thought.

Remembering what Parelli had said, she quickly assured herself that the chance was slim of the FBI ever finding out she was the same Annette Favia who had received nearly two and a half million dollars from the forum, transferred to a Swiss bank account held in the same name.

She could still recall what Parelli had said when she had first broached the idea of skimming money from the forum—she knew he was already doing the same.

'Unless you want too much, it's no problem, Anita. We've no audits and no receipts. Powers and Jameson are too busy to worry about the books I keep. Besides, senators are neophytes in the arcane art of moving money. Getting ourselves a bit of a nest egg is a sensible thing to do. Sure, I'll set up an account for you in Switzerland. It'll be in Zug, because the banks there don't ask awkward questions.' And then he'd given her a sly smile. 'You don't rat on me and I won't rat on you.'

Then, in early April, he had handed her a counterfeit passport in the name of Annette Favia. 'You'll need this to withdraw money from your account,' he had said.

She would now follow Powers' orders one last time before she disappeared. She didn't know where the despicable treasurer had gone, but her choice of destination was Switzerland. She had no idea how long she would stay, but the country was full of foreigners and she could make do with English.

She yawned a little, while waiting for her computer to start up. Then she booked a first-class ticket for Powers from Kansas City International to Honolulu with an overnight in Phoenix. He wouldn't be happy, but there weren't any direct flights. She booked him into a hotel in Phoenix as Mr McDonald. She smiled as she thought how annoyed Powers would be at this choice of name. She had his e-ticket sent to his official email account. Because of the six-hour time lag, she couldn't make the arrangements for Honolulu until later in the morning.

When she woke up at nine, she rang Powers to tell him he had an early afternoon flight to Phoenix. The conversation was very brief, as she had clearly woken him up.

She made some coffee and then her mobile rang. She thought it might be Powers again, but didn't recognize the number.

'Miss Faga, this is Jun Taira. We met at Senator Powers' birthday party in March. Remember?'

'Of course, I do. And your lovely wife Tomi. Are you in Washington?'

'No, I'm calling from Tokyo. I wanted to get in touch with Senator Powers, but his office said he is away. Since my business concerns the NAD Forum, I called the forum but I was told Mr Parelli is unavailable. So, I got your number. I'm sorry to bother you, but could you give the senator a message from me?'

'Certainly. He's in Kansas City and I'll be talking to him in a few hours.'

'Thank you. My message is confidential, but I know you are the senator's private secretary. Please tell him I've discussed with my brother the sizeable donation the senator asked me to make to the forum. Most regrettably, I've decided I must forego the privilege. I know the senator will be disappointed because he is working so hard to support Mr Bond. I hope to have a chance soon to apologize to him in person for this decision.'

'I'll tell him, Mr Taira. I know he'll be disappointed but I'm sure he'll understand. Thank you for calling.'

Anita packed up and was soon en route to New Hampshire. When she reached the outskirts of Manchester, she stopped, looked at her watch and realized she could now make the Honolulu arrangements for it would be morning there. She called the manager of the senator's condo only to find it had been rented out for a month. He was supposed to inform her whenever there were tenants. Luckily, she found a unit available in the Kahala Beach Apartments located next to the five-star Kahala Hotel. She arranged to rent it for a month and to have Mr McDonald picked up at the Honolulu airport.

Then, she made her last phone call to Powers. He still sounded a little worse for wear. Deciding he didn't have to know about the Japanese congressman's call, she gave him the details of the arrangements she had made and reminded him he was booked as Mr McDonald both in Phoenix and Hawaii. She quickly rang off before he could make any new demands.

Finally, before going on to her mother's, she stopped at a coffee shop with Internet service and booked a business class seat to Zurich for Annette Flavia on Sunday, 17 July. Powers and his lawyers could deal with the two apartments he had rented for her. They were his problem now. She would tell her mother that her job with Powers had come to an end and she wanted an extended vacation before she took up another one. Her mother wouldn't ask questions; she never had. As she left the coffee shop, she felt exhilarated, yet a little scared.

✪

As Anita arrived at her mother's in Vermont, the phone rang in Bess' apartment in New York.

'Hi, Bess.'

'Oh! Peri. Are you back in Boston? I thought you're going to stay in Paris for a while.'

'I *am* in Paris and will be in France for the foreseeable future. Or even longer.'

'Even longer? Sounds like you're going to become French.'

'Close to it! Alex asked me to marry him and I said *oui*.'

Bess was not surprised at all and very pleased.

'Wonderful! Congratulations! So, when's the wedding?'

'Sometime in September, here in Paris. Alex wants to go to Côte d'Azur for our honeymoon—his uncle has a large apartment on the shore. Can you and Nick come for the wedding?

'I'd love to! I'll talk to Nick and my boss and see if we can arrange it.'

'That would be great. But Bess, the reason I called was I've been wondering why there's been no news about the NAD Forum. It's so long since we sent those documents to the FBI. The only news I get in Paris is about conferences the forum is holding and my father still being Governor Bond's choice for VP as he seems to have a chance of getting nominated. Have you heard anything?'

'Nick and I have been talking about the same thing. There's no news here either about the FBI or Treasury or the Federal Election Commission starting an investigation. Nick's guess is that the lists we sent are hot potatoes politically, so the authorities might be investigating the forum on the QT. They don't want a big media circus a month before the Republican convention.'

'I hope Nick is right. But if the authorities don't want to indict the forum . . . my father . . . don't you think they ought to do it before Governor Bond gets nominated and puts my father on the ticket?'

'I agree. Let's see what happens during the next few weeks. If nothing happens soon, we'll have to think of something else.'

'Like what? What else can we do?'

'We may have to give what you sent to the FBI to newspapers or TV. But that would be our last resort. Call me again next Friday and we'll decide what to do if nothing happens by then. OK?'

'OK. I'll wait till then.'

'Congratulations again on your engagement! Give our best to Alex. *Au revoir.*'

Congresswoman Barrington picked up the phone on the first ring.

'Brad?'

'Yes. I hope this is safe enough for you. I asked you to go to my campaign manager's house because you were so worried about your phone being tapped the last time we talked.'

'What do you want to tell me? Your secretary said it was urgent.'

'In the past couple of days, a senator and two congressmen running for re-election told me they had been quizzed rather pointedly by the FBI about getting money from the forum. They were also asked whether they in turn had been giving any of that money to local Patriot groups who they suspect could be involved in serious crimes. I wanted to talk to you as soon as I could to tell you what I've told these people. And I want to advise you to get someone to say yes, your campaign got money from the forum but you weren't told about it. I persuaded the guy who handles all my campaign funds to say that, after discussing it with my campaign manager, the two of them decided to accept the money without my knowledge. If anyone prods further, they'll say they wanted to protect me, to make sure I didn't know anything about our campaign accepting any money that might be illegal.'

'They could get prosecuted, Brad. And the FBI is unlikely to believe them . . .'

'If they get into any legal trouble, I've promised to pay them a couple of million dollars each. No one gets a long jail term for violation of federal campaign finance laws. So they've agreed to take the risk for two million. The FBI will have a hard time proving I personally knew about the money from the forum. And to show I'm not in bed with Powers, I've made it clear that he is not being considered for VP.'

'OK, I'll take your advice. But where will I get two million dollars?'

'Evelyn, I've known you for a couple of decades. Don't talk nonsense. You've skimmed more than that from what the forum has been sending you.'

The congresswoman didn't respond and changed the topic.

'Brad, I'm worried. I've heard that a lot of the super delegates might vote for Higgins. You're being accused of being too close to the Patriots in your policies.'

'I'm very aware of all that. With the FBI nosing around and the papers and the pundits saying what they are saying, I might not get the nomination at all. Then I won't be President, and you won't be Secretary of Commerce, and our careers won't end with a bang.'

'Brad, let's not get overly pessimistic yet,' Evelyn said, trying to undo the grey mood she had set. 'You still have a shot at the nomination. Higgins is moving too far to the middle. In politics, nothing is certain. Let's batten down the hatches and stay optimistic. Telling Simon to get lost is a good start!'

'I'm going to do all I can to win this election. We have to realize the spirit of the Honolulu Pact.'

A few minutes after six, Dan Bronfenbrenner, Sam Ogden and Ben Perez met in the small conference room of the FBI headquarters for an emergency meeting Dan had called.

'What's up?' asked Sam, who was about to leave for the day. He was tired and hungry and worn out by the long days working on the task force.

'I thought you should know what Ben told me yesterday about some phone conversations Anita Faga had since Friday with several people, including a few with Powers who sounded drunk. Colin Yates got them taped. What's a bit surprising is how few calls she's made—I suspect she's either lying low or using her computer to communicate with people.'

'What did Powers want? And why has it taken all day to let me know?' Sam was irritated.

'Sorry, Sam,' said Ben apologetically. 'We don't have enough people to keep someone on the job all night, and Colin didn't hear the conversations until midday.'

'My apologies too, Sam,' Dan added. 'I didn't call the meeting until I had an idea to try out on both of you. Ben, tell Sam what you found out.'

'Powers told Faga that the "bastard Bond" had ditched him and he wanted to go into hiding. He wanted her . . . rather ordered her . . . to get him a ticket to Honolulu where he plans to go underground for a while at the condo he owns there; it turned out it wasn't available, so he's going to be staying at a rented place in the Kahala Beach Apartments complex.'

Ben summarized the conversations Anita had had with Powers and the call she took from Taira.

When Ben finished, Dan said, 'I've been thinking, and I've concluded this gives us a golden opportunity to catch XYZ or Xavier Yoshio Zagalo.

I managed to get his middle name out of G-1 at the Pentagon and a lot of background information too. We know he was born and raised in Honolulu and he was posted at Zama and Fort Shafter when Powers was there. We don't know where he is now, but if he's the X. Zeiss who's been getting regular payments, he's most likely based in or near San Francisco. My plan is to send an email to Zagalo from Powers asking to meet him in Honolulu. We have the code Powers used in his email to XYZ. When Zagalo shows up for the meeting, we'll nab both men.'

Sam looked thoughtful. 'You think he'll show up? Powers has been sending all these emails to him because they don't meet. Now, suddenly, if Powers wants to meet him in Honolulu, won't Zagalo be suspicious? I would.'

'He could be. So the email we send must sound like an order from a general to a soldier. And we'll send it before it becomes national news that Powers has been dumped and has gone underground. If we phrase the message carefully and add the code, the plan just might work. I've already called Frank Nguyen in our Honolulu field office to alert him about Powers' whereabouts, and I asked him to tell me what he could about the location. Frank said the condo's in the posh part of the city, right on the ocean, located between a luxury hotel and a golf course. It's on a dead-end street—easy to monitor all traffic, pedestrian and vehicular.'

'Could work,' Sam said aloud, having mulled this over in his head. 'If I were Powers, who now knows the forum's finances are being investigated, I'd even be worried that the FBI might get wind of my ties with Zagalo. In short, the last thing I'd want to do is to meet Zagalo. But what Powers thinks doesn't matter—it's what Zagalo thinks and does. All right. We've got the code. Let's send the email. If we're lucky, Zagalo will show up and we'll nab both. Cleaner to establish a direct tie between the two rather than just have emails.'

'Good. I'm glad you agree,' said Dan. 'I have to clear this with the director —I have an appointment with him after we finish here. If he has no objections, we'll send the message and I'll fly out to Honolulu. I want to make sure there won't be any slip-ups. Along with Frank's team in Honolulu, I'll also get Lisa Higashiguchi of the HPD, who's been in on this almost since the start.'

Then, looking squarely at Sam, Dan said, 'Sam, after that bombing in Spokane, I know how badly you want to get your hands on Zagalo. But I need you to stay here. I want you to take charge at this end while I'm away. We've got to get ready for the trial of Powers and Zagalo. And I want you to get in touch with the Frankfurt police about the final autopsy report on Senator Greenfield. It could be very important.'

Sam didn't hide his disappointment at not being in on the arrests, but he responded quietly, 'Fine. I understand.'

Then Dan turned to Ben and said, 'Make sure you have a tape of the conversation between Faga and Taira. We now have the additional evidence to show that Powers was soliciting money from a foreigner—strictly illegal.'

'Oh! And Ben, this reminds me . . . the Wessel tape that was turned over to us? Let's make sure we send it with the Faga–Taira tape to Justice and the Federal Election Commission.'

'What's the Wessel tape, Dan?' asked Sam. 'You've never mentioned it in any of our meetings.'

A little chagrined, Dan explained, 'We were sent a taped conversation Powers had with Ernst Wessel, Sr, the president of one of the largest grain traders in the country, and his son Ernst Wessel, Jr. On tape, Powers can be clearly heard saying the forum was rerouting money to Republican candidates. He even offers to change a law to allow for a cut in taxes on grain trading during a Bond administration in exchange for a ten-million-dollar donation to the forum. Wessel's son, who claims to have taped the conversion without his father's knowledge, turned it over to the Federal Election Commission in mid-April. A Republican member of the commission didn't like what the young Wessel said on tape about the Republicans, and about Bond in particular, so he just sat on the files.'

'So how did you come by it?' asked Sam.

'At a meeting at the end of June, a Democratic member of the commission learned about the tape, listened to it and sent it immediately to the FBI. I heard about it at an inter-divisional meeting but didn't think anything of it until we got that anonymous fax from Cambridge. It's more evidence of the illegal operation Powers has been running.'

'Looks like the noose is tightening around their necks,' Sam said with some satisfaction. 'So if the director approves our operation, when is Powers going to request this meeting with Zagalo?'

'Well, today is Wednesday. According to the phone call Faga made to Powers about his travel arrangements, he will arrive in Honolulu tomorrow. That's Thursday. Let's have him send the email to Zagalo on Friday—Zagalo should read it over the weekend. We'll have the office in Honolulu verify Powers has arrived and is in the condo. It may take Zagalo a couple of days to get to Honolulu, assuming he is in or near San Francisco. So let's ask for a meeting on Tuesday night. We want to make it seem as though Powers wants to meet Zagalo urgently, so Zagalo will go as soon as he can, without having time to think about it. I can leave on Saturday so I'll be able to see that everything is set up well before Powers and Zagalo meet on Tuesday.'

'What time do you want to set the appointment for?' enquired Ben.

'Let's say ten o'clock at night—late enough so no one will get hurt if Zagalo goes berserk.'

'And we've got to remember to end the message with K-E-K-O-A,' added Ben.

'I'm sure the Hawaiians would be unhappy about how that word is being misused!' remarked Sam wryly.

The terms of the Honolulu Pact were indelibly etched in his memory, as was the incident that had brought it about. His agreement with the general would never have come about had he not killed the bouncer at that bar in Japan. If he'd been caught, it could have been a charge of first-degree murder. He'd killed the bouncer intentionally, planning how in advance. But the bastard had deserved it.

He was in Kim's one-room flat the night she'd staggered in at half past two in the morning, her right eye swollen shut and the left side of her upper lip caked with congealed blood. He often waited for her to return from her weekend job as a bar hostess, but never before had anything like this happened. He had been shocked.

Kim had dropped to the floor wailing. He had moved over to comfort her, but she had squirmed out of his reach.

'Kim! Damn it! Who did this to you?'

Tears rolled down her cheeks, each tear reflecting the light of the naked sixty-watt bulb hanging from the ceiling.

'Toshi got drunk as usual,' she whispered through her sobs. 'Then Mama-san left early and asked me to close up after the last customer left. He was waiting for me. He . . . he . . . he took me. I fought like a wild cat but it was no use. He's too big and strong.'

'What?! Toshi the bouncer? That stupid ox? I knew he hankered after you . . . but how could he?'

'Well, he did. I feel so dirty. I have to take a shower.'

'You've got to call the police, Kim. He shouldn't get away with . . .'

'There's no point, Zabi. The police won't do anything. When the cops hear a stupid nineteen-year-old bar hostess say a yakuza raped her, they'll just laugh.'

'Kim, look at me. You're not a stupid bar hostess. You're a smart girl. You work at the PX all week and at the bar only on weekends to earn a little extra. Don't you ever say you're stupid. If you don't go to the police, I'll teach the swine a lesson. How dare he . . .'

'Don't even think about it, Zabi. He is as mean as a snake and a lot bigger than you. Just forget it.'

But he hadn't forgotten it. No one could do that to his Kimiko and get away with it.

Two days later, he had gone to the bar and called Toshi out to the back alley. Before the bouncer knew what the American GI wanted, he had stabbed him with his knife.

The Japanese yakuza, whose short-sleeved shirt exposed the tattoos covering both his arms, collapsed, clutching the knife plunged deep into his chest. He made a croaking sound with a gurgle, sounding more like an animal than a human. His body hit the ground with a thud. His arms and legs writhed and then stopped. All in a surprisingly short time. Zabi had pulled his knife out of the man's chest and wiped the blood off it, using the dead man's shirt. He remembered looking down at the body with disgust.

The very efficient Japanese police had interrogated everyone who had been in the bar that evening. They had quickly deduced that the killer was a steely-eyed American GI who frequented the bar, always asking Kim to wait on him, and someone who, they were told, spoke 'pretty good Japanese'. Kim had kept mum except to confirm that he was called Zabi—she had admitted this because she knew others in the bar had heard her call him by that name. So the police had come to the base looking for a steely-eyed soldier whose first or last name was Zabi and who spoke some Japanese.

But they didn't get anywhere in their search. The provost marshall made available the roster of all two and a half thousand soldiers at the base, but it didn't list anyone whose first or last name was Zabi or anything similar. When the local head of the Japanese police demanded that his officers be allowed to see and question all the soldiers, the provost marshall refused, saying that the commanding general wouldn't allow it because it would take days and completely disrupt the work of the base. He had told the police to come back when they knew which soldier they wanted to arrest, when they had his full name and some hard evidence, such as a witness to the murder. The Japanese police never returned because they had more pressing things to do than finding the murderer of a bouncer who, they quickly discovered, was part of the underworld and had a long record of serious crimes.

But he hadn't known at the time that the police had given up the search for Zabi the killer. He had waited to be called in by his commanding officer but the call never came.

Exactly ten days after the murder, he was surprised to be told to report to the commanding general's office. He was even more surprised to hear what the general had to say.

'At ease, Sergeant. Let me first make something clear. Since 1945, our soldiers, officers, their families and American civilians have committed a little more than twenty-four thousand serious crimes in occupied Japan—rapes, murders, hit-and-ran accidents . . . the list is long. Understandably, the Japanese are screaming their heads off, demanding we do something to curb these crimes. I'm most happy to oblige. So I'll make sure your good deed of getting rid of a worthless rapist doesn't add to crimes committed by Americans. If you're wondering how I know you're the one the police is after, Major Mike Shimabukuro, our very ingenious provost marshall who is fluent in Japanese, figured out that Zabi was short for Zabieru, the Japanese pronunciation for Xavier. When the major showed me your personnel record—your 201 file—it was easy for us to connect the dots. So, don't bother denying you killed the bouncer.'

He remained silent, surprised at how easily the major had caught him out.

The general went on.

'Sergeant, I've read your 201 file very carefully. You seem to have an interesting file. While your Battery A and B test scores are very high, for a smart soldier, you've got one of the lousiest records I've seen! You've been busted twice and even got kicked out of Officer Candidate School.'

He had wondered what the general was going to say next, but he had just dismissed him abruptly. Zabi heard nothing more from him until almost a month later, just after he received a surprise order telling him he would be rotated to Fort Shafter on Oahu in less than a month. A day or two after that, the commanding general had called him into his office again and asked him to do a favour for him.

'Robert Nakada of our transportation company is being accused of the attempted rape of a sixteen-year-old Japanese high-school student. Nakada says he met her at a coffee shop almost a month ago and one night last week they were kissing on a park bench. Suddenly, a cop showed up and she looked at him and screamed. The cop turned out to be her father's friend, Detective Oda from the Zama Police Department. The detective told the chief of the ZPD that the young girl said Nakada had attempted to rape her. He asked the chief for permission to come to the base to arrest him. The chief called me and told me that he personally doesn't think there is enough evidence to prosecute Nakada, but under the current situation he doesn't think it politic to stop the detective from going ahead with the arrest. Here's where I need your help. I want you to discourage the detective from trying to arrest Nakada.'

He had understood what the general wanted, but he didn't know how to go about it, so he had asked Kim to help him. She got the detective's address and also found out that forty-four-year-old Oda had a black belt in judo and a family consisting of a daughter from a first marriage and a second wife who had recently borne him a son.

He had spent a couple of days patrolling Oda's house in the western part of Zama and then late one night he had stolen into the house. He didn't have to break in because it was so hot that the family had left their sliding doors open to the night air. He had gone into the child's room and quietly done the deed.

He knew the family would see the long looped rope over the baby's head the next morning and would find the attached note he had managed to write in childlike Japanese: *Nakada o taihosuruto, anata no kazoku ga taihen kiken desu*—his translation of 'If you arrest Nakada, your family will be in grave danger.'

He hadn't made a sound, and had got out of the house the same way he had come in. He had seen no one as he left the yard and walked away, and knew if someone had seen him, they wouldn't think he was an American soldier as he was dressed like a Japanese.

The general had never mentioned this matter again, but he knew that Nakada hadn't been arrested. Just before he went to Fort Shafter, he heard Nakada had been transferred to a base in Korea.

He had arrived at Fort Shafter in Honolulu just a few days before General Powers took command of the same base. There, his relationship with the general had gradually evolved. First, there had been an implicit understanding that he would do whatever the general asked of him in exchange for a choice of jobs on the base within the military occupational specialities he had qualified for—medic and ordnance. He usually chose working in demolition because he liked playing with explosives.

The general hadn't asked him to do much. His most memorable duty was to get rid of a demanding mistress for him. He smiled as he remembered her reaction when, after a carefully planned exchange of words, he had demonstrated the power of hydrochloric acid (a bottle of which he had purloined from the base machine shop) by burning a gaping hole through the carpet in her car. She had never appeared again.

He remembered how, some months after he had come to Fort Shafter, one incident had made him eternally indebted to the general. He had befriended a specialist in demolition who had done two tours in Iraq and who was teaching him how to make and diffuse improvised explosive devices. One night when the two had been drinking together, the inebriated sergeant said he reminded him of an incompetent Iraqi who had blown himself up when making an IED. He had flown off the handle at the insult. What started out as a squabble had ended up in blows. He caught the sergeant off balance with a hard jab to his jaw, and the man had fallen hard, crashing his skull against the metal edge of his bed. The man had died almost instantly. So he had killed the sergeant, albeit unintentionally.

Even though he had taken care to erase his fingerprints from the glasses they were drinking from and every other place else he thought he had touched, the authorities got on to him and started to grill him. He claimed he was nowhere near the sergeant's room at the time of his death because he was running a personal errand in town for the general. The general confirmed his statement, giving him an alibi the authorities dared not question. He knew right then that henceforth he would have to carry out anything the general asked of him. He now owed the general far more than after he killed the yakuza in Japan because he had killed an American in Hawaii, and there was no statute of limitations for murder in the US, unlike the fifteen-year statute of limitations in Japan.

The general never said a word about this incident either, but within a few months, the implicit understanding had become what the general called the Honolulu Pact. The general had spelt out the terms of the pact and they had shaken hands on it—the first and only time they had ever shaken hands. 'Sergeant, you do everything I ask of you, and I'll guarantee you the best of everything even after you leave the army. But once you're out of the army, we'll NEVER meet.'

After both of them had left the army, he had helped Powers win the Senate election, and continued to carry out numerous questionable jobs, secretly amused at what the general—now senator—asked him to do each time, so contradictory to his upright public reputation. And then, last autumn, the general had broken the agreement, just the once, when he had met with him secretly in Honolulu and given him a series of assignments to be executed over the coming year. The pact had become extremely lucrative. Since January he had been paid generously to cover the expenses of each assignment plus a bonus of fifty thousand dollars on the successful completion of each. The jackpot was the promise of two million dollars after he finished his last assignment just before the coming election in November.

With a smile, he thought of the nearly one million dollars in a bank in San Francisco, most of it from the bonuses he'd received since the beginning of the year. And in November he would get the two million. What a great life he could have with three million dollars!

Today, he had slept in till past ten—he was sleeping too much, to catch up on the months of sleep lost on tense assignments and because he was slightly bored since his last assignment in Frankfurt. He missed the excitement and the challenges. So he lolled round the flat until noon and then went to San Francisco to see Phuong, a Vietnamese barmaid who reminded him of Kim. He spent the afternoon in her dingy room and then drank far too much at her bar, finally returning to his place in Sausalito late in the evening.

He hadn't checked his email all day, decided it was better to do it before he turned in, and logged in on his phone.

There was a message from the general!

Meet me at #4022 Kahala Beach Apartments, 4999 Kahala Avenue, Honolulu at 2200, Tuesday, July 19. Ring 8537 at Bldg #4 for access.
KEKOA

He stared at the email for a long time, baffled by why the general would break a crucial part of the Honolulu Pact. Why did they have to meet? But, then again, the general had broken the pact once last autumn. Perhaps, this was equally important.

Something bothered him. The message didn't sound quite like the general. He would have expected 'rendezvous point at' instead of 'meet me at'. On the other hand, it did say '2200' instead of '10 p.m.'. The email had to be from the general. No one else knew this email address. And then the message did end with KEKOA, their secret code.

He sat back and continued to ponder over why the general would want to break the pact and meet. What was so important? And why in Honolulu of all places? As far as he knew from the news, the general was busy campaigning for Governor Bond somewhere on the mainland. He figured meeting at night would make them less likely to be noticed. But why were they to meet at a condo in Kahala instead of at the general's own condo on the Gold Coast?

He couldn't help wondering whether the general had decided to get him arrested by the Honolulu Police when he showed up. But he could get him arrested here in Sausalito. So that didn't make sense either. Then, if he *were* arrested, he could easily implicate the general. He was certain his bank in San Francisco could identify which banks had been wiring money to his account and the police could trace this to the general and his organization.

He considered the general being under duress, coerced by someone, the FBI perhaps or the US marshalls. But this would mean the authorities had somehow learnt about all the general's operations and had made him send this email. This too was inconceivable as he was sure he would have got wind of it earlier.

Even less likely was the possibility of the authorities having somehow found out everything, without the general's knowledge. So they had sent the email to catch him. But if the FBI had unravelled his identity, they would likely send in agents to take him by surprise and arrest him at home—the whole plot seemed far too complicated to be real.

He was getting nowhere. He had to decide what to do.

He tried to focus his thoughts. Should he go meet the general? There could be good reason for his wanting to see him despite their pact. Or should he ignore the email and clear out of Sausalito as soon as possible? He didn't know where he would go. If he were going to Japan, perhaps he ought to go via Hawaii in case the meeting was not a trap.

He went to the kitchen and made himself a cheese sandwich. As he chewed slowly, he came to a firm decision. He had to know what was going on, and this meant he had to go to Honolulu.

He searched online, found an economy seat on a morning flight to Honolulu for the following day and booked it. He chose a window seat almost at the back of the plane. He wanted to be lost in the crowd and also see who else might be on the flight. Then he reserved a room at the Hilton Hawaiian Village, the largest hotel in Honolulu with over three thousand rooms. He would be just one among thousands of guests.

He packed quickly, taking clothing for Hawaii and Japan. He took both his passports: a legitimate one in his own name and a second issued to Aaron Zobel, the one he had used to go to Frankfurt. He had six credit cards and IDs in various names and a little over ten thousand dollars in cash. If the general had been coerced into sending that email, the credit cards could be dangerous to use. He put almost two thousand dollars in all in his many pockets and his wallet and stashed the rest in a travel money belt as he often did on assignments. Then, he carefully packed his carry-on with other essentials, checking and rechecking every detail, and went to bed.

Sunday morning he was up early because of the three-hour time difference between California and Hawaii. He went to the Rainbow Lanai for a buffet breakfast, dressed like a tourist and wearing sunglasses. He had been watchful from the minute he stepped off the plane, but he didn't think he had seen anyone—policeman or FBI agent—tailing him.

At the Hilton, he had checked in under the name of Donald Zingaro, using a California driving licence and a credit card issued in the same name. He had been given a double room on the eighth floor of the Rainbow Tower with a commanding view of the ocean and Diamond Head to the far left. He had spent the afternoon exploring the area and relaxing, and then had *mahi-mahi*, his favourite island fish, for dinner. It felt odd to be here in Waikiki like a tourist instead of the local boy he had been until he enlisted in the army.

Now, after a good night's sleep and a filling breakfast, he was ready to investigate the condo where the general had asked to meet him. For this, he rented an inconspicuous black Toyota.

He drove round Diamond Head to the Kahala area, and near the end of Kahala Avenue, just past the Waialae Beach Park and the neighbouring country club, he found the gated condo complex with its quartet of four-storey-high buildings. He slowly drove past the entrance, noting the booth for the security guards, next to which two uniformed guards were chatting.

There was no place to park on this narrow street, so he turned round and went back to the parking lot at the beach park. Many locals were lugging barbecue equipment, swimming gear, ice chests, snorkelling equipment and even chairs to the beach for a Sunday outing. He found a spot to leave the car, and, donning his dark sunglasses and baseball cap, he walked back to the condo complex and asked one of the guards if he could walk round the complex. Not unless he was a resident or a guest, he was told. Unwilling to mention the general's name, he thanked the guard and walked on towards the adjacent luxury hotel. Before he even got there, he found an employee directing traffic, keeping out sightseers. He waved a greeting at the man, went on to the hotel, walked into the lobby as if he was staying there, and then down to the lower level and out onto the beach.

To the left of the hotel's property was the golf course with greens that came down to the waters' edge. So he turned right and walked back towards the beach park, past the condo complex and the clubhouse belonging to the golf course. As he passed the condo complex, he saw a young security guard making his rounds. The complex was surrounded by a high iron fence, easy to climb over, but certainly not with all the people round. He circled back through the beach park and down Kahala Avenue to the golf course and stood in front of the shop outside as if waiting for someone. As far as he could tell in the quarter of an hour he had been there, the security guards mainly functioned as traffic police and errand boys. They all seemed to be bored rent-a-cops, armed with nothing more than their walkie-talkies.

This recce was getting him nowhere, so he drove to the Kahala Mall located a mile away and bought swimming trunks, a subdued blue Aloha shirt and rubber thong sandals. After a quick lunch at the California Pizza Kitchen, he returned to the park, changed into his new clothes in the toilet and spent the rest of the afternoon examining the complex from the ocean side. He found a stone bench on the short promontory between the condo complex and the hotel. The bench was shaded by a tree and hidden by chest-high shrubs from passers-by, giving him a comfortable place from which he could survey the sidewalk in front of the complex.

In the two hours he spent on the beach, he saw five wedding parties, numerous passers-by and the guards on their rounds. He was quick to note that the guards were better than he had first thought: they didn't follow the same routes and made their rounds at random times. In all the time he spent there, he never caught sight of the general, and couldn't determine which of the buildings was no. 4 where the general was staying.

He decided he had to get inside, which proved easier than he had thought. A large key opened the gate to the pool area, but often a couple of groups would enter at the same time. He followed a man with three children; when the father opened the gate, he entered with them, saying, 'Thanks, my wife has the key.' The father joked, 'No problem, just so long as you're not a burglar!'

He walked round the pool, up a low flight of stairs and came out into what looked like a tropical park with a *koi* pond running through it between the middle buildings. When he got to the mid-point of this narrow garden, he saw that all four buildings were connected by a walkway running through them. He now knew the lay of the land and how to enter the complex easily at night, but he had no intention of meeting the general there and getting trapped inside one of the fences.

After a long swim, he returned to his hotel and had a Japanese meal at the Hilton's Benihana. The restaurant was full of a noisy group of Japanese tourists, and no one paid him any attention. By eight he was back in his room. He went out onto his lanai and began to brood over what he ought to do next.

He had already decided he wouldn't meet the general inside the complex. He also decided it would be best to meet him before the time mentioned in the email, in case this was a trap. It had to be tomorrow night. The safest place was somewhere in the open from where it would be relatively easy for him to flee if required. He finally settled on the beach park at midnight.

But how would he get this message to the general? If this was a trap, sending an email would tell the authorities exactly how to catch him.

And then he hit upon an idea. He would go over to the Kahala Hotel's flower shop in the morning and ask to have a flower arrangement delivered to the general by early afternoon. He would enclose a gift card with a message:

Please meet me at 2400 tonight at picnic tables in beach park west of golf club. KEKOA

He knew he was taking a big chance, maybe the biggest in his life, but he just couldn't think of an alternative if he wanted to see Powers to find out what was really going on.

Lisa couldn't sit still. She had been in a state of high anticipation since Friday when Captain Kalani had called her into his office as soon as she arrived at work. He had told her about the FBI setting a snare for the serial killer and that she was to be part of the action.

'Here!? In Honolulu? When?' Lisa asked, open-mouthed.

The captain had laughed at her reaction. 'Yes, here, in Honolulu. It's been set up for Tuesday night in Kahala. The FBI wants you and two men from HPD to be part of the team. On Tuesday, they will also need our uniformed men. The head of the task force has specifically asked for you because of your earlier involvement in the Sasaki killing. And apparently you're the only law enforcement agent who's seen the killer.'

She hadn't been able to put her mind to anything on Friday, and yesterday she had gone over all the notes she had made of the case, to bring them up to date. She had gone through her wardrobe and ended up buying a new bathing suit for the casual beachwear dress code she'd been given. She was to meet Dan Bronfenbrenner at nine on Sunday morning—today.

Lisa was checking her emails for the umpteenth time when the door to the large office she was in opened and Captain Kalani ushered in Agent Bronfenbrenner.

Lisa stood up and greeted the two men, looking quizzically at Dan. He looked attractive in his khaki pants and light-blue button-down shirt. But she had been told to dress for the beach and the mall and had come to work in a very short muumuu over her new swimsuit and strappy sandals.

'Hi, Lisa,' he said, and noticing her look, added, 'Yes, I know I look like an FBI agent, but give me five minutes.' He thanked the captain for his cooperation and for giving up part of his weekend for him.

As soon as the captain left, Dan disappeared, reappearing a few minutes later in shorts, a T-shirt, sandals, a baseball cap and dark glasses.

Lisa smiled at him. 'Much better, but you need an Aloha shirt to look local.'

'OK, you're the expert here in Honolulu. You can coach me, so we can pretend to be a couple hanging out on the beach and not a pair of cops. Let's go!'

Dan pulled out a map of the city from a canvas bag he had slung over his shoulder and Lisa explained exactly where they were going, the layout of the condo complex and its location. Then they set off for Kahala in Dan's white rental car.

He told Lisa that local FBI agents had already done some groundwork. One of them had gone to see the manager of the condos on Friday to explain that they had a very important political figure staying in building no. 4 under an assumed name, and they were providing extra security because of the series of homicides of Congressional candidates. The agent had told the manager the FBI would appreciate it if the security men stayed extra vigilant, discreetly. Agent Nguyen had learnt that there was an empty condo in the building in question and had got permission to use it for the operation. He had also got copies of the keys needed to enter the grounds and the buildings. Dan added that the complex's security men would be given more details on Tuesday, the day of the operation.

Dan and Lisa parked in the garage reserved for the FBI's unit. Then they set out to look round the complex. They went up and down the various stairs, noted doors that needed keys and those that didn't, and checked out the parking space for Mr McDonald's condo—it was empty.

'My stomach's on DC time,' Dan declared, so Lisa suggested they go to the Kahala Mall for an early lunch at the California Pizza Kitchen. Afterwards Lisa helped Dan buy an Aloha shirt, and then the two officers drove back to the beach park where they left the car. Taking Lisa's beach towels, they made their way along the beachfront past the golf club and the condo complex to the hotel. Dan kept looking for likely spots to place an agent. 'The only place I can see for an agent to wait without attracting attention is on one of the benches on that little promontory,' he noted, as they entered the grassy hotel grounds.

They took a leisurely swim in the ocean in front of the hotel, and while basking in the sun, Dan filled Lisa in on all that had happened since their meeting in Washington. 'We are now sure you were right—there is only one killer and he's probably the same guy you saw at Sasaki's party. You'd make a great FBI agent, you know, but I don't suppose you'd ever want to leave this isle of paradise!' he added.

By mid-afternoon they were thirsty and had had enough sun, so Dan suggested they go into the hotel and get something to drink.

Lisa hesitated and then decided she had nothing to lose. 'Dan, you gave me a lovely French dinner in DC. I'd like to reciprocate and invite you to dinner tonight at Hoku's, here at the hotel; it's known to be one of the best restaurants on the island.'

Dan grinned and accepted immediately. 'That'd be great! From tomorrow it's going to be all business—we have to work out the logistics of the operation in detail and arrange to have the condo under tight surveillance from Tuesday morning—so it's lovely to have an evening in paradise with a charming companion!' he said with a twinkle in his eyes.

On late Monday afternoon, four days after his arrival in Honolulu last Thursday, Powers was sitting on his lanai with a glass of rum in hand, staring at the garage of the hotel next door. He was thoroughly bored and disgruntled and the rum he had been sipping for the past hour was giving him a headache. For the past two days, he had been bothered by what he thought was a distinct loss of sensation on his left side.

He had been met at Honolulu International by a limo driver and taken to the Kahala Beach Apartments where he had been shown into a large, two-bedroom unit. But unlike his own condo on the Gold Coast next to Diamond Head, which had a great view of the ocean, this faced a multi-storey parking garage. After the condominium manager left, giving him the keys, he had explored the kitchen and found nothing. Cursing Anita for failing to have the place stocked, he had supper at a ground-floor restaurant at the hotel next door. He hated eating at a tucked away corner table, but knew he had to remain inconspicuous. He made up for it by rushing through his meal, and paid in cash instead of using the credit card in his name.

On Friday morning, he wracked his brains to think of someone he could ask to get provisions. He didn't want to go shopping because he thought it demeaning for a senator; besides, he couldn't take the risk of being identified. Shortly after eight, he heard the loud noise of a vacuum cleaner in the hall. He opened the door and saw a middle-aged Latino woman. Her English was halting but she quickly understood what he wanted and readily agreed to go; he tipped her fifty dollars. She said he had to wait until her lunch break, and promised to run any errands for him and to keep his presence in the condo a secret. He tipped her another fifty to go get two suitcases he had stored in his locker in the basement of his Gold Coast condo.

On Friday and Saturday, he had watched Fox intermittently all day. But he had stopped after he had seen an interview Bond had given. When asked if he had a running mate in mind, Bond had laughed and said, 'It's too early. First I have to win the nomination. And since I'm from Minnesota, I'm considering a Southerner to balance the ticket.'

Since his arrival, Powers had been living like an inebriated animal, pacing round his spacious apartment as if it was a cage. For fear of being seen, he had gone out only once to study the lay of the land. While down by the pool, he had picked up a couple of paperbacks from the library. He had tried to read them but the print seemed wavy. Increasingly bored, his sustained drinking giving him a continuous headache and the numbness on his left side now palpable, Powers felt like screaming. He had little appetite, so he kept drinking. This helped dull the indignation he felt at what Bond had done to him and the vague sense of growing desperation.

He was furious with Bond. He was also obsessively anxious over Bond's claim that the FBI was investigating the forum's funds. Was that true or had Bond just made it up as a reason to drop him from the nomination? What if it was true? Would he be able to put all the blame on Parelli? Even in his current mental state, he had to admit this was not possible.

And why had Parelli suddenly disappeared? He hadn't been too surprised because he knew Parelli was a crook and had been skimming money. He figured the man had wanted to make a getaway before his embezzlement was discovered and his job terminated in November. But why just now? Was Parelli's disappearance linked to the unravelling of everything?

And why wasn't Anita answering his calls? They all went into her voice mail. He reckoned she had taken a holiday as he was away in Hawaii. But she had never gone away for days at a stretch without letting him know where she was, and she always answered her phone. He wondered what might have happened. Had she disappeared too? *Unlikely*, he reasoned, *Anita has always been so reliable.*

Now, seated in his lanai, Powers was a physical wreck. To top it all, he was almost paranoid with worry. To try to escape from his anxieties, he had spent almost half an hour earlier in the day combing news channels but hadn't heard his name being mentioned. How long could he live like this, he wondered. *Have I become worthless like my old man?*

Just as he thought he ought to eat something, the doorbell rang and he got up to open the door. To his surprise, he was handed a huge arrangement of tropical flowers by a short Asian man in a deliveryman's uniform. He insisted he hadn't ordered it, but the man said it was a gift. Powers set the heavy arrangement down on the coffee table and saw a gift card. He was unnerved when he read the message:

Please meet me at 2400 tonight at picnic tables in beach park west of golf club. KEKOA

His head was abuzz with questions. *Why does Zagalo want to meet? Why in Hawaii? How did he learn where I am? Surely he remembers the Honolulu Pact. Has something gone horribly wrong that I don't know about?*

Powers felt dizzy. He plopped down on the sofa and read the card again. *What if Zagalo hadn't sent the message with the flowers? Was it possible the* authorities had found out about Zagalo and forced him to send this message? It didn't make sense. If this was a trap, it was unnecessary. If the authorities knew where he was, they could just come and get him.

No, the message must be from Zagalo. It's got the right code word. And if Zagalo had been arrested for murder, it would've been headline news and I'd have seen it.

Could Zagalo have sent the message to warn me that the authorities had found out and that I should leave the condo?

Should I just ignore the message?

The questions came in quick succession, as did every counter-response. The dull pain in his head made it hard to think. He stood up jerkily, went to the corner of the bedroom and began to scrabble about in one of the suitcases the Latino woman had brought for him from his condo. He quickly found his M15 .45-calibre pistol and a spare magazine kept in a small lacquered box he had bought in Japan.

He hefted the pistol to get a feel of it again. He no longer cared who had sent the message. He would go to the park at midnight and see who showed up. With the gun he would be protected.

A dark-haired man of medium build dressed in dark pants and a dark T-shirt got out of a black car and walked down Kahala Avenue, crossed Kealaolu Street, walked past the park to its car park and turned right towards the shore. It was ten. He saw two couples engrossed in each other and a group of young men packing up their van to leave. The man walked to the picnic tables and then onto the beach, and looking about casually, sat down on the sand. After a quarter of an hour, he stood up and went to the large public toilet. He came out a few minutes later, looked about and then walked round the building to the rear. Had anyone been looking, they might have wondered why he didn't reappear. Gradually the few remaining people left the beach park.

A few minutes before midnight, an elderly man tottered down the beach from the direction of the condos and approached the picnic tables. Although he thought he had been observant, he was startled when he heard the voice behind him.

'General, I thought we ought meet today instead of tomorrow like you'd asked. I thought someone might have coerced you to send me that email. Why did you want to see me?'

Even in the very dim light, it was clear the general was befuddled.

'Whadda ya mean I sent you a message? I told you we'd NEVER meet. Why did *you* ask to see me?'

'I got an email signed KEKOA on the email address only you know.'

Suddenly, the general became angry and began to yell, his words so slurred now it was almost hard to understand what he was saying.

'Thissh the best ploy you can come up . . . to asssk me to pay . . . the two million now? . . . Can't wait . . . few months? Heard my forum's . . . inveshtigated? . . . thought funds might be frozen huh? . . . worried about your money, eh?'

'No, no, General,' the young man said quietly, trying to calm him down. 'I have no doubt you'll pay me what you've promised . . . out of your own pocket if necessary. You've always been very generous.' He paused. 'But if you didn't send the email, someone else did. If it was the FBI or somebody else in law enforcement, they're coming to get me . . . and you too . . . tomorrow night.'

'NO WAY!' the general roared. I'm absolutely sure no one knows about the Honolulu Pact. They can't.'

'But General, if you didn't send me the email, who did?'

'No one. You didn't get an email. You're making it up. You've broken our pact!'

'Why would I do that, sir?' The young man was worried about the older man's tone.

'You want to shake me down, don't you? Threaten me to tell the authorities what I've been asking you to do. You've come to blackmail me! Don't forget I know what a clever, devious bastard you are! Now get away from me. Go! And never come near me again. That's an order!'

'General, listen to me, I . . .'

Before he could finish his sentence, he saw the general clumsily pull out something from his belt with his right hand. The young man grew fully alert.

The general raised his right hand gripping a pistol. But he was slow, and the time it took for the general to aim the pistol at him was enough for the young man to kick the general's groin with his right foot. The general cried out and collapsed on the sand, dropping the pistol as he covered his groin with both hands. The young man kicked the pistol away and grabbed the general from behind, wrapping his right arm round the general's neck. He pulled up the general to his feet.

Holding the general, he looked round. There was no one in the park or on the beach as far as he could see. He furiously debated what to do next. He could knock out the general and run, but the general would come round soon and could alert the police. He could shoot and kill the general using the general's pistol and then run, but someone might hear the gunshot, and the police could be alerted right away. He needed time to get away.

While he was wondering what to do, the general suddenly grabbed at his arm and shoved him in an effort to break loose.

The young man reacted immediately. No longer thinking, he tightened his right arm round the general's neck and dragged him across the narrow beach into the ocean. The general desperately tried to free himself, squawking loudly. But he was no match for the younger man who pushed the old man's head under water and got on top of him, preventing the general from raising his head above the water. The generals arms and legs flailed wildly, then his body became limp and, within moments, totally inert.

The young man dragged the body into deeper waters, gave it a shove and watched it sink. He stood looking to see whether the general's body would stay submerged. It didn't. It floated up and, face down, moved gently with the waves, washing slowly out to sea with the ebbing tide.

He looked round again but couldn't see anyone. He waded back to shore, where he looked for the pistol but couldn't see it in the dark. So he gave up and went to the shelter of the toilet where he took off his clothes and wrung them out as best he could. Then, he quickly put them back on and walked rapidly to his parked car and sped away towards Diamond Head.

Parelli found the midday sun on Ishigakijima too hot. This wasn't the only thing he disliked about this subtropical isle, located to the west of Okinawa. He had only been here for a week, yet he found life here a torment. He hated the food—too much fish!—and Ginko's family was a pain. They spoke almost no English and he felt isolated and claustrophobic on this small island; he could well do without the beautiful beaches and the colourful flowers.

But this morning his spirit had buoyed because today he was leaving, never to return. Thanks to Goro, his new local contact, in a few hours he was going to carry out the plan he had conceived in Tokyo. He looked at his Rolex and hoped Goro wouldn't be long. There was no shade on the beach. Without thinking, Parelli fanned himself with the envelope containing his one-line note that read: 'Sayonara, Ginko. No money, no point in living.' He heard what sounded like a motor in the distance. Peering down the narrow road, he watched Goro's truck drive into view.

Without waiting for Goro to pull up and stop, Parelli started to undress down to his underwear. He put the envelope into the pocket of his jacket, making sure it was partially exposed. He carefully folded his jacket, shirt and trousers and made a small pile of them on the beach. He placed his shoes and socks next to them. Hesitating a little, he removed his Rolex and placed it gingerly on top of the socks, fleetingly wondering why he hadn't left the watch alongside his wedding ring, passport and wallet for Ginko to find in the room they had shared at her father's house.

Goro got out of his truck and greeted Parelli, handing him a new set of clothes. Parelli felt his undershirt to check that a plastic bag, bulkier than he liked, was still tied securely to his waist. He greeted Goro in return and quickly put on the new set of clothes Goro had purchased with money Parelli had given him two nights ago.

Meeting Goro had been serendipitous. Parelli had thought he might be stuck on this blasted island for weeks, if not months. But he couldn't take the company of either his wife or her family, and so within a day or two of his arrival, he had started going down the road to a seedy bar. Here he had struck up an acquaintance with middle-aged Goro who had once worked for an Australian trading firm in Fukuoka. Goro eagerly wanted to practise his sketchy English, and the two men had taken an instant liking to each other.

Parelli learnt that Goro was now a truck driver hauling goods for Ginko's father. At first they had pussyfooted round their relationship with Ginko's family and how they felt about them. Then, after a few beers one night, Parelli had started complaining about life with his in-laws and this had struck a chord with Goro. He groused that he had to work like a serf because Ginko's father had a virtual monopoly on everything on the island—from foodstuff to furniture, TVs and other electronic products, almost all of which came from the main islands of Japan via Naha on the island of Okinawa.

Goro had spoken about how greedy Ginko's father was and Ginko, whom he'd known in high school, was just like her father. Parelli replied, 'My wife is a grabby shrew. I can't take any more of her lambasting me about a deal that went wrong in Tokyo.' Parelli would have told Goro details had he asked, but all Goro had done was give him a knowing smile.

Two nights ago, Parelli had asked Goro to help him carry out his plan to escape the island and his in-laws. He promised to make it worthwhile. Goro thought Parelli's plan was crazy but feasible. So Goro had agreed to get Parelli clothes, drive him to the airport and buy him a ticket to Fukuoka. Parelli had promised to pay him five hundred dollars when he dropped Parelli at the airport and to send him another five thousand when he accessed his bank accounts off the island. He had no intention of sending Goro the money he promised, but he thought Goro knew all along. The five hundred was probably sufficient for what Goro was doing; besides, there was the excitement of it.

Goro had said that they would set a time for Parelli's departure once he had checked the tides. When they met at the bar the previous night, Goro had suggested Parelli leave the following day.

'The tide will begin to ebb from about ten and you can expect a pretty nasty eddy at about a hundred metres out into the bay. You said Ginko knows you're a lousy swimmer, so she will believe you walked into the bay, swam out a bit and got caught in the eddy, getting swept out to sea. Over the years, we haven't found the bodies of a dozen or more people because of the strong eddy. And there are sharks too just outside the bay. So the police and Ginko will likely give up looking for your body after a couple of hours.'

Everything had gone as smoothly as Parelli had hoped. After he landed in Fukuoka, he had purchased a carry-on suitcase, some underwear and a bulky jacket so he wouldn't raise suspicions by travelling without luggage. He was able to get a seat on the next flight to Hong Kong. Once there, he knew he would be home free if his fake passport passed muster. He would go to a decent hotel where he would get a comfortable room in which he could ensconce himself for a while. It should be easy to open a bank account and have as much money as he needed wired from the four accounts he already had—one each in Singapore, Luxembourg, Zug and George Town.

He realized how tense he had been for the past couple of days only after he boarded the Hong Kong flight and fastened his seat belt. At last he was on his way to a new life, unencumbered by his reputation in the US and his silly wife, who had seemed so exotic when he had met her at the bank where they were both working in Tokyo. His accounts in foreign banks held a total of four million dollars he had skimmed from the NAD Forum, but he had let Ginko think they were broke when the Monet had proven to be a fake, as he had been thinking of leaving her for months now.

Siphoning the money had been easy. He had been dealing mostly with illegal donations and disbursements, for which no one ever asked for receipts. For the legal funds relating to forum activities, such as conferences and publications, he had underlings keep the accounts, and he had been so meticulous in ensuring they were all accurate that no one would suspect what he was doing with the accounts he kept himself. Powers was always too busy or uninterested in the details.

Parelli knew he would, unfortunately, have to let Ginko get the house money, but that wouldn't come to much because it was so heavily mortgaged. She would get it all because Lou Parelli was now presumed dead, his body washed out to sea.

He reflected on the loss of the five million or more from the Monet painting—he found that loss most galling. Professor Mary Furness of Boston College, who he had been told was an impeccably honest expert, had sworn that she was almost a hundred per cent sure it was a genuine Monet. But the expert they had taken it to in Tokyo said it was an excellent forgery. So had the second and third experts who had been asked to authenticate it. They had all tested it and confirmed the painting had very cleverly produced *craquelure* but it had been artificially done very recently by slowly heating the painting. Parelli couldn't help wonder whether Furness had been incompetent or whether the couple who sold him the painting had somehow managed to make a switch. How they did it he would never know. Ginko, of course, had a nervous breakdown—the tipping point for him when he knew he had to walk out.

He wondered whether Anita Faga had managed to escape without getting caught by the FBI. *What a complex person! She was so enamoured of Powers that she failed to see he was just using her.* But Anita had had enough foresight to realize she might one day need to escape. She knew about his illegal money transactions, his diverting of forum funds, and realized that she would be implicated if the senator was caught. Parelli had got her the false passport from Mr West—the master forger and good friend of a casino owner in Atlantic City, who always sought Parelli's help to launder money.

He remembered when Anita had come to see him unannounced one day in March. She had come straight to the point and broached the idea of building her nest egg just as he had—she knew what was going on in the forum. Parelli hadn't made a fuss nor was he surprised. He smiled and said it would remain 'their little secret'.

Parelli thought it wise to do what Anita had asked. He knew it was unlikely the accounts would be audited—that would be the last thing Powers would want. So the only way Powers could find out about millions missing was if someone told him. Anita had implied such a threat, so he felt he did well to comply.

Parelli had been concerned about getting through immigration at Hong Kong International Airport, but he needn't have worried. The bored official had taken a cursory look at Lloyd Parnell's American passport and admitted him, saying, 'Welcome to Hong Kong.'

Mr Parnell breathed a silent sigh of relief and walked out through the airport. Now all he had to do was find a decent hotel, buy a new wardrobe, and then, perhaps, find a Suzie Wong who would charm him.

Lisa managed to answer her phone on the fourth ring. Why was anyone calling her at half past six in the morning? She didn't recognize the caller.

She was jolted wide-awake by what she heard.

'Lieutenant, this is Sergeant Doug Messina. Sorry to wake you up. A couple of octopus fishermen found a body in the ocean off the Waialae Beach Park. They called in half an hour ago and I got here ten minutes ago with Ron Watanabe.'

'Have you identified the victim?'

'No, Lieutenant. It's a man probably in his sixties, a haole, slightly overweight, tall—maybe six feet or more. He has a full head of grey, almost white, hair.'

Lisa's heart thumped.

'You think he drowned?' she asked, trying not to sound alarmed.

'Could be, but the victim is fully dressed, so we are treating it as a suspicious death. I've just called in the doctor and the crime scene investigating team. Ron said I should call you though you aren't on the duty roster today. He said he was one of the guys briefed with you by an FBI agent for a big stakeout tonight, and he thinks the victim could be one of the men the agent described. And he said the location fits . . .'

Lisa had heard enough.

'Sergeant, I'll be there in fifteen minutes,' she shouted into the phone and rang off.

Half an hour later, Lisa phoned Dan at the Hawaiian Village.

'Oh, Lisa . . . what's up?' he began, surprised to hear from her so early.

'Bad news, Dan. Powers' body was found this morning just after sunrise by a couple of guys out fishing for octopus. They found him at the beach park where we were yesterday. He was in the water about forty feet from the shore. His body was lodged against the breakwater that juts out from the side of the canal. Looks like he was drowned, but we can't be sure. A pistol was found on the sand but it hasn't been fired recently. I just got here ten minutes ago, and the investigating teams are just arriving so I can't tell you more yet. But I thought you would want to come out right away.'

Stunned, Dan said nothing for several seconds. He swore, then apologized to Lisa and asked, 'Have you got an APB out on Zagalo?'

'I've already phoned the sergeant in charge of bulletins. Zagalo's photo is also being sent out to all police, airlines and the TSA.'

'OK, I'll join you as soon as I can.' The phone went dead almost before his last words.

Dan called a joint meeting of the FBI and the HPD for half past one that same day. He was clearly mortified by the turn of events and apologized, saying it was entirely his fault. Lisa knew how bad he felt.

'I had planned for surveillance to begin this morning, thinking Zagalo might want to check out the surroundings before meeting Powers. But I should've realized such a careful killer would be devious enough to want to change the time and place of the meeting to avoid a trap,' Dan said regretfully.

Preliminary reports were made. The tentative cause of Powers' death was declared to be by drowning because there had been water in his lungs. The gun on the beach had only his fingerprints on it. The apartment the senator had been staying in had not been broken into. The police had woken up the two security guards who had been on night duty at the condominium complex, but neither of them reported seeing anything out of the ordinary while on duty. Neither saw the senator leave the complex nor had there been any visitors for him. A few residents had returned in the wee hours, but they had parked their vehicles in the garage and gone to their condos using the lift, which required a building key to operate.

All the airlines serving Honolulu, interisland and overseas, were contacted immediately, but no one by the name Zagalo had flown out in the past twenty-four hours, nor was anyone by that name scheduled to fly that week. They seemed to be at a dead end.

Dan and Lisa were both depressed. Dan hadn't had any lunch, so when the meeting broke up, he suggested they go have a snack. She took him for local food to the *ramen* shop across from the HPD's main entrance and introduced him to Japanese noodles in soup island-style.

As Dan ate hungrily, his phone rang. It was Sam Ogden calling from DC.

'You're sure working late,' Dan said.

'I thought you'd want the news from Frankfurt as soon as we got it. The police faxed a report. The English is a bit hard to decipher, but the thoroughness of their investigation ought to put us to shame. They did a check with the airlines and the tapes of the CCTV cameras at the passport control booths at Frankfurt Airport and confirmed that a guy who looks like Zagalo left for Chicago on a Lufthansa flight within eight hours of the death of Senator Greenfield. The name on his passport was Aaron Zobel.'

'Wow! I like German efficiency. We've already put an APB out on Zagalo. So we need to send one out on Aaron Zobel immediately.'

'That's right,' said Sam. 'There's more. As required by German law under the circumstances—no evident cause of death, finding a murdered woman's body at the same time—the Germans did a thorough high-powered autopsy. They used the gas chromatography–mass spectrometry test—GC/MS, I think it's called—on the tissues of some internal organs.'

'Sounds like something these meticulous Germans would do! Spare me the forensic mumbo-jumbo. What did the lab find?'

'The report concluded that the senator ingested a chemical substance identical to aconitine, which can cause a heart attack. How soon depends on how much of the stuff the person ingests. They sent the lab report with the molecular structure of . . .'

'Sam, I couldn't care less about the molecular structure. Did they say how one gets hold of—what was it?—aconitine?'

'Yes, they did. The poison can be extracted from a plant called *eisenhut*. I looked it up—it's wolfsbane in English. Grows in colder parts of the world. This isn't the first homicide in Germany in recent decades resulting from this poison, which is why the German forensic toxicologist checked for it.'

'Hats off to the Germans! Sam, I really appreciate your getting this info to me today. We'll make sure that Powers' body is checked for aconitine. Anything else to report?'

'Yeah, it looks like Faga has gone underground, just like Parelli. I guess we dropped the ball on this one too, but who would've thought we needed to worry about keeping tabs on her, when she was the one who led us to Powers and Zagalo?'

'What do you mean *gone underground*?'

'I called her a week ago and gave her a general report on what we found in Powers' computer—the stuff he deleted. I told her virtually nothing. Then I called her yesterday to tell her a bit more because I had promised her I would, but she didn't answer her phone. The senator's office told me she's taken leave while he's out of town. So I had a few agents check. Her apartment here in DC has been cleared of her personal belongings. So too has her apartment in Cambridge, and her mother says she's on vacation between jobs. Left some personal belongings and her car with her mother, but didn't tell her where she was going.'

'Thanks, Sam, for the thorough job. I'm sure one reason you're still in the office and calling me is because you're dying to know what's happening here! Things aren't going well at all.'

Dan quickly gave Sam an update.

'We also found a note in Powers' apartment that Zagalo had sent to Powers asking to meet at midnight last night at the beach park near where he was staying. That's where his body was found. Since Powers was fully dressed, it's possible it wasn't an accident and Zagalo may have drowned him. That's all we know at present,' Dan finished, and heard Sam exclaim in surprise at the other end.

Dan continued: 'I promise to call you as soon as I have something more to tell you. Now go home, Sam!'

Dan turned to Lisa and related to her the part of the conversation she hadn't heard. Then he added, 'Looks like you were right all along, Lisa. I bet Steve Sasaki too died of aconitine poisoning.'

Dan pushed away his nearly empty bowl of noodles and put his head in his hands.

'Looks like we've blown it on all accounts. Powers is dead, Anita and Parelli have disappeared, and who knows how many Congressional candidates and others have been murdered. *And* our murderer is still on the loose. If he hasn't flown out, where could he be on this small island? Could he take a boat anywhere?'

'Oh, Christ! Wait a minute!' exclaimed Lisa. 'I don't think the APB was sent to harbours and cruise ships. He might have hired someone to take him to another island and take a flight from there!'

'OK, let's get to work,' declared Dan. We have to get Aaron Zobel's name sent out on the APB and we have to make sure that ships and harbours are notified. It would be just like the guy to hitch a ride on a freighter or hire a private pilot or captain to take him off Oahu. Let's go.'

By Thursday, life at the HPD had returned to some normalcy for Lisa. Dan had been assured by the forensic toxicologist that, since she knew exactly what she was looking for, she could test Powers' body for aconitine. He had decided there was nothing more he could do in Honolulu, so he had returned to Washington on a red-eye flight on Wednesday. Lisa had gone back to regular duty, but Dan had requested she be the liaison between the FBI and the HPD to follow up on the search for Zagalo.

To Lisa's great disappointment, so far there were no clues at all. Major hotels had been contacted, but with the thousands of rooms in Honolulu, all they had managed to do was check the guest lists, and nothing had surfaced. Knowing Zagalo was born and had grown up in Honolulu, the FBI along with Lisa's pal Sergeant Pat Foletta and two other officers of the HPD looked for friends and relatives who might be hiding him or whom he might have contacted. So far, they had come up with nothing.

Lisa's only consolation was that she and Dan had formed a strong friendship, with an attraction that went well beyond that. Dan had said that he had leave coming up and would like to spend it in Hawaii. Lisa had said she'd be delighted to be his guide. She thought he had wanted to hug her when they parted, but there were far too many officers round for that. Captain Kalani had sensed their feelings and had teased Lisa about her FBI connections.

But Lisa, who managed to keep up her usual cheery disposition on the surface, was crushed at the thought that the murderer had got away. She was desultorily looking over reports that had piled up on her desk, when Pat burst into the room waving a sheet of paper.

'Lisa, look at this! I've been checking the list of muggings and other crimes that have taken place over the past week. Among the usual bar fights and domestic violence reports is this one of a Japanese tourist being mugged in the wee hours of Tuesday morning. A forty-one-year-old Japanese man, medium build, dark hair, who was visiting Honolulu with a group of men from his company. He had serious injuries, including head wounds, and was taken to Queen's. Lost his wallet including his passport. Don't you think this is a bit too much of a coincidence?'

'What? Let me see that!' Lisa almost shouted. She snatched the report from Pat, read the piece herself and said, 'The guy's name is Norio Koga. I'm calling Queen's to see if he's still in the hospital.'

Fifteen minutes later, after being put on hold twice and talking to three different people, Lisa learnt that Mr Koga was still in the hospital but no longer in the ICU. Yes, he could speak a bit of English, but his wife, who had arrived yesterday, knew the language better. Yes, he was conscious but in a lot of pain and so heavily medicated. Yes, he could withstand an interview but it should be short. Lisa said she would be there as soon as she could make it.

While Lisa was on the phone, Pat printed out the full report on the mugging. Lisa read it carefully and called Sergeant Victor Consillio, who was identified as the case officer. The sergeant was far more informative on the phone than in the report he had written.

Mr Koga had left a bar around two in the morning with the seven men he had come with. The bar's duty manager had told the sergeant that the group had had a lot to drink and, about half an hour before they left, a local man who spoke decent Japanese had joined the group and stood everyone a round of double whiskeys. The manager confirmed they were drunk when they staggered out. The sergeant said Mr Koga somehow had been separated from the rest of the group and was roughed up rather badly—he had been thrown against the wall of the building and had suffered a concussion and serious bruises on his face and on the right side of his upper body. He was robbed of his wallet, passport and all the money he had inside his jacket. Someone from his group went back to look for him, found him lying unconscious in a passage next to the bar and went into the bar to call the police. Mr Koga had been taken to Queen's and admitted to the ICU. The local who had stood them drinks was a suspect, but no one knew who he was and none had ever seen him before. The sergeant said the description he was given fit hundreds, if not thousands, of men.

Responding to Lisa's questions, Sergeant Consillio added that he had interviewed the people who worked at the bar and the hospital and had also got the names of the people in the group, but they had returned to Japan on Tuesday, with the exception of one man who had stayed in Honolulu until the victim's wife arrived.

After talking with Sergeant Consillio, Lisa rushed to the hospital. When she walked into the hospital room, Mrs Koga stood up and bowed slightly and greeted Lisa in English. 'Do you have any news?' she asked.

Lisa greeted her in her best school Japanese: '*Hajimemashite*. Nice to meet you. Thank you for letting me come when your husband has been so badly hurt. I am so sorry this happened to him. We are still working on the case, though we think we know who the mugger was. I need to ask your husband some questions about the incident. I hope that's all right.'

'*Maagah?*' a puzzled Mrs Koga asked. Lisa answered slowly enunciating each word.

'The person who attacked your husband and stole his passport and wallet.' Mrs Koga nodded in understanding.

Lisa looked at the man lying on the bed and found his eyes on her. He had an ordinary face, black hair cut short, indistinguishable from many a Japanese American man, except for the bruised right eye and a large bandage on the side of his head. She approached him and asked Mr Koga in Japanese whether he would answer some questions. '*Hai* . . . Yes,' he hoarsely replied.

Using Japanese and English and taking a very long time, Lisa learnt key information that Sergeant Consillio had not given her. The friendly local had been especially friendly towards Mr Koga. When they left the bar, Mr Koga hadn't felt well and knew he was going to throw up. The local had pushed him gently on the back to guide him to the three-foot gap between the bar and the next building, where Mr Koga had been sick. He knew the local was there, to help him he had thought, but the next thing he knew his wallet was being removed from his back pocket and his passport and papers from inside his jacket. He tried to push the hands back even as he retched, and the next thing he knew, he had been slammed against the side of the building and struck hard on his face and body. After the first several blows, he remembered nothing.

Lisa had to know one more thing: 'Did you see his eyes? *Kare no me wo mimashitaka?*'

'*Hai, kimi no warui me deshita,*' Mr Koga answered visibly cringing.

Seeing the puzzled expression on Lisa's face, Mrs Koga clarified, 'My husband says his *me* . . . his eyes . . . were scary.'

Lisa now had no doubt it was Zagalo. It had to be! She was about to thank the Kogas and leave, but Mr Koga motioned he had more to say. He told her that when the local sat next to him round the crowded table, their arms had touched and he remembered the man's shirt had been wet.

Lisa could hardly wait to get out of the hospital room. She stayed a few minutes more thanking the couple for their help and wishing Mr Koga a speedy recovery. She was barely out in the corridor before she called the sergeant in charge of issuing the APBs and asked her to contact all airlines to check whether a Mr Norio Koga had flown out on Tuesday or Wednesday.

Two hours later, the call came in from United Airlines. A Mr Norio Koga from Saga Prefecture in Kyushu had flown to Tokyo on one of their morning flights on Tuesday.

Lisa sat at her desk, her eyes blurred on her computer. Powers was dead. And Sasaki. And possibly close to twenty other people. All killed by Zagalo. And now they had lost him. She didn't even want to speculate on the chance of their catching him in Japan. She felt tears rolling down her cheeks as she pulled out her phone to call Dan.

He was much more anxious than when he had used the counterfeit American passport at Frankfurt Airport. He forced himself to stay calm as he went up to the 'Japanese Only' window at immigrations in Narita Airport. Using a stolen Japanese passport, he knew he had to keep his answers to all questions as short and simple as possible. If he didn't, the passport control officer was likely to ask why a man carrying a Japanese passport in the very Japanese name Norio Koga was speaking Japanese like a foreigner.

He was in luck. The officer glanced at him, barely looked at a few pages in the passport, stamped it and motioned him to move on. With only a small suitcase, he got through customs as easily. Once out in the crowded airport lobby, he went to a bank and changed two thousand dollars into yen, enough to meet his needs for the next several days. He didn't want to use the credit cards Powers had given him if he didn't have to, and certainly not Koga's, because he would run the risk of being traced by the authorities.

He went out of the arrival area to the pavement outside the building. Nearly four in the afternoon, it was as hot as it was in Honolulu. His throat was scratchy from car exhaust and cigarette smoke. He looked round and found the shuttle-bus stop for the airport hotels and boarded the first one that came along. Within a few minutes he arrived at the Tobu Hotel where he was given a small room on the eighth floor.

Despite being so used to travelling and to airport hotels and to being alone in strange places, this time was different. There was no place he had to go for an assignment. He found himself at a loose end. He longed to contact Kim, but he had lost touch with her years ago and he had no idea how to look her up. Finally, fatigue got the best of him and he fell asleep.

His body still on Hawaii time, he woke up long before the restaurant opened for breakfast, so he made his way by hotel shuttle and then by train to Tokyo Station where he had breakfast at a cafe before boarding a bullet train to Sendai.

He was going to see Dr Ito because his great uncle was the only person in Japan he knew he could trust. And he wanted to thank the doctor for sending him the dried roots of *torikabuto* last December. He hoped the old man was still alive. He liked the crazy but engaging doctor with whom he had spent a few days almost a decade ago. And Dr Ito was not likely to tell anyone he had a visitor. He would stay with him a few days and decide what to do next. He might stay in Japan for a while and then go back to the US after it became safer for him to do so. Since he was not going to get the two million dollars Powers had promised him, he had to plan his finances carefully. But he was sure that all the money his banker in San Francisco was managing for him would do for several years at least.

At a little before eleven a taxi dropped him off at Dr Ito's house. He was shocked to see how it had changed since the first time he had been there. The gutters drooped on one side and a veranda sagged badly. He guessed the 2011 Tohoku earthquake had damaged the house and it looked as if it hadn't been repaired since.

Today, instead of the attractive young woman who had greeted him last time, a short elderly woman came to the door. 'Who are you? What do you want?' she asked him suspiciously, in Japanese.

'I'm a relative of Dr Ito. He knows me well. Tell him the son of his favourite niece from Hawaii is here,' he replied in Japanese.

'Oh! It's you, Yoshio-san. For the past few months, since his health has been failing, he often talks about you. I think he wants to see you. Did he get in touch with you? Did he ask you to come?'

'No. He didn't ask me to come. I just happened to be in Japan and I wanted to come visit. What's wrong with him?'

'He has some sort of cancer he says. Being a doctor he says he knows there is no point in getting debilitating treatment at his age. Don't tell him I told you anything. Do come in.'

He removed his shoes and followed her into the house and into the doctor's formal guest room where he had spent so many hours a decade ago, only now the room was dominated by a huge altar. The old woman disappeared to tell Dr Ito he had a visitor.

Within a few minutes, Dr Ito came into the room, smiling broadly. The welcome was as warm as it had been on his first visit but the old man had changed so much that he found him barely recognizable. He no longer resembled the look-alike he had seen recently on the train from Portland to California. Dr Ito still had white hair but it was now so thin his pate showed and he looked haggard and bent over.

'Oh, my! My *torikabuto* sorcerer and a soldier in the war-against-useless-people! Welcome. I've been thinking about you often of late. Nice to see you again after so many years, my boy!'

The old man's English was still intact but he was now shuffling rather than walking.

'Get us some lunch,' the doctor said to the old woman. 'Whatever you have will do. We have a lot to catch up on.'

As the old woman left the room, Dr Ito explained who she was: 'Mrs Ishida lost all her family in the tsunami of 2011. She comes in everyday for a couple of hours—not like my Misako who stayed with me after her divorce. But she cleans and cooks for me, and does all my shopping. She is a good woman.'

Dr Ito didn't ask what he had been doing since they had last met. Instead, he started talking about himself.

'I'm getting ready to go. We Japanese tend to become religious . . . spiritual . . . as we grow old. But organized religions are for mental weaklings. Too many silly myths and nonsensical logic. So I made up my own god, one who will forgive me for all the bad things I've done in my ninety-two years. My god is omnipotent because he created our limitless universe, so it's easy for him to forgive me. I pray to him many times a day, burning a bit of incense. I'm not sure he likes the smell, but it makes me feel reverential. Do you believe in a god?'

'I don't think so. We have churches and temples in Honolulu but I've never gone to one.'

'You ought to pray to my god and ask for forgiveness. We must all do *shokuzai*.'

'*Shokuzai*? I don't know that word.'

'The original meaning of the Chinese character for *shoku* is to give something precious in exchange for something, and *zai* is crime. So it means you give up what you value most to be forgiven for all the crimes you've committed.'

'Have you decided what you will give up?'

'I think about it everyday. That's why I pray to my god everyday.'

Then Dr Ito fell silent, and his head drooped as if he had fallen asleep. He awoke with a jerk when the old lady brought in a tray with their lunch of *miso* soup, broiled sardines, pickles and rice. After lunch, the doctor went off to take a nap.

Unsettled by the strange conversation and still feeling jet-lagged, the young man went out and wandered round the unkempt garden. Then, he went into the old man's laboratory where he was trained many years ago. It was obvious the room was no longer used. It had been cleaned out and was now just an empty room.

He went back to the house and sat down on the narrow wooden veranda, dangling his legs over the edge. He was sure Dr Ito knew he was dying. The old man's talk about *shokuzai* had rankled him and he couldn't stop thinking about it.

He knew he couldn't stay here long. Not with a dying old man who was now more monk than doctor and seemed even crazier than when he had first met him. Where could he go next? With the money he had in San Francisco, he could live for several years somewhere in Japan. But where would he stay and what would he do? Thinking about the future gave him a headache. He calmed himself recollecting what his mother often said: '*ashita wa ashita no kaze ga fuku*'—'tomorrow, tomorrow's wind will blow'. *Whatever will be, will be*, he repeated to himself.

It was hot out on the veranda, so he went back inside and lay down in the doctor's small sitting room. He must have slept a couple of hours before Mrs Ishida shook his shoulder. 'Dinner's ready. Dr Ito is already having a drink. I made a special dinner for you two. I'm going home now,' she said.

He washed up and went to the guest room where he found Dr Ito sipping saké from a small earthen *choko*. The low lacquered table was laden with dishes—grilled salted fish, chicken and leeks on skewers, boiled vegetable dishes, various kinds of mountain greens and local pickles. He knew Mrs Ishida must have worked very hard all afternoon to produce this feast. The aroma from the delicacies almost overcame the lingering odour of incense emanating from the large altar.

Dr Ito raised his saké cup and said, 'Sit and join me, my boy. Mrs Ishida made all of this just for you. There's no soup, but to welcome you I'm giving you my last bottle of the best saké this area can produce.' The old man poured the rice wine from a green glass bottle into a *choko* and handed it to him. 'Drink up.'

The young man joined the old doctor in a toast. *Excellent wine*! He was ravenous and the food delicious, so he ate and drank his fill. Dr Ito drank cup after small cup of saké, but ate very little.

Over dinner, he listened to Dr Ito talk more about *shokuzai* and his made-up god. The old man began to list the worst things he had done in his life. He claimed to have sent away eight people, maybe nine or ten—'I lost count,' he admitted. Some had suffered heart attacks because the doctor needed their insurance money. Others had been terminally ill and he didn't want them to suffer any longer. 'I don't really think that counts as a bad thing, do you?' he asked.

But that was a rhetorical question, as the doctor rambled on to say he had also had to punish those who deserved to die. 'And in the course of my research, I also killed countless innocent animals. Even horses. I need to be forgiven for those deaths too.' He chattered on, stopping only to refill his little *choko* and his nephew's as well.

Then all of a sudden, the old man sat up straight and looked him in the eye. 'Yoshio, now you tell me the terrible things you've done and I'll ask my god to forgive you.'

He mumbled something the old doctor failed to understand. 'Speak up. I didn't understand what you said.'

The young man just stared at the old man.

'Come on. You've scarcely led a blameless life!' exclaimed Dr Ito.

Though he had had a lot to drink, the old man didn't sound inebriated. 'You can at least tell me what you used the *torikabuto* for, the batch I sent you just before the end of last year.'

Again the young man said nothing, but bit his lip.

'I may be old and dying but I'm not stupid. Why did you suddenly come to Japan? Are the police after you?'

He wondered what Dr Ito knew. He tried to hide his anxiety, but the old man had seen his eyes.

'I read about the series of political deaths in the US, you know. I keep myself well informed, read the news, hear what they say. So, am I wrong in thinking you had a hand in them?'

He shook his head, dumfounded by his great-uncle's ability to put two and two together.

Seeing that his nephew didn't refute the statement, Dr Ito went on: 'So, then, having sent so many people away, don't you think you should do *shokuzai?*'

The young man drank another *choko* of saké to stall for time. The green bottle was nearly empty now. And he could feel his face getting red and his heart beating faster. He wasn't used to saké.

'How do you feel?' Dr Ito asked, almost like he would his patients.

'What do you mean?' the young man responded, a little surprised by the question.

'Whatever your reasons were, you ended many lives. You need my god's forgiveness. For that, you need to give up the thing that's *most* important to you . . . just as I am going to do . . . and I am going to help you. I really want to be forgiven and so should you. I am your teacher and you are my disciple.' The old man's voice trailed away.

The young man's head was beginning to feel woolly. He poured out the last of the delicious saké and downed it. What was the old man prattling on about? Exasperated, he raised his voice and asked, 'What *are* you talking about?

The old man, looking very contented, said with a smile, 'Life. Yours and mine. That's what we will give up to get forgiveness.'

'Nonsense! I'm not giving up my life. I don't want to die. I'm not old and sick like you.'

'Ah! So you know I am dying. You are still young and healthy. But only for an hour . . . maybe two at most. I will be gone soon too. I am doing what I need to do. It has been an interesting life. Very exciting too. And I want you to know that I am helping you absolve . . . do your *shokuzai* as well. I know you came to Japan because it is a matter of time before the police in America get you. It is better for you to come with me . . . to go where we are going, instead of living a fugitive's life in Japan.'

He couldn't comprehend what the old doctor was saying. Where was he to go with him? What for? For a made-up god? He couldn't think any more. He felt the heat rise in his chest and tears welled up in his eyes. All at once he knew what the old man had done. He knew how reliable the aconitine was, especially in alcohol. The bile rose in his throat as he realized he hadn't long to live. He felt helpless as he watched his great-uncle lean back and close his eyes, a benign smile lighting up his face.

At a quarter past nine the following morning, a police car arrived at Dr Ito's residence in response to a call from a sobbing old lady who had reported two deaths. In a room that reeked of incense and vomit, the two officers found the lifeless body of an old man, his hands folded over his chest in a position of prayer. The table, laden with the remains of an elaborate meal, was covered in vomit at the side opposite where the old man lay. The stench nearly made the younger officer retch.

Then the nearly incoherent Mrs Ishida led the police to an adjoining room where the body of a much younger man lay sprawled on the floor, his eyes wide open, reflecting terrified despair. The sliding door to the veranda was open, the room was in disarray with a tea kettle and a glass overturned, water soaking the tatami matting. The mess suggested that the young man had struggled in vain to overcome the effect of whatever had killed him.

Mrs Ishida said the young man had arrived only the day before. 'If he hadn't come, none of this would have happened,' she cried.

In a guest room on the second floor, the junior officer found a small carry-on suitcase with clothes and a small, black leather case of toiletries. In a jacket neatly folded beside these, he found a wallet containing almost fifteen thousand yen, six credit cards and IDs, each issued to a different name, and two savings passbooks from a bank in San Francisco. In an inside pocket was a Japanese passport issued to Norio Koga. He took the passport downstairs and compared the dead men's faces with the picture in the passport. Puzzled, he shook his head.

He handed the passport to the senior officer who exclaimed, 'This is the one stolen in Honolulu! We got an urgent notice about this from the National Police Agency only this morning.'

The senior officer went upstairs and went through the dead young man's belongings very carefully. At the bottom of the case of toiletries he found eight thousand US dollars in cash and two American passports, one for Aaron Zobel and the other for Xavier Yoshio Zagalo.

The senior officer interrogated Mrs Ishida for nearly fifteen minutes, then called his superior at the Sendai Police Department, who in turn called the National Police Agency.

Filini's restaurant in the Radisson Blu Hotel at Zurich Airport was unusually busy. A line had formed at the entrance. It was just after seven and many were getting restless at the long wait. Then, a hostess came out and announced that unfortunately there would be quite a wait for a table for one or two, but if there were groups of three or four, she could seat them immediately.

A well-dressed Japanese man in his sixties, who had been chatting in fluent English with a scholarly-looking woman speaking with a slight German accent, looked at his companion questioningly. She nodded, so he looked round and asked if anyone would care to join them. A young man looked up from his mobile. 'Sure, that'd be great,' he said with a strong American accent. At that, an attractive young woman, who had been reading the *International Herald Tribune*, asked the three, 'May I join you?'

Within minutes the four were seated, menus were brought and orders were taken for drinks and food. As usual in a Swiss restaurant, once orders were taken, customers had to be prepared for a long wait.

'I ate here last night and the food is very authentic Italian, which is why I was in line again tonight,' explained the young woman. 'Thank you for letting me join you,' she said to the Asian man.

'Glad to hear the food is good. My name is Sada. I'm from Tokyo. And my friend here is Professor Gertrud Baum from the University of Duisburg-Essen in Germany.'

The young man introduced himself. 'I'm Zach Cunning, a reporter for CNN. I've been posted to China, but on my way there, I'm taking two weeks leave to go hiking in the Alps.'

'My name is Annette Favia. I'm a secretary, here on a break between jobs. I'm hoping to travel round the country for a while.'

For the next few minutes the conversation turned to why they were staying at the airport hotel in Zurich. The Japanese and the German were attending a conference here. Annette had chosen the hotel for convenience, and the young American because he had got a big discount on a room.

The waiter brought their wine, and the CNN reporter changed the subject.

'Say, Annette, I guess you know about the mysterious death of Senator Powers—it's still headline news in the *IHT*.'

'Yes. Very tragic. Some people are saying he would've been the running mate for Governor Bond should Bond get the Republican nomination,' she responded, barely audibly.

'Tragic? I don't mean to speak ill of the dead or to trample on your politics, but he was the kind of a senator we can do without. His book, *The New American Destiny*, is his version of *Mein Kampf*—a fascist manifesto for the extreme right wing and a call to arms not to give in to the leftists, further dividing Americans.'

Annette shot back, 'I know what the senator said in his book. He expressed his concerns to try to stop America from sliding into socialism and from being at the mercy of foreign powers because of the enormous national debt.'

Professor Baum gave a short laugh. 'You Americans bandy about terms without really understanding what they mean. The Republicans aren't fascists, nor are the Democrats socialists. You're using them as epithets. Don't they teach you the meaning of these terms in your schools?'

The two Americans, surprised and rather chagrined, looked at the blunt-speaking German. 'Yes, Professor, you're right. We often use these words carelessly,' Zach said, abashedly. 'I stand corrected.'

The Japanese tried to lighten the conversation. 'No need to apologize, Mr Cunning. These days, even a lot of educated Japanese criticize almost everything our conservative government does as being anti-capitalist or even socialist. They don't realize the government has many important roles to play.'

The German professor launched into a veritable tirade.

'Frau Favia and Herr Cunning, please don't take this personally, but from the Western European perspective, too many Americans don't understand what Professor Sada has just said. They bitterly complain about what the government does when it is doing what it must do. Health insurance is a case in point. Only the government can provide health insurance to everyone at a reasonable cost. So all the advanced economies, except the US, have national health insurance. So many Americans consider everything the government does a socialistic encroachment on their freedom and free market. To me, the debates among the parties in the US are more about squabbles between ideologues than about how to solve vital issues through compromise.'

More than a little overwhelmed by the German professor's vehement words, the two young Americans remained silent. The Japanese professor tried to calm the waters. 'For me, the central problem facing all of us in the democratic, advanced capitalist economies comes down to this: capitalism is the most effective production system for maintaining efficiency, but at the cost of creating winners and losers. I used to believe capitalism, left to its own devices, would eliminate poverty. Instead, I see increasing poverty and a growing disparity in income distribution. And, sadly, in emerging economies, such as China and India, income distribution is becoming more unequal as these countries adopt a more free market system—capitalism,' he said quietly.

The German professor spoke up again, this time her voice tinged with regret: 'What concerns me no less is that the increasing lack of equality in income breeds a perception of a lack of fairness in our societies. People feel helpless about rectifying this, and despair spawns violence. I've been reading about the murders of the political candidates in America. Since most of the candidates killed have been Democrats and moderate Republicans, my guess is some extreme right-wing sociopaths are responsible for these murders. I don't know enough about the Patriots, but it could be them.'

Annette, who had been very quiet up to now, asked in a small voice, 'I'm very interested in what you say. So you think income disparity and the inability of politicians to solve problems have led to right-wing violence in order to get politicians on the far right into office?'

'Yes, in that economic problems often lead to political extremism,' said Professor Baum. 'But don't get me wrong. The extreme right wing doesn't have a monopoly on violence. Far from it. There have been many cases of left-wing extremists who have resorted to murder and all manner of violence. In Germany after World War II, we had the notorious Baader–Meinhof gang, a violent left-wing militant group of urban guerrillas. This grew into the Red Army, which had groups in other countries—the Japanese had their Red Army, as did several other countries from the 1970s until almost the end of the century. Extremism on both ends of the political spectrum breeds violence. And when this happens, we are often faced with a megalomaniac such as Ivan the Terrible, Robespierre, Hitler, Stalin, Idi Amin . . . Well, I shouldn't go on. I don't want to dishearten everyone so much that we can't enjoy our dinner.'

At this point their appetizers were served, and for a few minutes the group concentrated on the food. When Zach had wolfed down his salad, he looked at the professors and said, 'I thought we were going to have only polite chitchat at dinner. But I'm grateful to both of you for giving me a lot of things to consider as I do my job. The media clearly has to take a lot of blame, because we focus on the extreme things people say, and I suspect that divides the country even more. We have to be more even handed and focus on what brings people together, what the parties—and countries—have in common, and how we can work together.'

'I hope you will focus on the right things then,' smiled the Japanese professor. 'And with energetic, hard-working, young people like you, you may just be able to pull it off. Now if you will excuse me,' he said as he finished his stuffed eggplant, the only item he had ordered, 'I have had a long day at the conference and am not fully adjusted to the time difference. So I will leave you to enjoy your dinners. I'll pay on the way out.' And with that, he stood up, bowed slightly to the three and went over to the desk at the entrance to settle his bill.

'An amazing man. Very good English too.' remarked Zach.

Professor Baum laughed. 'I'm not sure you realize how amazing. He's recently retired from Japan's top university, he's the most respected economist in Japan and he's considered to be a top candidate for the first Nobel Prize in Economics to go to a Japanese. We were very lucky to get him as the keynote speaker for our international conference on formulating a coherent and broad-based political economic theory . . . eclectic canons that help the Left and the Right to start finding ways to compromise on major issues of our day.'

As the remaining three diners ate their main courses and ordered dessert and coffee, conversation turned to travel. Professor Baum offered suggestions to Annette and Zach as to what they should try to see while in Switzerland. Hearing monosyllabic responses from Annette, the other two got the distinct impression that she was self-occupied and possibly a bit lonely. Sensing it, the German urged her to go to small inns in villages where she would find friendly Swiss, instead of continuing to rattle about in Zurich. Annette said she appreciated the German's suggestions and would first visit Zug, where she had a friend.

After dinner, the professor, the reporter and the secretary went up to the desk to pay for their meals. But the man in charge smilingly told them the bill had already been taken care of.

On the same day twelve time zones away, Lisa was trying to relax over a cup of coffee on her lanai in Honolulu. Even though it was a balmy Friday morning and she had the day off, Lisa was finding it hard to unwind. She was still keyed up by the aftermath of Powers' death and the failure to capture Zagalo. The only solace for the past few days had been the emails going back and forth between her private email account and Dan's. They were writing about all the things they might do and places they might visit when everything had been cleared up—Dan had no idea how long it would take, but he said he would certainly come to Hawaii as soon as possible.

Lisa heard her phone ring and ran inside to answer it. It was a very excited Dan calling from Washington.

'Lisa, I think we've got Zagalo! I've had a fax from the National Police Agency in Japan.'

'Where is he? Where did they find him?'

'He's dead. In Sendai . . . a couple hours north of Tokyo, by train.'

'Dead? What? What happened?'

'The police in Sendai answered a call yesterday morning and found two bodies, one of a very old man and one of a man in his thirties. The younger man had three passports: one for Norio Koga, one for Aaron Zobel and one for Xavier Yoshio Zagalo. The report said the Sendai police suspect it was a murder-suicide, not uncommon in Japan, though it's unclear who the killer was. Under Japanese law, in cases like this, a complete autopsy is mandatory. And because there has to be a formal identification of Zagalo, they asked whether we could send over his fingerprints. The report said Zagalo might have been a relative of the old man. It's a sketchy report and the NPA doesn't have all the details yet. But they were kind enough to let us know as soon as the Sendai police were certain they had found our suspect.'

'Did they say what the cause of death was?'

'No. The police haven't determined it yet. They were told the old man had terminal cancer but they can't determine the cause of death until an autopsy has been done. Because Zagalo vomited so much, they are testing the leftover food and drinks and all the tableware for poison. I've suggested they test for aconitine. Sam is sending the NPA relevant parts of the German forensic report on Senator Greenfield, with that recommendation. It's too early for me to make a press statement, but I had to let you know that I'm really certain we got him. At least our taxpayers have saved a lot of money because there won't be a trial!'

Lisa was so overwhelmed by everything Dan had just told her that she was silent for a long moment.

'I don't know if we'll ever find out what really happened. But at least Zagalo is dead. And so is Powers,' Dan said with a sigh.

'And so are some twenty other people,' Lisa said softly. Then, with fervency, she added, 'May the murders be at an end!'